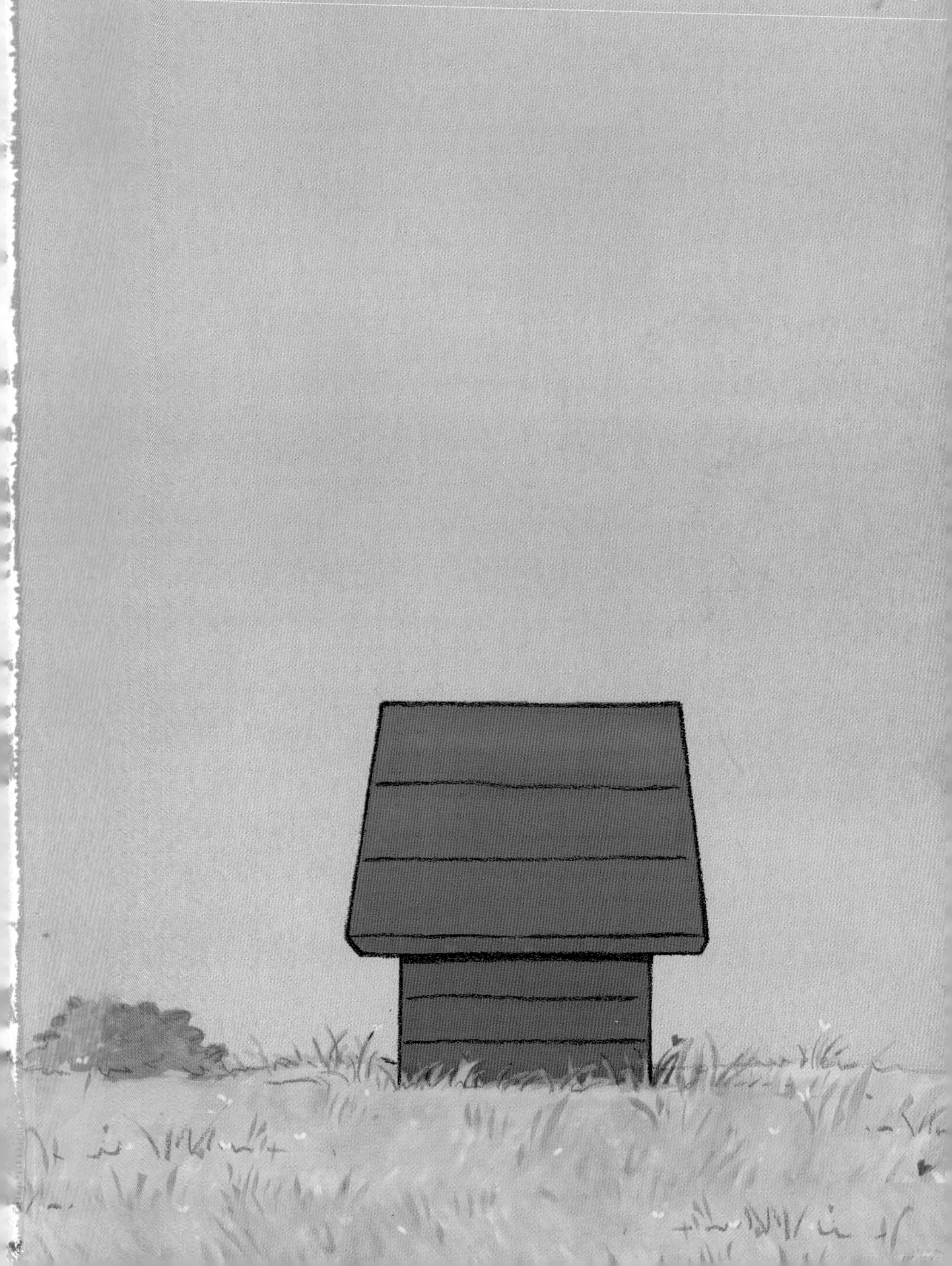

PEANUTS® GRAPHIC NOVELS

Adventures with Linus and Friends!

Charles M. Schulz

SIMON SPOTLIGHT

New York London Toronto Sydney New Delhi

PEANUTS®

by Schulz

SIMON SPOTLIGHT
An imprint of Simon & Schuster Children's Publishing Division
1230 Avenue of the Americas, New York, New York 10020
This Simon Spotlight edition March 2023
Peanuts and all related titles, logos, and characters are trademarks of Peanuts
Worldwide LLC © 2023 Peanuts Worldwide LLC.
"Happiness Is a Warm Blanket" © 2011 Peanuts Worldwide LLC.
"Umbrella Fella," "Fast 'n Furrious" © 2012 Peanuts Worldwide LLC.
"Lucy's Loophole" © 2014 Peanuts Worldwide LLC.
"Give It a Shot," "Balloon Bother," "Ewe First" © 2015 Peanuts Worldwide LLC.
"Security Blanket Science" © 2016 Peanuts Worldwide LLC.
"Beagles and Blazers" © 2023 Peanuts Worldwide LLC.
Most stories in this volume were originally published in the PEANUTS
comic series by Boom Studios 2011–2016.
For information about special discounts for bulk purchases, please contact
Simon & Schuster Special Sales at 1-866-506-1949 or business@simonandschuster.com.
Manufactured in China 1022 SCP
2 4 6 8 10 9 7 5 3 1
ISBN 978-1-6659-2706-2 (hardcover)
ISBN 978-1-6659-2705-5 (paperback)
ISBN 978-1-6659-2707-9 (ebook)

Contents

Cover art by Scott Jeralds

Happiness Is a Warm Blanket 7

Based on the animated special written by Stephan Pastis and Craig Schulz • Pencils by Bob Scott and Vicki Scott • Inks by Ron Zorman • Colors by Brian Miller • Letters by Bryan Stone

Umbrella Fella 86

Story by Shane Houghton • Art by Matt Whitlock • Colors by Lisa Moore

Fast 'n Furrious 92

Story by Vicki Scott • Pencils by Bob Scott and Vicki Scott • Inks by Paige Braddock • Colors by Nina Kester

Classic Peanuts by Charles M. Schulz 97

Lucy's Loophole 98

Story by Caleb Monroe • Art by Robert Pope • Colors by Lisa Moore • Letters by Steve Wands

Classic Peanuts by Charles M. Schulz 100

Give It a Shot 101

Story by Jeff Dyer • Art by Robert Pope • Colors by Lisa Moore • Letters by Steve Wands

Classic Peanuts by Charles M. Schulz . . . 106

Classic Peanuts by Charles M. Schulz . . . 107

Balloon Bother 108

Story and Layouts by Bob Scott • Pencils by Scott Jeralds Inks by Justin Thompson • Colors by Lisa Moore • Letters by Steve Wands

Classic Peanuts by Charles M. Schulz . . . 120

Ewe First 121

Story and Pencils by Vicki Scott • Inks by Paige Braddock •
Colors by Nina Kester • Letters by Donna Almendrala

Classic Peanuts by Charles M. Schulz . . . 125

Security Blanket Science 126

Story by Jeff Dyer • Art by Robert Pope • Colors by Lisa Moore •
Letters by Steve Wands

Classic Peanuts by Charles M. Schulz . . . 131

LOL Lucy 132

Story and Pencils by Vicki Scott • Inks by Paige Braddock •
Colors by Donna Almendrala • Letters by Alexis E. Fajardo

Classic Peanuts by Charles M. Schulz . . . 138

Leaf it to Linus 139

Story by Jeff Dyer • Art by Robert Pope • Colors by Nina Taylor
Kester • Letters by Steve Wands

Classic Peanuts by Charles M. Schulz . . . 147

Beagles and Blazers 148

Story by Charles M. Schulz, adapted by May Nakamura • Art by
Scott Jeralds • Letters by Bryan Stone

Classic Peanuts by Charles M. Schulz . . . 158

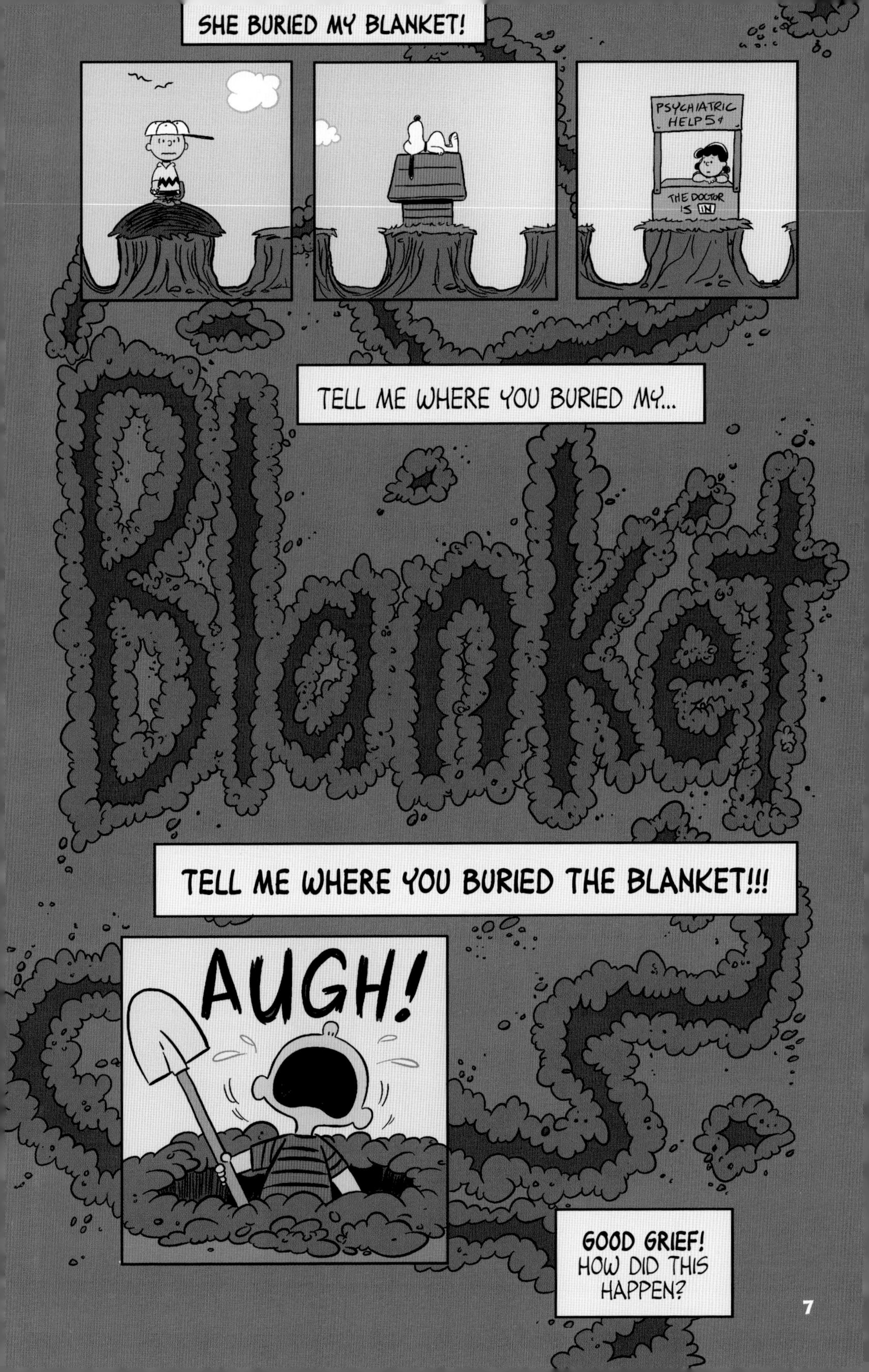
SHE BURIED MY BLANKET!
PSYCHIATRIC HELP 5¢
THE DOCTOR IS IN
TELL ME WHERE YOU BURIED MY...
Blanket
TELL ME WHERE YOU BURIED THE BLANKET!!!
AUGH!
GOOD GRIEF! HOW DID THIS HAPPEN?

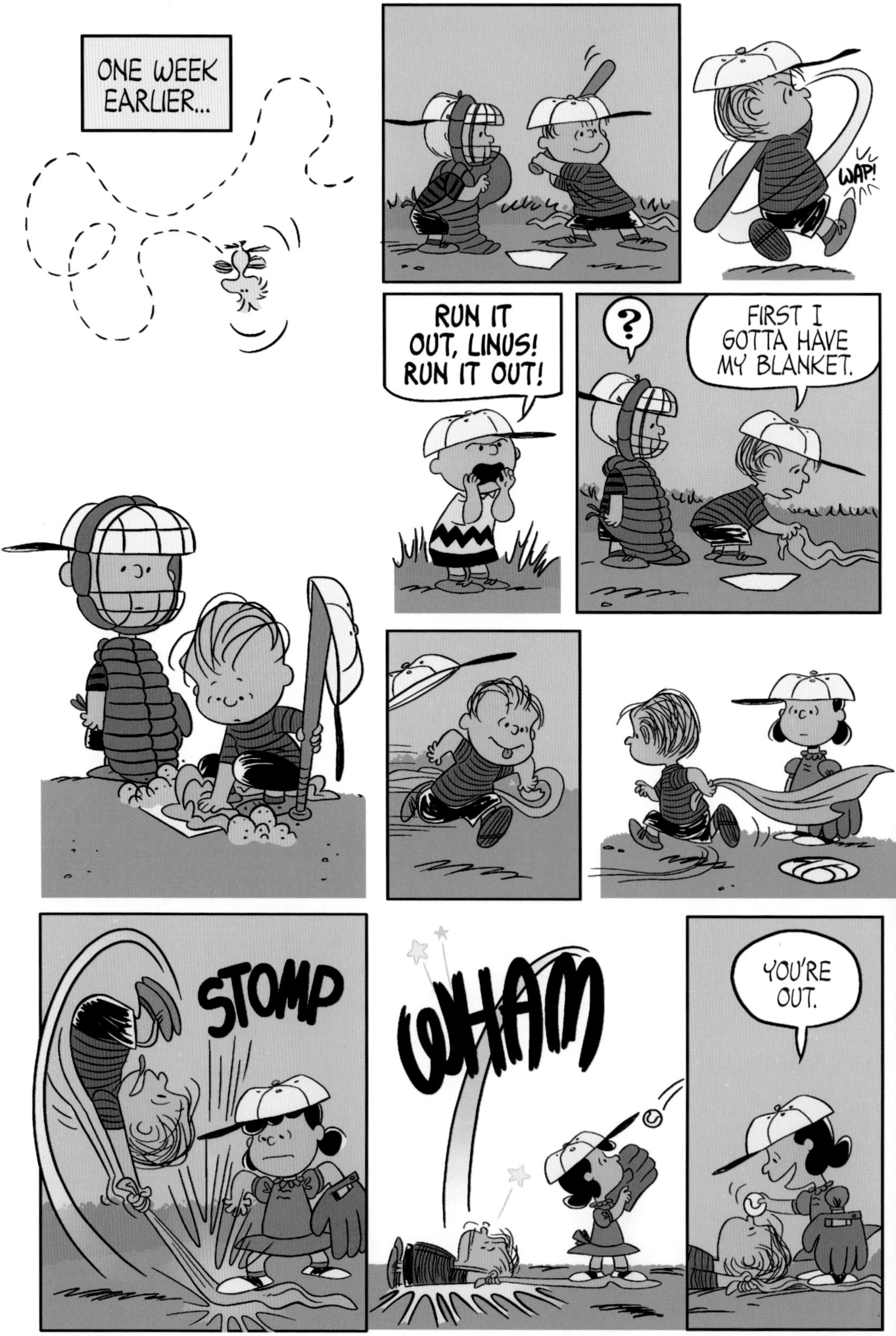
ONE WEEK EARLIER...
WAP!
RUN IT OUT, LINUS! RUN IT OUT!
?
FIRST I GOTTA HAVE MY BLANKET.
STOMP
WHAM
YOU'RE OUT.

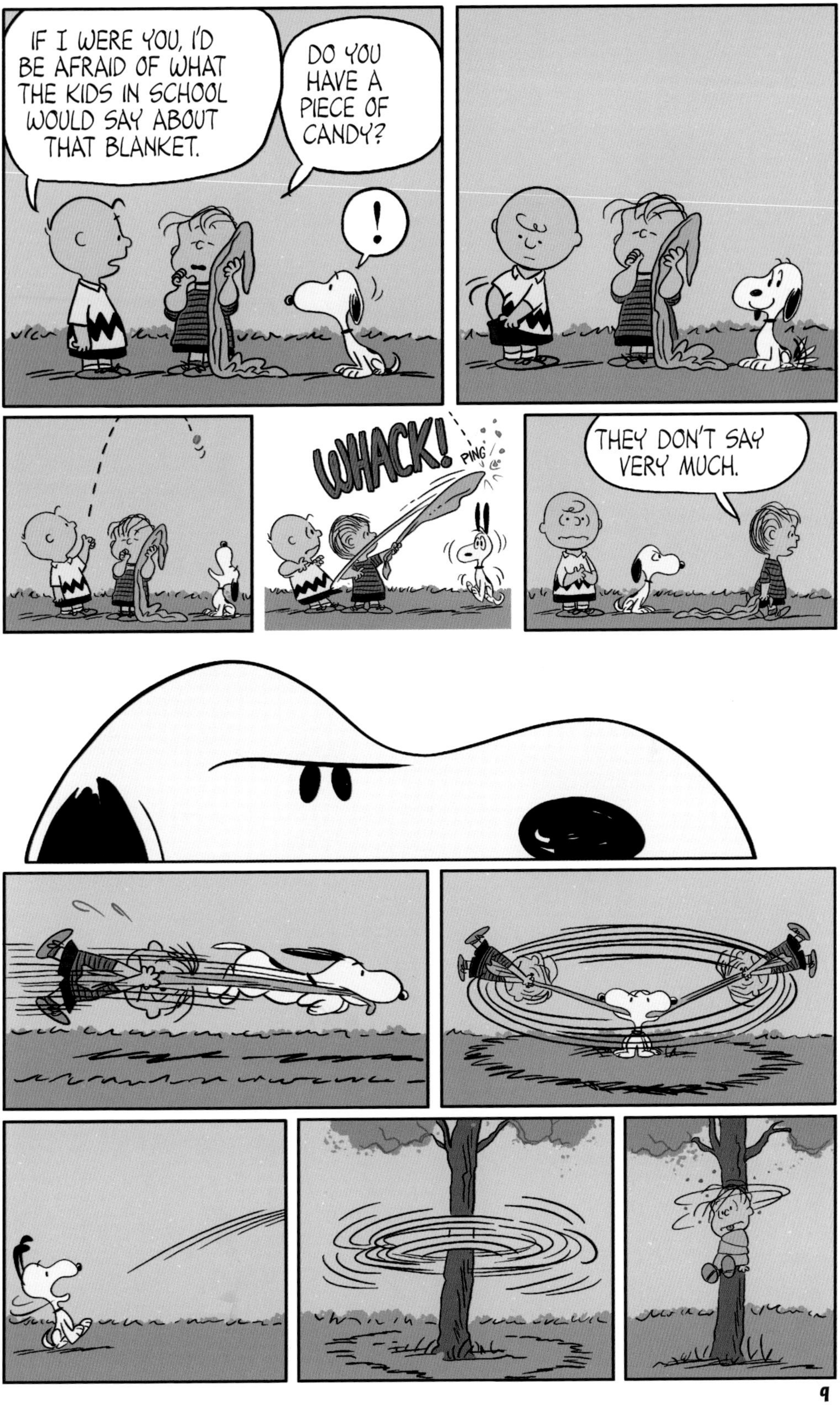

IF I WERE YOU, I'D BE AFRAID OF WHAT THE KIDS IN SCHOOL WOULD SAY ABOUT THAT BLANKET.
DO YOU HAVE A PIECE OF CANDY?
!
WHACK!
PING
THEY DON'T SAY VERY MUCH.

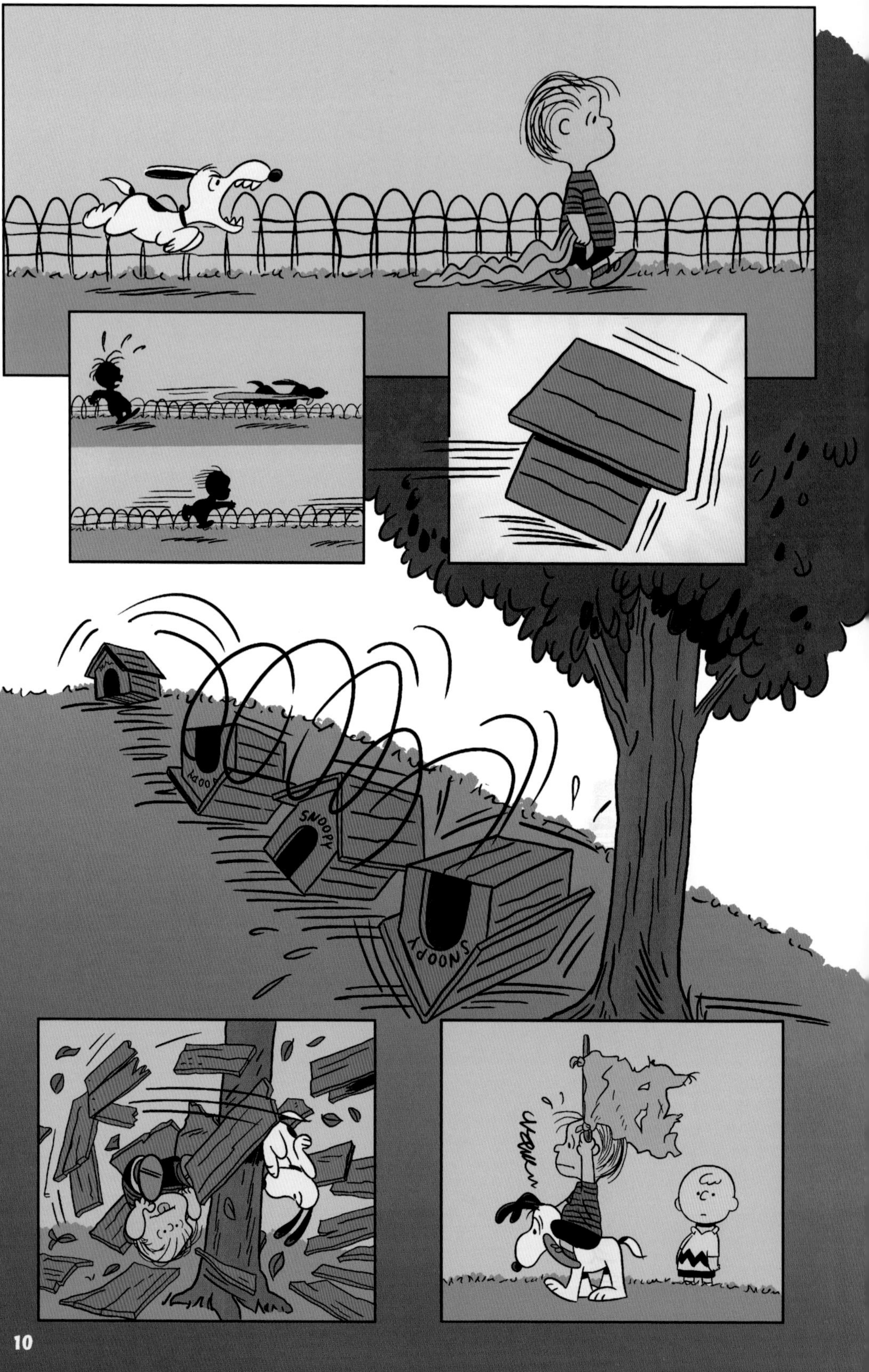
SNOOPY
SNOOPY

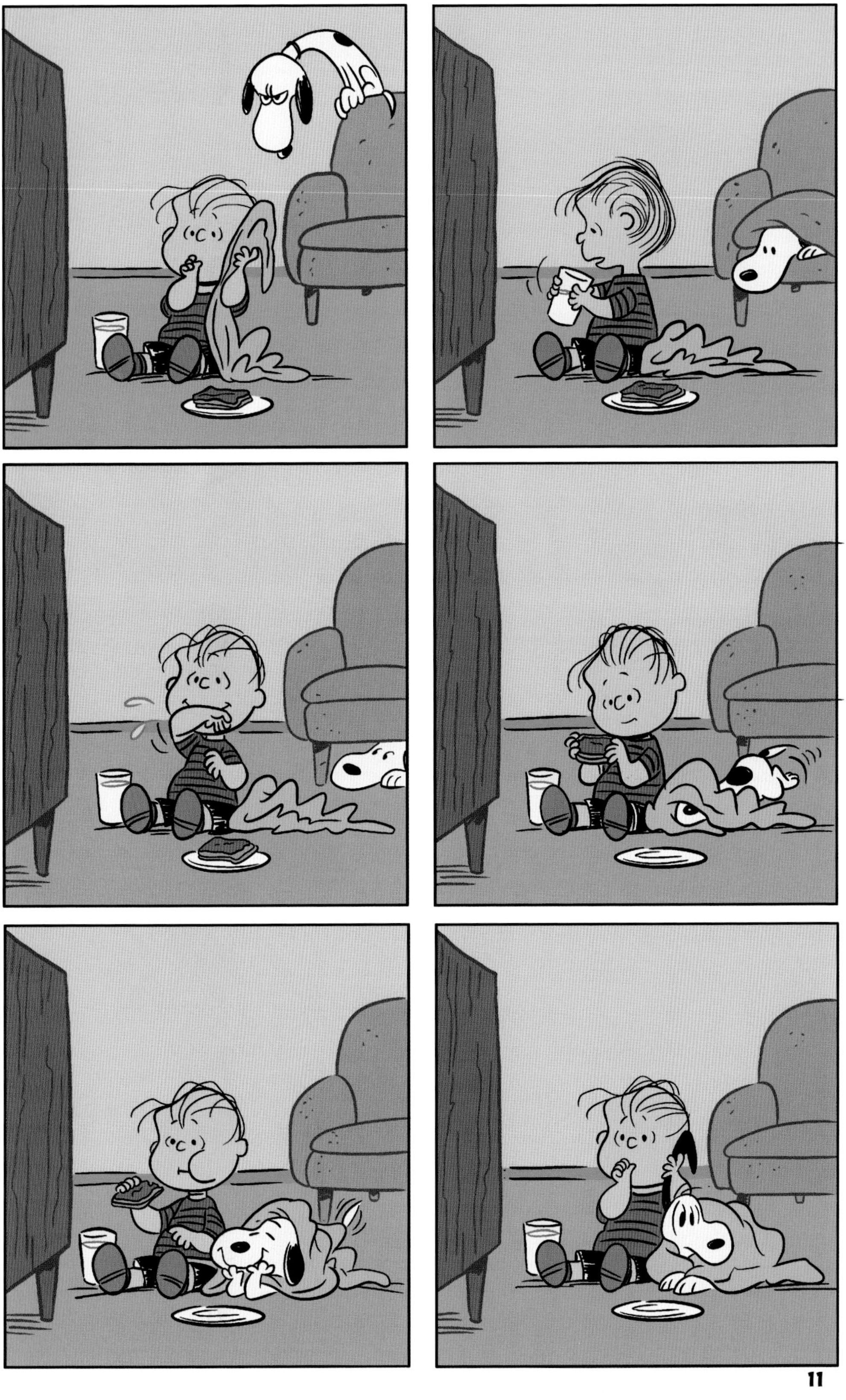

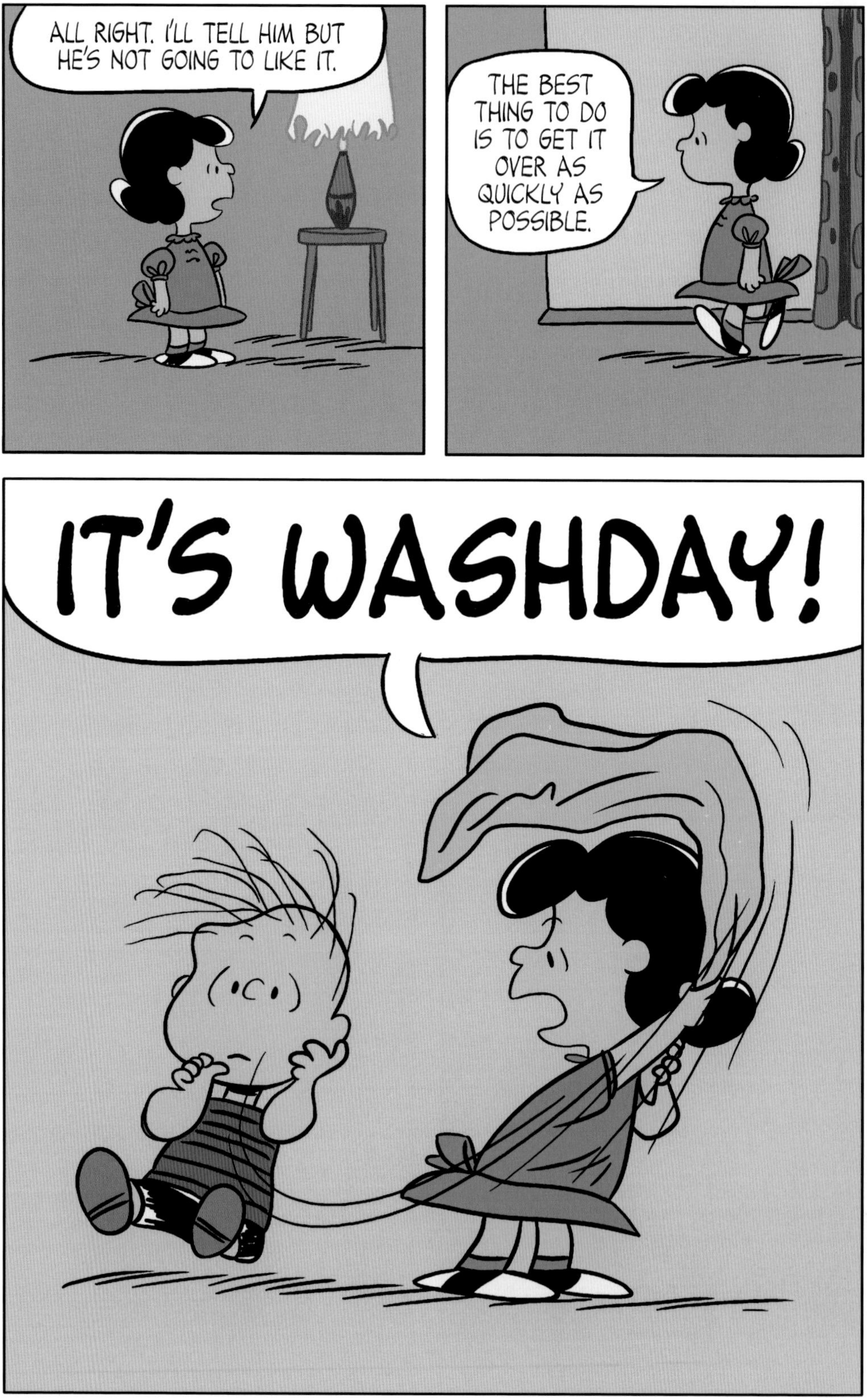
ALL RIGHT. I'LL TELL HIM BUT HE'S NOT GOING TO LIKE IT.
THE BEST THING TO DO IS TO GET IT OVER AS QUICKLY AS POSSIBLE.
IT'S WASHDAY!

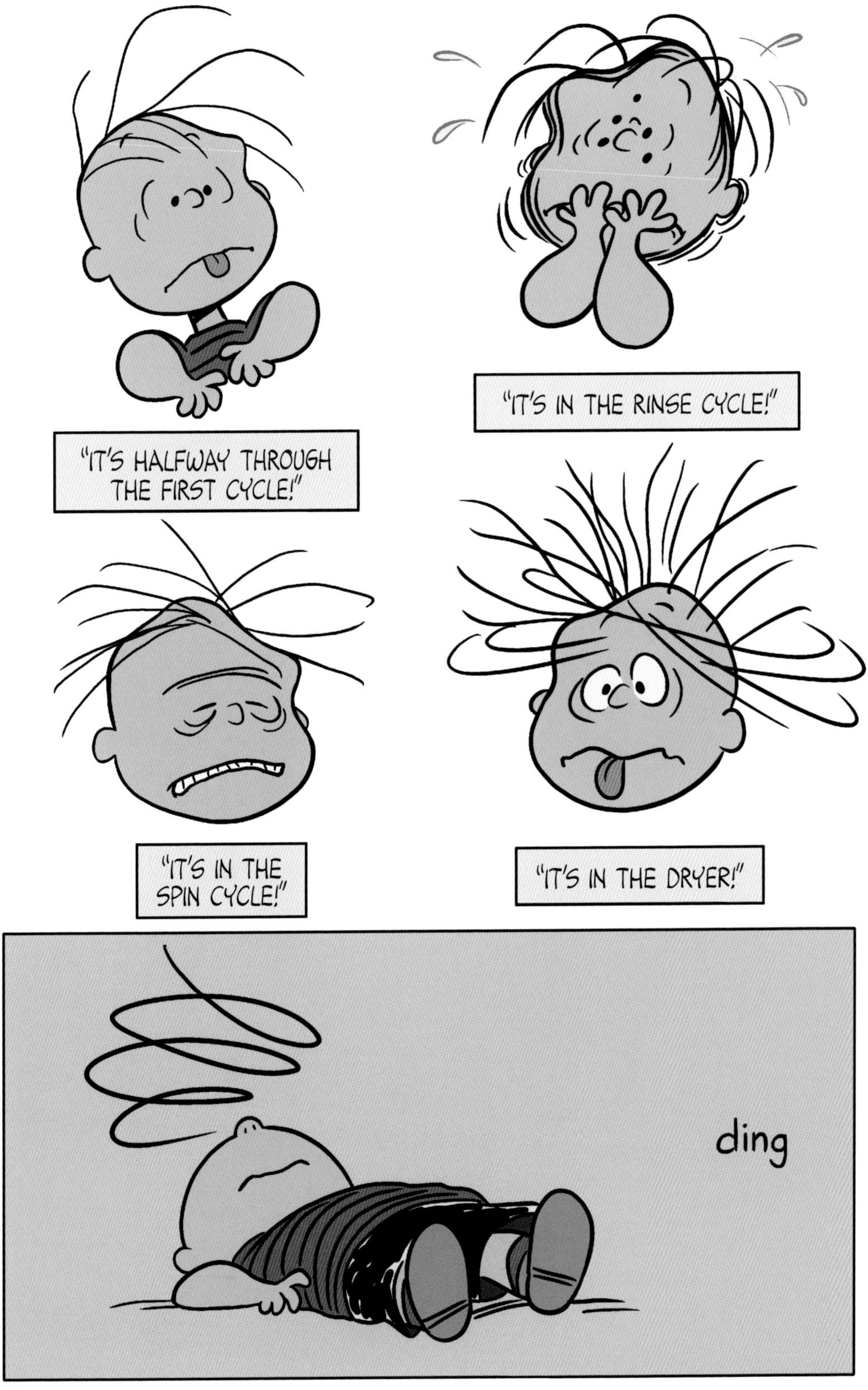
"IT'S HALFWAY THROUGH THE FIRST CYCLE!"
"IT'S IN THE RINSE CYCLE!"
"IT'S IN THE SPIN CYCLE!"
"IT'S IN THE DRYER!"
ding

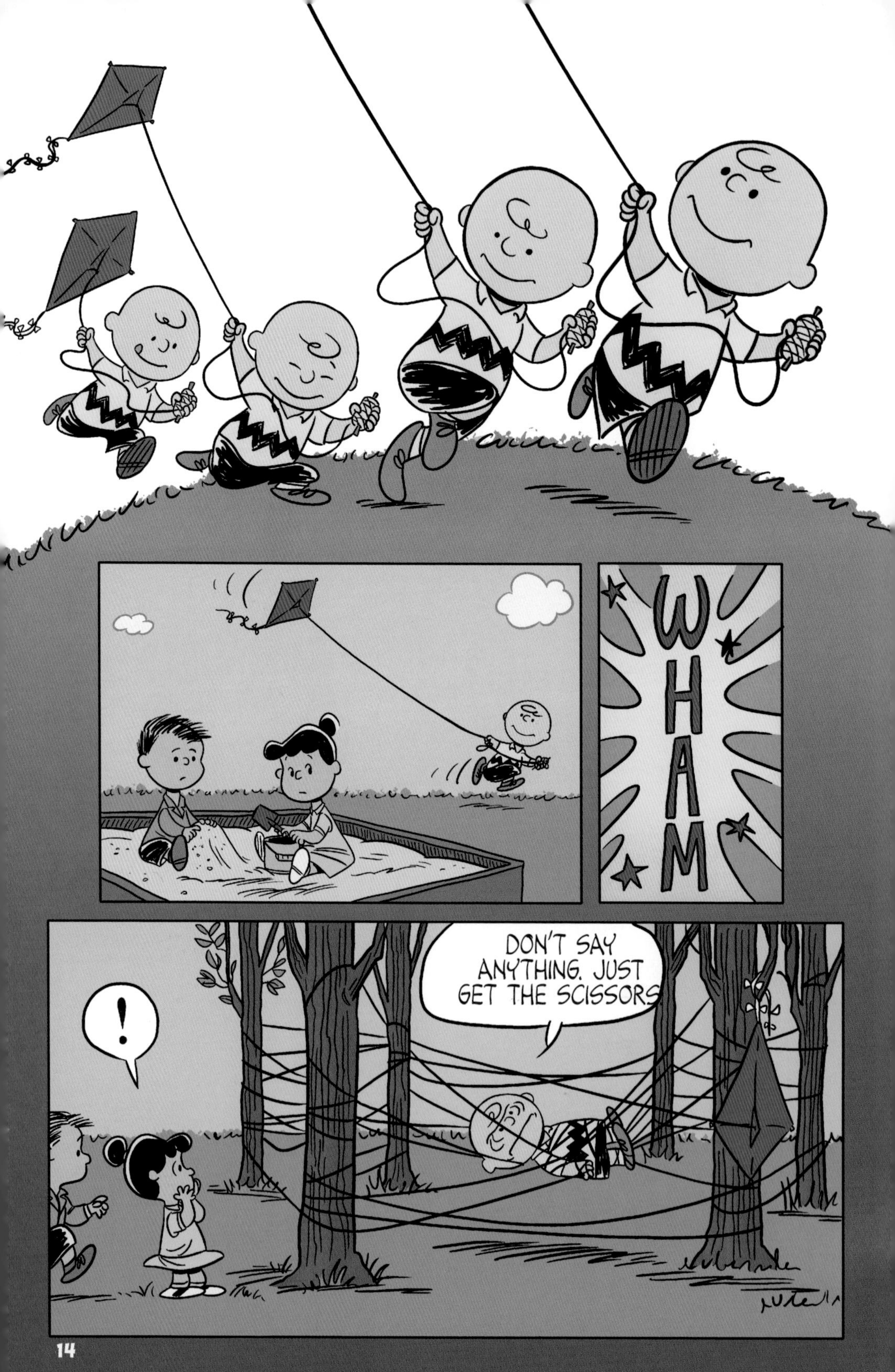
WHAM
DON'T SAY ANYTHING. JUST GET THE SCISSORS.
!

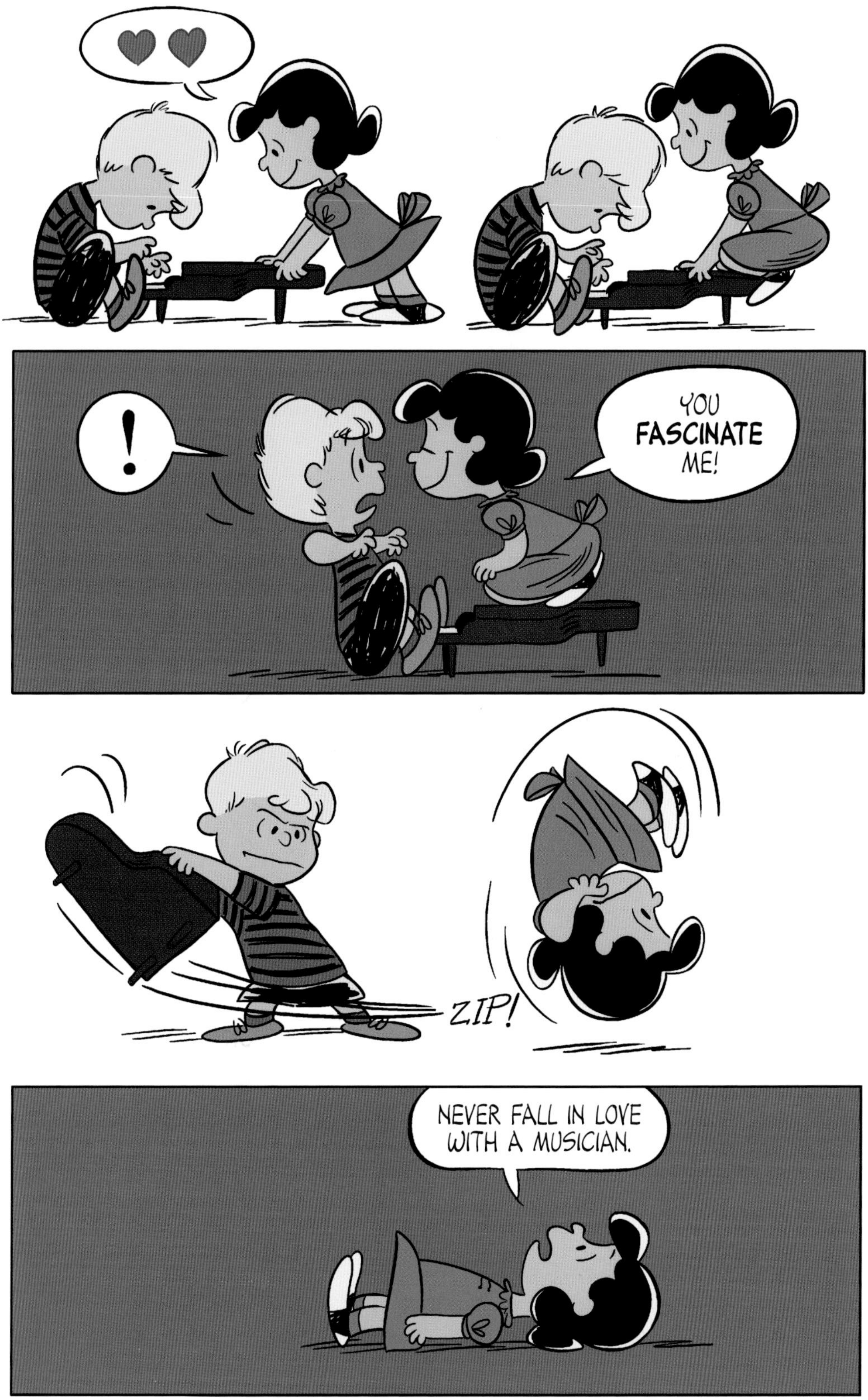
!
YOU FASCINATE ME!
ZIP!
NEVER FALL IN LOVE WITH A MUSICIAN.

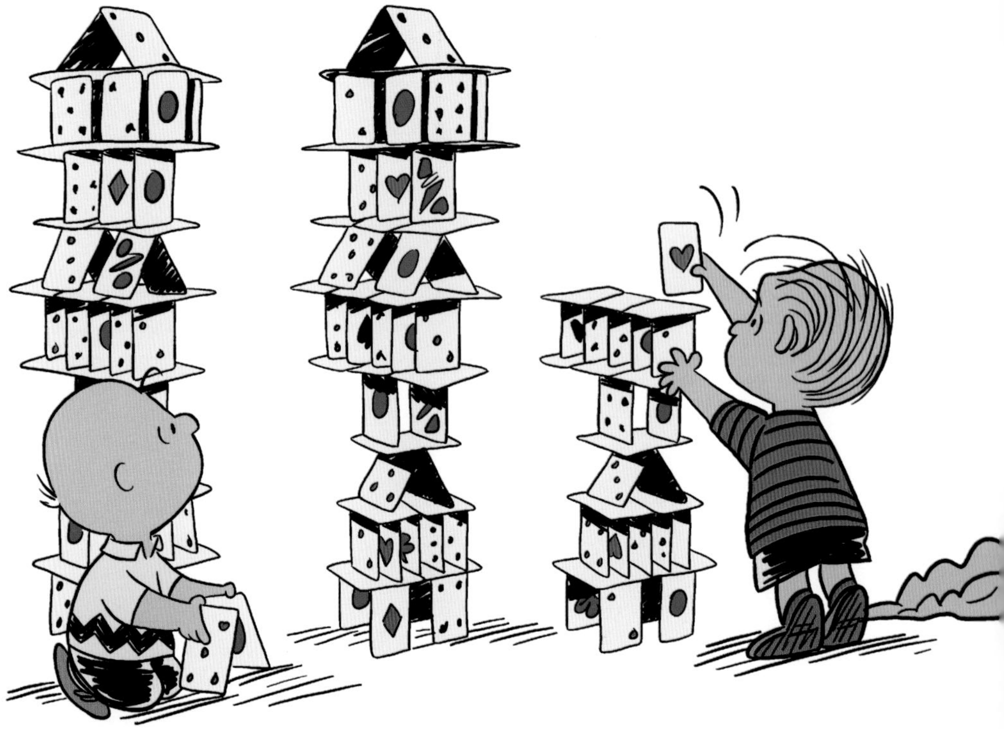

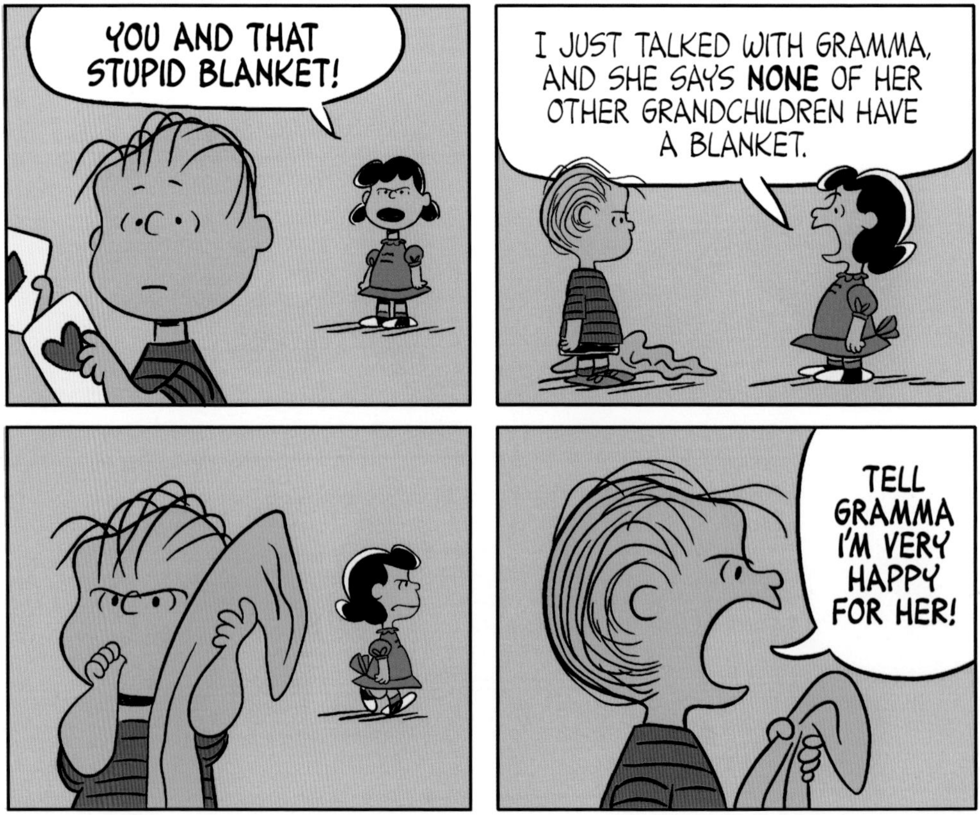
YOU AND THAT STUPID BLANKET!
I JUST TALKED WITH GRAMMA, AND SHE SAYS **NONE** OF HER OTHER GRANDCHILDREN HAVE A BLANKET.
TELL GRAMMA I'M VERY HAPPY FOR HER!

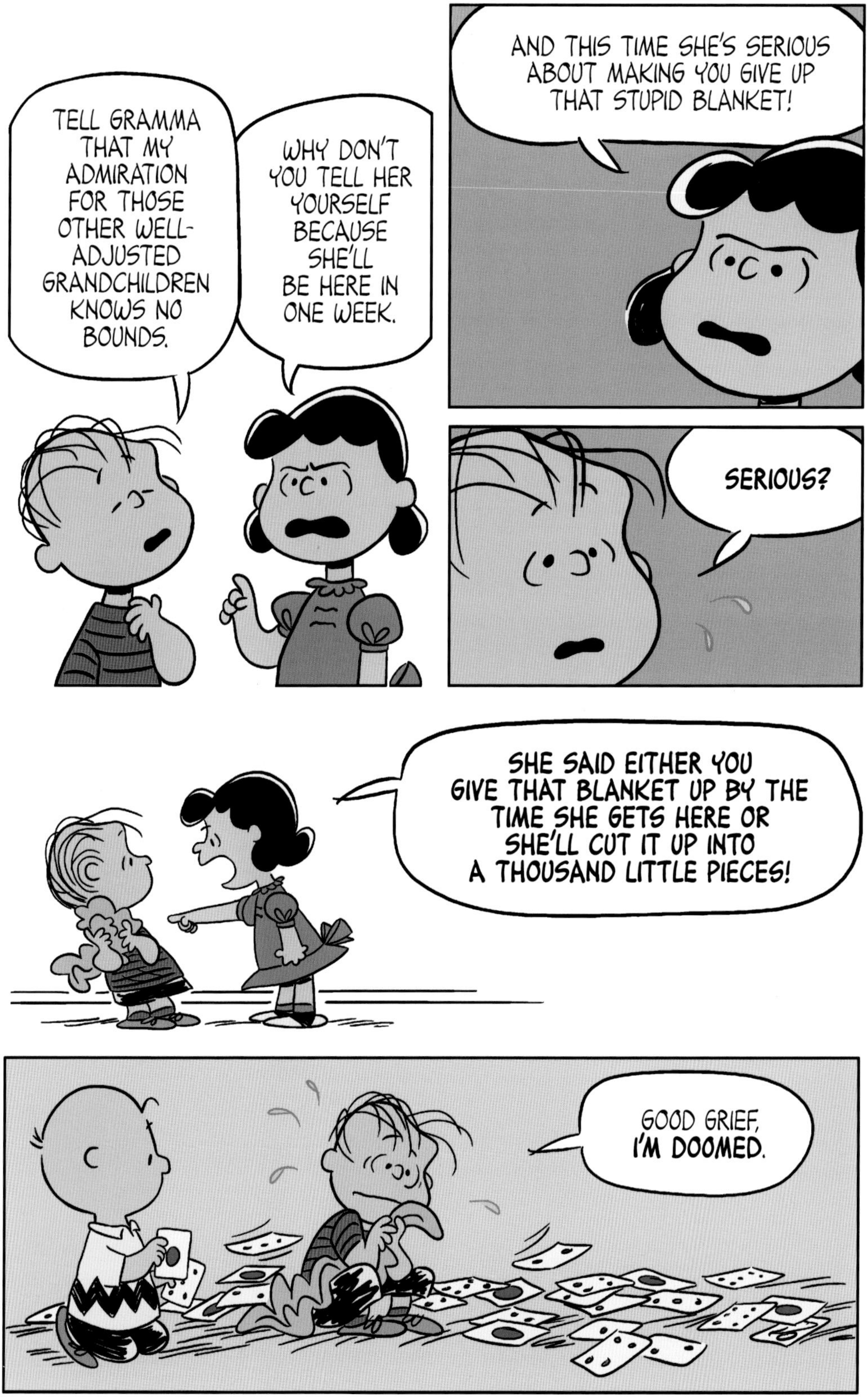
TELL GRAMMA THAT MY ADMIRATION FOR THOSE OTHER WELL-ADJUSTED GRANDCHILDREN KNOWS NO BOUNDS.
WHY DON'T YOU TELL HER YOURSELF BECAUSE SHE'LL BE HERE IN ONE WEEK.
AND THIS TIME SHE'S SERIOUS ABOUT MAKING YOU GIVE UP THAT STUPID BLANKET!
SERIOUS?
SHE SAID EITHER YOU GIVE THAT BLANKET UP BY THE TIME SHE GETS HERE OR SHE'LL CUT IT UP INTO A THOUSAND LITTLE PIECES!
GOOD GRIEF, I'M DOOMED.

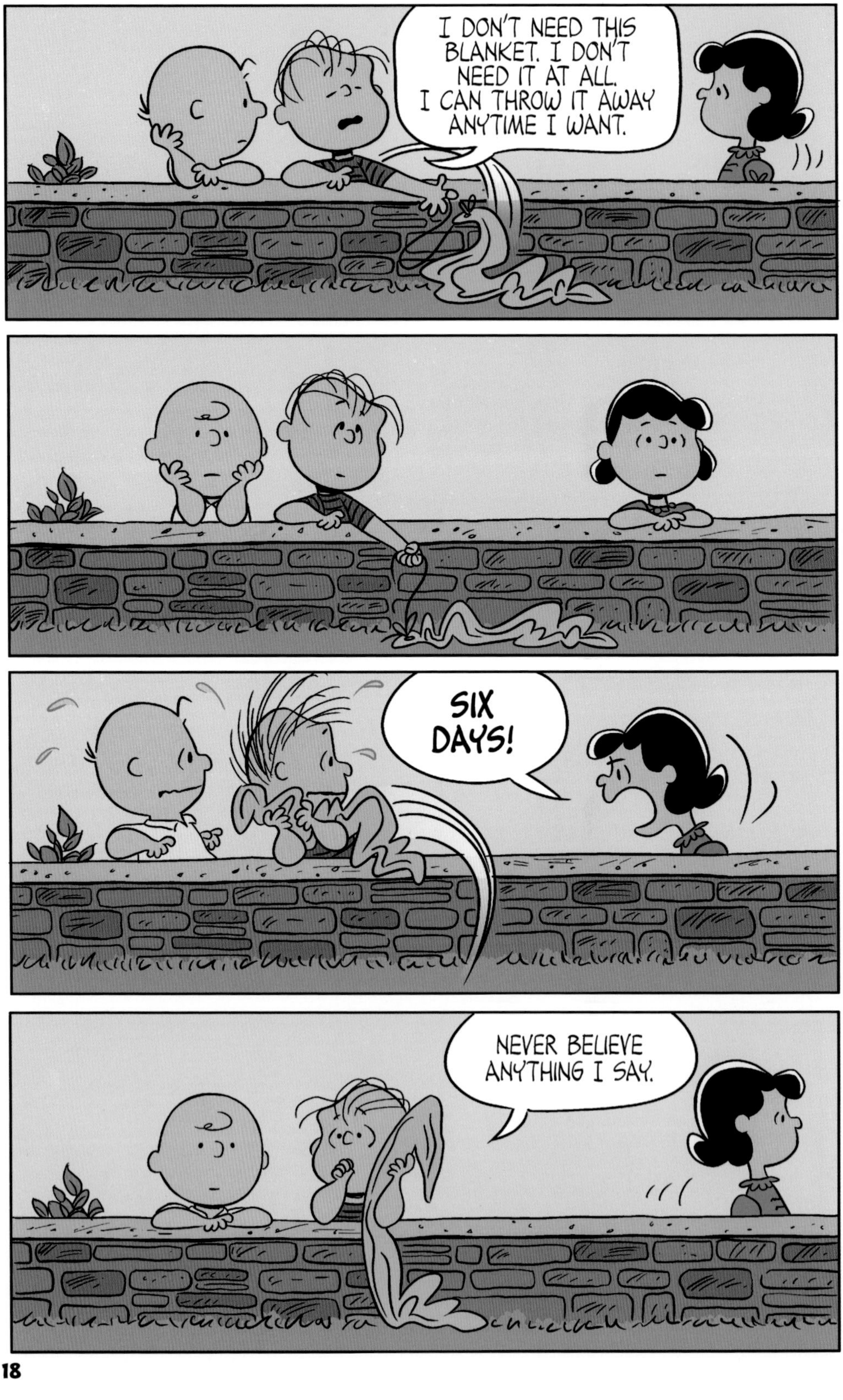
I DON'T NEED THIS BLANKET. I DON'T NEED IT AT ALL. I CAN THROW IT AWAY ANYTIME I WANT.
SIX DAYS!
NEVER BELIEVE ANYTHING I SAY.

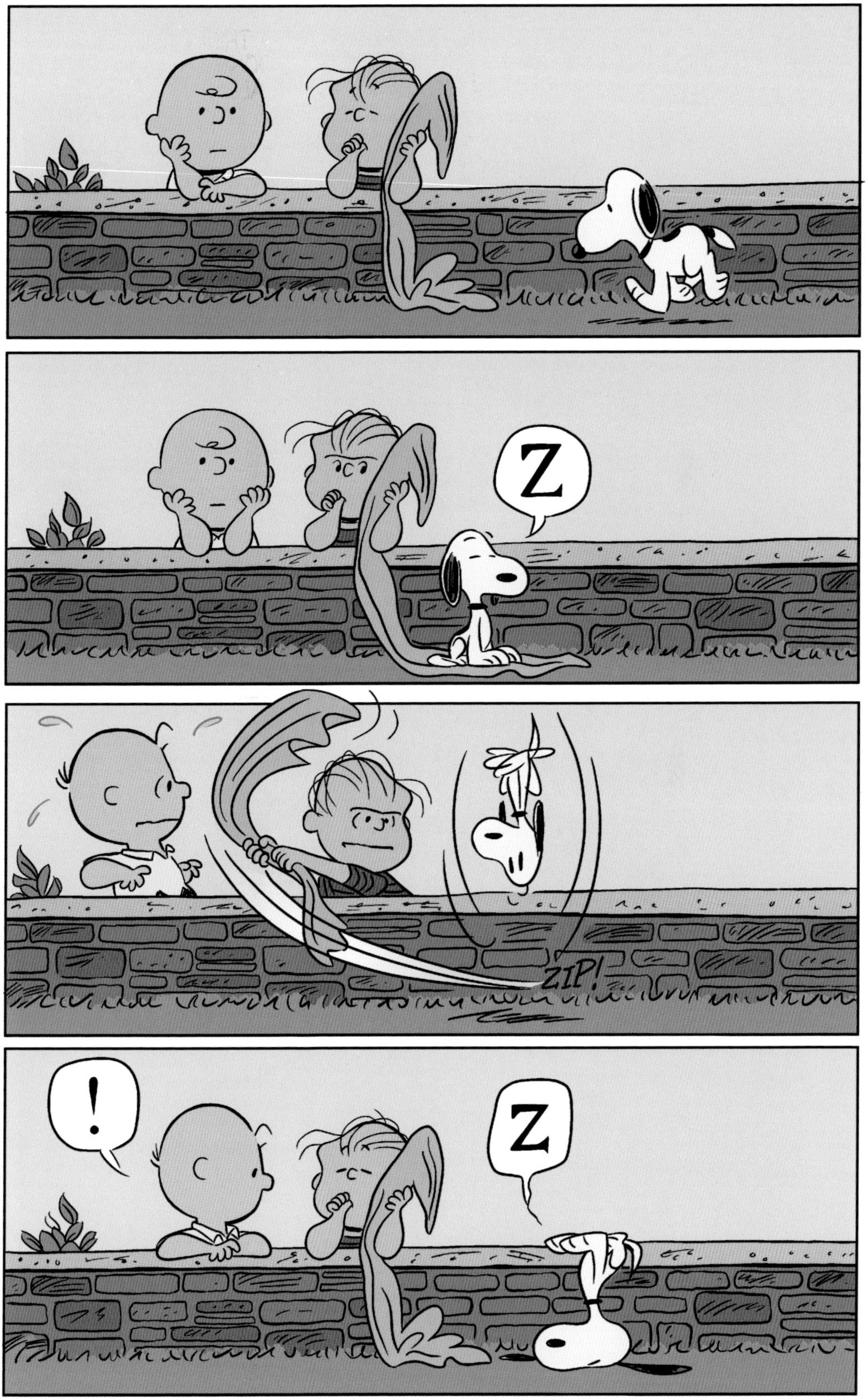
Z
ZIP!
!
Z

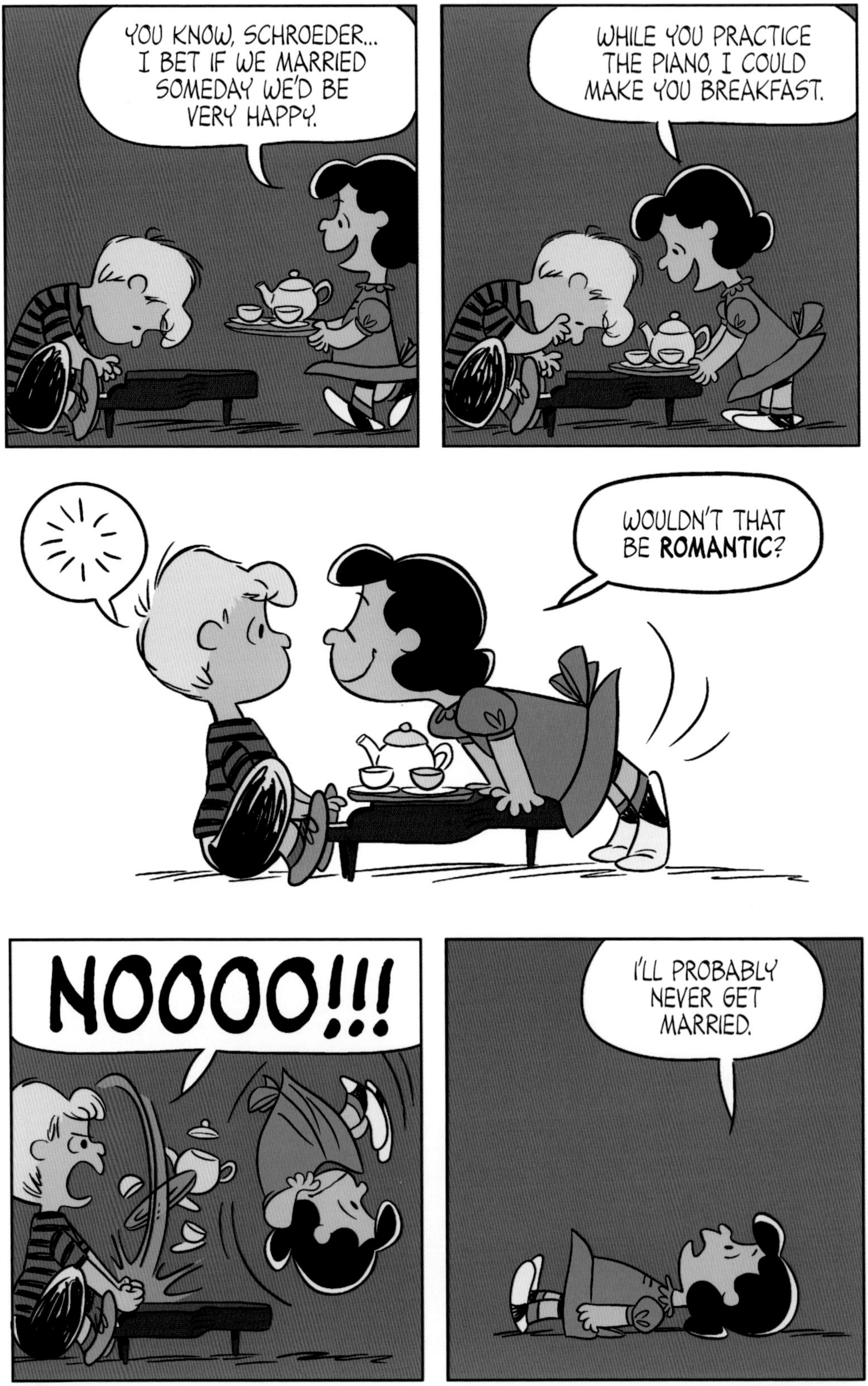
YOU KNOW, SCHROEDER... I BET IF WE MARRIED SOMEDAY WE'D BE VERY HAPPY.
WHILE YOU PRACTICE THE PIANO, I COULD MAKE YOU BREAKFAST.
WOULDN'T THAT BE **ROMANTIC**?
NOOOO!!!
I'LL PROBABLY NEVER GET MARRIED.

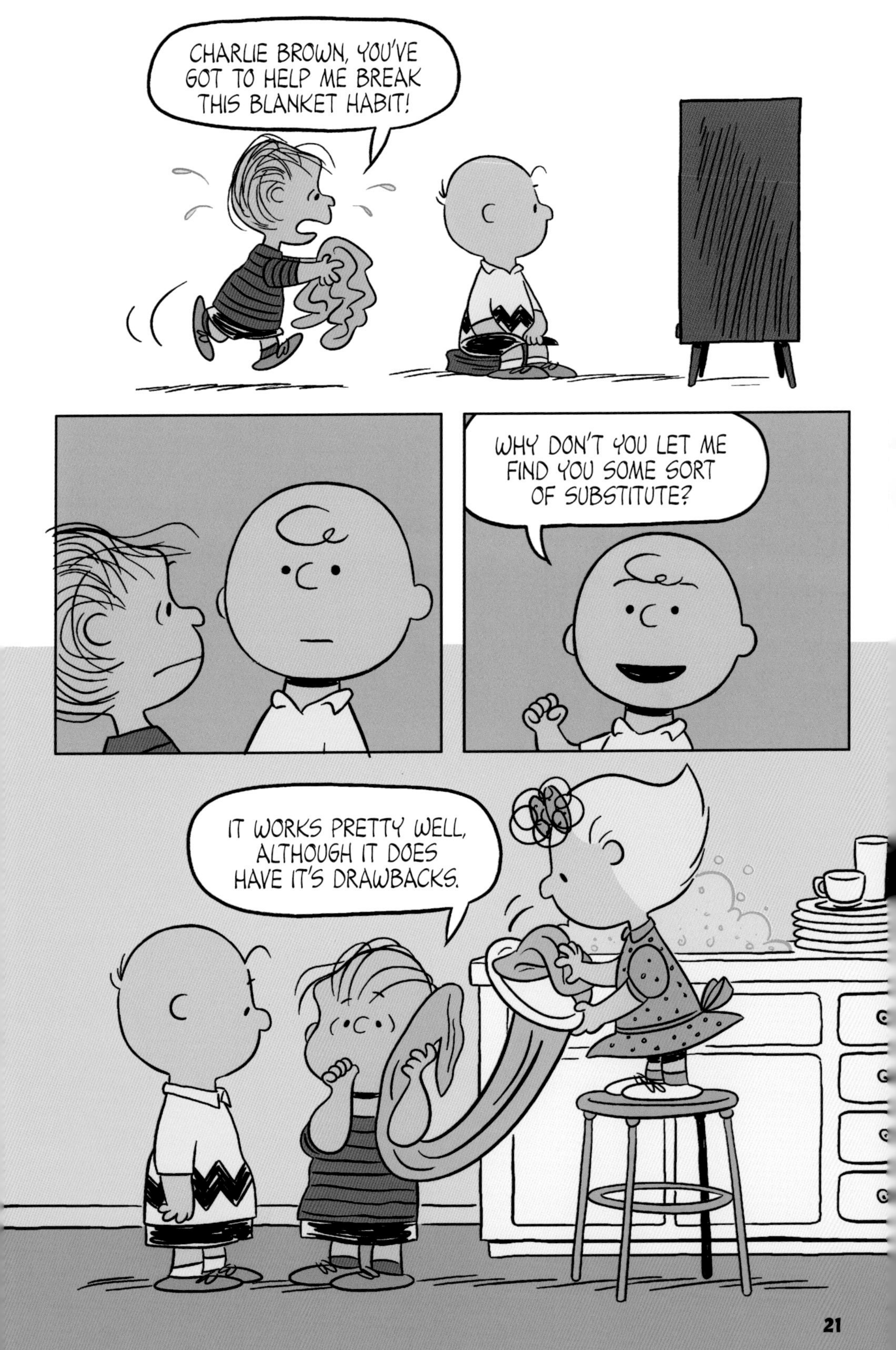
CHARLIE BROWN, YOU'VE GOT TO HELP ME BREAK THIS BLANKET HABIT!
WHY DON'T YOU LET ME FIND YOU SOME SORT OF SUBSTITUTE?
IT WORKS PRETTY WELL, ALTHOUGH IT DOES HAVE IT'S DRAWBACKS.

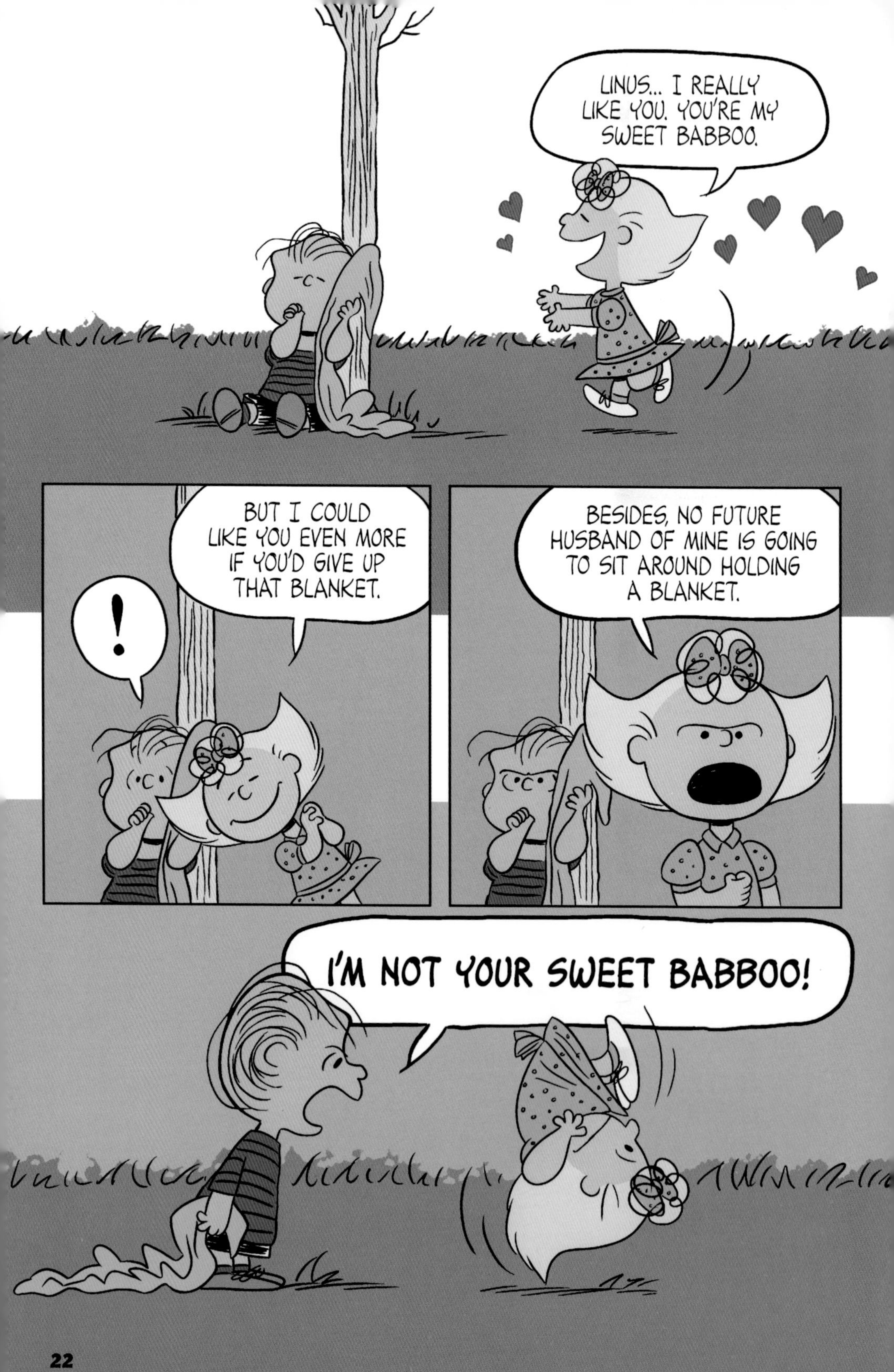
LINUS... I REALLY LIKE YOU. YOU'RE MY SWEET BABBOO.
!
BUT I COULD LIKE YOU EVEN MORE IF YOU'D GIVE UP THAT BLANKET.
BESIDES, NO FUTURE HUSBAND OF MINE IS GOING TO SIT AROUND HOLDING A BLANKET.
I'M NOT YOUR SWEET BABBOO!

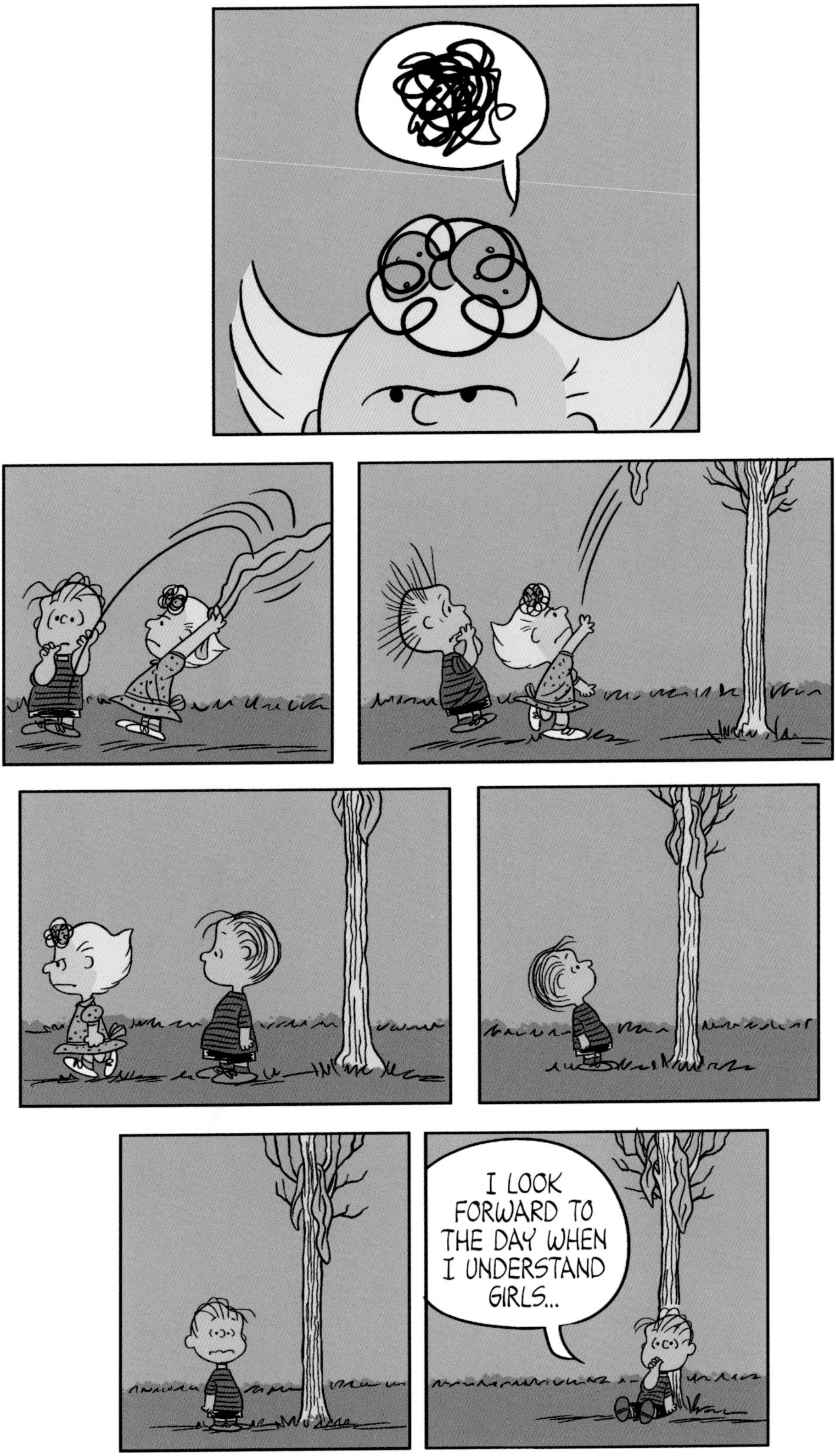
I LOOK FORWARD TO THE DAY WHEN I UNDERSTAND GIRLS...

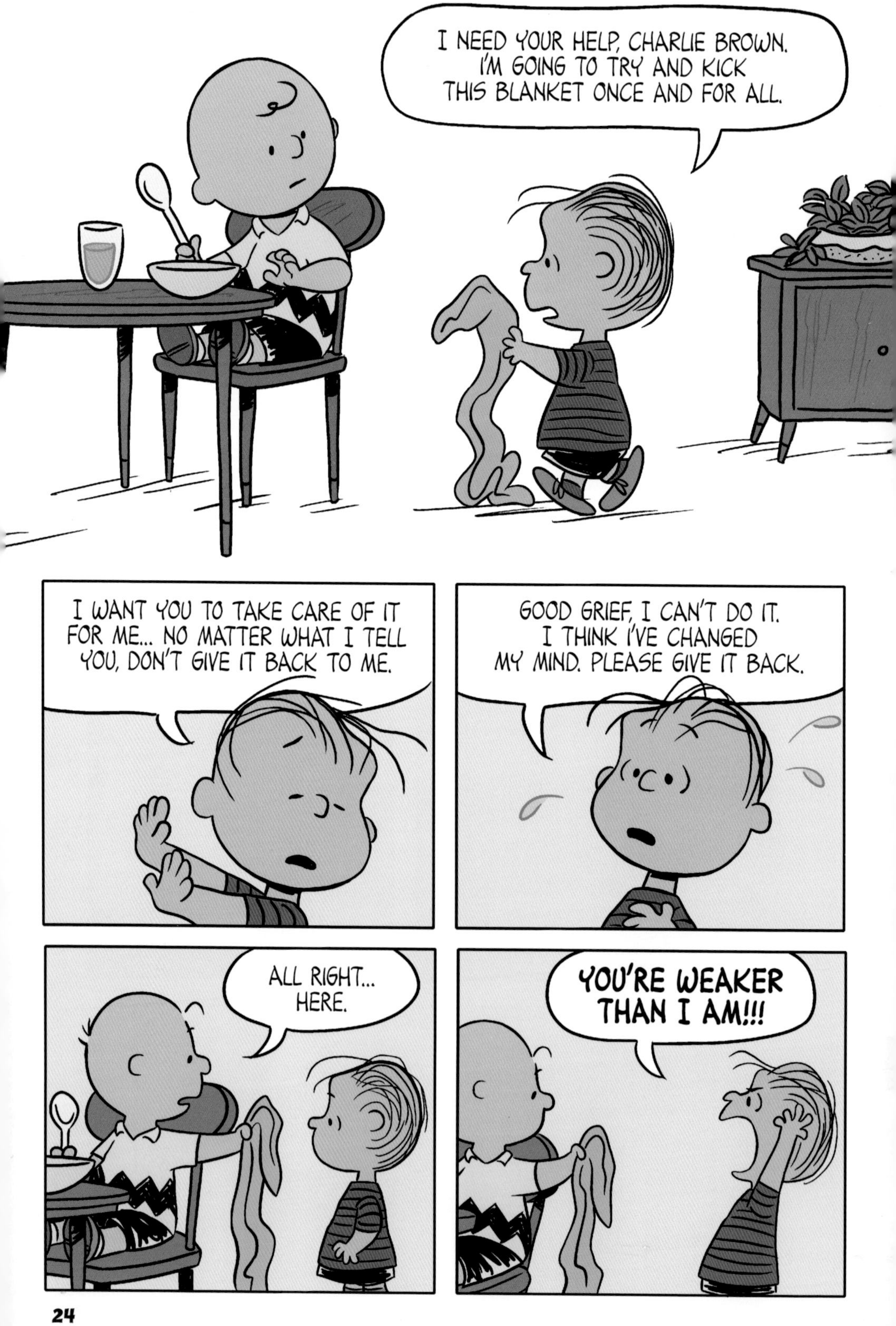
I NEED YOUR HELP, CHARLIE BROWN. I'M GOING TO TRY AND KICK THIS BLANKET ONCE AND FOR ALL.
I WANT YOU TO TAKE CARE OF IT FOR ME... NO MATTER WHAT I TELL YOU, DON'T GIVE IT BACK TO ME.
GOOD GRIEF, I CAN'T DO IT. I THINK I'VE CHANGED MY MIND. PLEASE GIVE IT BACK.
ALL RIGHT... HERE.
YOU'RE WEAKER THAN I AM!!!

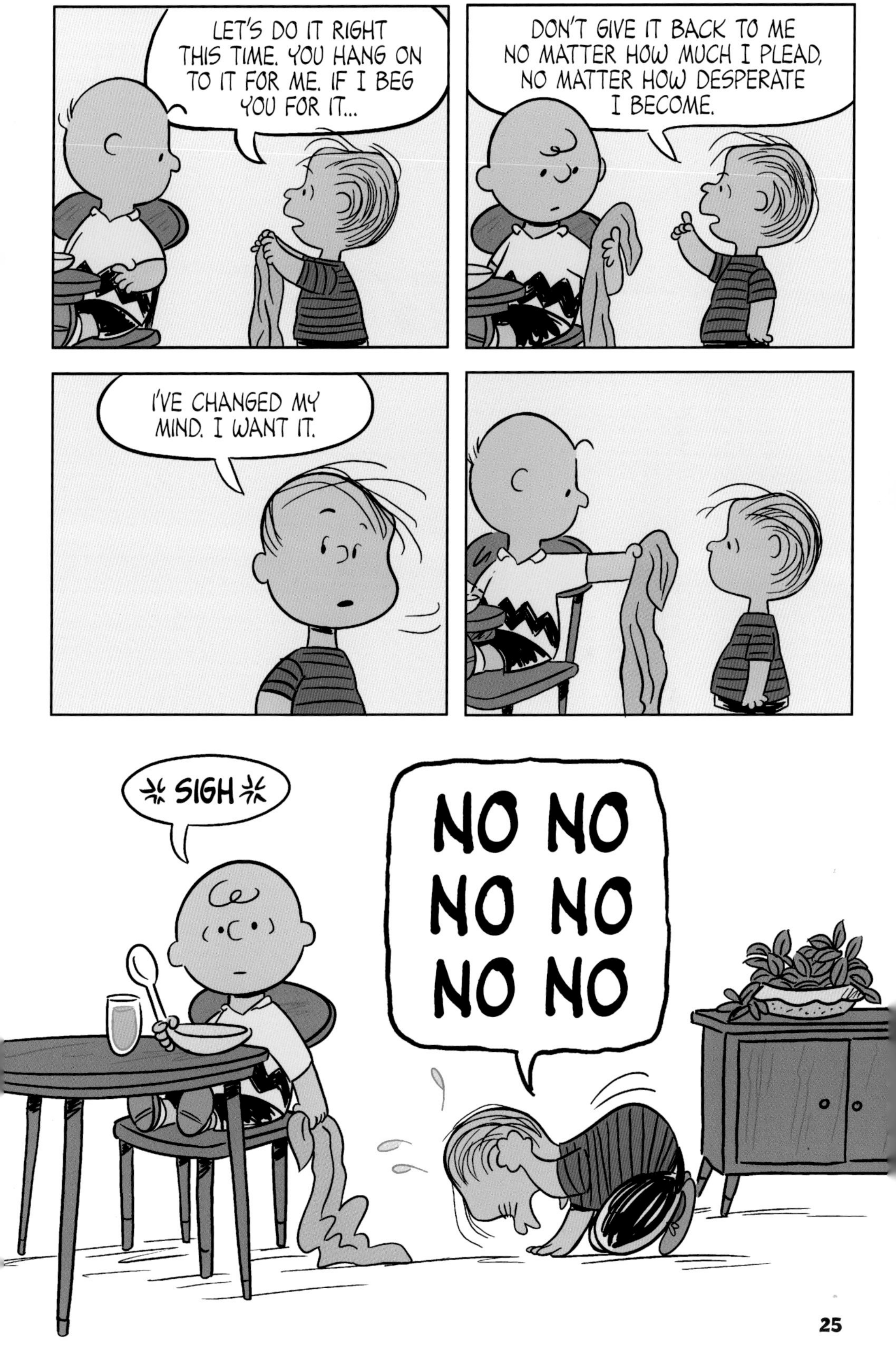
LET'S DO IT RIGHT THIS TIME. YOU HANG ON TO IT FOR ME. IF I BEG YOU FOR IT...
DON'T GIVE IT BACK TO ME NO MATTER HOW MUCH I PLEAD, NO MATTER HOW DESPERATE I BECOME.
I'VE CHANGED MY MIND. I WANT IT.
SIGH
NO NO NO NO NO NO

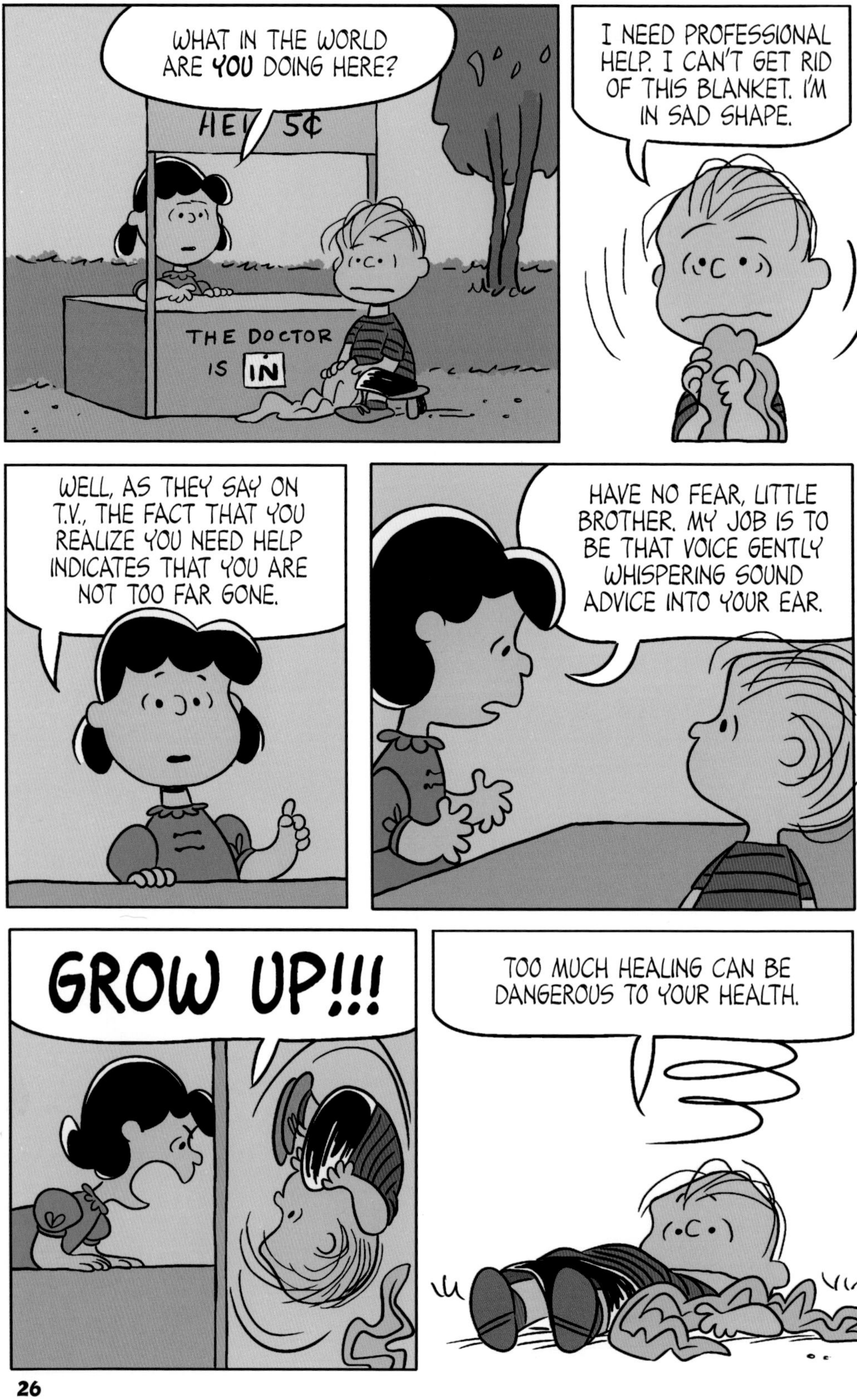
WHAT IN THE WORLD ARE **YOU** DOING HERE?
HE 5¢
THE DOCTOR IS IN
I NEED PROFESSIONAL HELP. I CAN'T GET RID OF THIS BLANKET. I'M IN SAD SHAPE.
WELL, AS THEY SAY ON T.V., THE FACT THAT YOU REALIZE YOU NEED HELP INDICATES THAT YOU ARE NOT TOO FAR GONE.
HAVE NO FEAR, LITTLE BROTHER. MY JOB IS TO BE THAT VOICE GENTLY WHISPERING SOUND ADVICE INTO YOUR EAR.
GROW UP!!!
TOO MUCH HEALING CAN BE DANGEROUS TO YOUR HEALTH.

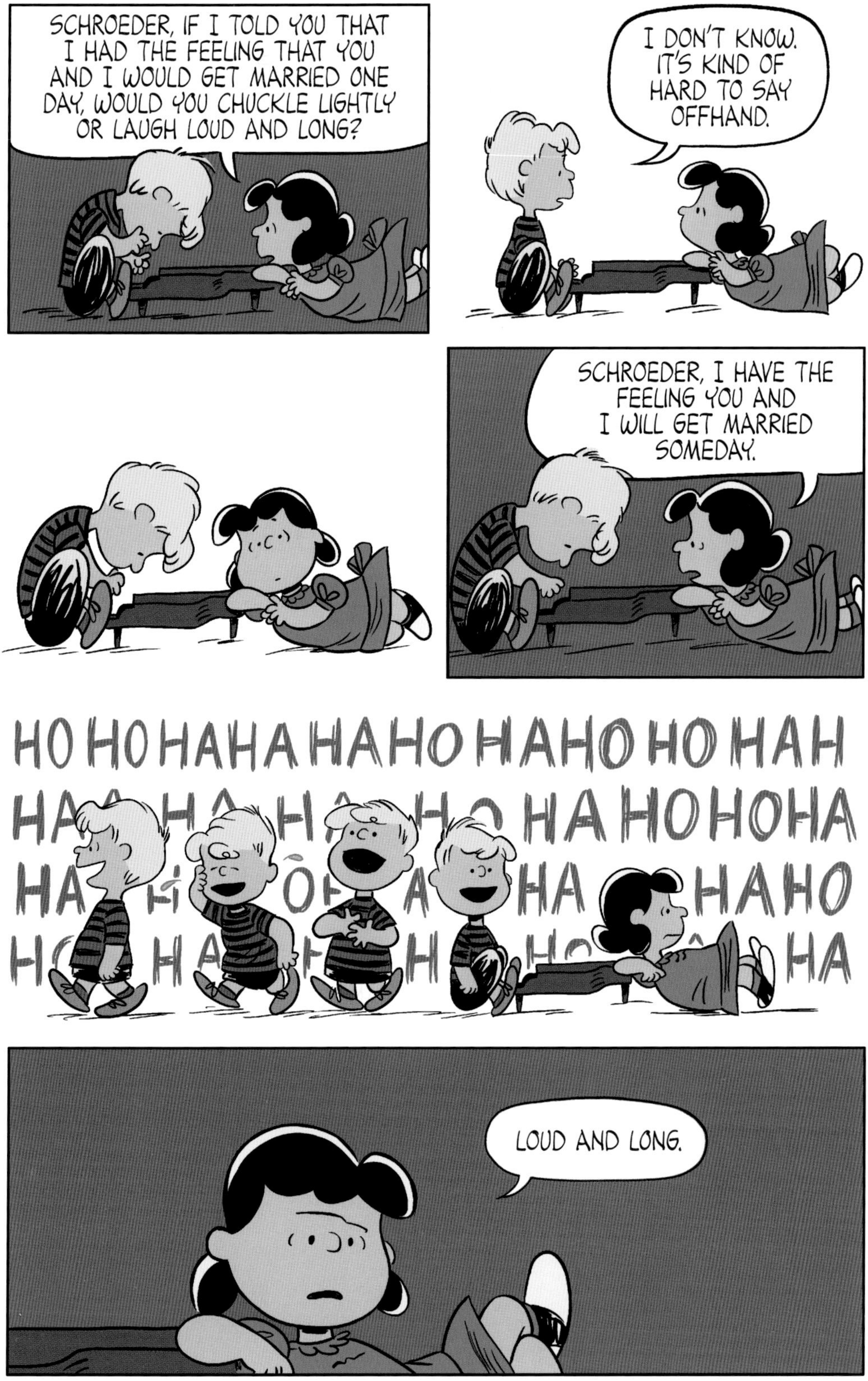
SCHROEDER, IF I TOLD YOU THAT I HAD THE FEELING THAT YOU AND I WOULD GET MARRIED ONE DAY, WOULD YOU CHUCKLE LIGHTLY OR LAUGH LOUD AND LONG?
I DON'T KNOW. IT'S KIND OF HARD TO SAY OFFHAND.
SCHROEDER, I HAVE THE FEELING YOU AND I WILL GET MARRIED SOMEDAY.
HO HO HA HA HA HA HO HA HO HO HO HAH
LOUD AND LONG.

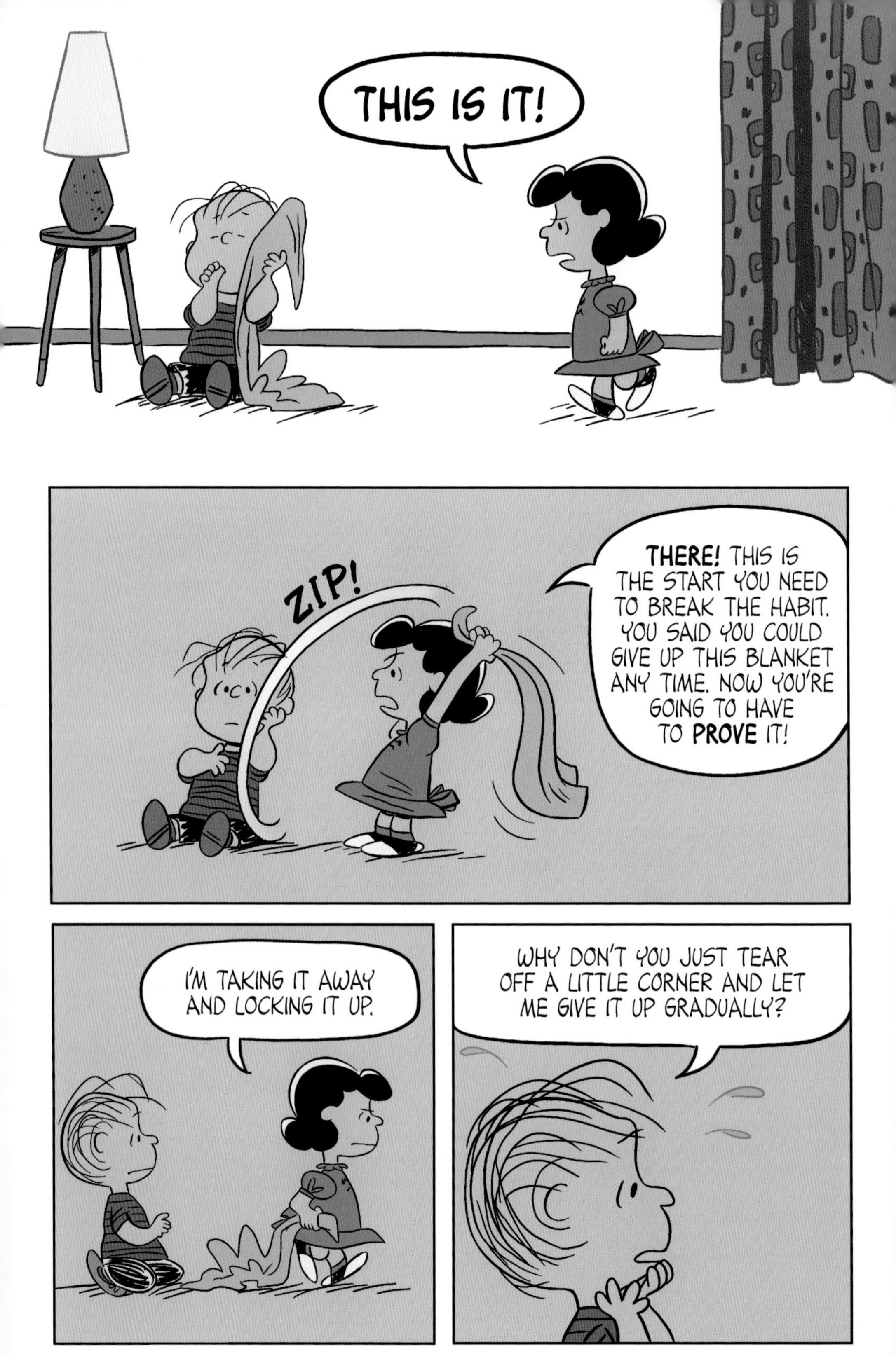
THIS IS IT!
ZIP!
THERE! THIS IS THE START YOU NEED TO BREAK THE HABIT. YOU SAID YOU COULD GIVE UP THIS BLANKET ANY TIME. NOW YOU'RE GOING TO HAVE TO PROVE IT!
I'M TAKING IT AWAY AND LOCKING IT UP.
WHY DON'T YOU JUST TEAR OFF A LITTLE CORNER AND LET ME GIVE IT UP GRADUALLY?

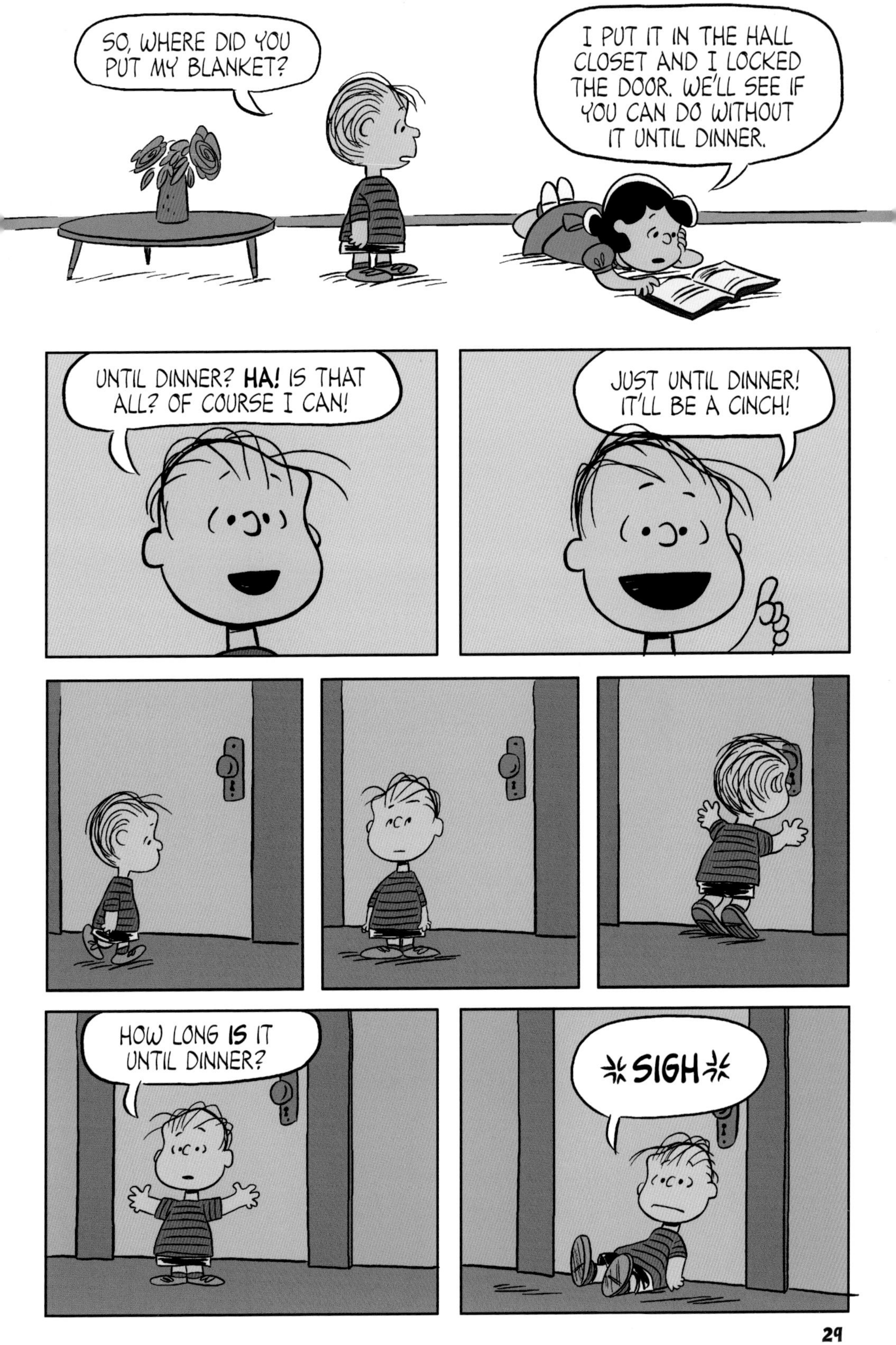
SO, WHERE DID YOU PUT MY BLANKET?
I PUT IT IN THE HALL CLOSET AND I LOCKED THE DOOR. WE'LL SEE IF YOU CAN DO WITHOUT IT UNTIL DINNER.
UNTIL DINNER? HA! IS THAT ALL? OF COURSE I CAN!
JUST UNTIL DINNER! IT'LL BE A CINCH!
HOW LONG IS IT UNTIL DINNER?
SIGH

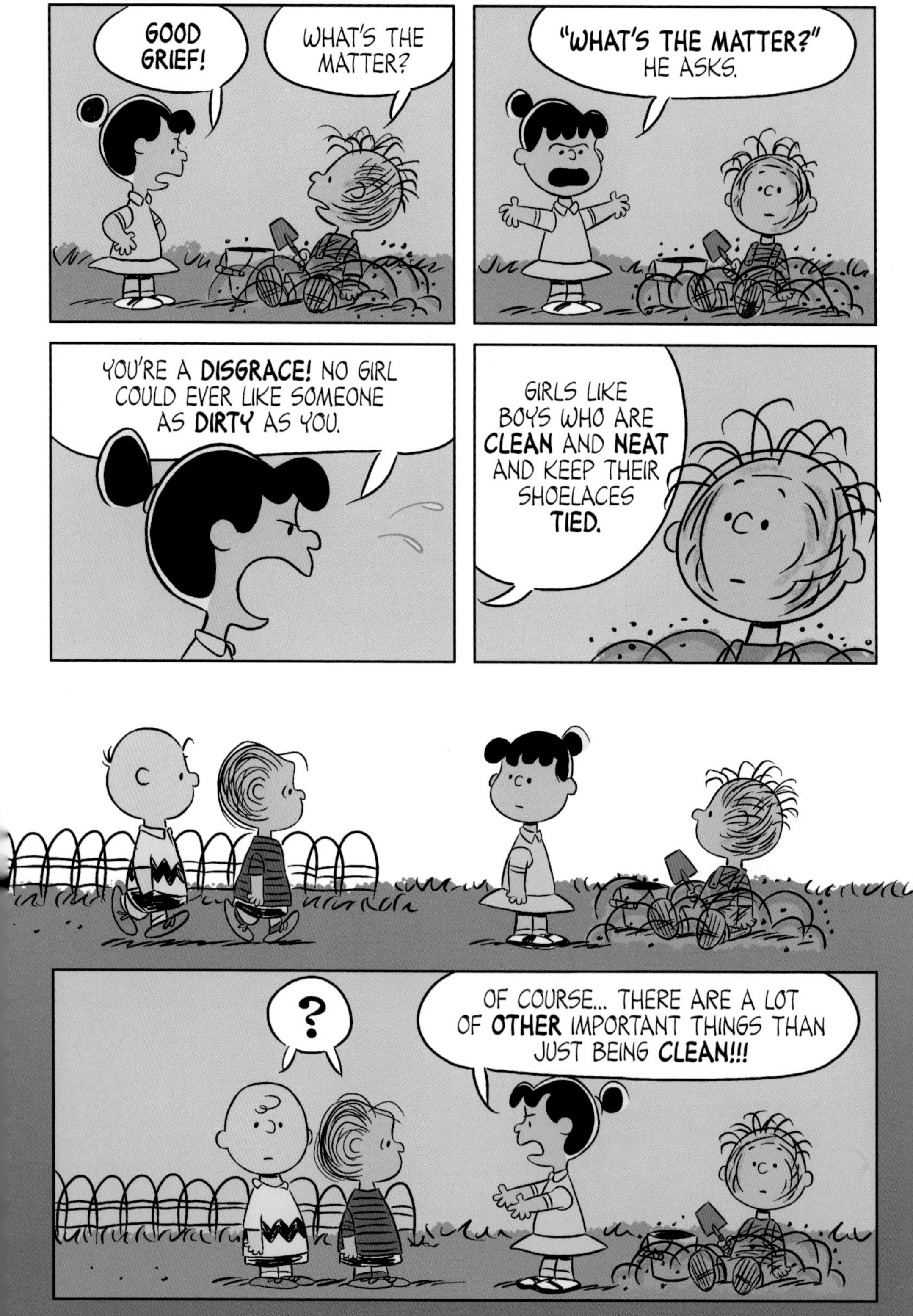
GOOD GRIEF!
WHAT'S THE MATTER?
"WHAT'S THE MATTER?" HE ASKS.
YOU'RE A DISGRACE! NO GIRL COULD EVER LIKE SOMEONE AS DIRTY AS YOU.
GIRLS LIKE BOYS WHO ARE CLEAN AND NEAT AND KEEP THEIR SHOELACES TIED.
?
OF COURSE... THERE ARE A LOT OF OTHER IMPORTANT THINGS THAN JUST BEING CLEAN!!!

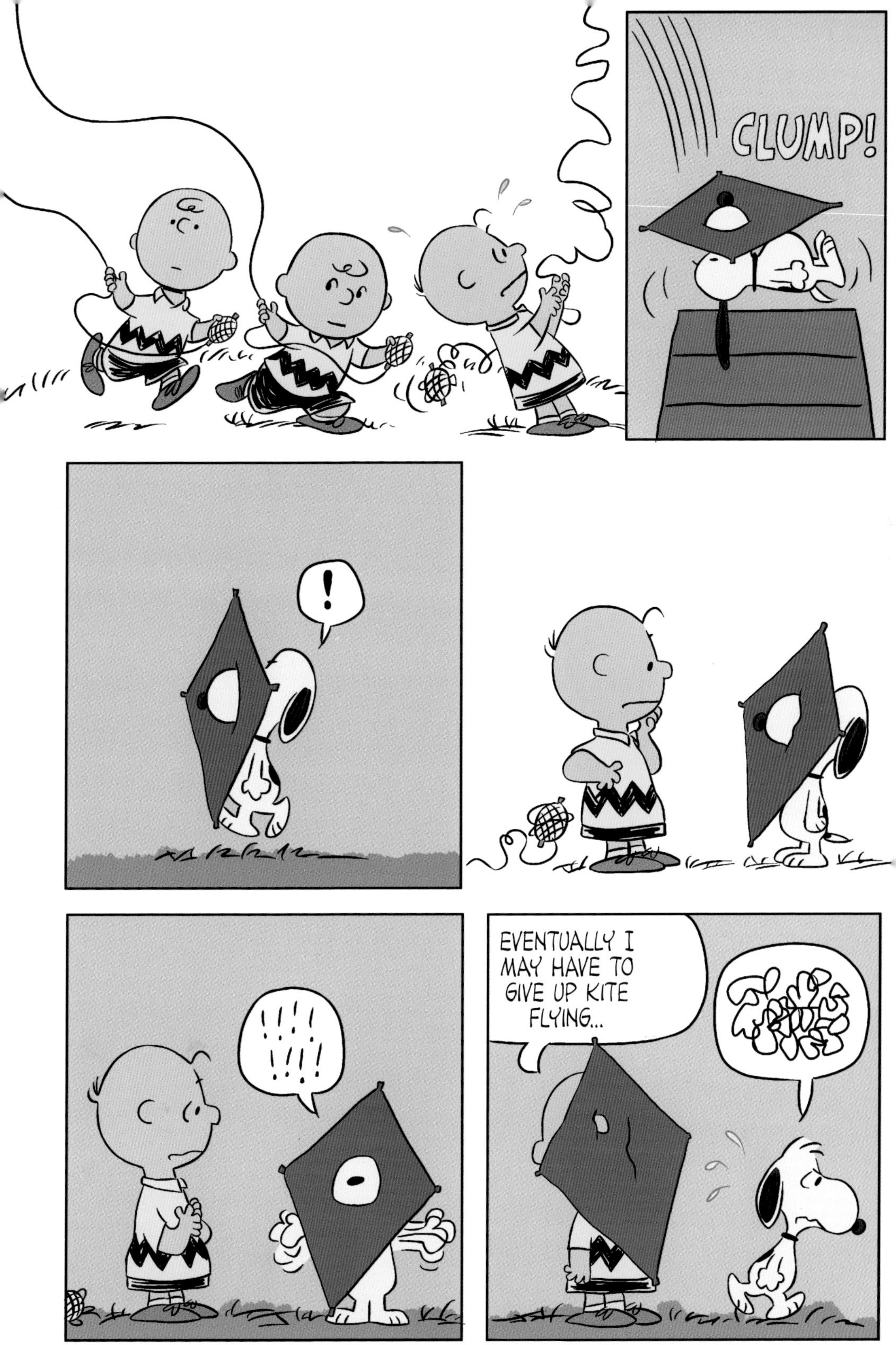
CLUMP!
!
!!!!
!!!!
EVENTUALLY I MAY HAVE TO GIVE UP KITE FLYING...

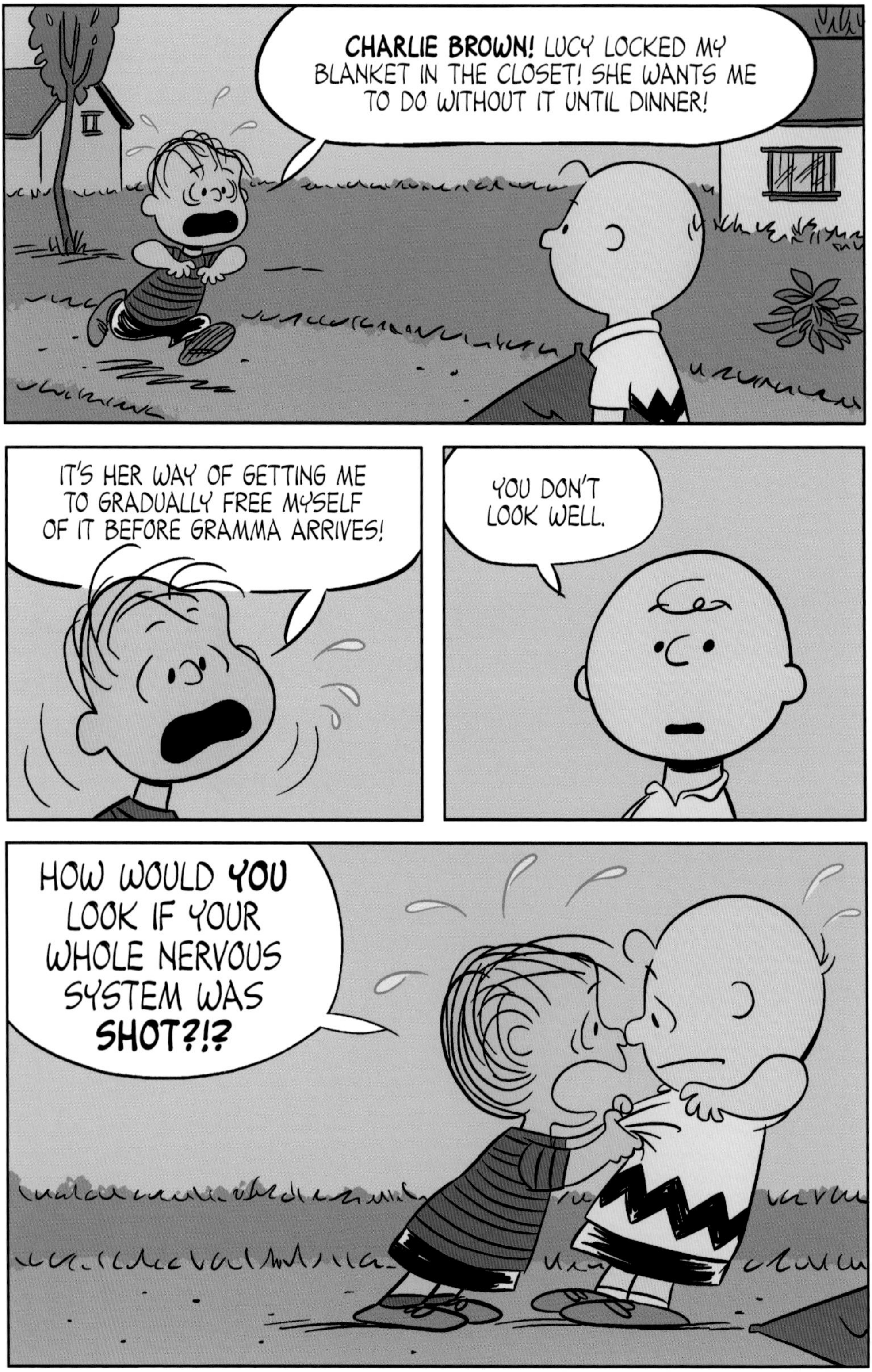
CHARLIE BROWN! LUCY LOCKED MY BLANKET IN THE CLOSET! SHE WANTS ME TO DO WITHOUT IT UNTIL DINNER!
IT'S HER WAY OF GETTING ME TO GRADUALLY FREE MYSELF OF IT BEFORE GRAMMA ARRIVES!
YOU DON'T LOOK WELL.
HOW WOULD YOU LOOK IF YOUR WHOLE NERVOUS SYSTEM WAS SHOT?!?

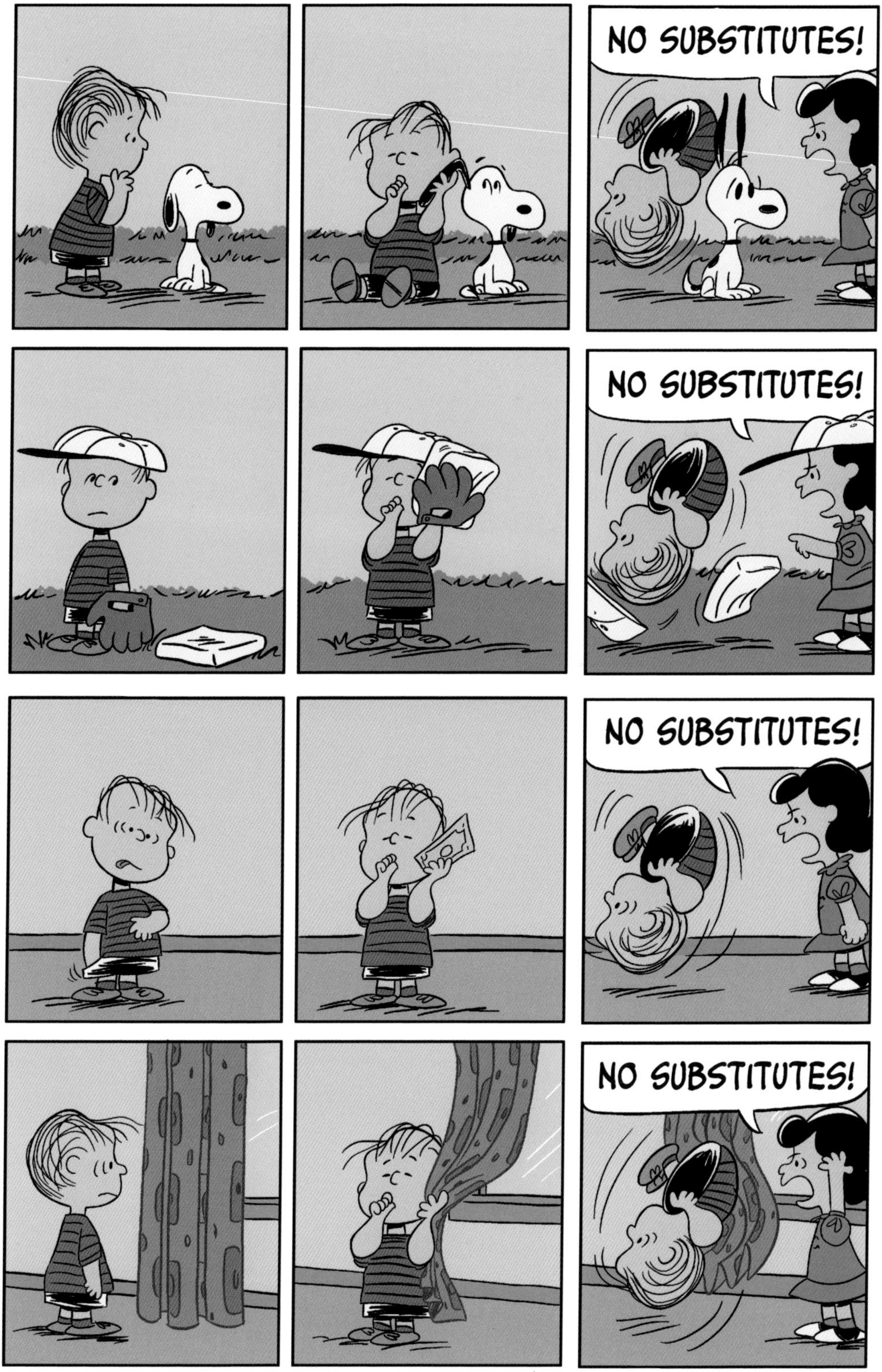
NO SUBSTITUTES!
NO SUBSTITUTES!
NO SUBSTITUTES!
NO SUBSTITUTES!

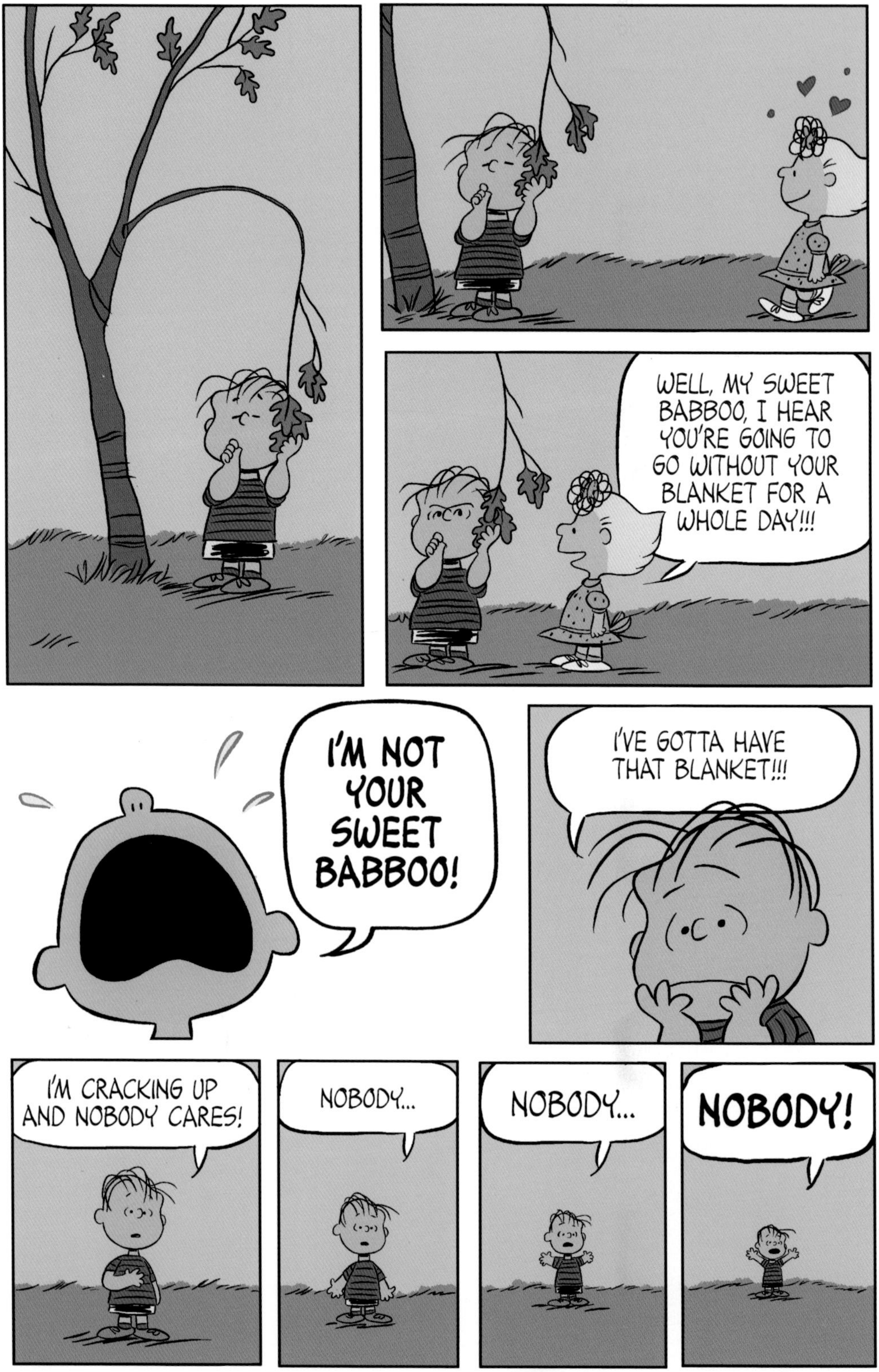
WELL, MY SWEET BABBOO, I HEAR YOU'RE GOING TO GO WITHOUT YOUR BLANKET FOR A WHOLE DAY!!!
I'M NOT YOUR SWEET BABBOO!
I'VE GOTTA HAVE THAT BLANKET!!!
I'M CRACKING UP AND NOBODY CARES!
NOBODY...
NOBODY...
NOBODY!

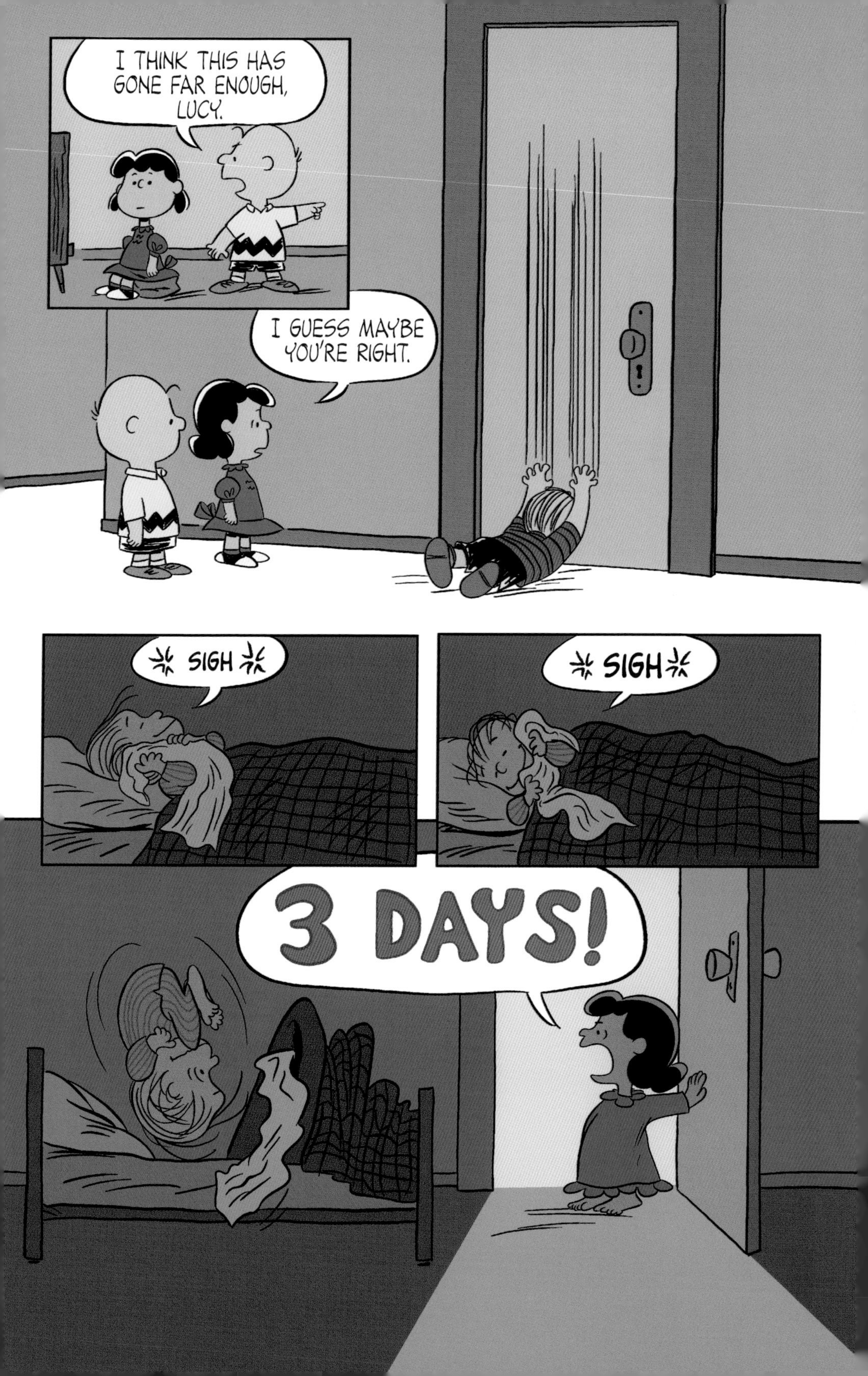
I THINK THIS HAS GONE FAR ENOUGH, LUCY.
I GUESS MAYBE YOU'RE RIGHT.
SIGH
SIGH
3 DAYS!

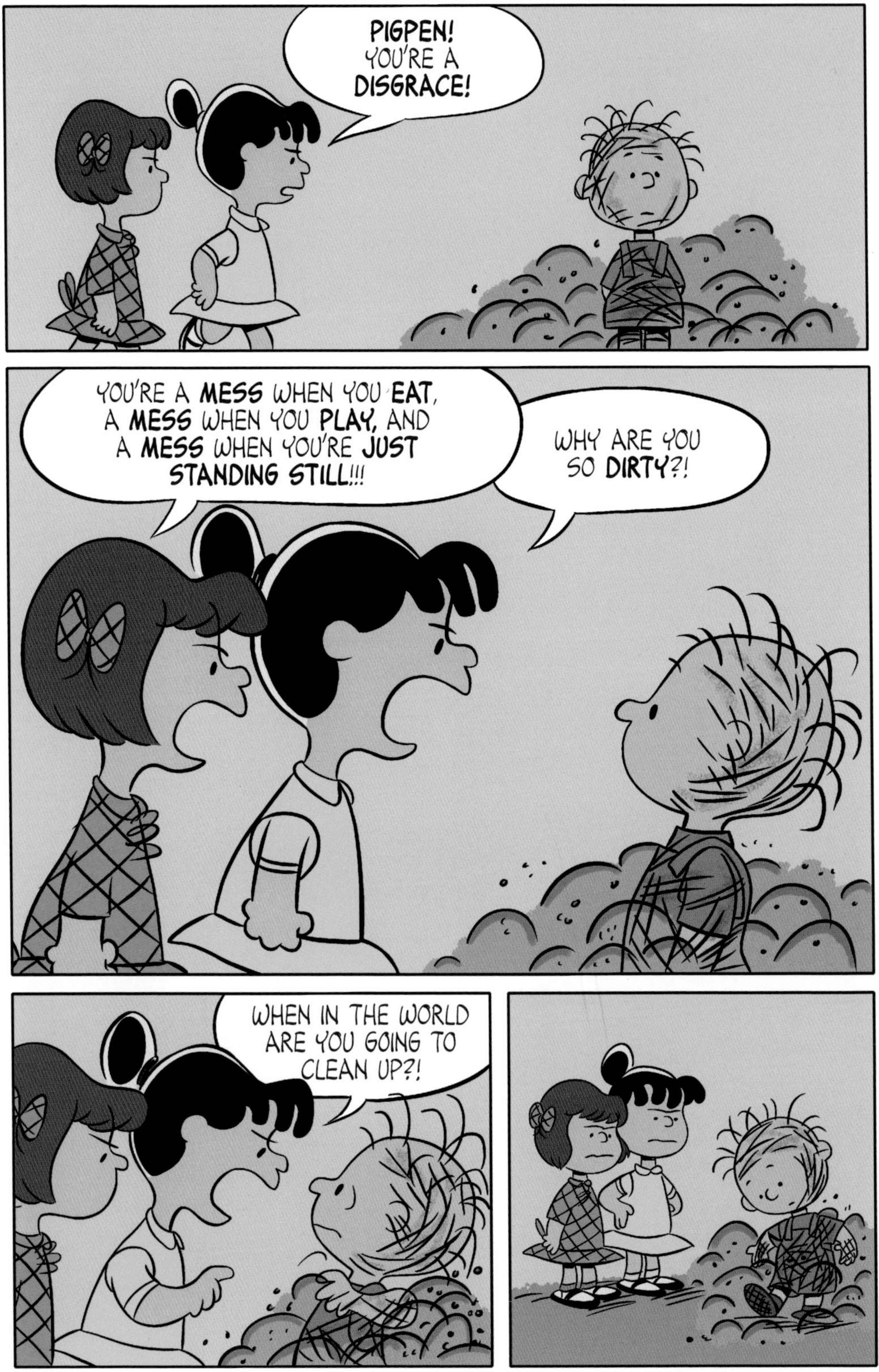
PIGPEN! YOU'RE A DISGRACE!
YOU'RE A MESS WHEN YOU EAT, A MESS WHEN YOU PLAY, AND A MESS WHEN YOU'RE JUST STANDING STILL!!!
WHY ARE YOU SO DIRTY?!
WHEN IN THE WORLD ARE YOU GOING TO CLEAN UP?!

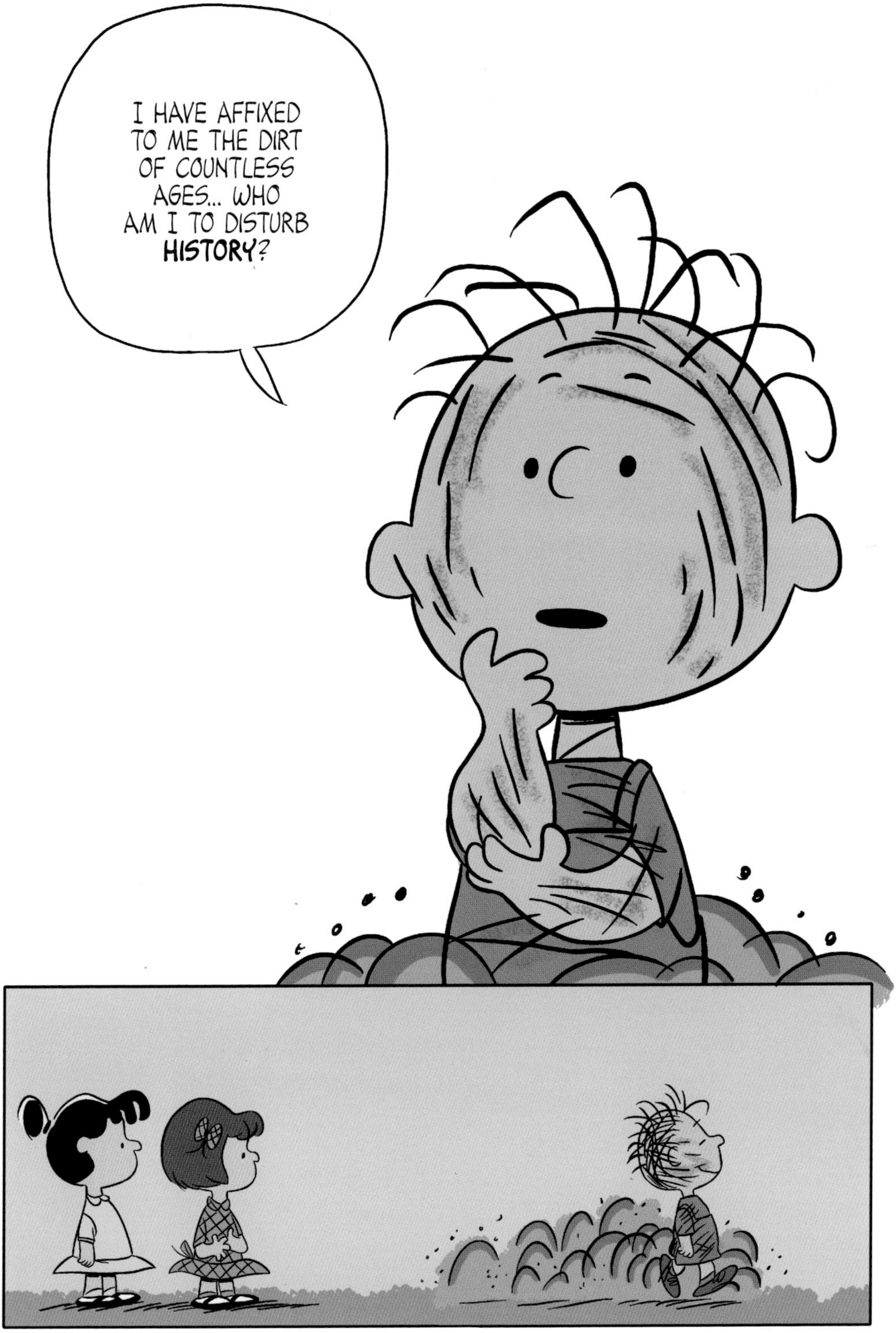
I HAVE AFFIXED TO ME THE DIRT OF COUNTLESS AGES... WHO AM I TO DISTURB **HISTORY**?

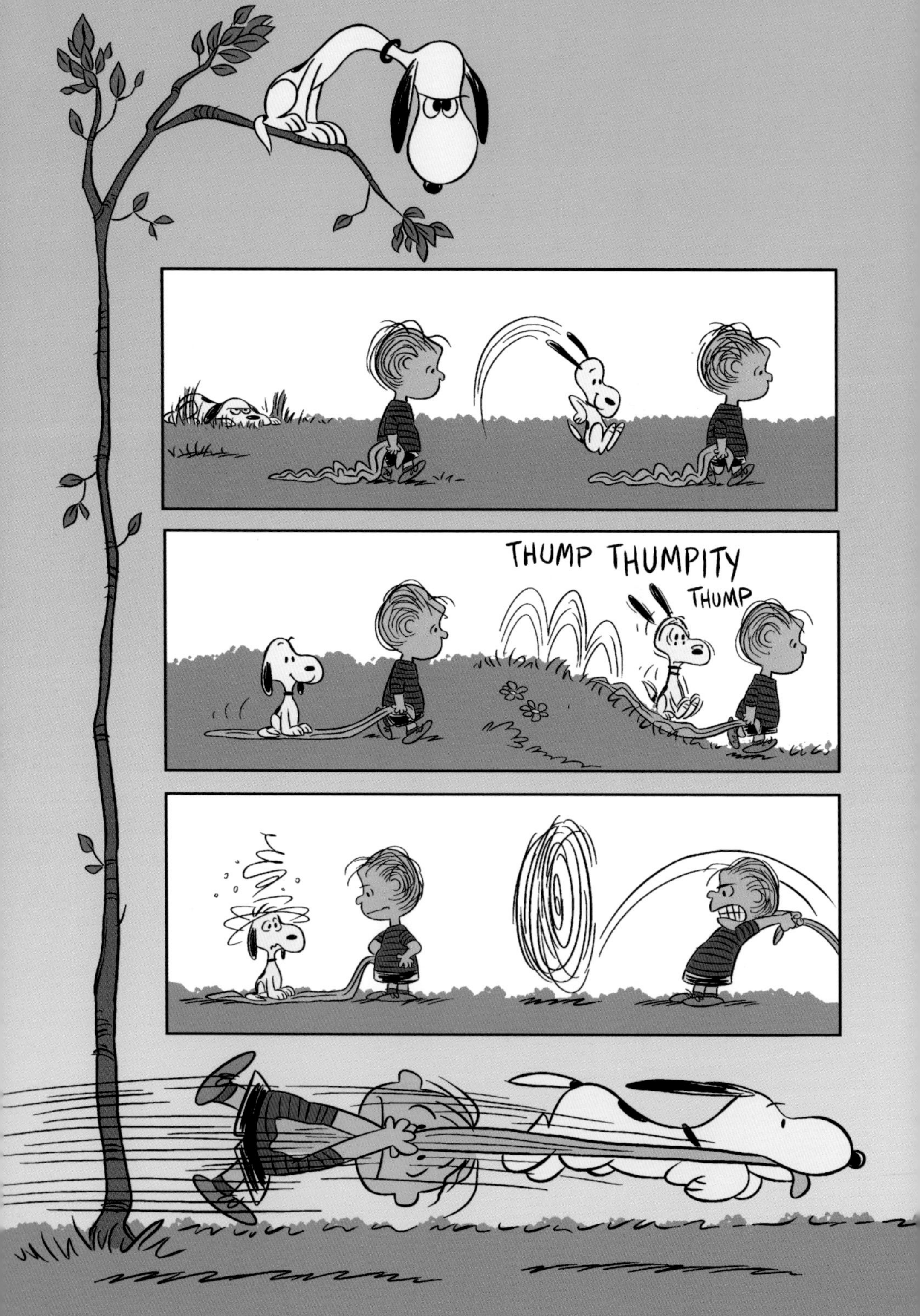
THUMP THUMPITY
THUMP

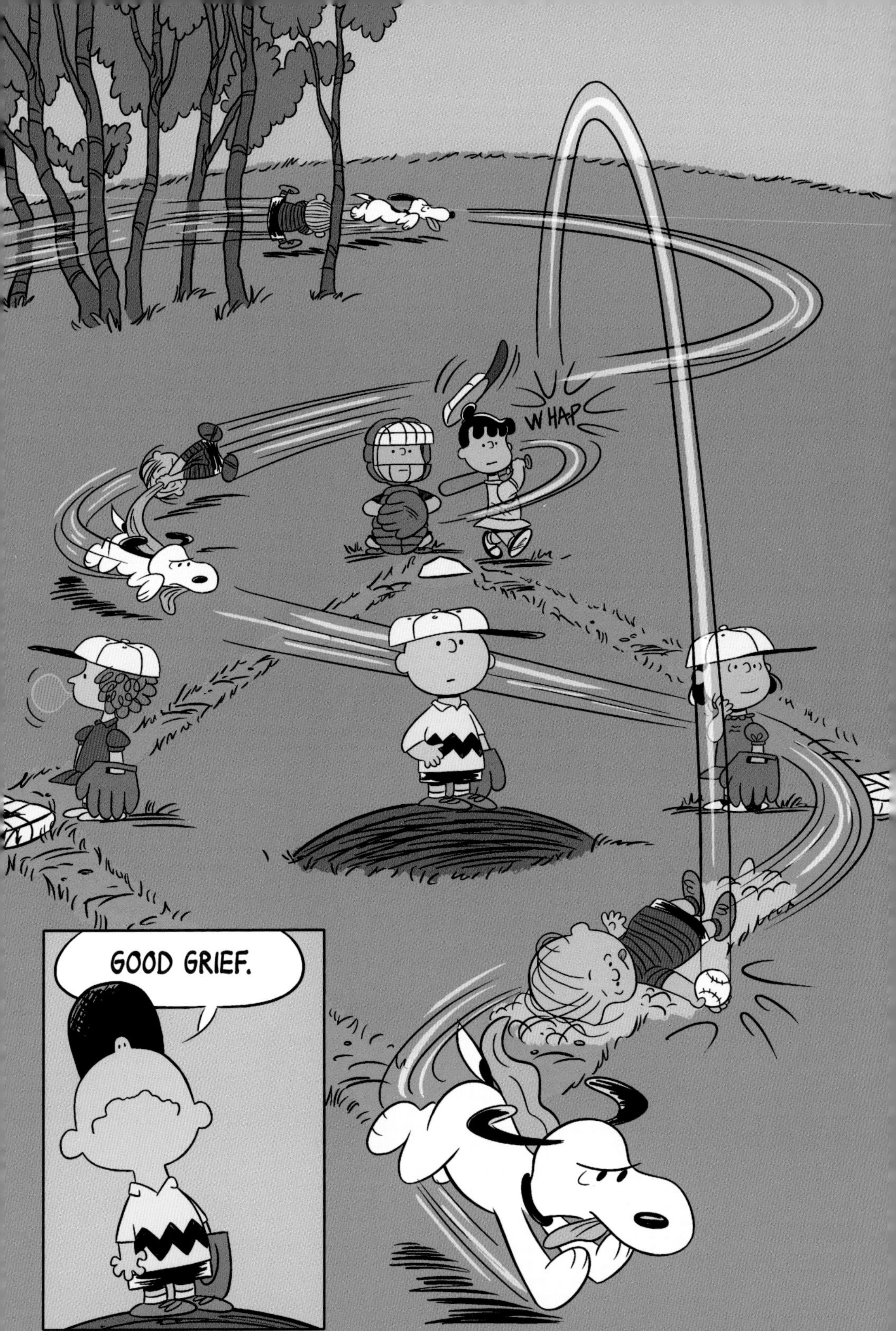
WHAP
GOOD GRIEF.

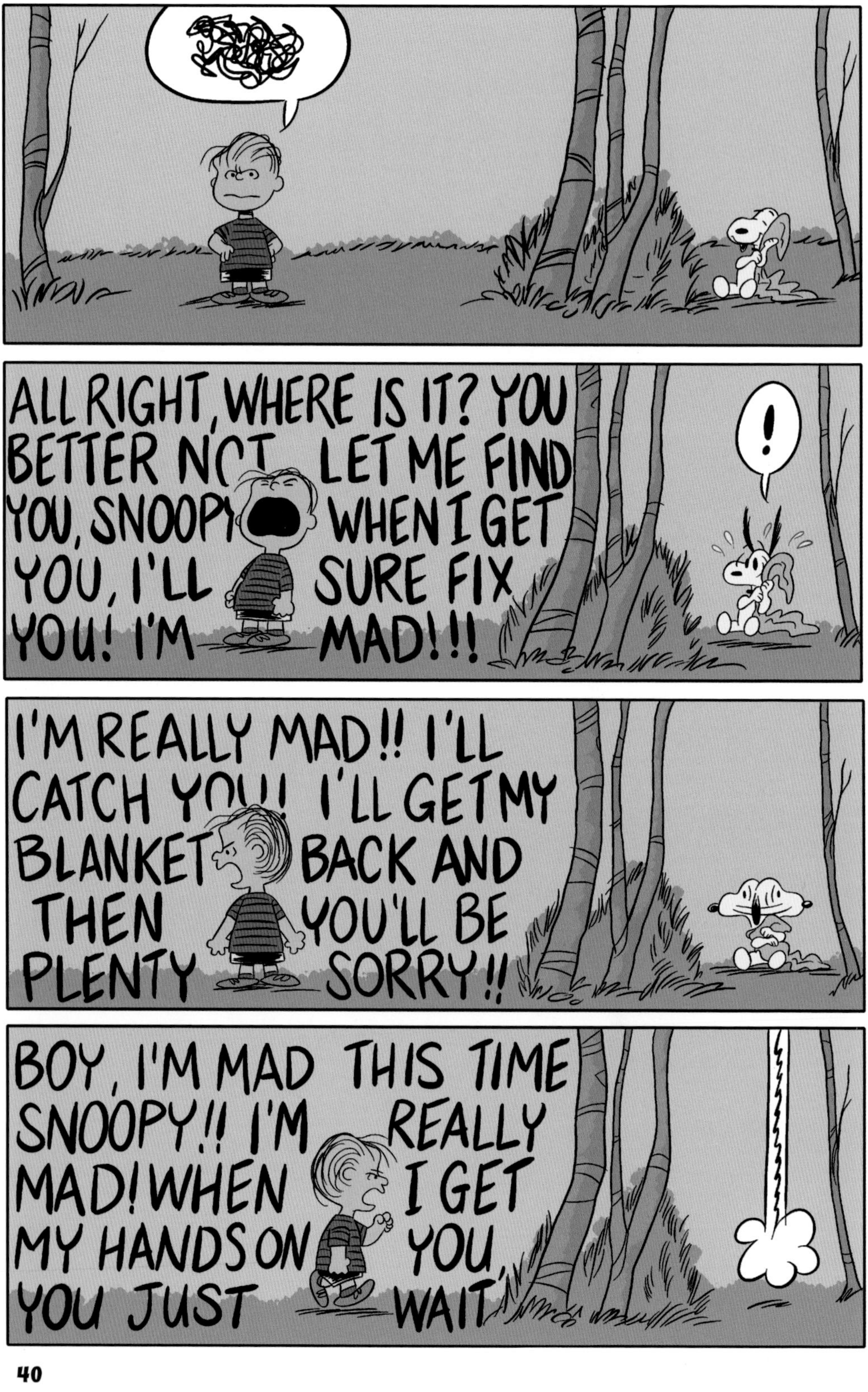
ALL RIGHT, WHERE IS IT? YOU BETTER NOT LET ME FIND YOU, SNOOPY WHEN I GET YOU, I'LL SURE FIX YOU! I'M MAD!!!
!
I'M REALLY MAD!! I'LL CATCH YOU! I'LL GET MY BLANKET BACK AND THEN YOU'LL BE PLENTY SORRY!!
BOY, I'M MAD THIS TIME SNOOPY!! I'M REALLY MAD! WHEN I GET MY HANDS ON YOU, YOU JUST WAIT

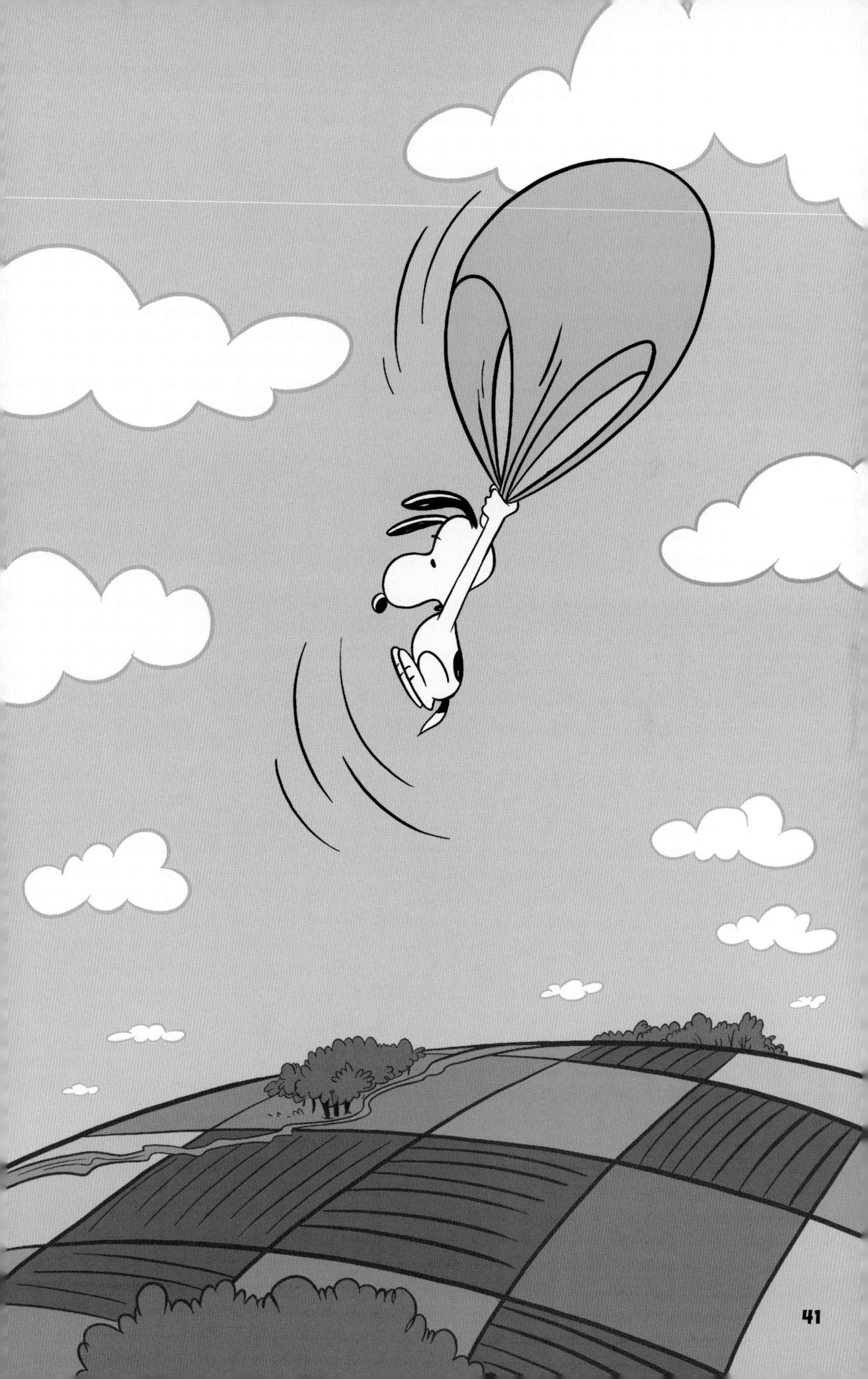

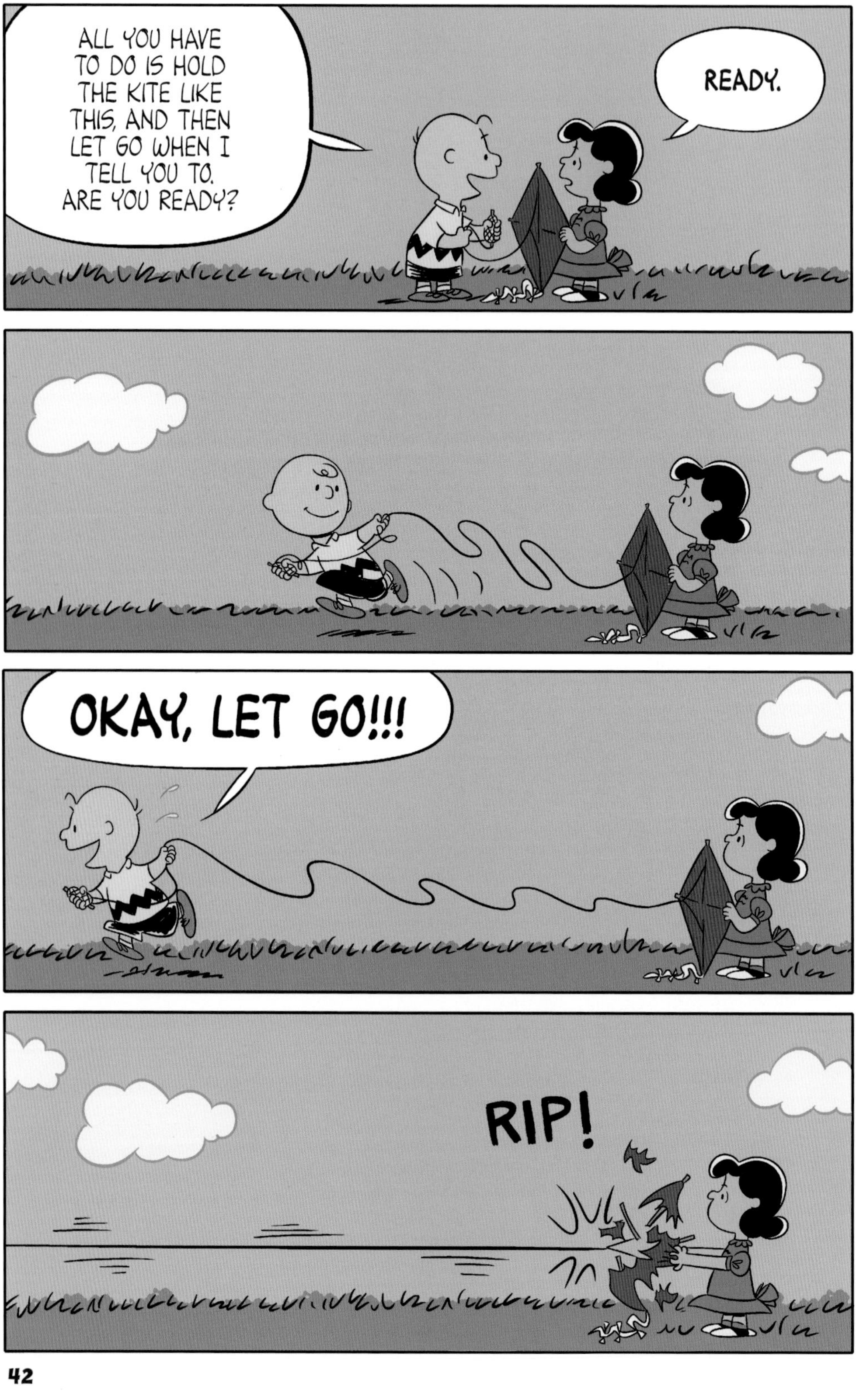
ALL YOU HAVE TO DO IS HOLD THE KITE LIKE THIS, AND THEN LET GO WHEN I TELL YOU TO. ARE YOU READY?
READY.
OKAY, LET GO!!!
RIP!

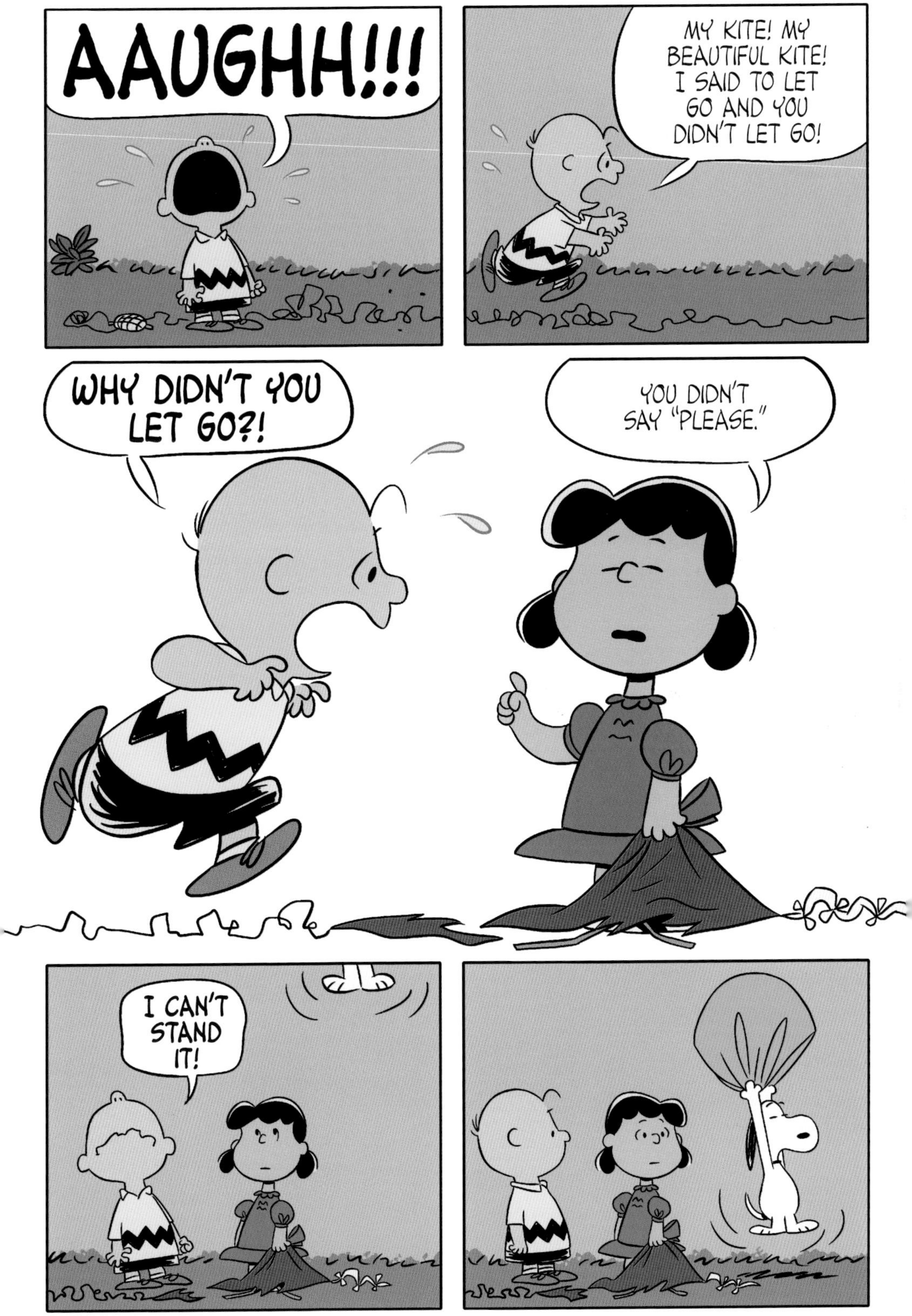
AAUGHH!!!
MY KITE! MY BEAUTIFUL KITE! I SAID TO LET GO AND YOU DIDN'T LET GO!
WHY DIDN'T YOU LET GO?!
YOU DIDN'T SAY "PLEASE."
I CAN'T STAND IT!

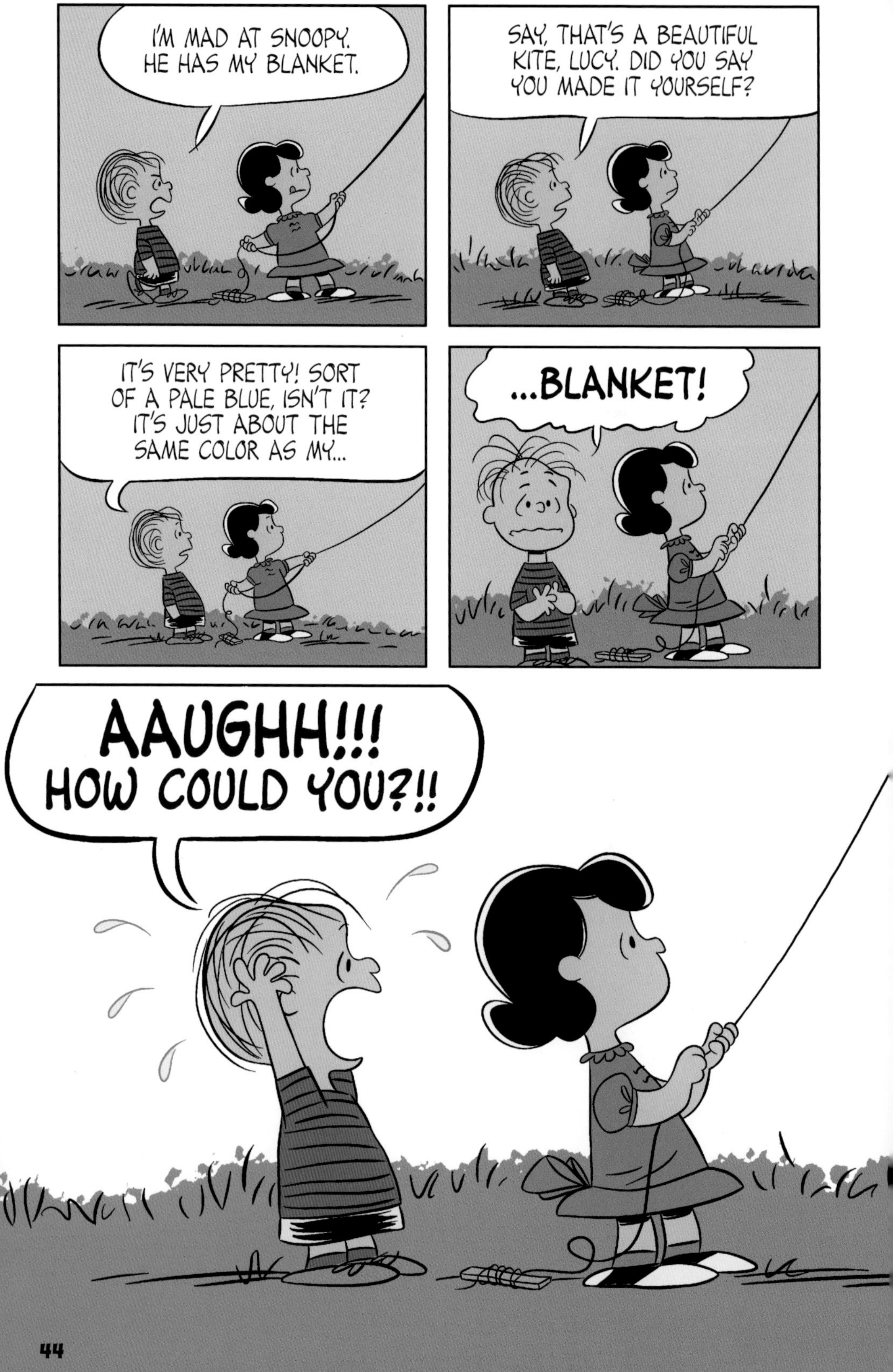
I'M MAD AT SNOOPY. HE HAS MY BLANKET.
SAY, THAT'S A BEAUTIFUL KITE, LUCY. DID YOU SAY YOU MADE IT YOURSELF?
IT'S VERY PRETTY! SORT OF A PALE BLUE, ISN'T IT? IT'S JUST ABOUT THE SAME COLOR AS MY...
...BLANKET!
AAUGHH!!! HOW COULD YOU?!!

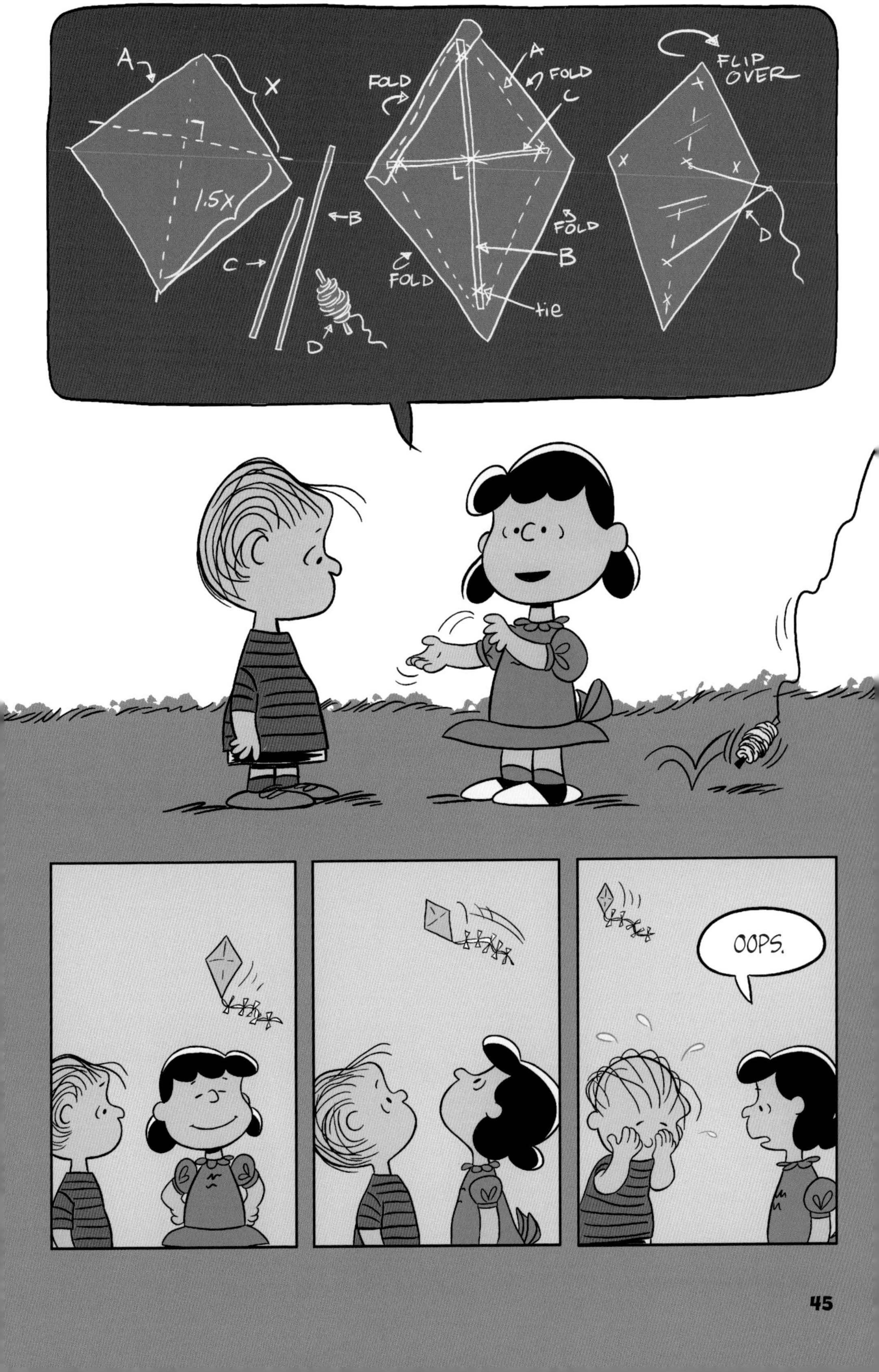
A
X
1.5X
C
B
D
FOLD
A
FOLD
C
L
FOLD
B
FOLD
tie
FLIP OVER
D
OOPS.

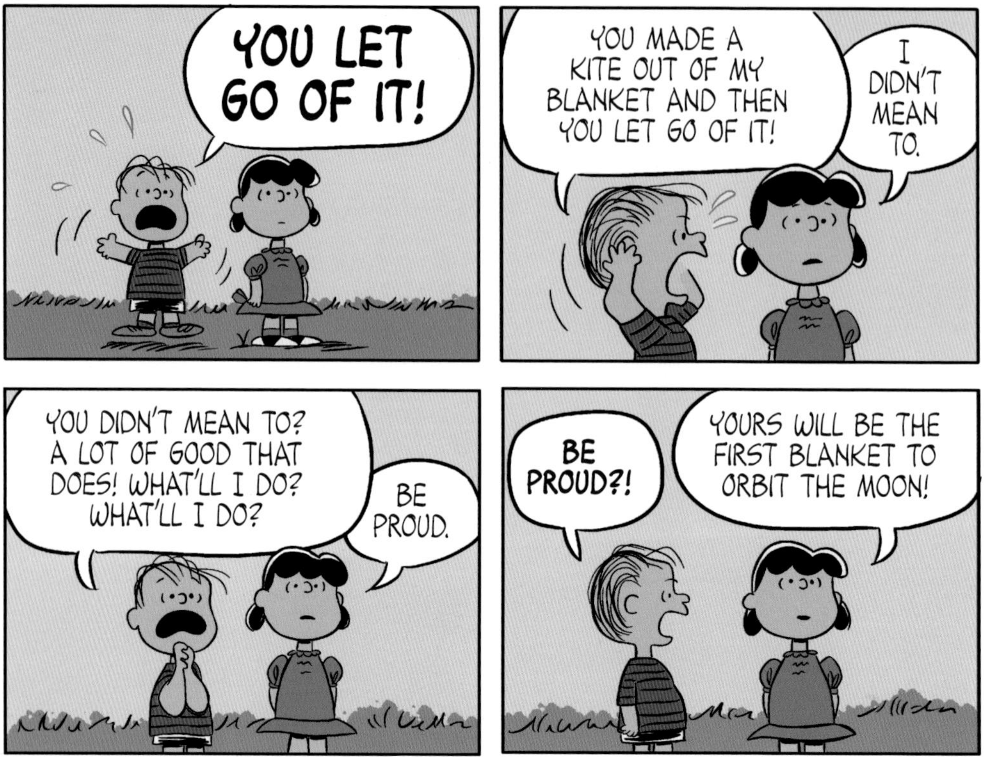
YOU LET GO OF IT!
YOU MADE A KITE OUT OF MY BLANKET AND THEN YOU LET GO OF IT!
I DIDN'T MEAN TO.
YOU DIDN'T MEAN TO? A LOT OF GOOD THAT DOES! WHAT'LL I DO? WHAT'LL I DO?
BE PROUD.
YOURS WILL BE THE FIRST BLANKET TO ORBIT THE MOON!
BE PROUD?!

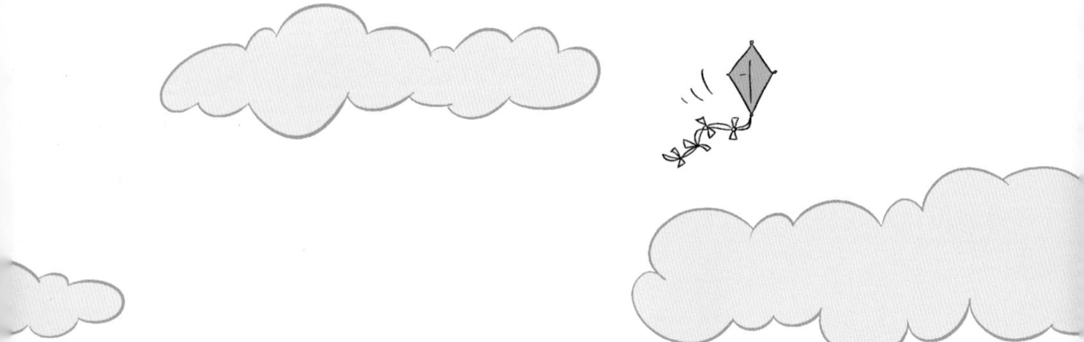

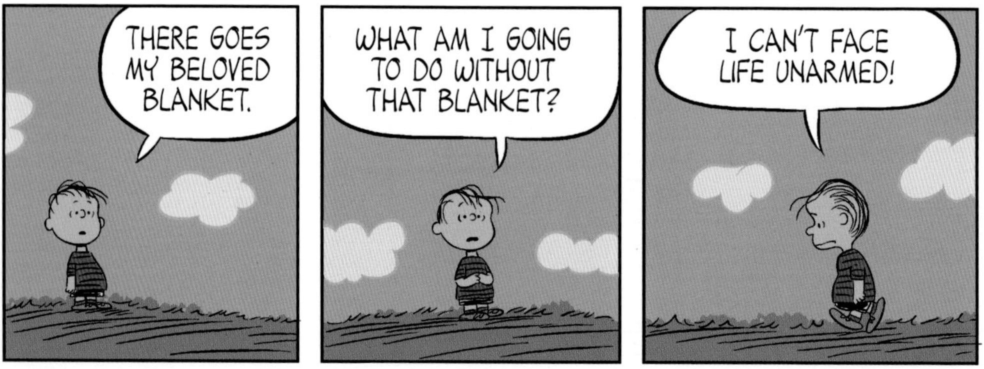
THERE GOES MY BELOVED BLANKET.
WHAT AM I GOING TO DO WITHOUT THAT BLANKET?
I CAN'T FACE LIFE UNARMED!

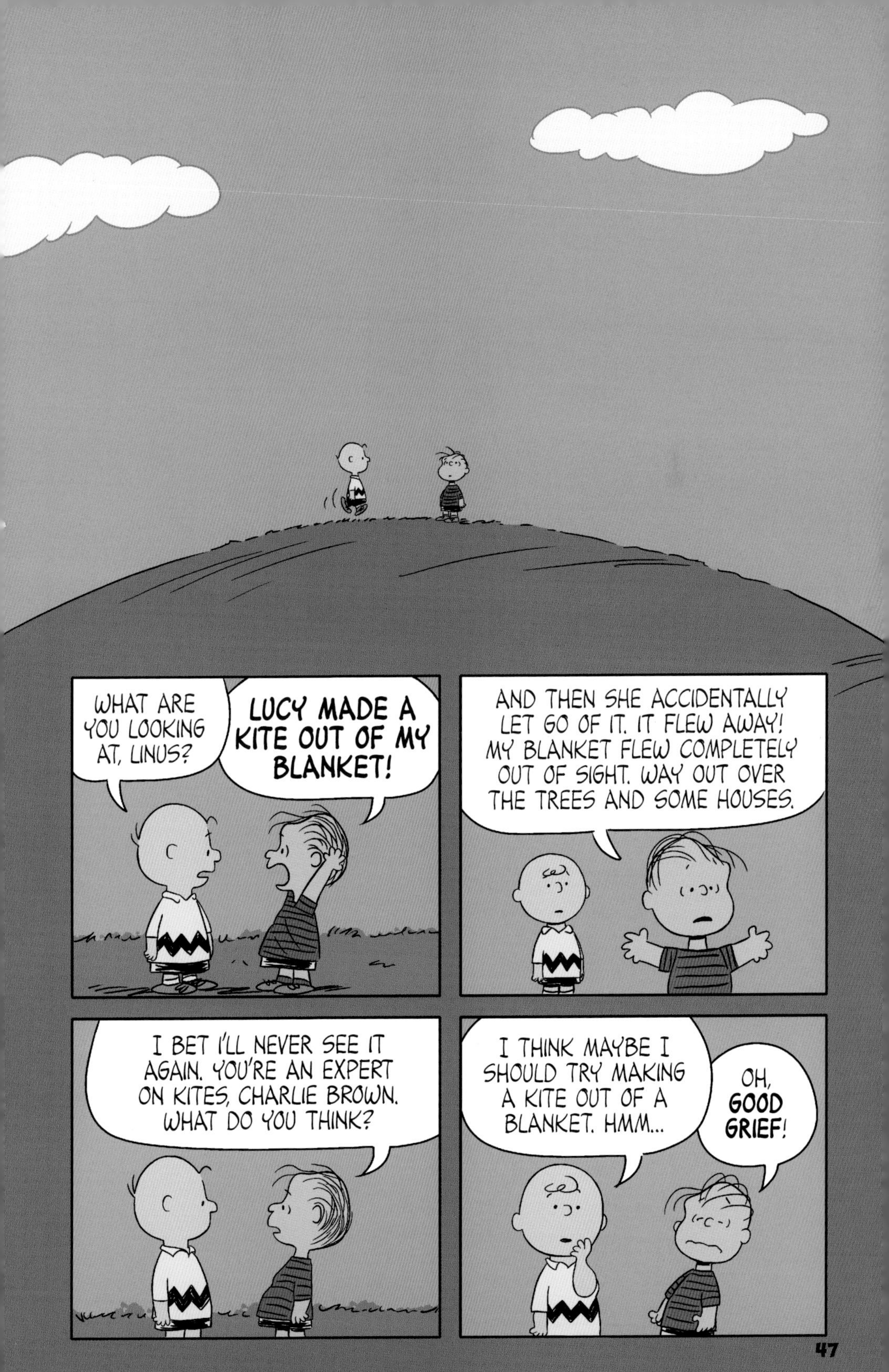
WHAT ARE YOU LOOKING AT, LINUS?
LUCY MADE A KITE OUT OF MY BLANKET!
AND THEN SHE ACCIDENTALLY LET GO OF IT. IT FLEW AWAY! MY BLANKET FLEW COMPLETELY OUT OF SIGHT. WAY OUT OVER THE TREES AND SOME HOUSES.
I BET I'LL NEVER SEE IT AGAIN. YOU'RE AN EXPERT ON KITES, CHARLIE BROWN. WHAT DO YOU THINK?
I THINK MAYBE I SHOULD TRY MAKING A KITE OUT OF A BLANKET. HMM...
OH, GOOD GRIEF!

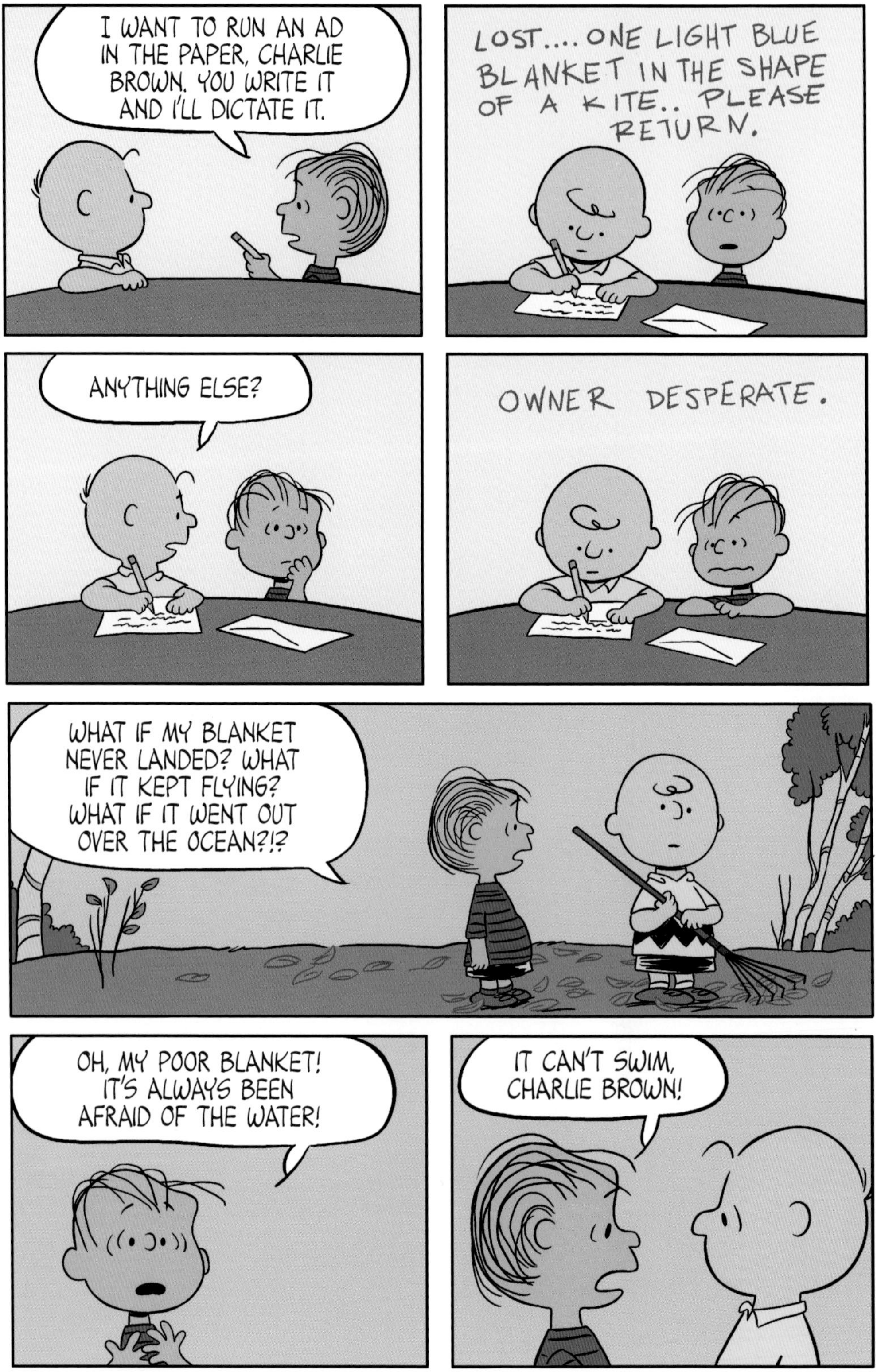
I WANT TO RUN AN AD IN THE PAPER, CHARLIE BROWN. YOU WRITE IT AND I'LL DICTATE IT.
LOST.... ONE LIGHT BLUE BLANKET IN THE SHAPE OF A KITE.. PLEASE RETURN.
ANYTHING ELSE?
OWNER DESPERATE.
WHAT IF MY BLANKET NEVER LANDED? WHAT IF IT KEPT FLYING? WHAT IF IT WENT OUT OVER THE OCEAN?!?
OH, MY POOR BLANKET! IT'S ALWAYS BEEN AFRAID OF THE WATER!
IT CAN'T SWIM, CHARLIE BROWN!

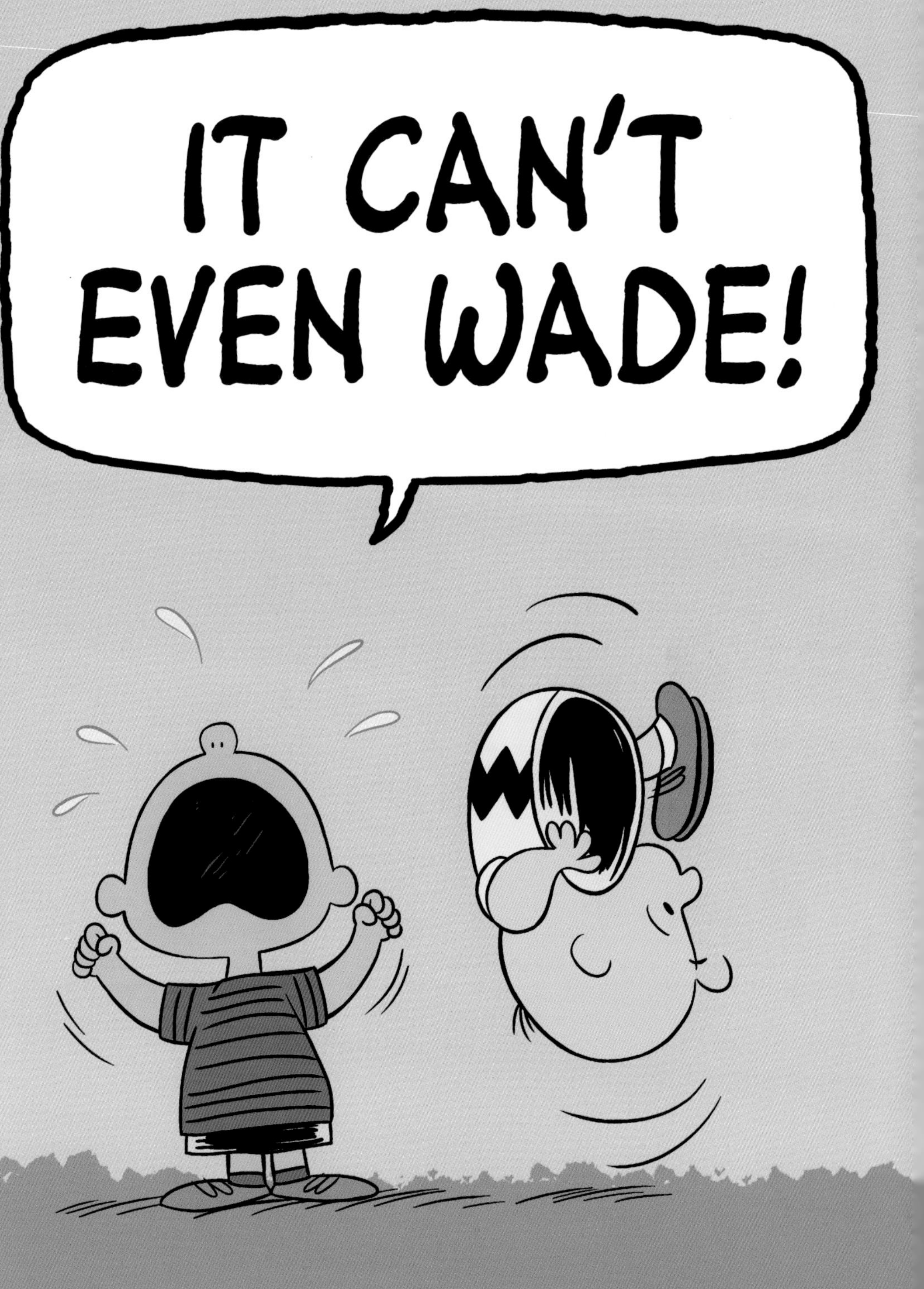
IT CAN'T EVEN WADE!

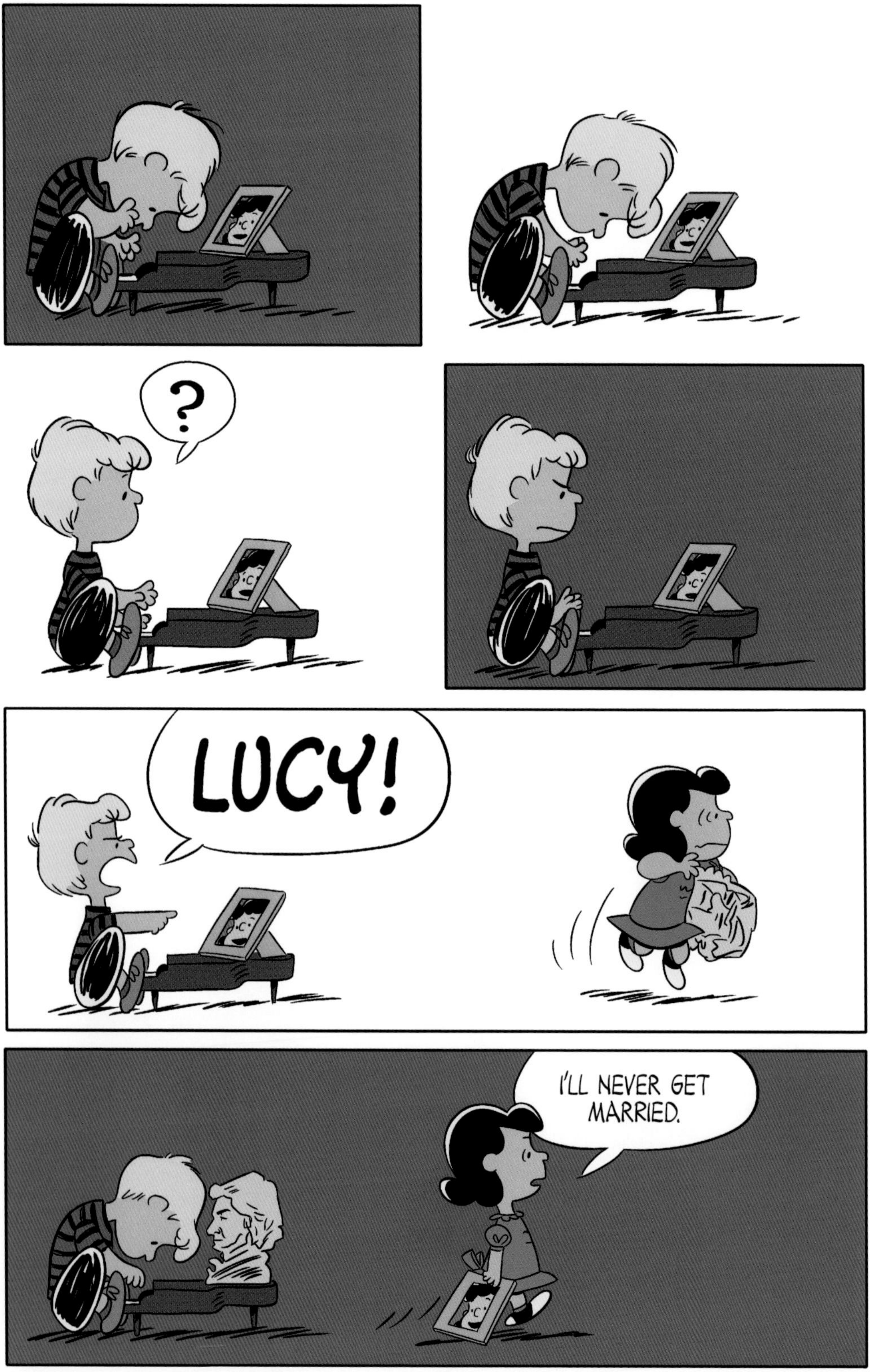
?
LUCY!
I'LL NEVER GET MARRIED.

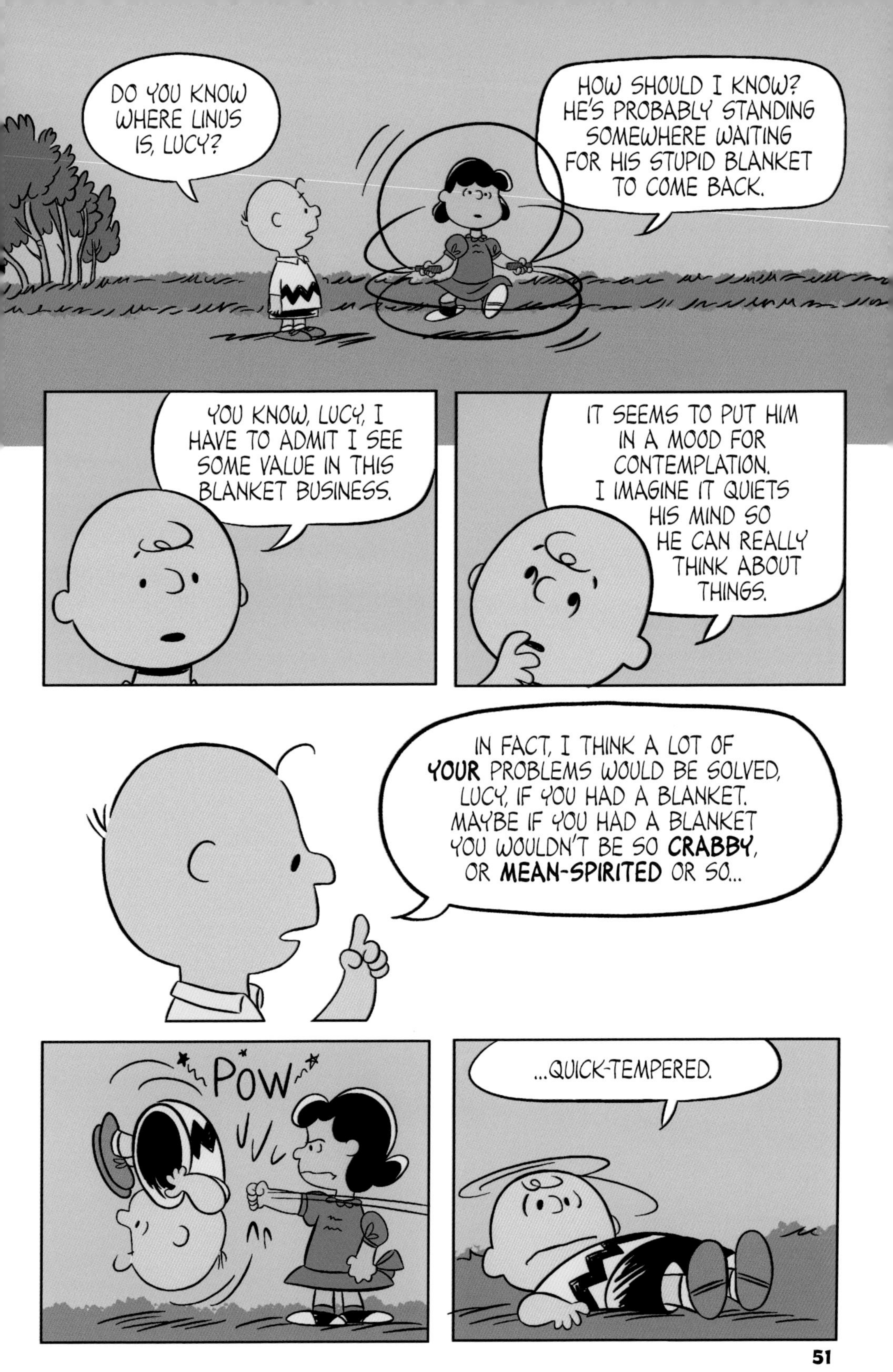
DO YOU KNOW WHERE LINUS IS, LUCY?
HOW SHOULD I KNOW? HE'S PROBABLY STANDING SOMEWHERE WAITING FOR HIS STUPID BLANKET TO COME BACK.
YOU KNOW, LUCY, I HAVE TO ADMIT I SEE SOME VALUE IN THIS BLANKET BUSINESS.
IT SEEMS TO PUT HIM IN A MOOD FOR CONTEMPLATION. I IMAGINE IT QUIETS HIS MIND SO HE CAN REALLY THINK ABOUT THINGS.
IN FACT, I THINK A LOT OF **YOUR** PROBLEMS WOULD BE SOLVED, LUCY, IF YOU HAD A BLANKET. MAYBE IF YOU HAD A BLANKET YOU WOULDN'T BE SO **CRABBY**, OR **MEAN-SPIRITED** OR SO...
POW
...QUICK-TEMPERED.

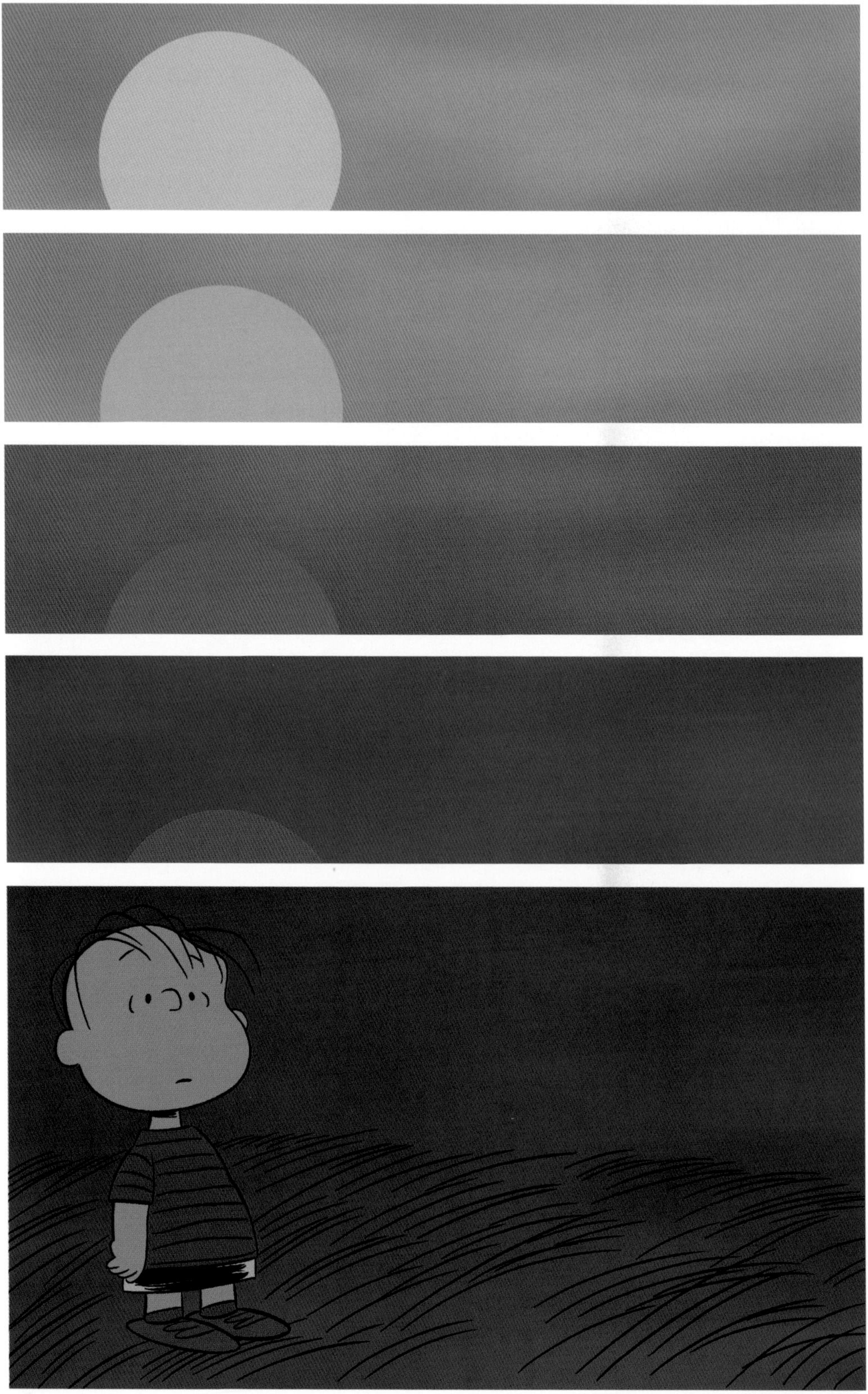

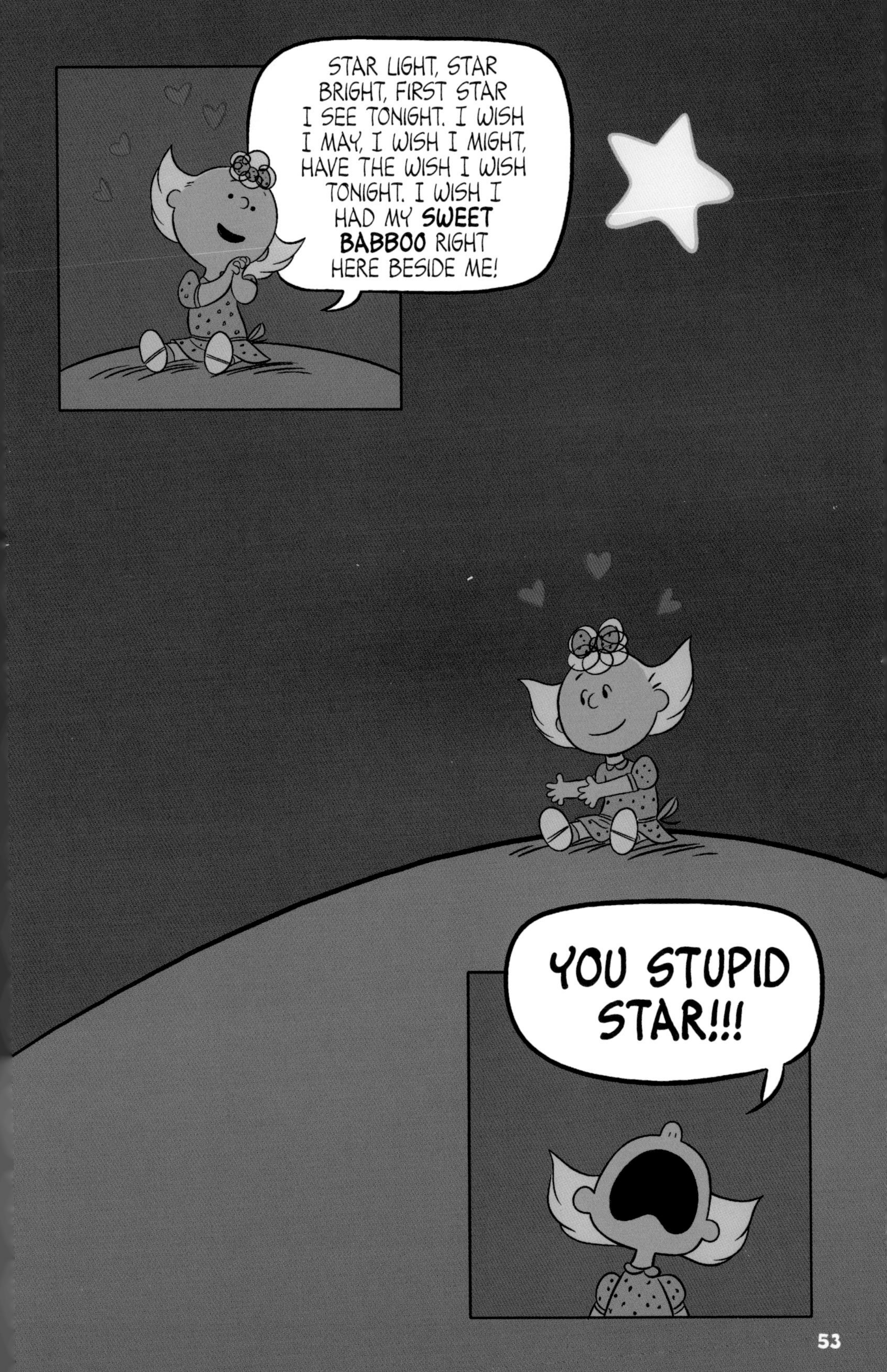
STAR LIGHT, STAR BRIGHT, FIRST STAR I SEE TONIGHT. I WISH I MAY, I WISH I MIGHT, HAVE THE WISH I WISH TONIGHT. I WISH I HAD MY **SWEET BABBOO** RIGHT HERE BESIDE ME!
YOU STUPID STAR!!!

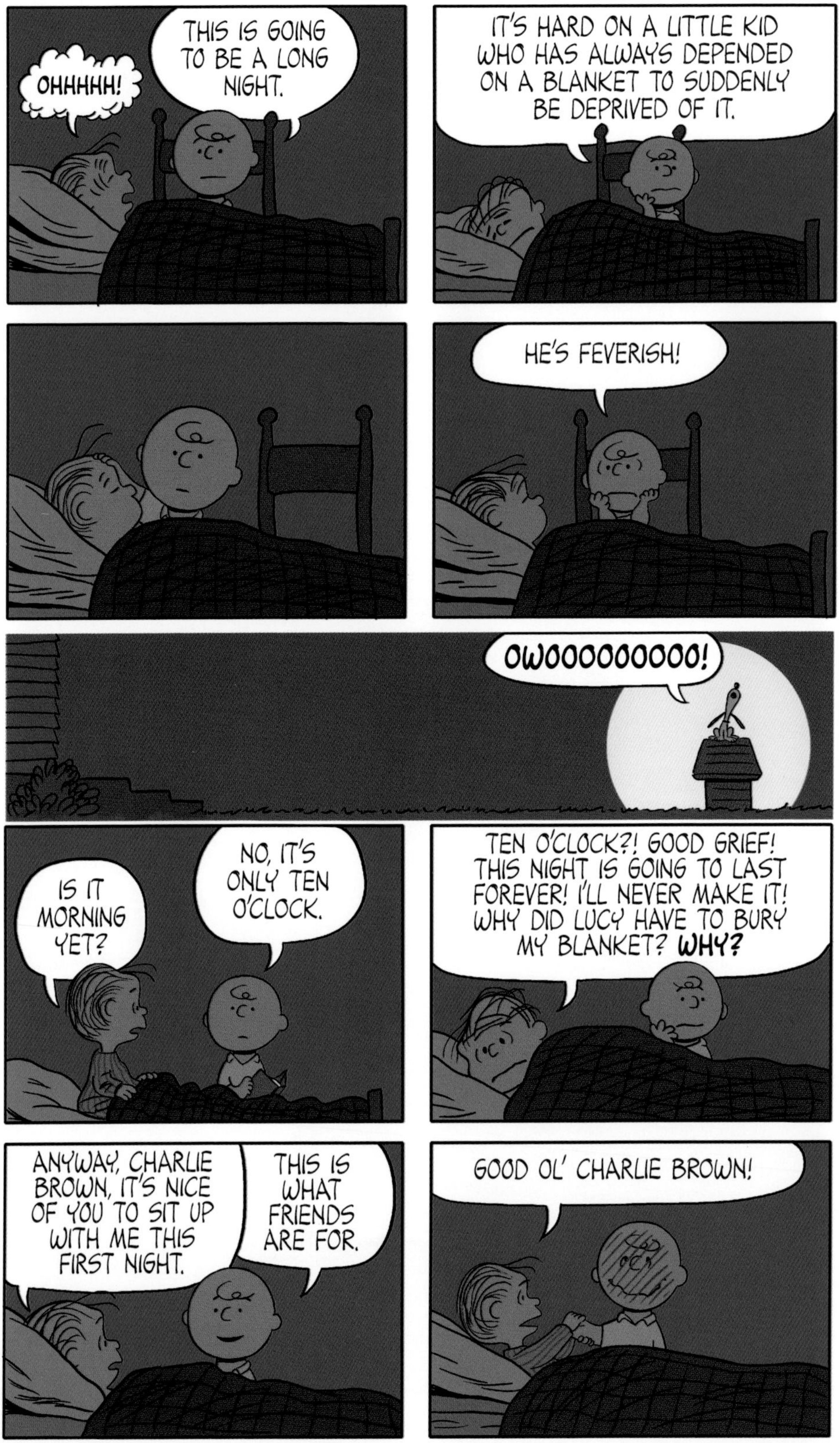
OHHHHH!
THIS IS GOING TO BE A LONG NIGHT.
IT'S HARD ON A LITTLE KID WHO HAS ALWAYS DEPENDED ON A BLANKET TO SUDDENLY BE DEPRIVED OF IT.
HE'S FEVERISH!
OWOOOOOOOOO!
IS IT MORNING YET?
NO, IT'S ONLY TEN O'CLOCK.
TEN O'CLOCK?! GOOD GRIEF! THIS NIGHT IS GOING TO LAST FOREVER! I'LL NEVER MAKE IT! WHY DID LUCY HAVE TO BURY MY BLANKET? WHY?
ANYWAY, CHARLIE BROWN, IT'S NICE OF YOU TO SIT UP WITH ME THIS FIRST NIGHT.
THIS IS WHAT FRIENDS ARE FOR.
GOOD OL' CHARLIE BROWN!

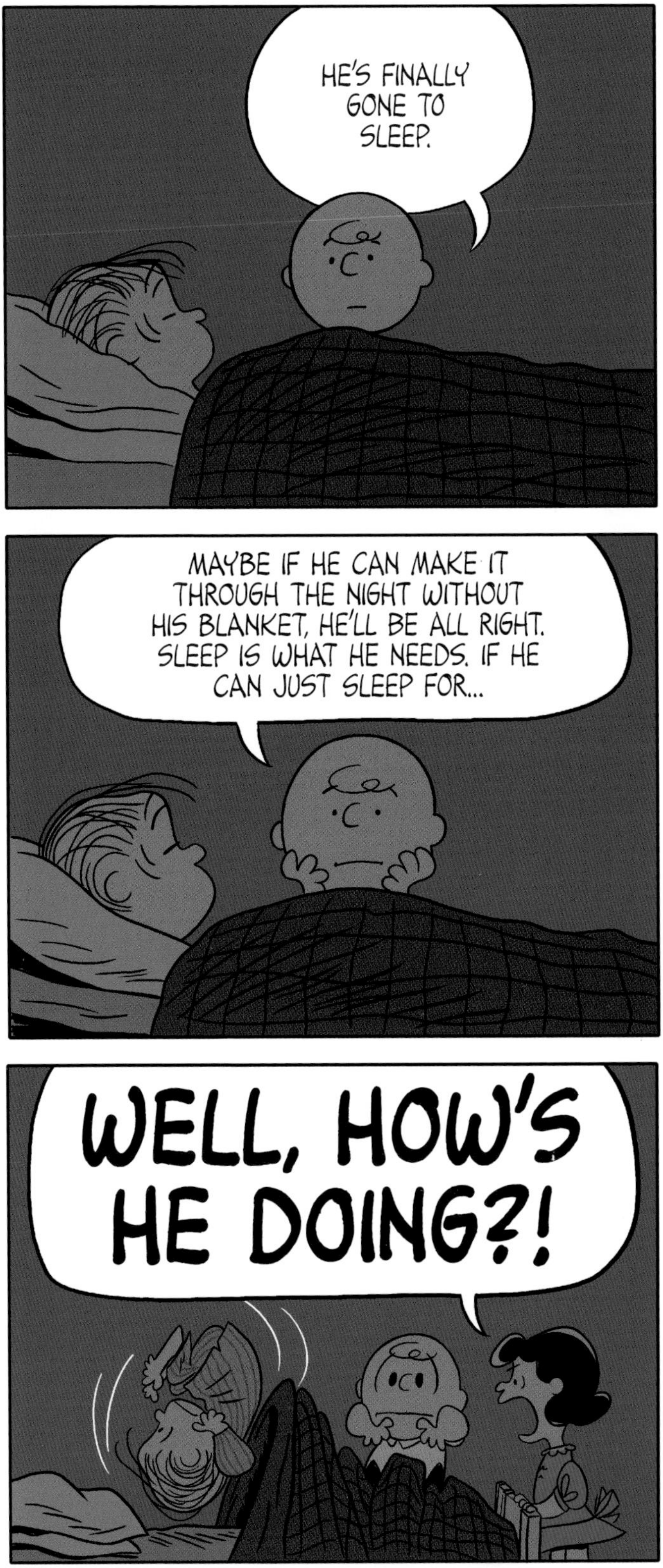
HE'S FINALLY GONE TO SLEEP.
MAYBE IF HE CAN MAKE IT THROUGH THE NIGHT WITHOUT HIS BLANKET, HE'LL BE ALL RIGHT. SLEEP IS WHAT HE NEEDS. IF HE CAN JUST SLEEP FOR...
WELL, HOW'S HE DOING?!

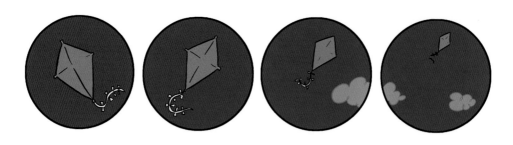

BAM
BAM
BAM

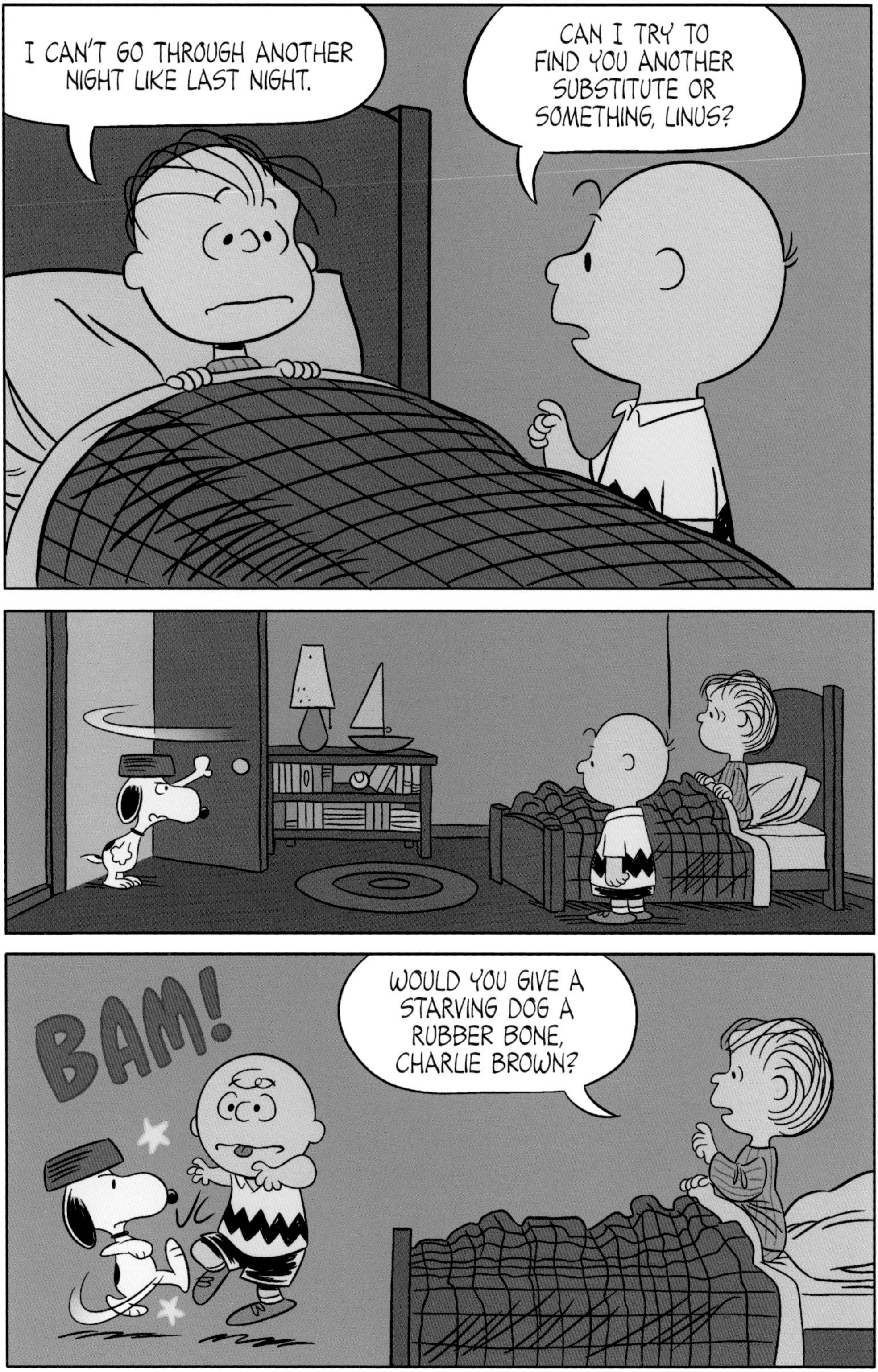
I CAN'T GO THROUGH ANOTHER NIGHT LIKE LAST NIGHT.
CAN I TRY TO FIND YOU ANOTHER SUBSTITUTE OR SOMETHING, LINUS?
BAM!
WOULD YOU GIVE A STARVING DOG A RUBBER BONE, CHARLIE BROWN?

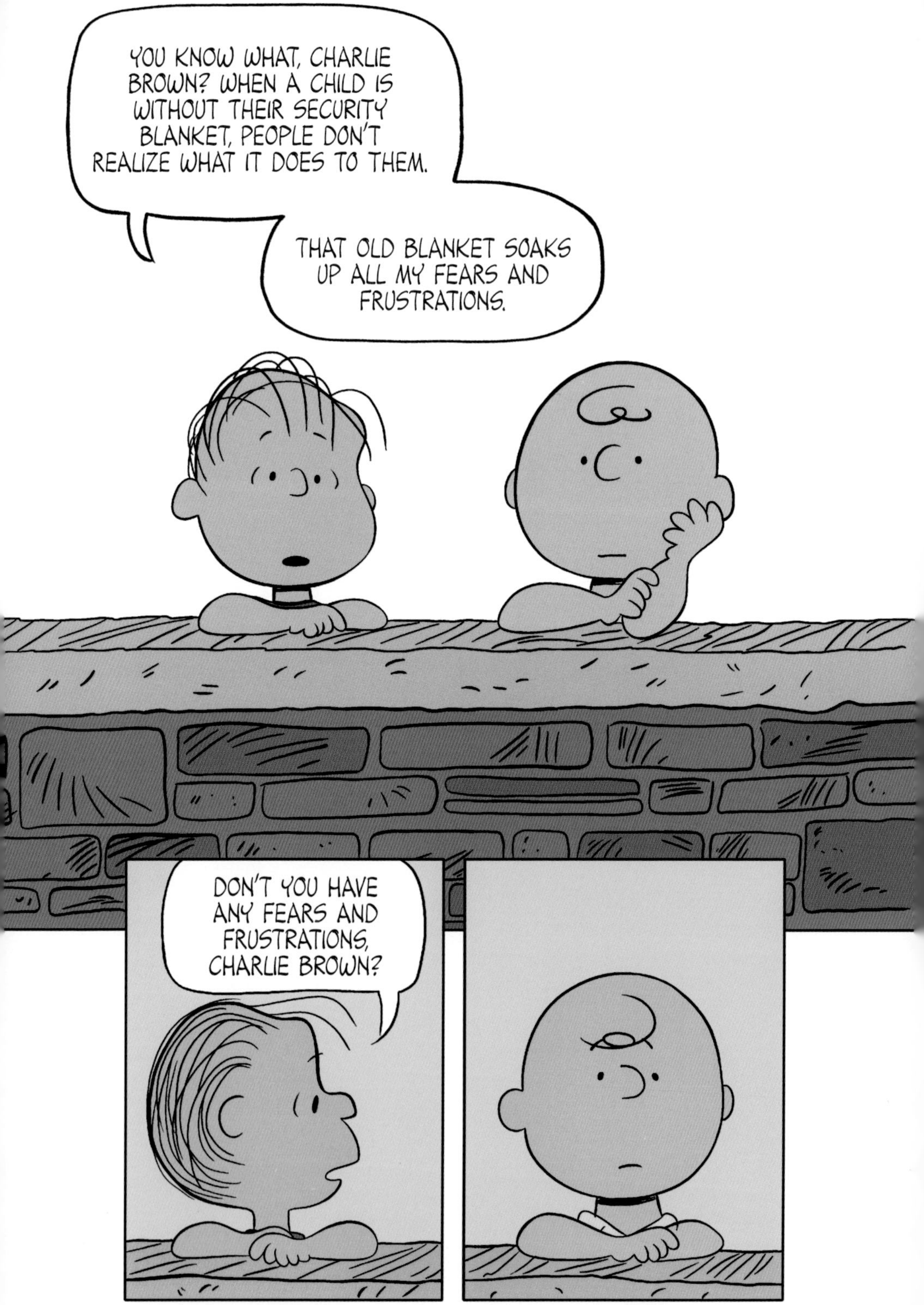
YOU KNOW WHAT, CHARLIE BROWN? WHEN A CHILD IS WITHOUT THEIR SECURITY BLANKET, PEOPLE DON'T REALIZE WHAT IT DOES TO THEM.
THAT OLD BLANKET SOAKS UP ALL MY FEARS AND FRUSTRATIONS.
DON'T YOU HAVE ANY FEARS AND FRUSTRATIONS, CHARLIE BROWN?

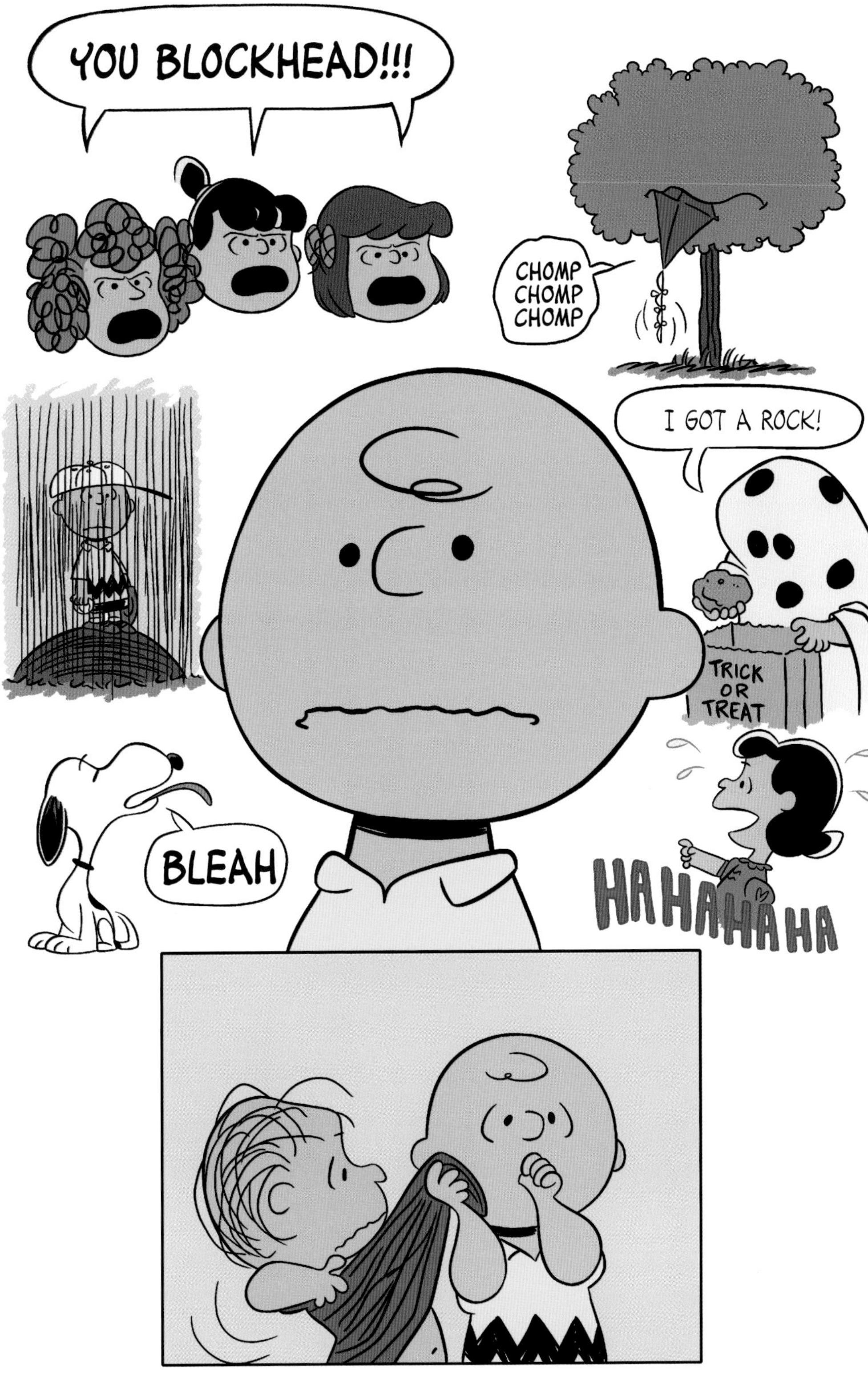
YOU BLOCKHEAD!!!
CHOMP CHOMP CHOMP
I GOT A ROCK!
TRICK OR TREAT
BLEAH
HAHAHAHAHA

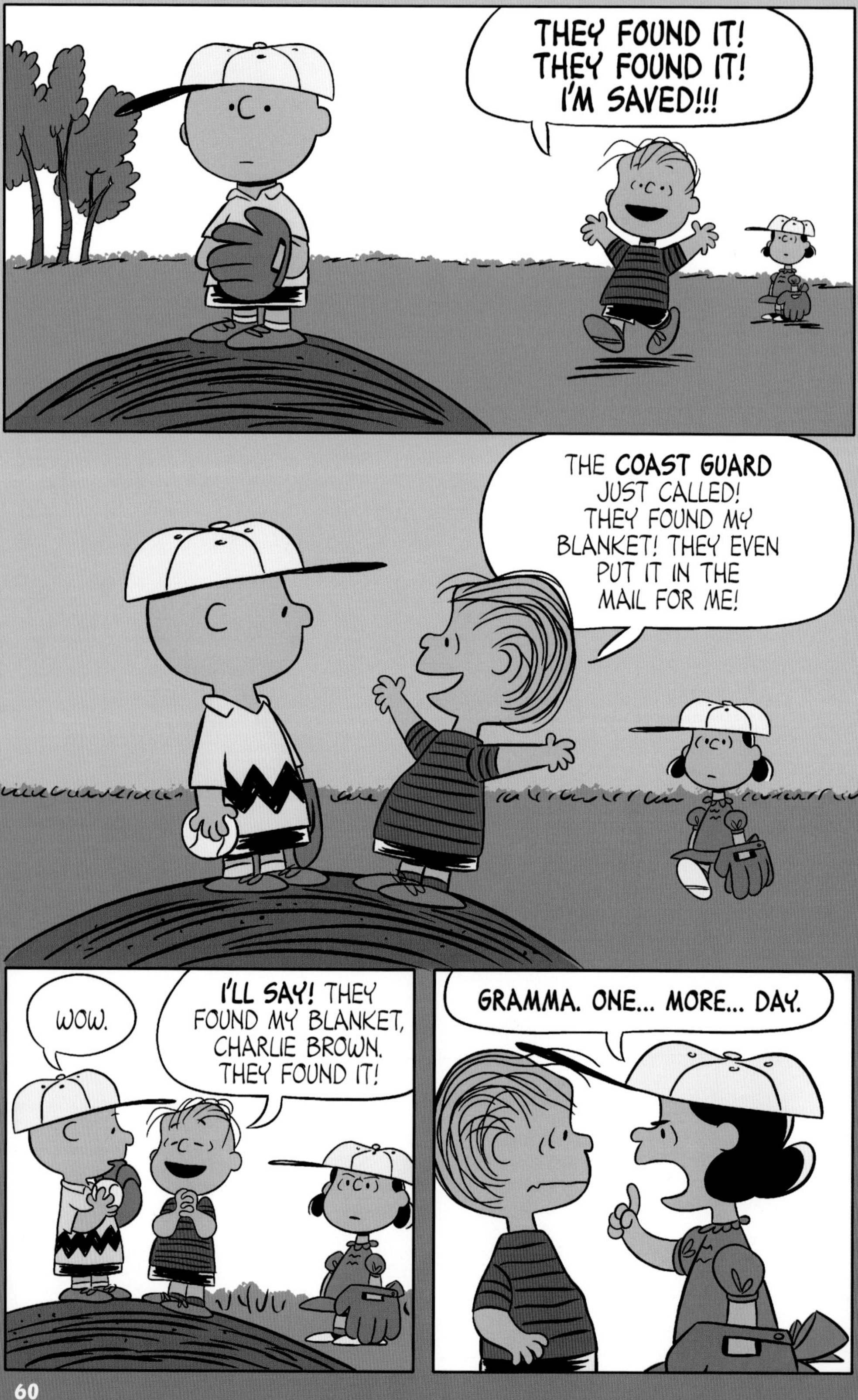
THEY FOUND IT! THEY FOUND IT! I'M SAVED!!!
THE **COAST GUARD** JUST CALLED! THEY FOUND MY BLANKET! THEY EVEN PUT IT IN THE MAIL FOR ME!
WOW.
I'LL SAY! THEY FOUND MY BLANKET, CHARLIE BROWN. THEY FOUND IT!
GRAMMA. ONE... MORE... DAY.

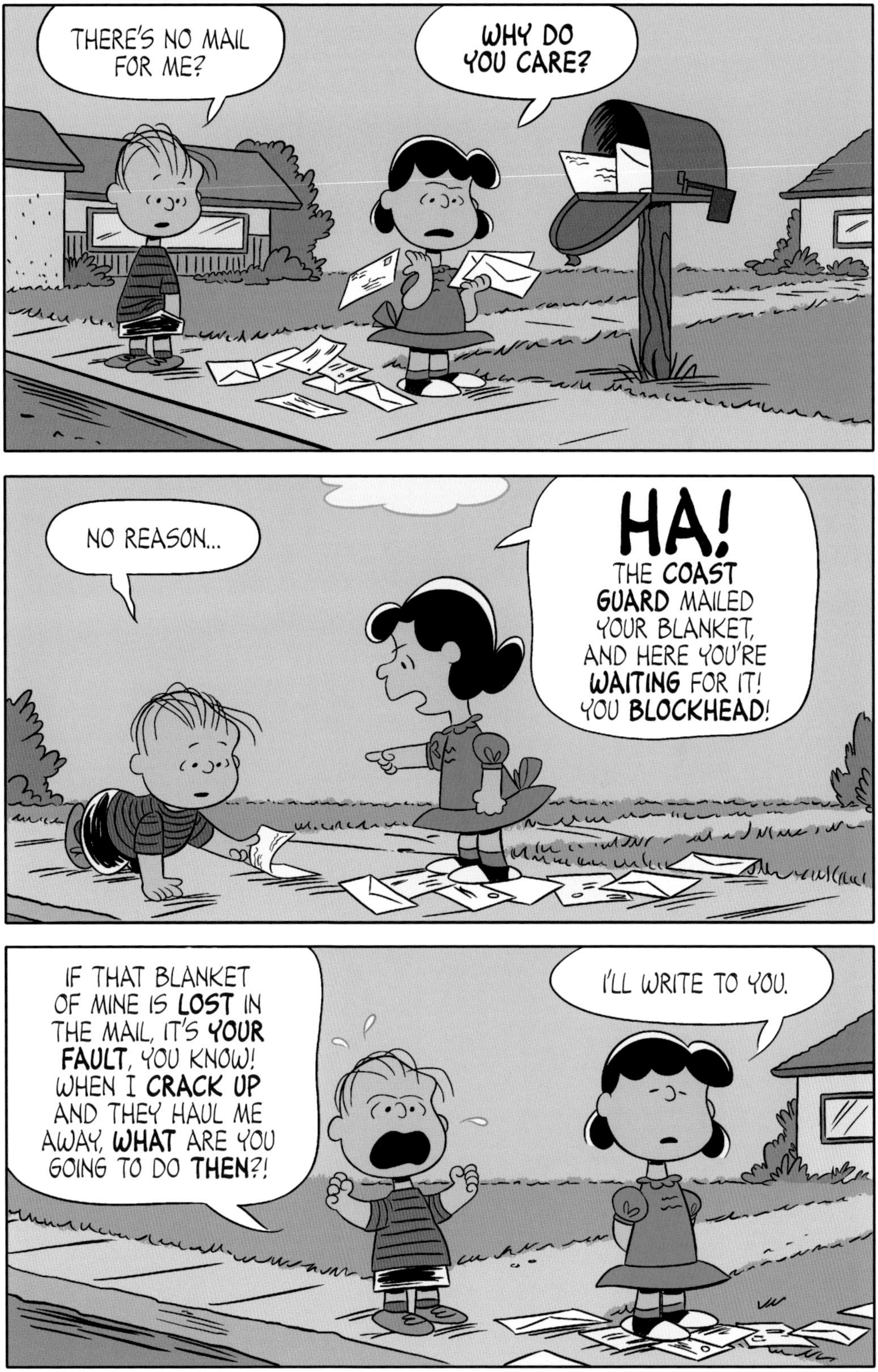
THERE'S NO MAIL FOR ME?
WHY DO YOU CARE?
NO REASON...
HA! THE COAST GUARD MAILED YOUR BLANKET, AND HERE YOU'RE WAITING FOR IT! YOU BLOCKHEAD!
IF THAT BLANKET OF MINE IS LOST IN THE MAIL, IT'S YOUR FAULT, YOU KNOW! WHEN I CRACK UP AND THEY HAUL ME AWAY, WHAT ARE YOU GOING TO DO THEN?!
I'LL WRITE TO YOU.

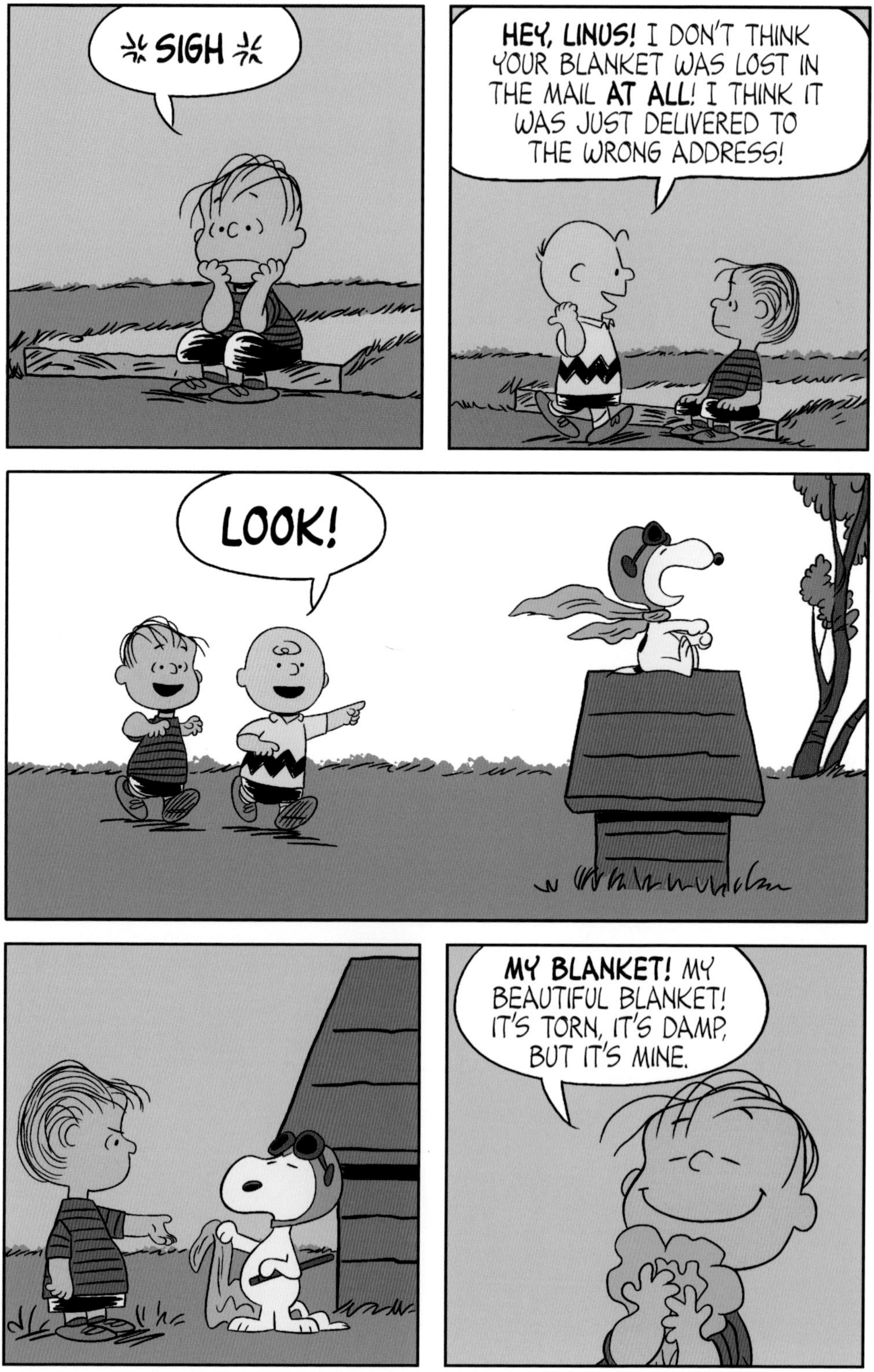
SIGH
HEY, LINUS! I DON'T THINK YOUR BLANKET WAS LOST IN THE MAIL AT ALL! I THINK IT WAS JUST DELIVERED TO THE WRONG ADDRESS!
LOOK!
MY BLANKET! MY BEAUTIFUL BLANKET! IT'S TORN, IT'S DAMP, BUT IT'S MINE.

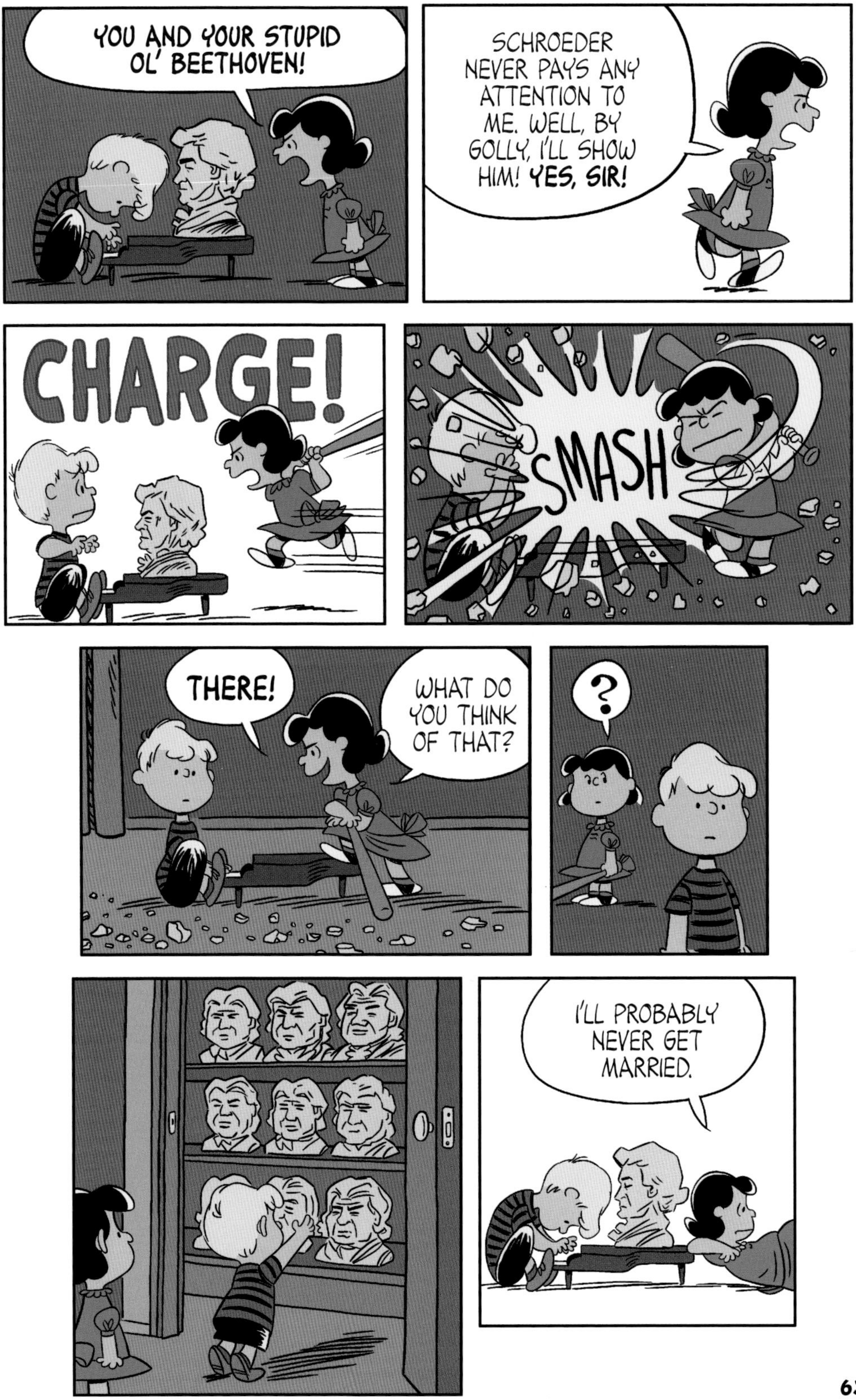
YOU AND YOUR STUPID OL' BEETHOVEN!
SCHROEDER NEVER PAYS ANY ATTENTION TO ME. WELL, BY GOLLY, I'LL SHOW HIM! YES, SIR!
CHARGE!
SMASH
THERE!
WHAT DO YOU THINK OF THAT?
?
I'LL PROBABLY NEVER GET MARRIED.

WELL, THAT'S THAT.

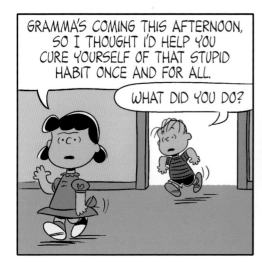

GRAMMA'S COMING THIS AFTERNOON, SO I THOUGHT I'D HELP YOU CURE YOURSELF OF THAT STUPID HABIT ONCE AND FOR ALL.

WHAT DID YOU DO?

I BURIED IT.

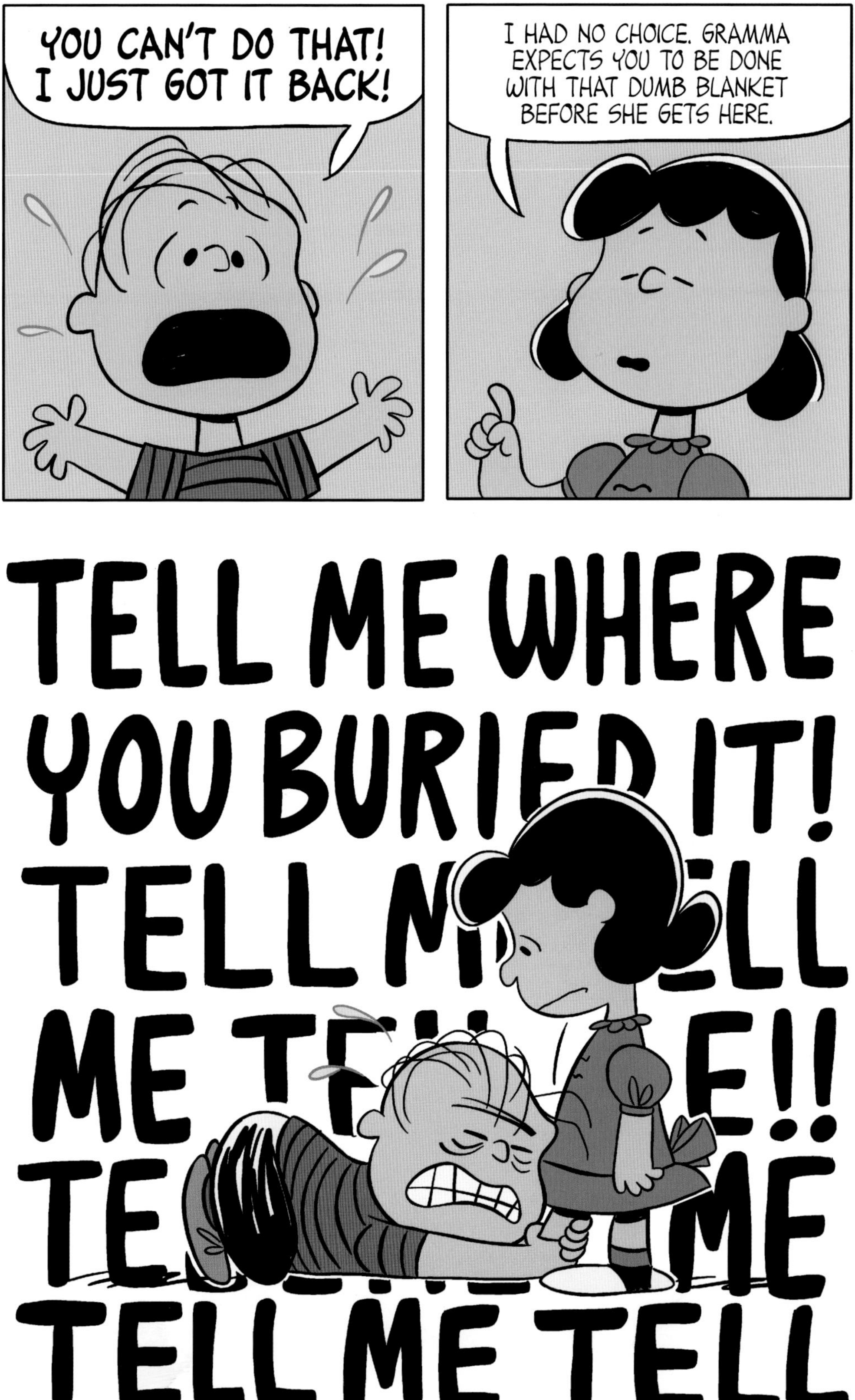
YOU CAN'T DO THAT! I JUST GOT IT BACK!
I HAD NO CHOICE. GRAMMA EXPECTS YOU TO BE DONE WITH THAT DUMB BLANKET BEFORE SHE GETS HERE.
TELL ME WHERE
YOU BURIED IT!
TELL M ELL
ME TE E!!
TE ME
TELL ME TELL

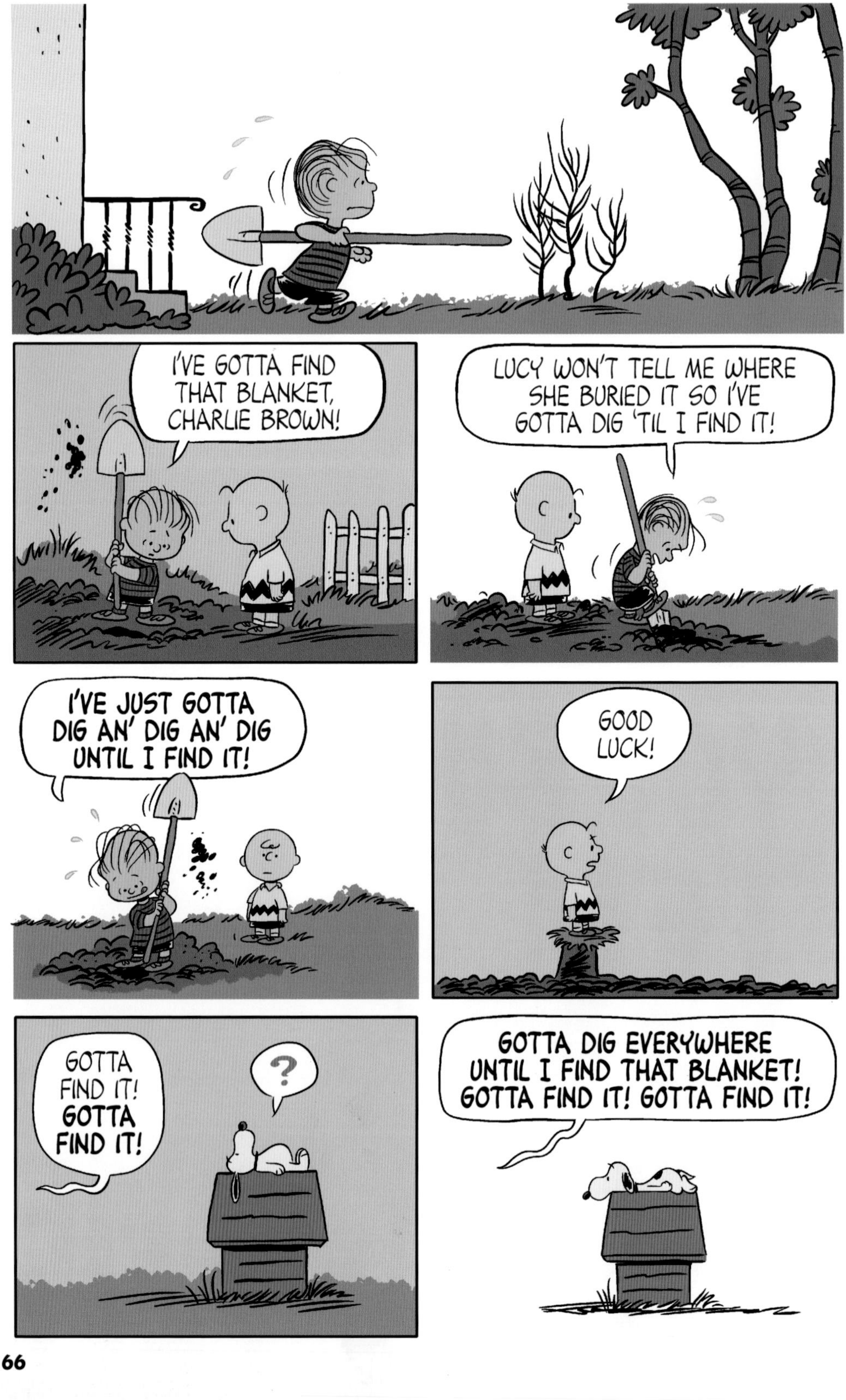
I'VE GOTTA FIND THAT BLANKET, CHARLIE BROWN!
LUCY WON'T TELL ME WHERE SHE BURIED IT SO I'VE GOTTA DIG 'TIL I FIND IT!
I'VE JUST GOTTA DIG AN' DIG AN' DIG UNTIL I FIND IT!
GOOD LUCK!
GOTTA FIND IT! GOTTA FIND IT!
?
GOTTA DIG EVERYWHERE UNTIL I FIND THAT BLANKET! GOTTA FIND IT! GOTTA FIND IT!

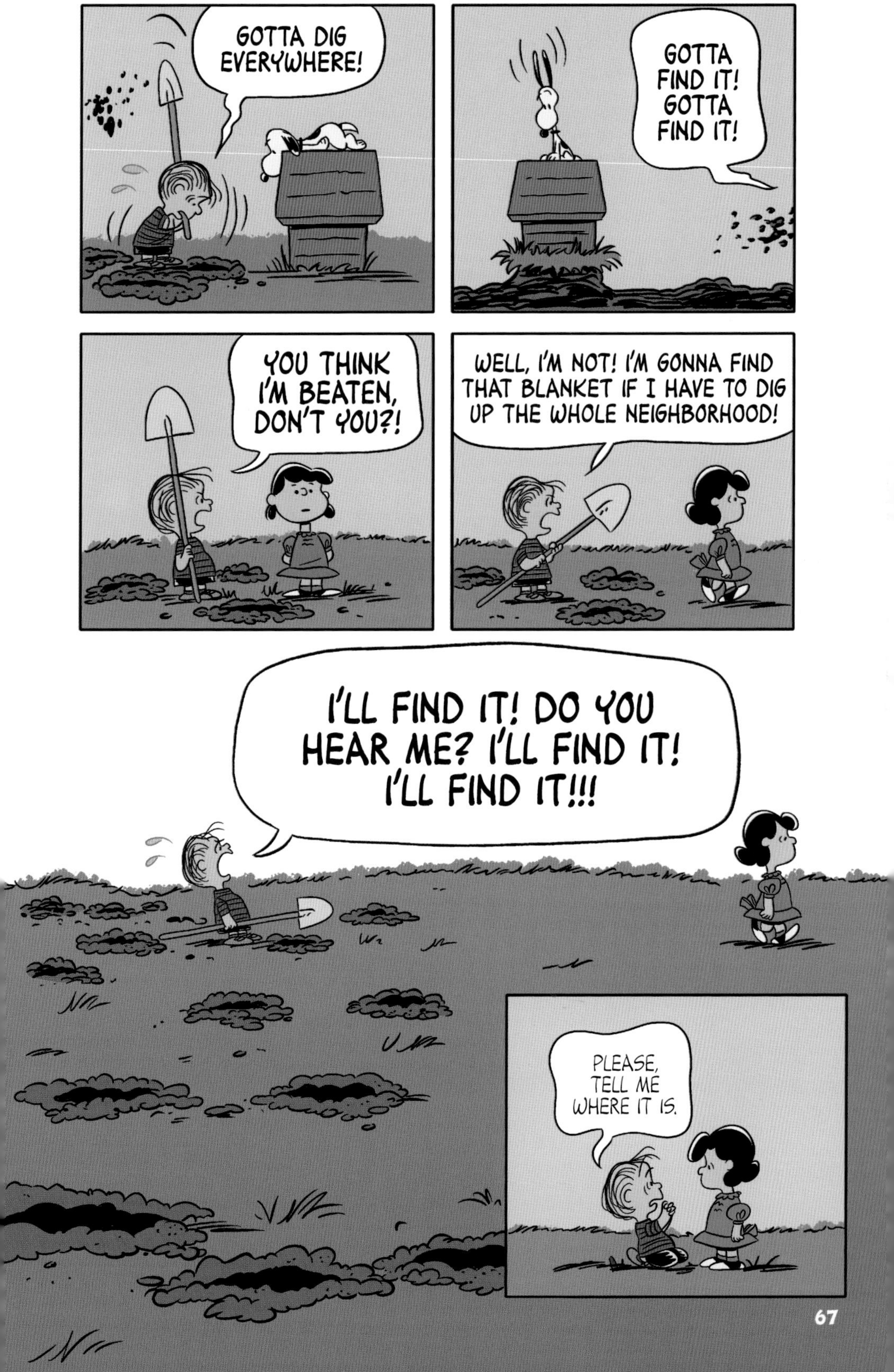
GOTTA DIG EVERYWHERE!
GOTTA FIND IT! GOTTA FIND IT!
YOU THINK I'M BEATEN, DON'T YOU?!
WELL, I'M NOT! I'M GONNA FIND THAT BLANKET IF I HAVE TO DIG UP THE WHOLE NEIGHBORHOOD!
I'LL FIND IT! DO YOU HEAR ME? I'LL FIND IT! I'LL FIND IT!!!
PLEASE, TELL ME WHERE IT IS.

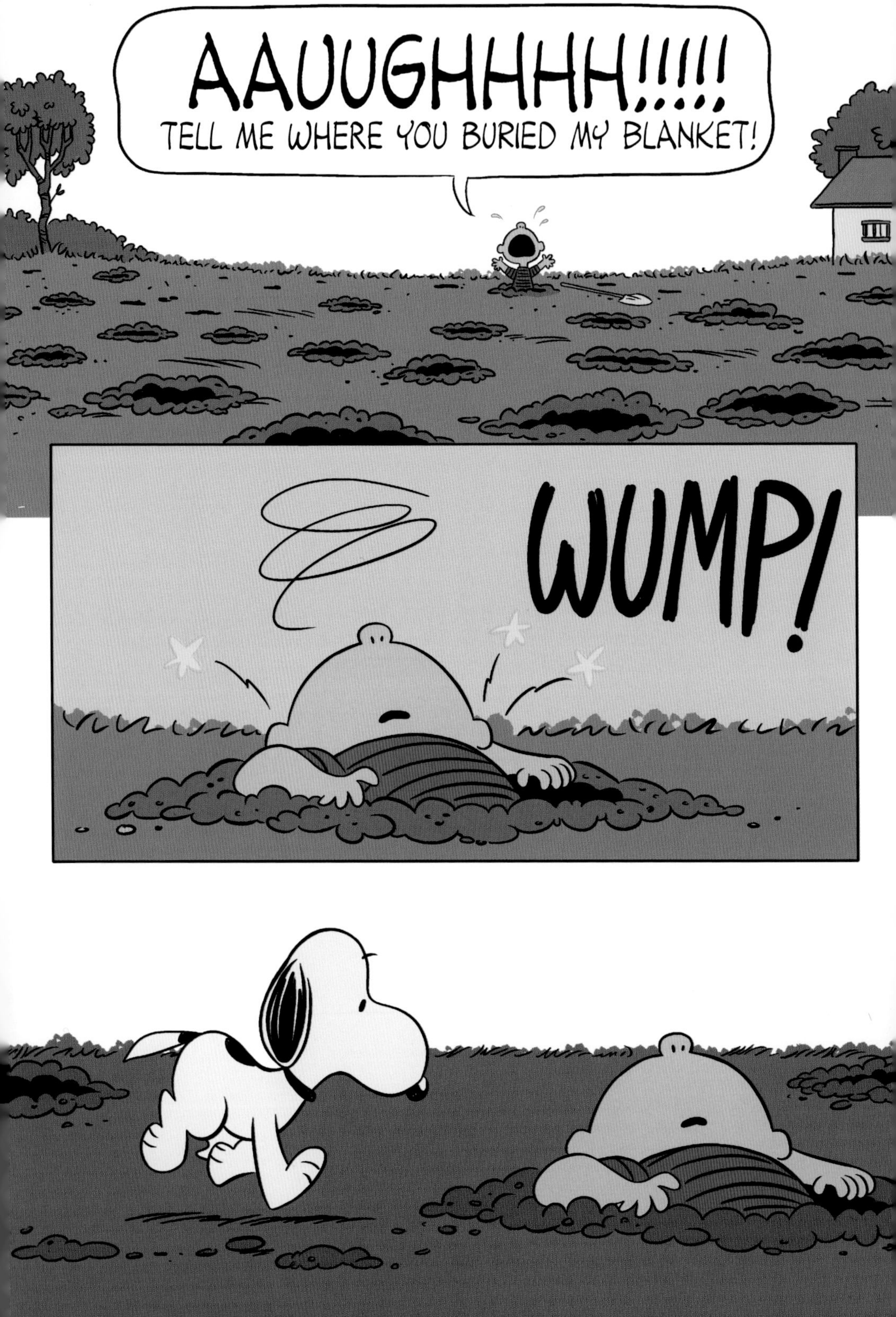
AAUUGHHHH!!!!!
TELL ME WHERE YOU BURIED MY BLANKET!
WUMP!

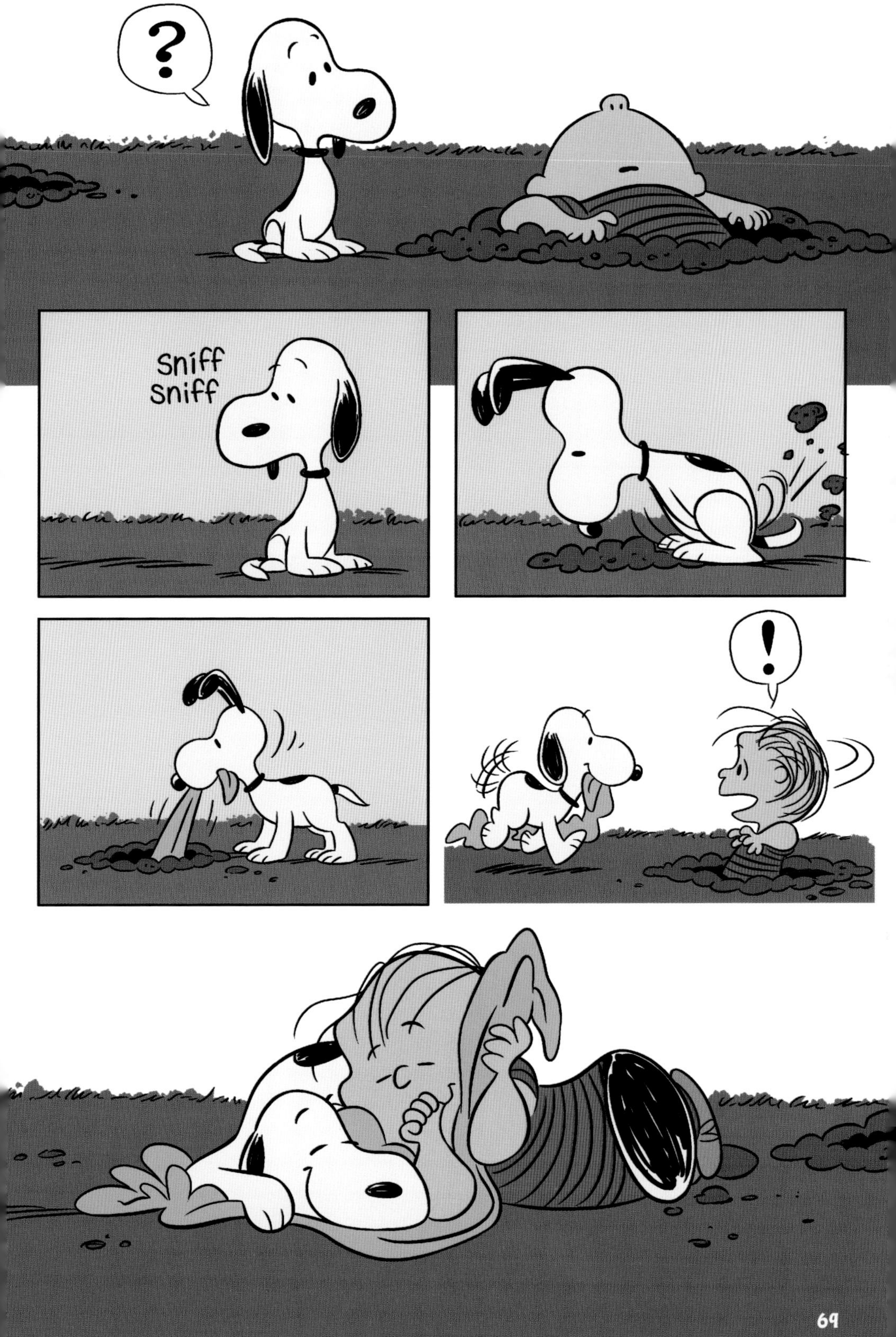
?
Sniff
sniff
!

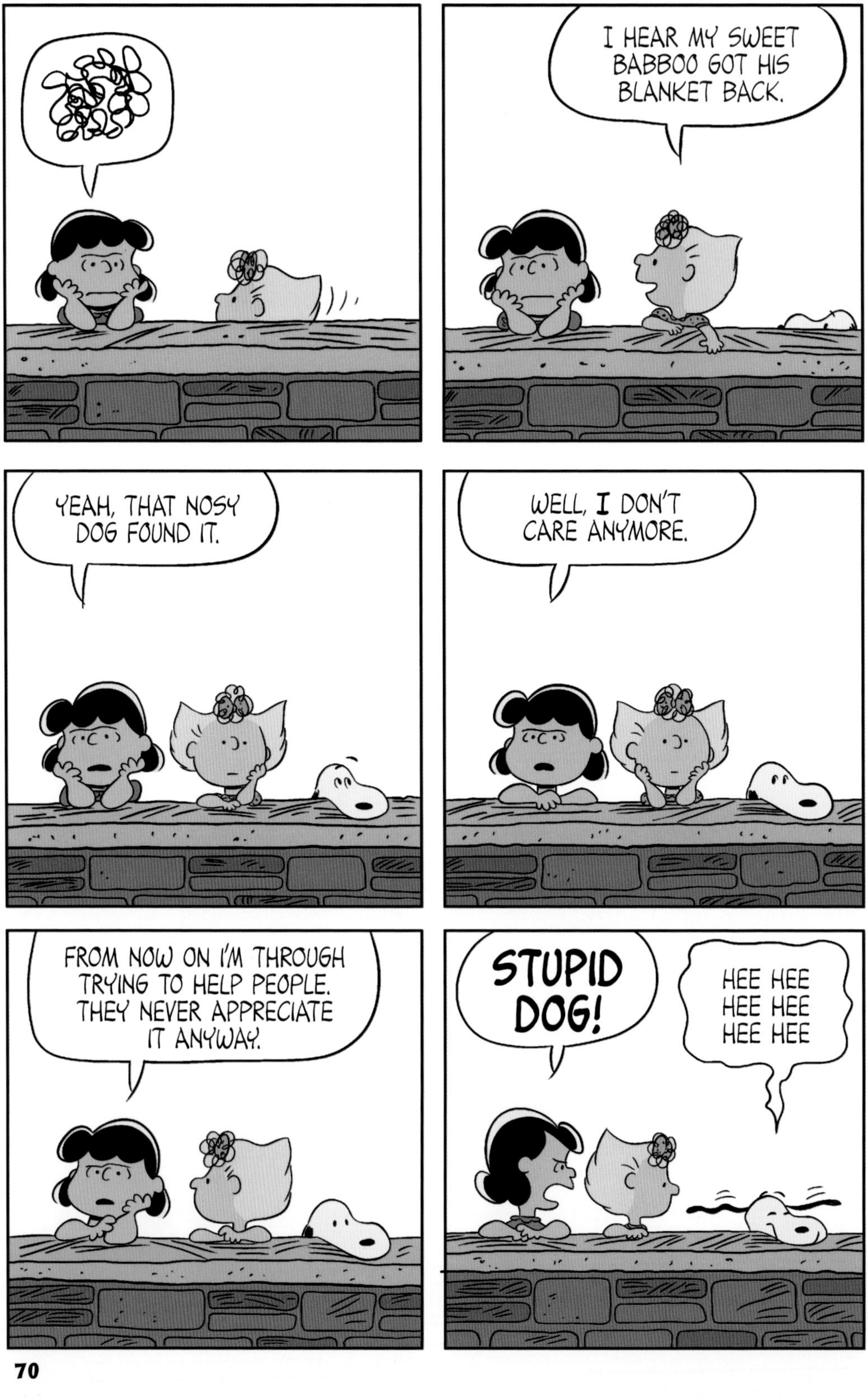
I HEAR MY SWEET BABBOO GOT HIS BLANKET BACK.
YEAH, THAT NOSY DOG FOUND IT.
WELL, I DON'T CARE ANYMORE.
FROM NOW ON I'M THROUGH TRYING TO HELP PEOPLE. THEY NEVER APPRECIATE IT ANYWAY.
STUPID DOG!
HEE HEE HEE HEE HEE HEE

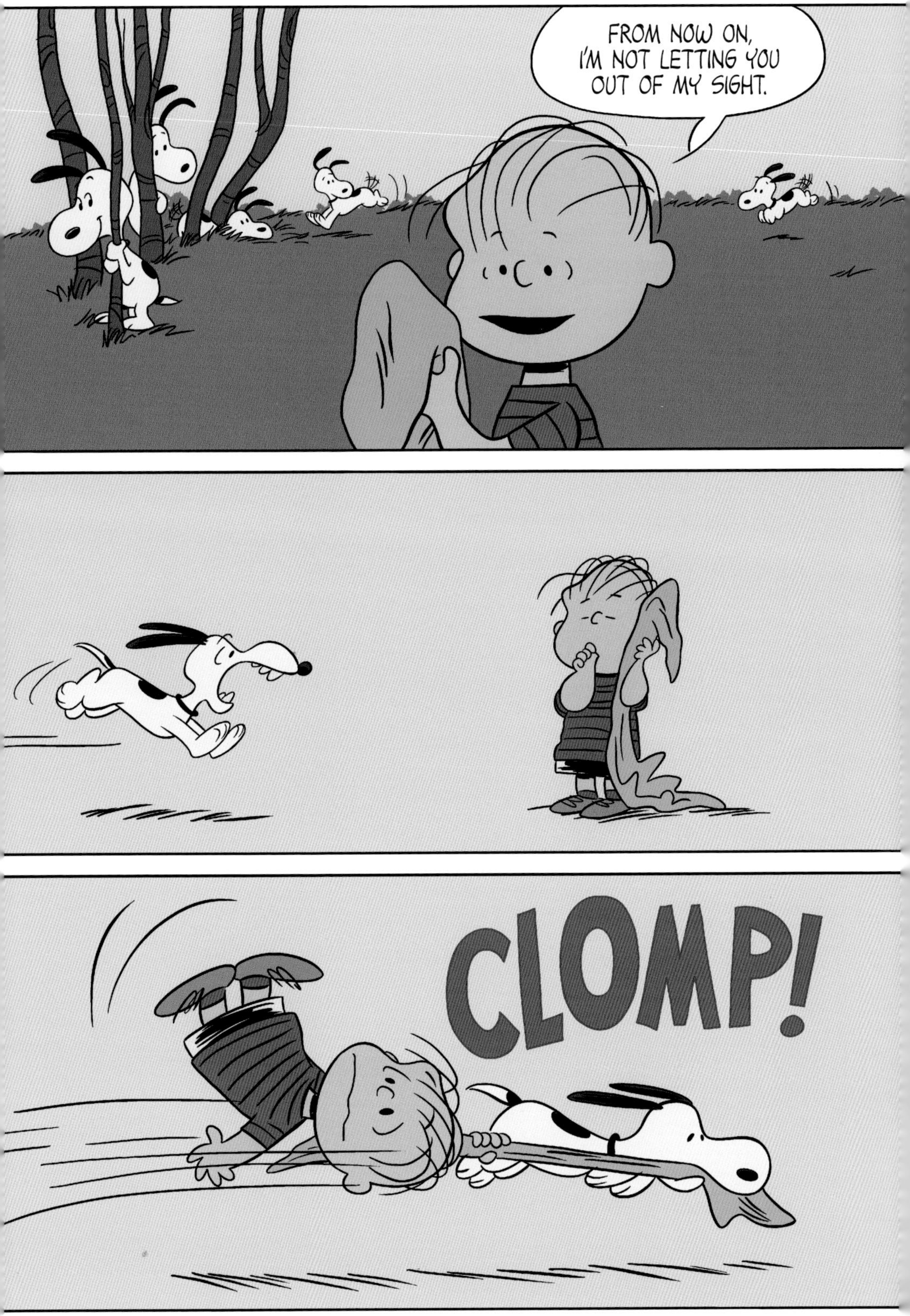
FROM NOW ON, I'M NOT LETTING YOU OUT OF MY SIGHT.
CLOMP!

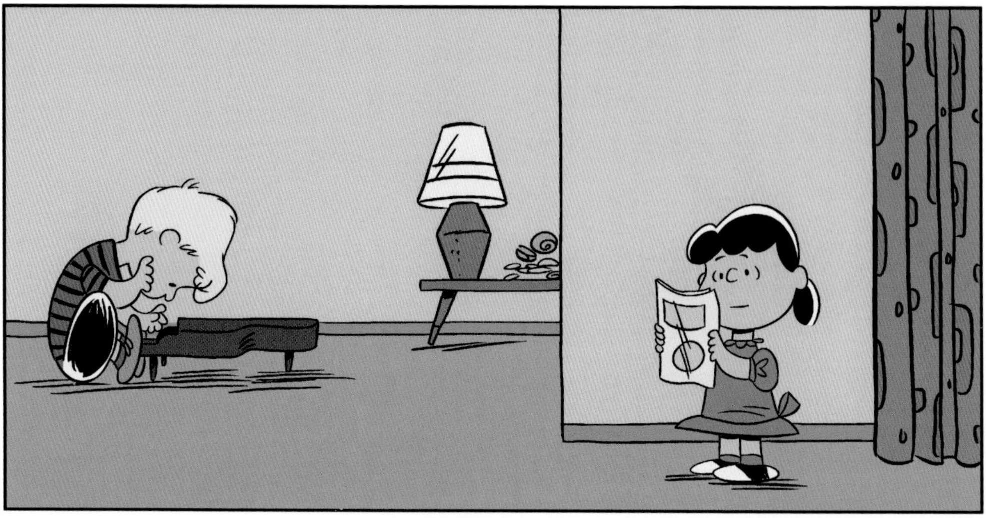

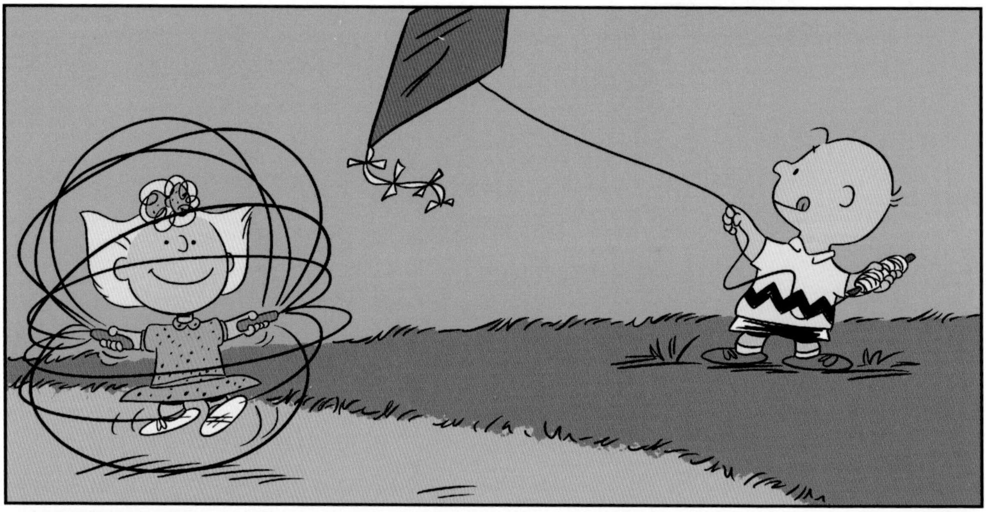

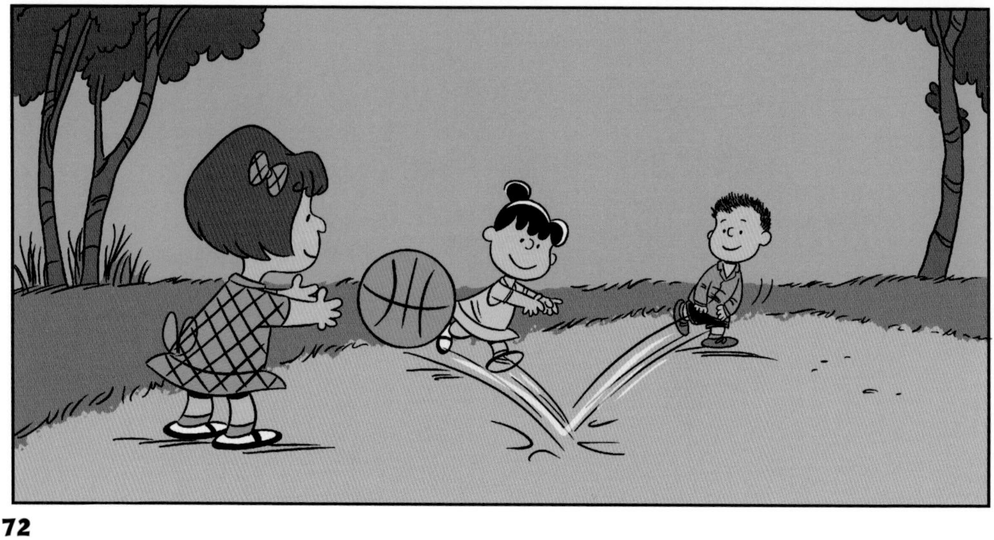

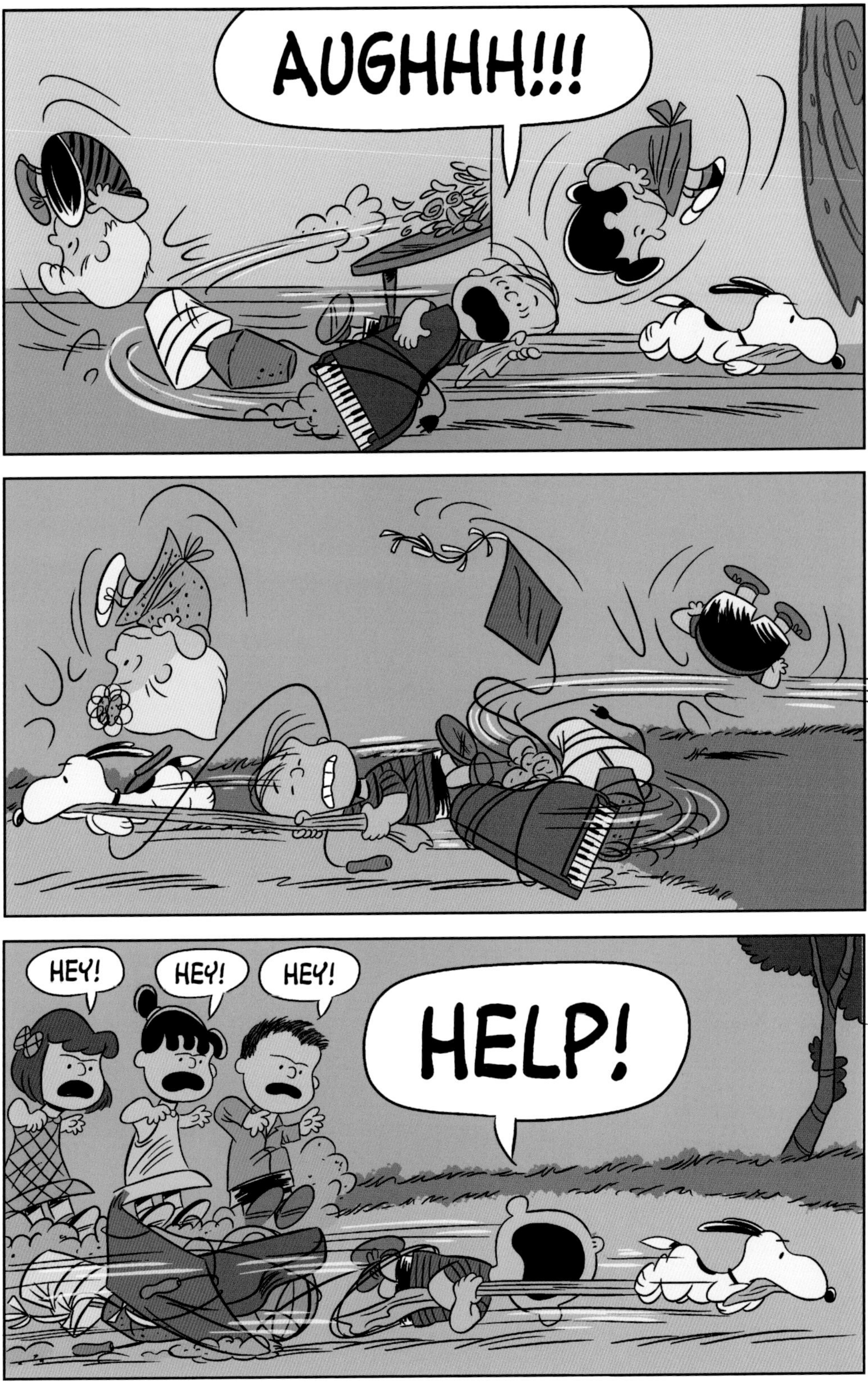
AUGHHH!!!
HEY!
HEY!
HEY!
HELP!

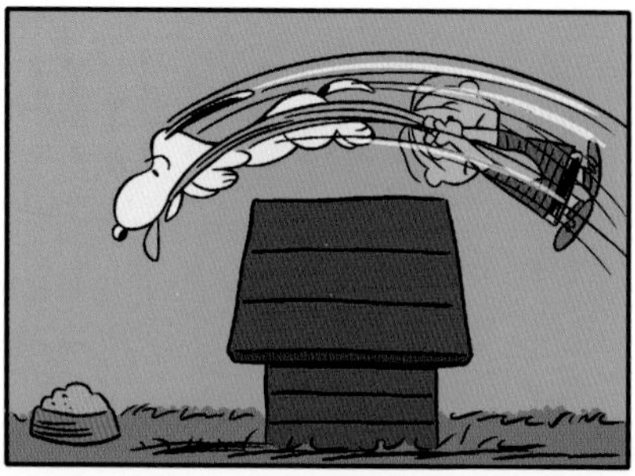

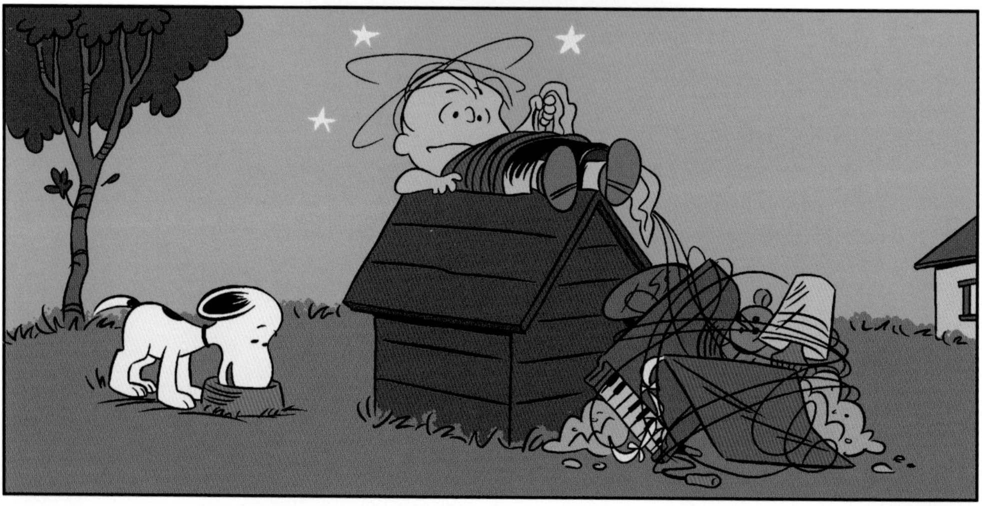

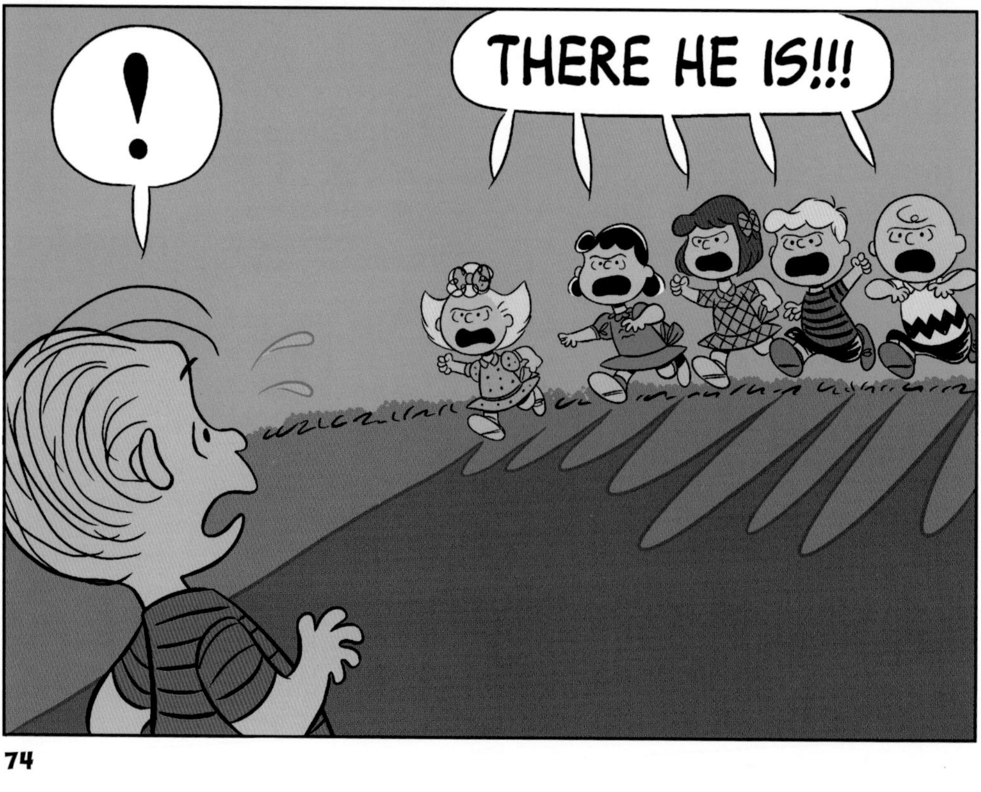

!
THERE HE IS!!!

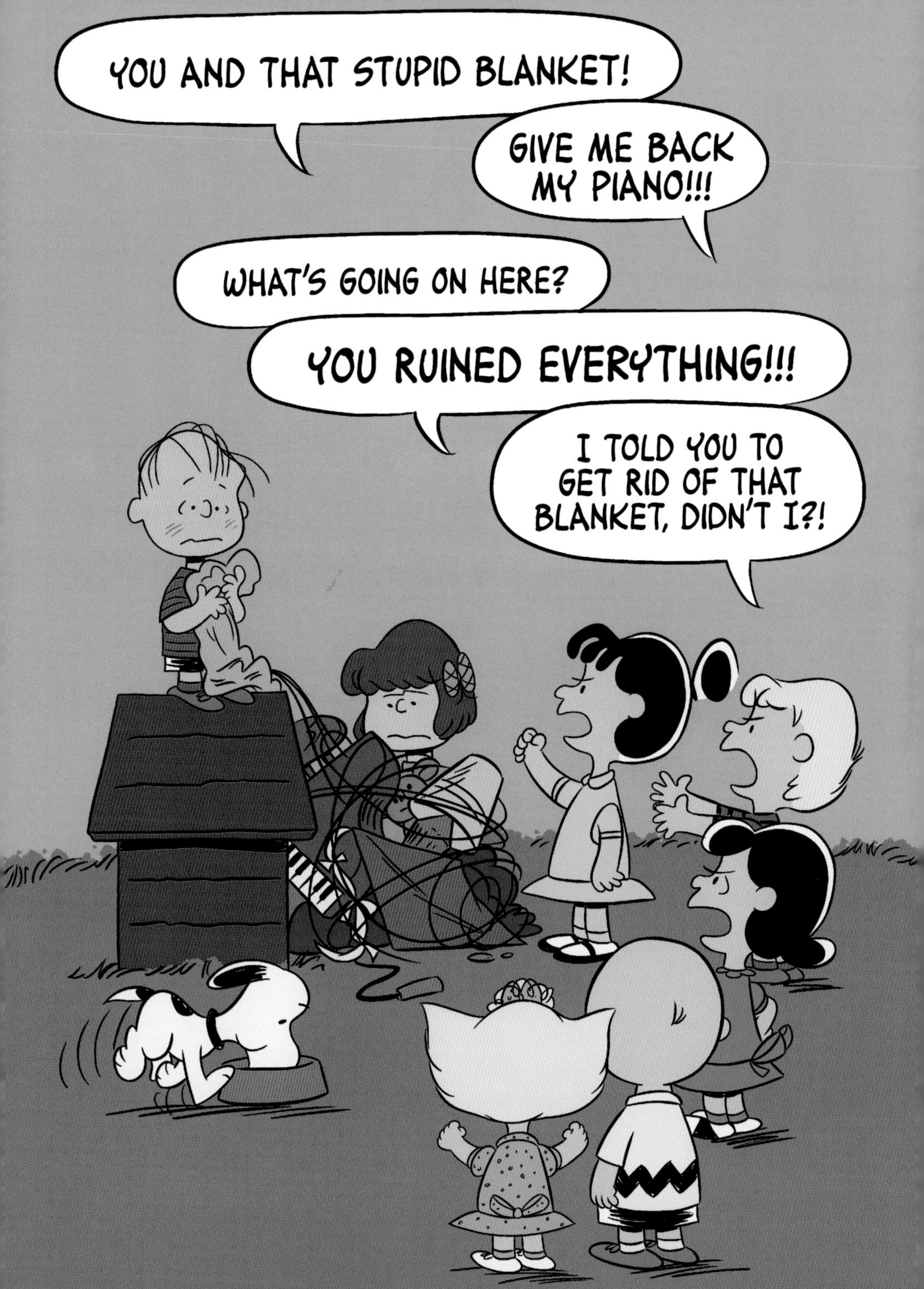
YOU AND THAT STUPID BLANKET!
GIVE ME BACK MY PIANO!!!
WHAT'S GOING ON HERE?
YOU RUINED EVERYTHING!!!
I TOLD YOU TO GET RID OF THAT BLANKET, DIDN'T I?!

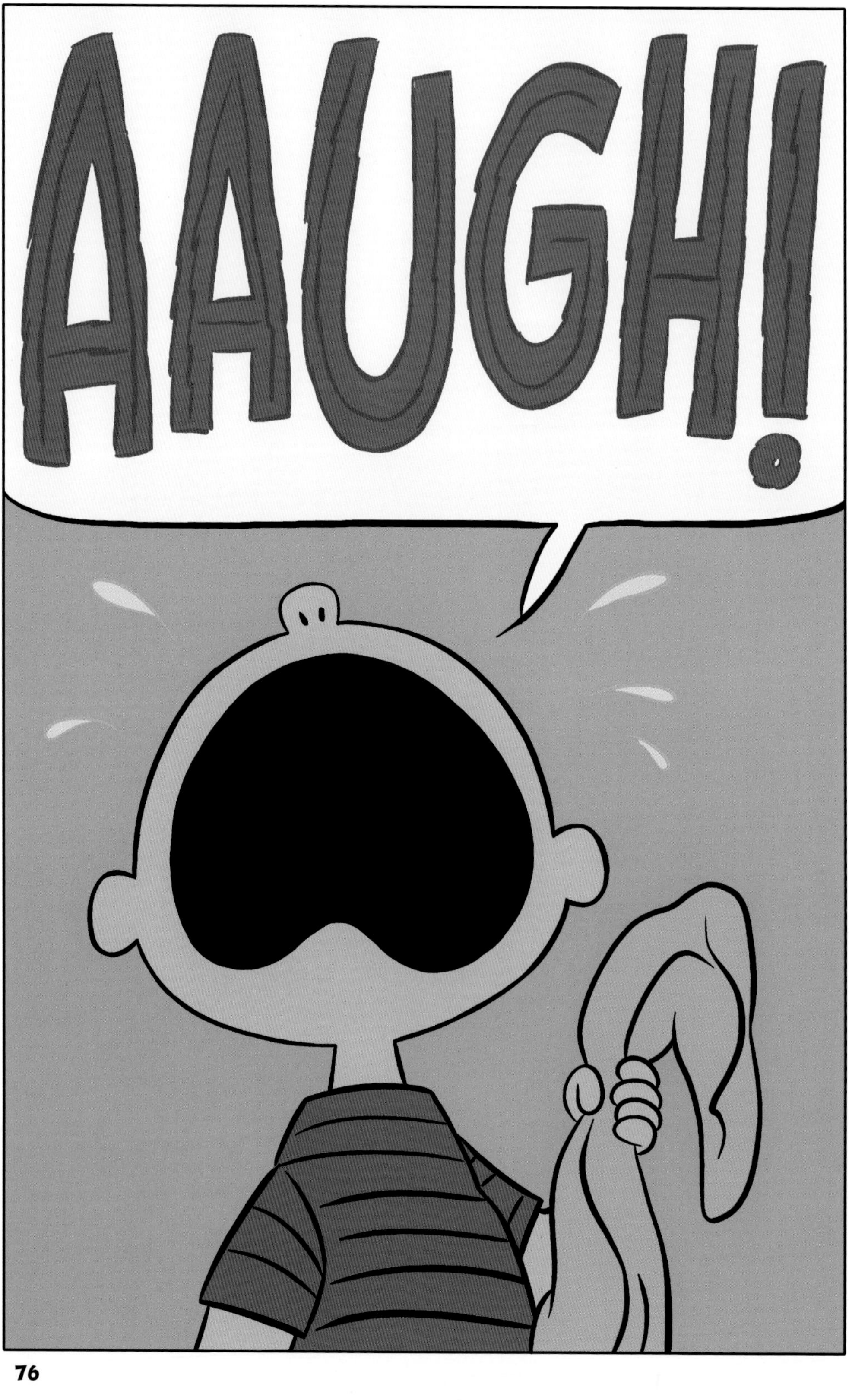
AAUGH!

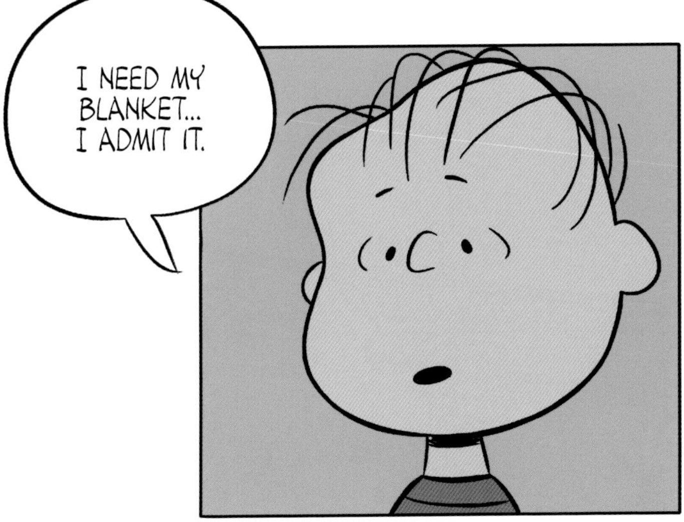
I NEED MY BLANKET... I ADMIT IT.

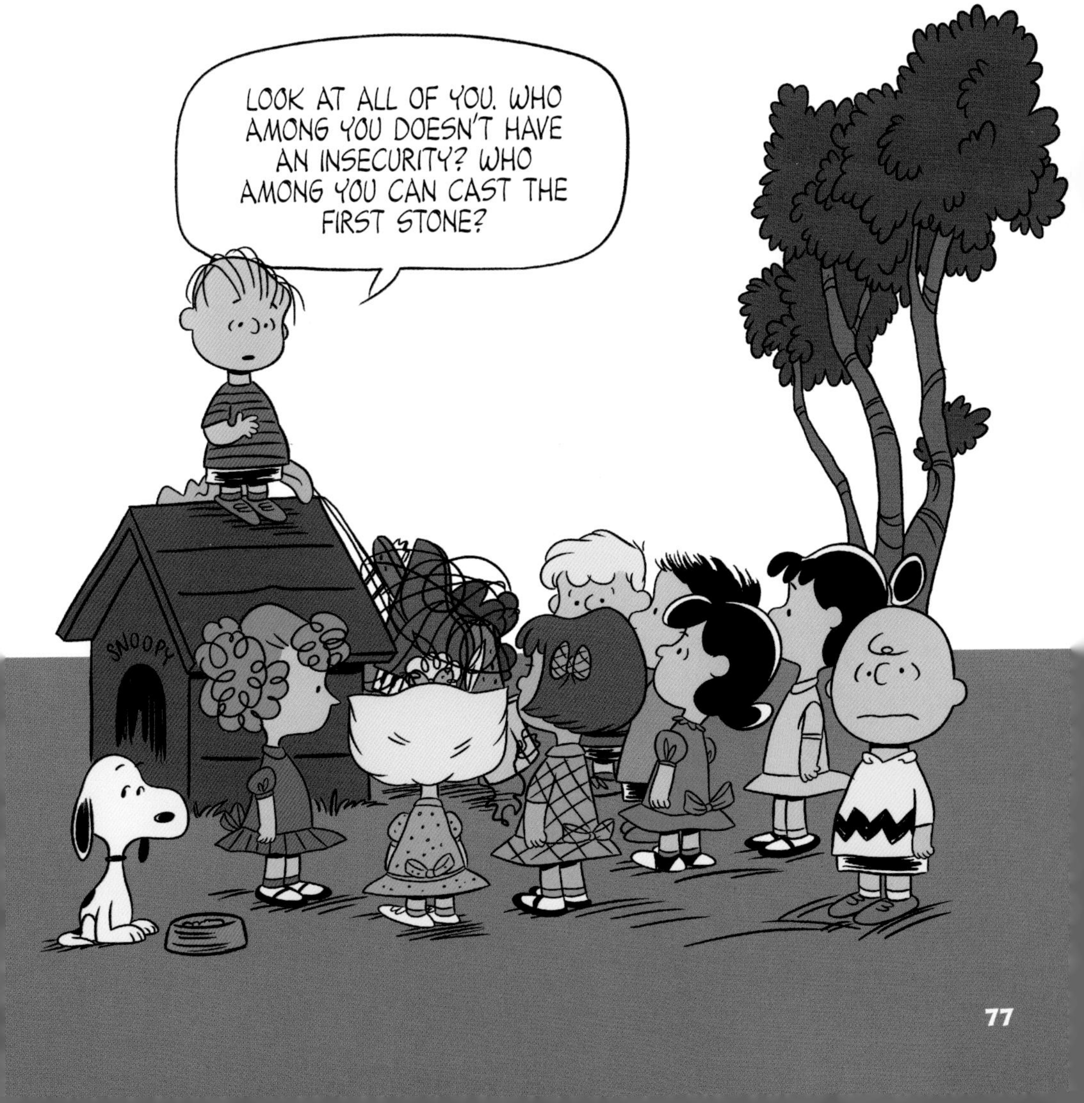
LOOK AT ALL OF YOU. WHO AMONG YOU DOESN'T HAVE AN INSECURITY? WHO AMONG YOU CAN CAST THE FIRST STONE?
SNOOPY

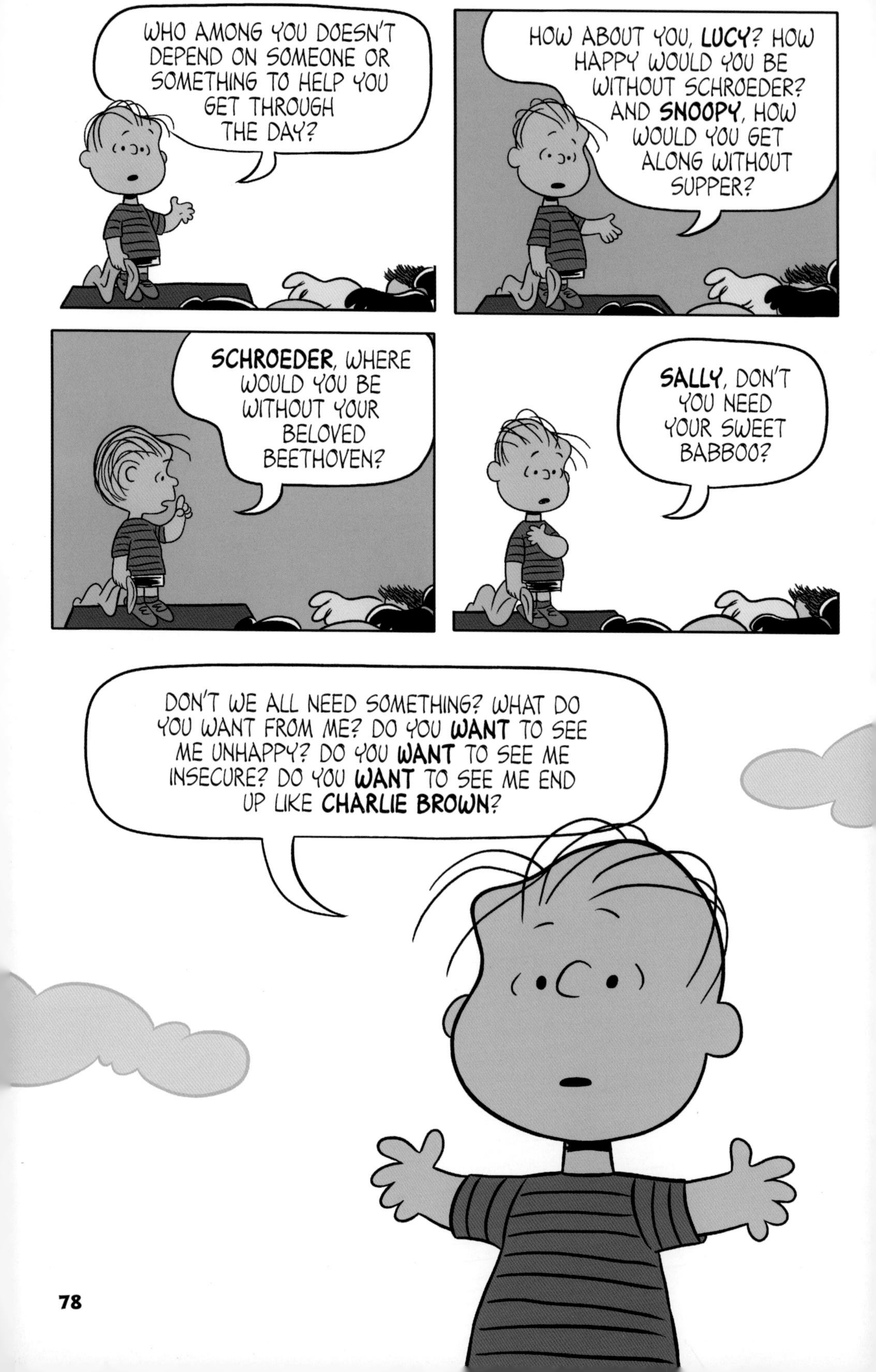
WHO AMONG YOU DOESN'T DEPEND ON SOMEONE OR SOMETHING TO HELP YOU GET THROUGH THE DAY?
HOW ABOUT YOU, LUCY? HOW HAPPY WOULD YOU BE WITHOUT SCHROEDER? AND SNOOPY, HOW WOULD YOU GET ALONG WITHOUT SUPPER?
SCHROEDER, WHERE WOULD YOU BE WITHOUT YOUR BELOVED BEETHOVEN?
SALLY, DON'T YOU NEED YOUR SWEET BABBOO?
DON'T WE ALL NEED SOMETHING? WHAT DO YOU WANT FROM ME? DO YOU WANT TO SEE ME UNHAPPY? DO YOU WANT TO SEE ME INSECURE? DO YOU WANT TO SEE ME END UP LIKE CHARLIE BROWN?

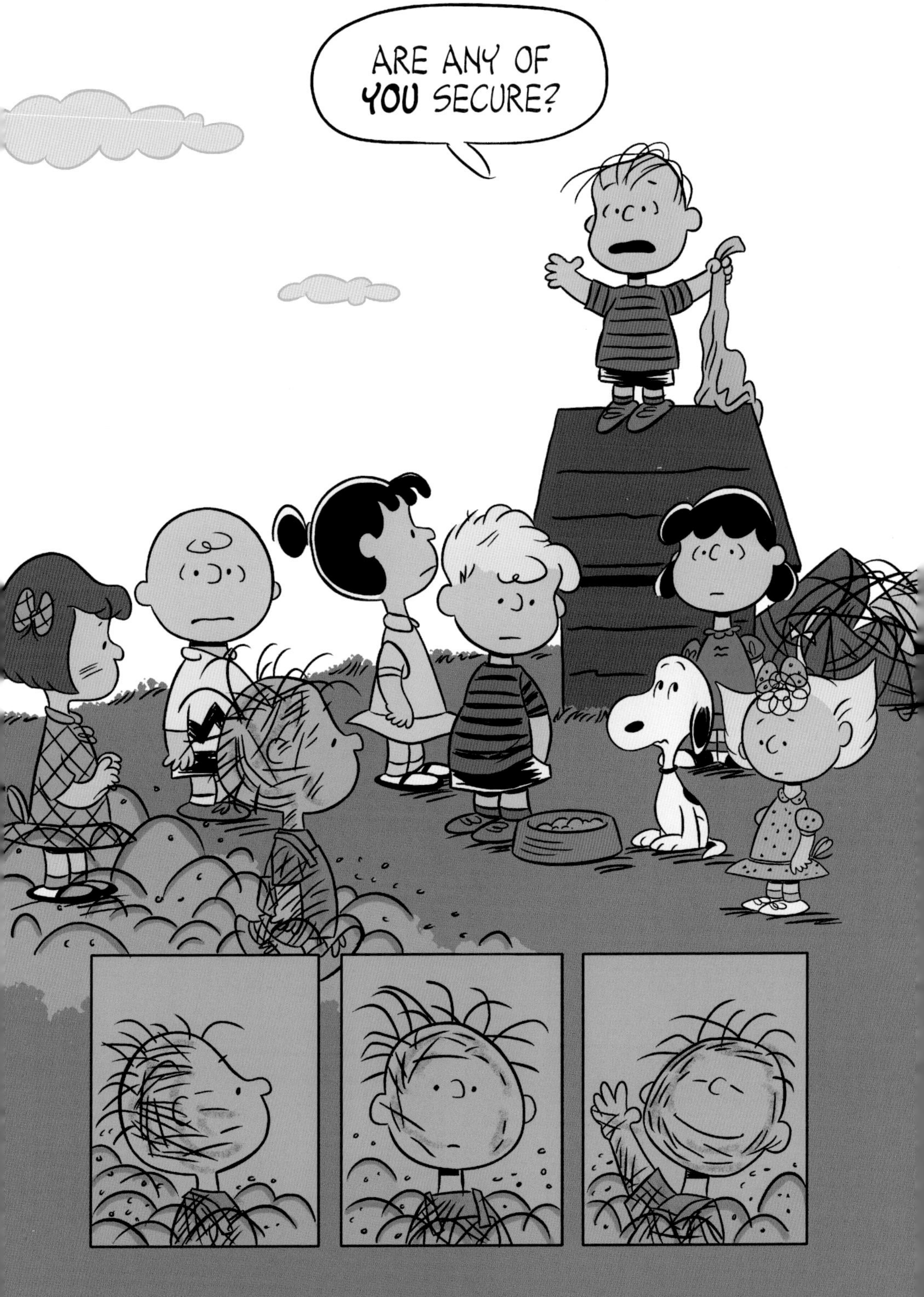
ARE ANY OF YOU SECURE?

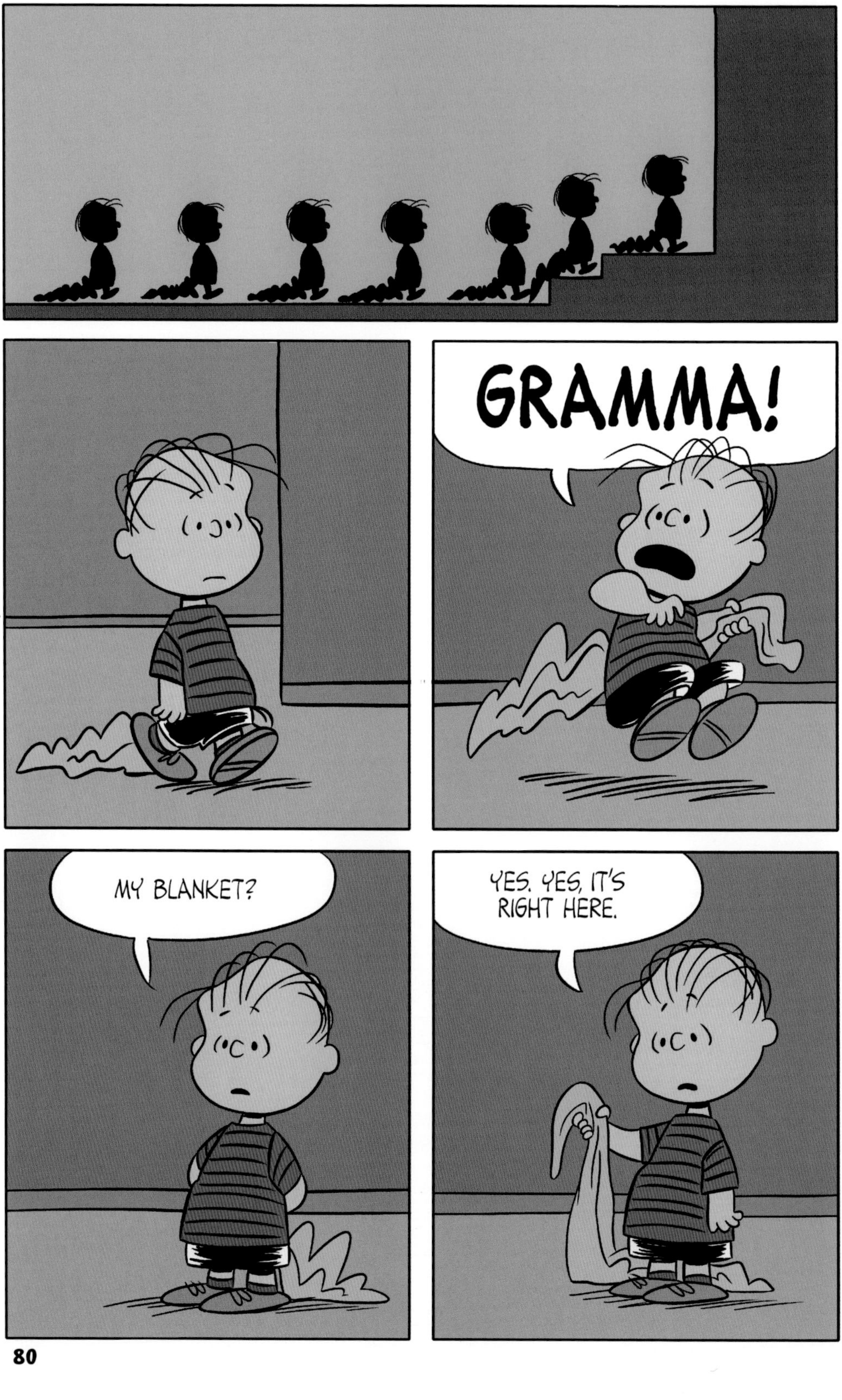
GRAMMA!
MY BLANKET?
YES. YES, IT'S RIGHT HERE.

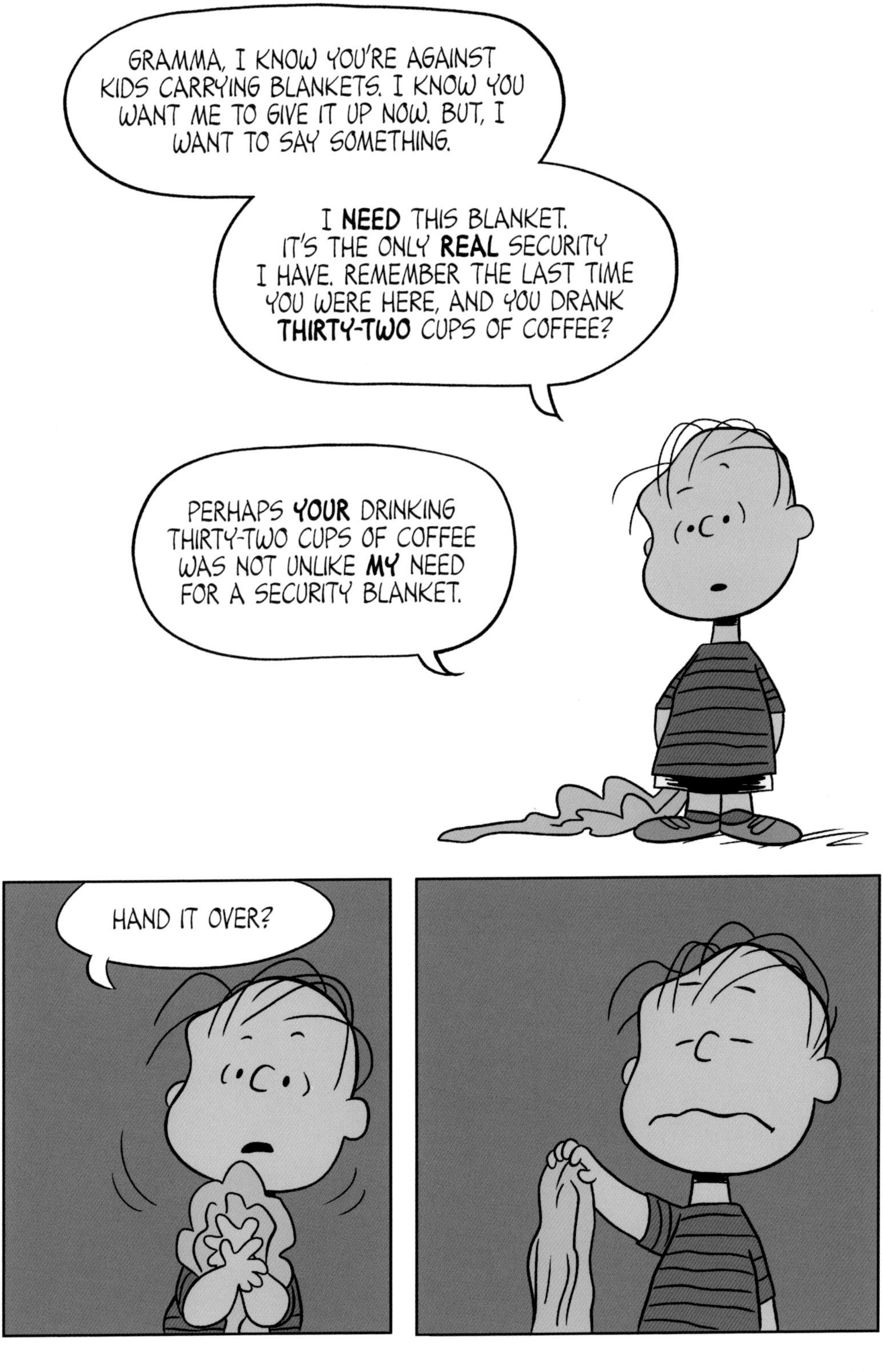
GRAMMA, I KNOW YOU'RE AGAINST KIDS CARRYING BLANKETS. I KNOW YOU WANT ME TO GIVE IT UP NOW. BUT, I WANT TO SAY SOMETHING.
I **NEED** THIS BLANKET. IT'S THE ONLY **REAL** SECURITY I HAVE. REMEMBER THE LAST TIME YOU WERE HERE, AND YOU DRANK **THIRTY-TWO** CUPS OF COFFEE?
PERHAPS **YOUR** DRINKING THIRTY-TWO CUPS OF COFFEE WAS NOT UNLIKE **MY** NEED FOR A SECURITY BLANKET.
HAND IT OVER?

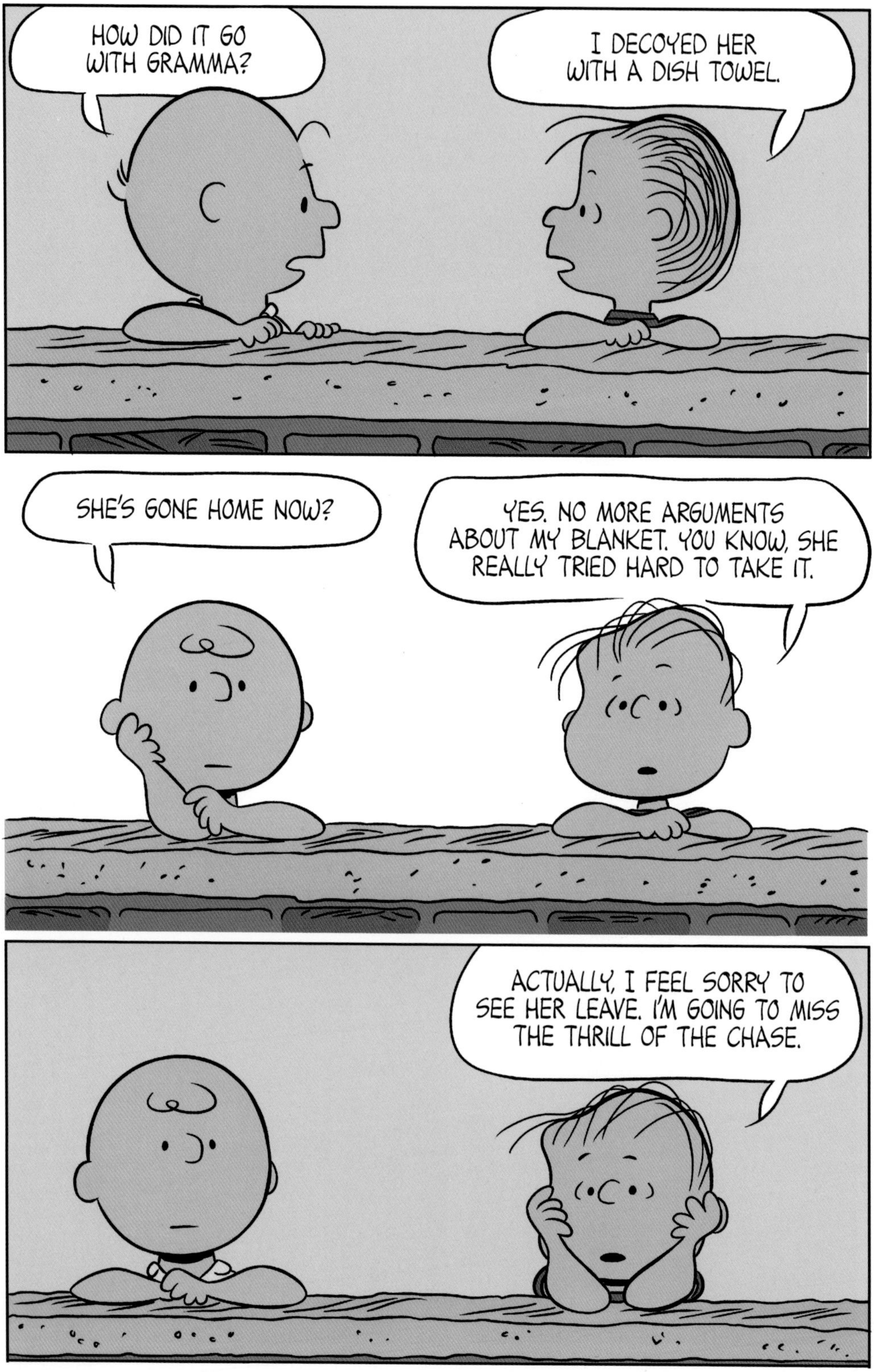
HOW DID IT GO WITH GRAMMA?
I DECOYED HER WITH A DISH TOWEL.
SHE'S GONE HOME NOW?
YES. NO MORE ARGUMENTS ABOUT MY BLANKET. YOU KNOW, SHE REALLY TRIED HARD TO TAKE IT.
ACTUALLY, I FEEL SORRY TO SEE HER LEAVE. I'M GOING TO MISS THE THRILL OF THE CHASE.

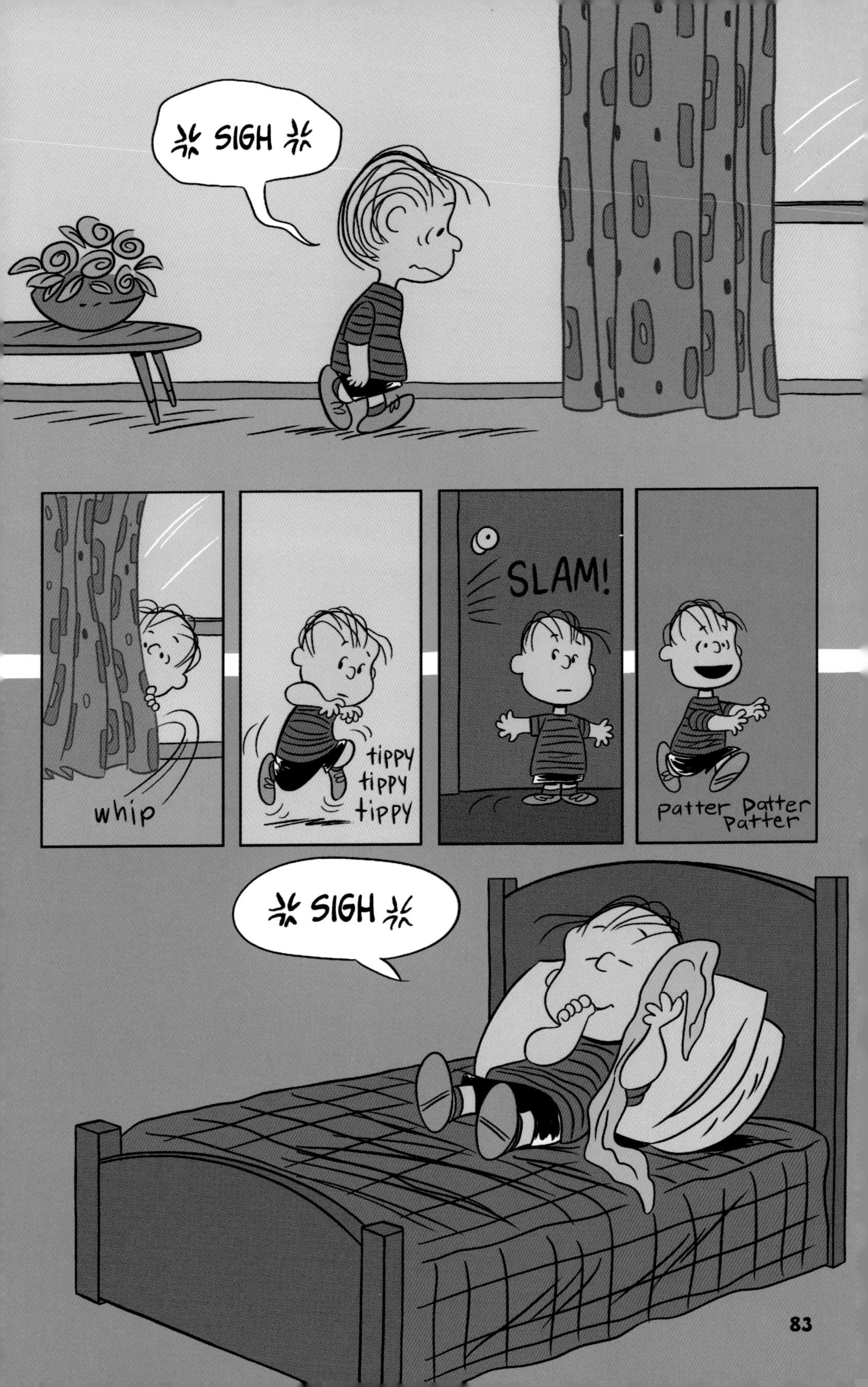
SIGH
whip
tippy
tippy
tippy
SLAM!
patter patter
patter
SIGH

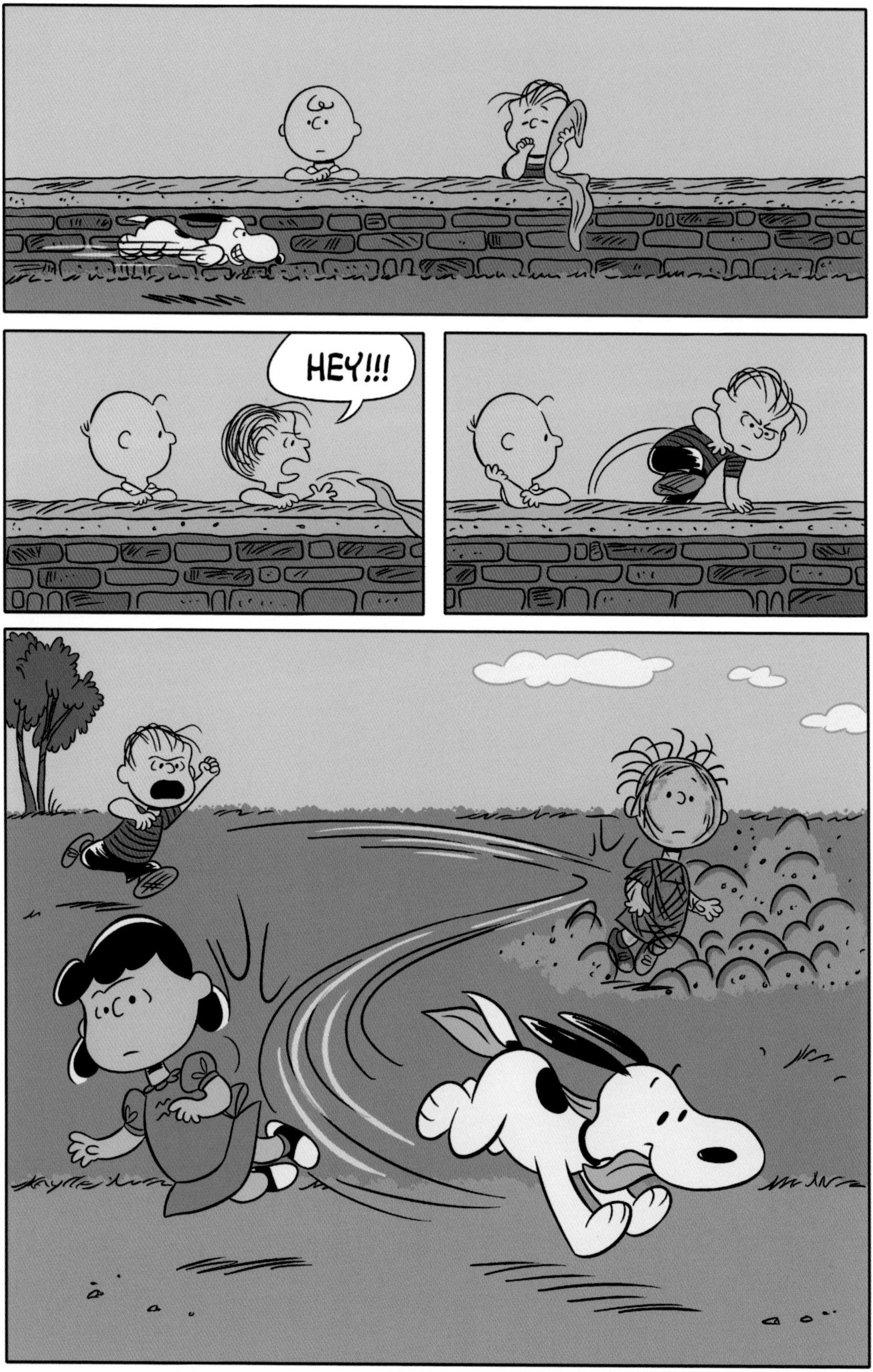
HEY!!!

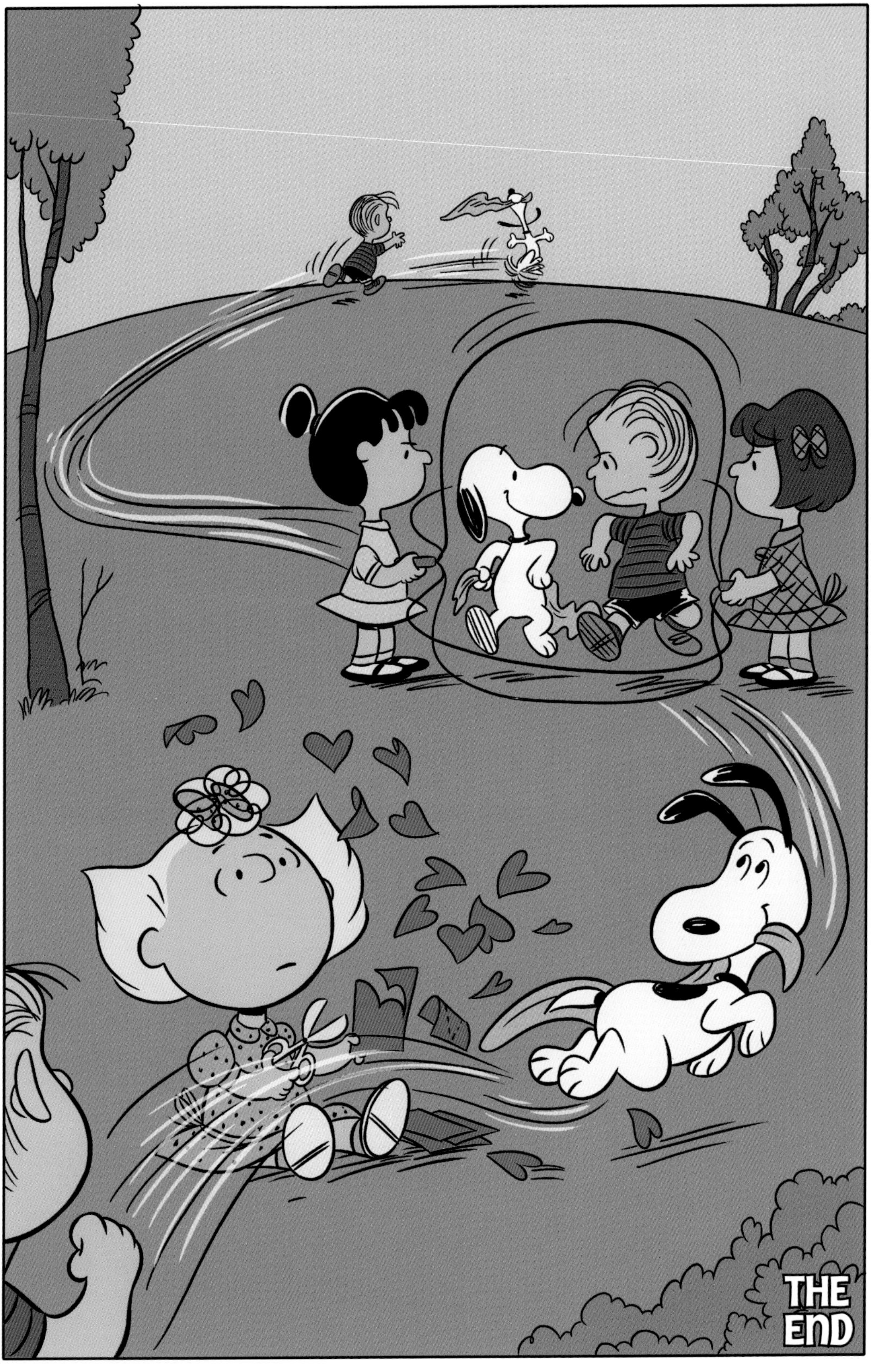
THE END

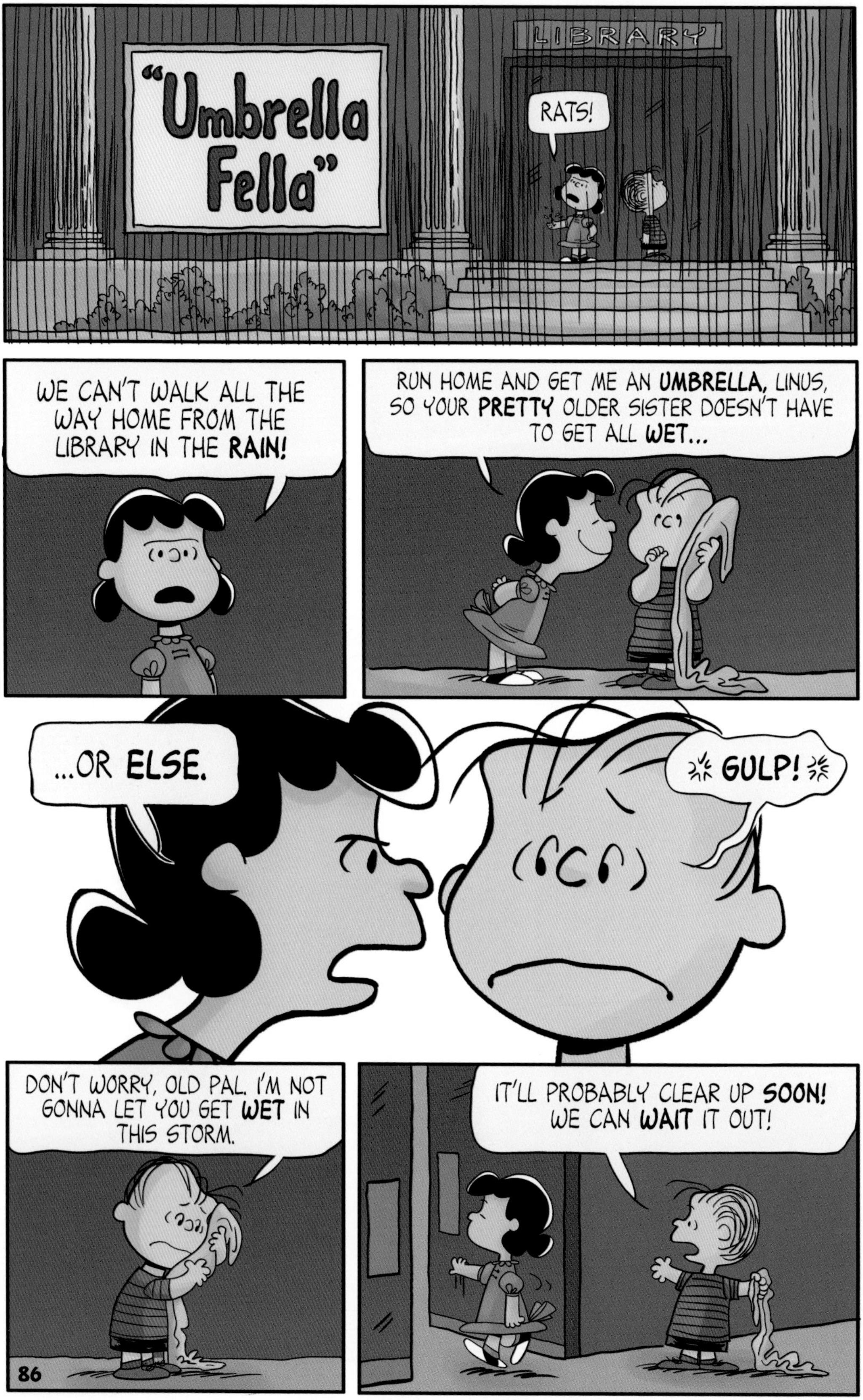

"Umbrella Fella"
LIBRARY
RATS!
WE CAN'T WALK ALL THE WAY HOME FROM THE LIBRARY IN THE **RAIN!**
RUN HOME AND GET ME AN **UMBRELLA,** LINUS, SO YOUR **PRETTY** OLDER SISTER DOESN'T HAVE TO GET ALL **WET**...
...OR **ELSE.**
GULP!
DON'T WORRY, OLD PAL. I'M NOT GONNA LET YOU GET **WET** IN THIS STORM.
IT'LL PROBABLY CLEAR UP **SOON!** WE CAN **WAIT** IT OUT!

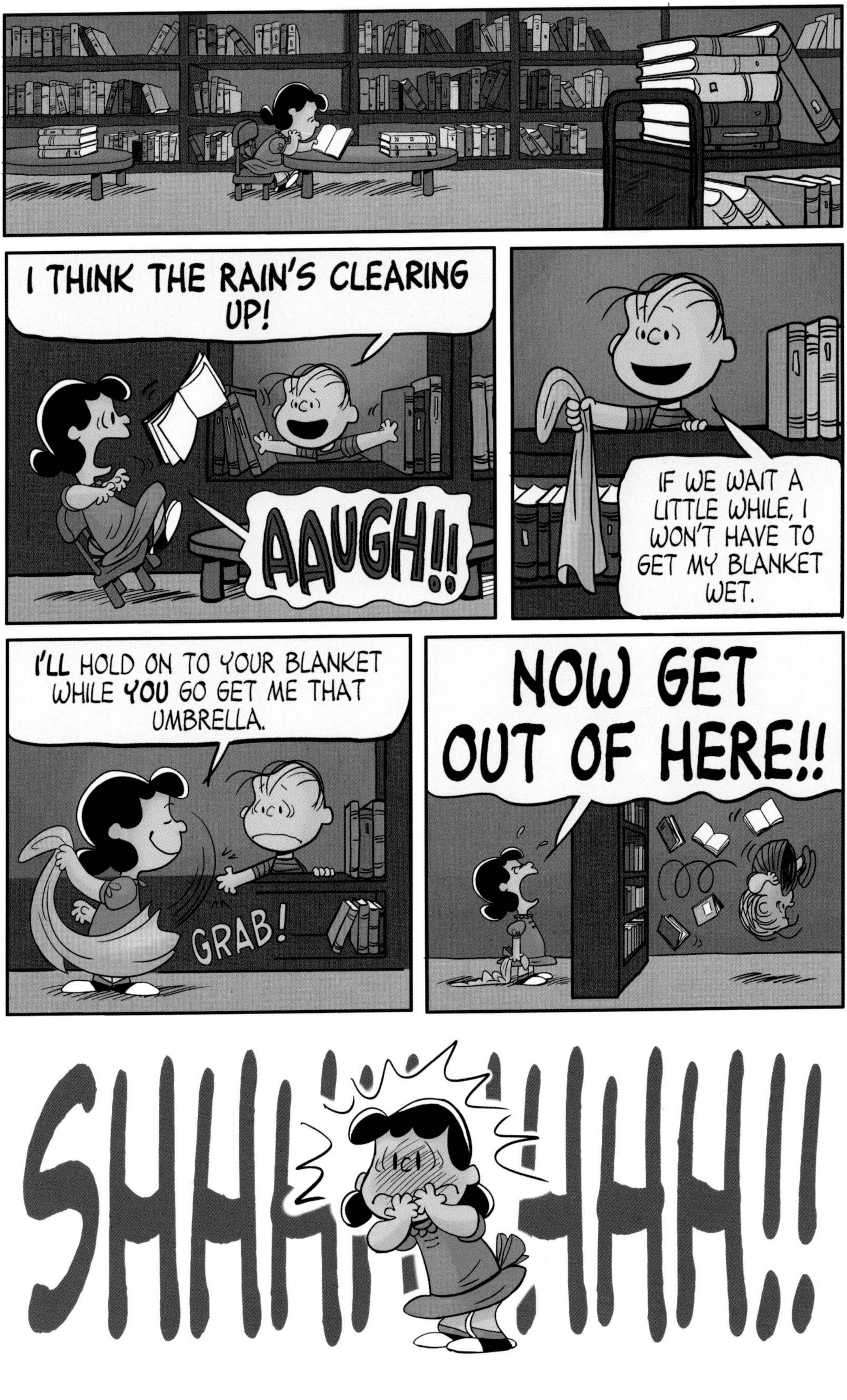

I THINK THE RAIN'S CLEARING UP!
AAUGH!!
IF WE WAIT A LITTLE WHILE, I WON'T HAVE TO GET MY BLANKET WET.
I'LL HOLD ON TO YOUR BLANKET WHILE YOU GO GET ME THAT UMBRELLA.
GRAB!
NOW GET OUT OF HERE!!
SHHHHHHH!!

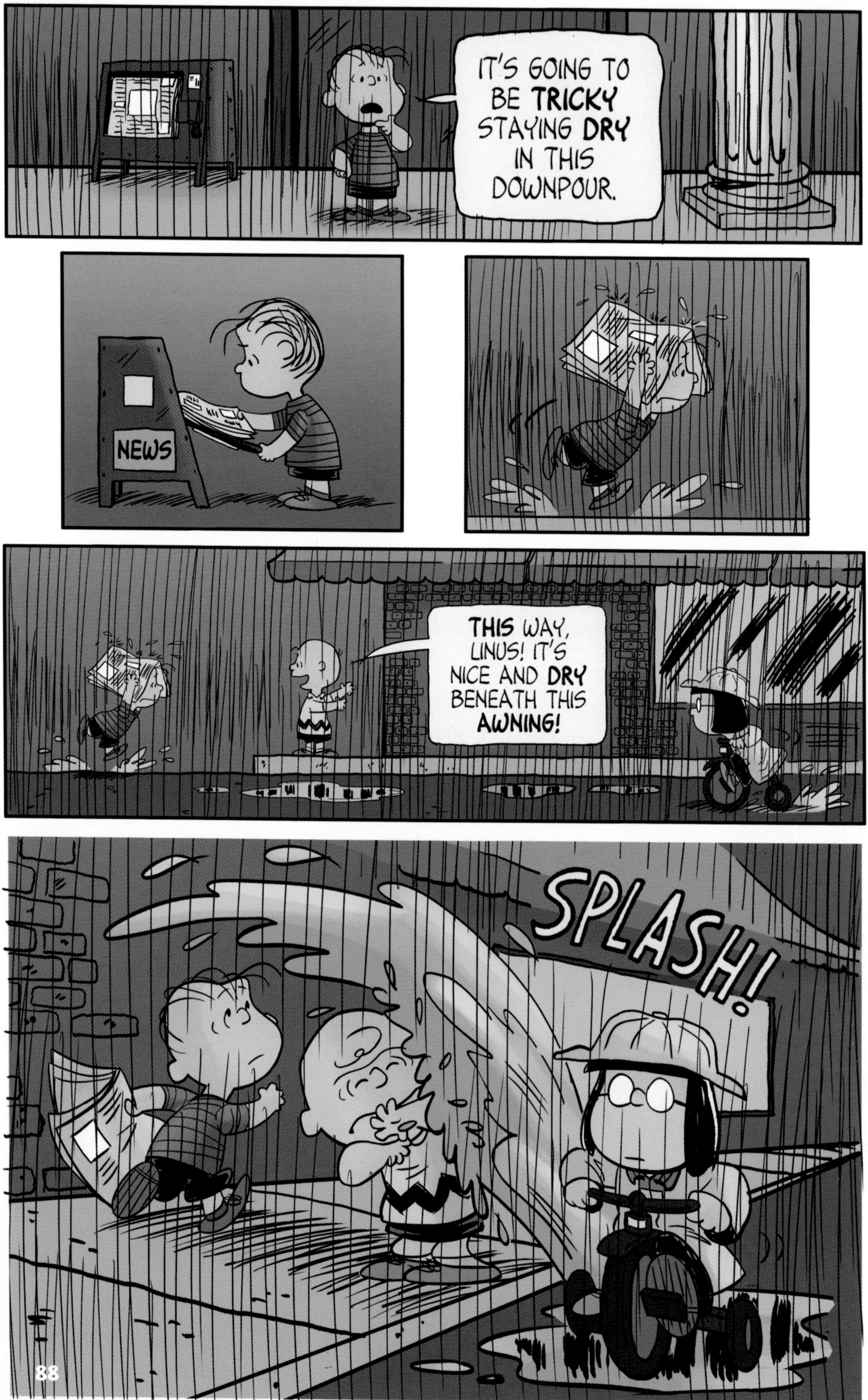
IT'S GOING TO BE TRICKY STAYING DRY IN THIS DOWNPOUR.
NEWS
THIS WAY, LINUS! IT'S NICE AND DRY BENEATH THIS AWNING!
SPLASH!

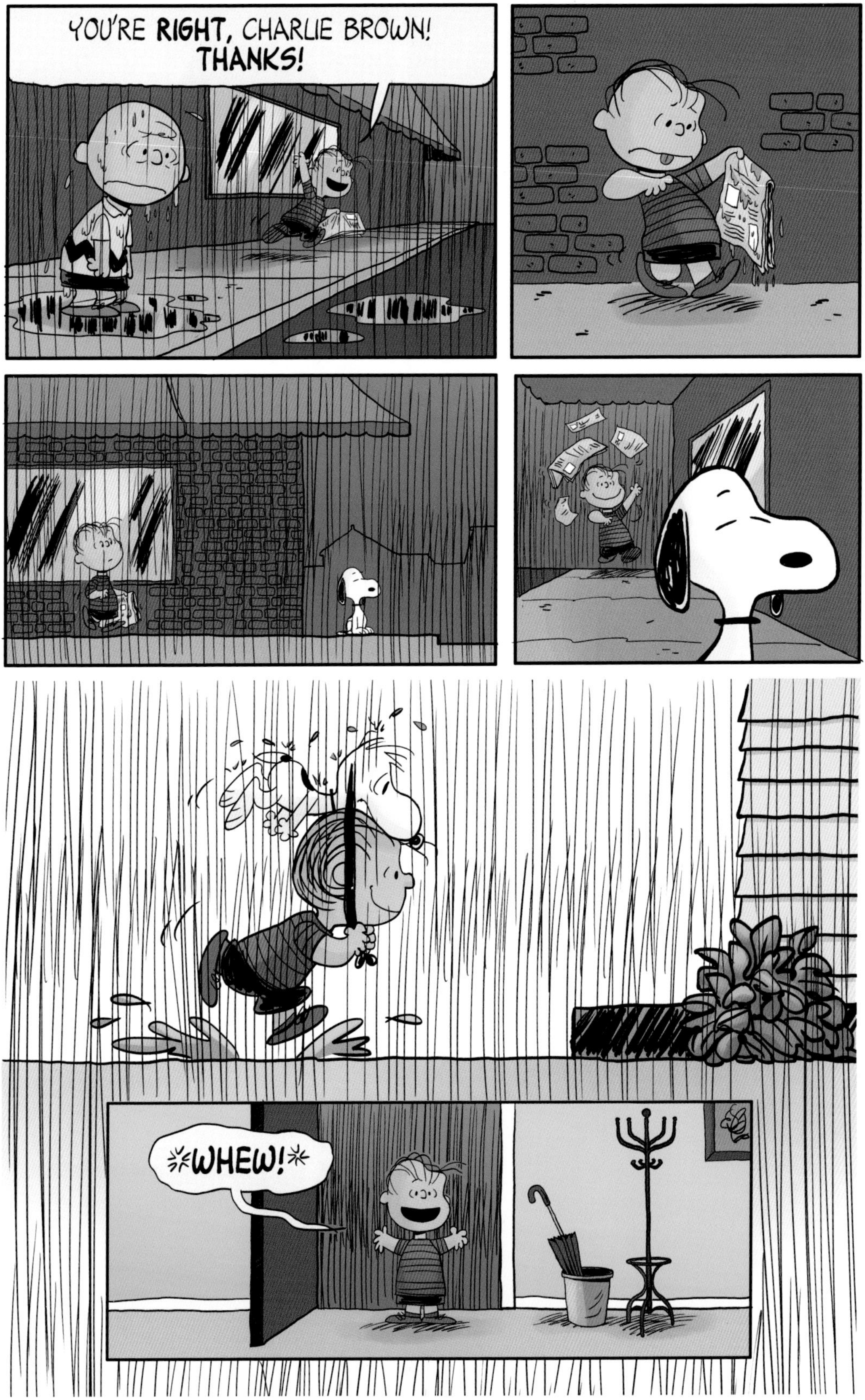
YOU'RE **RIGHT**, CHARLIE BROWN! **THANKS!**
WHEW!

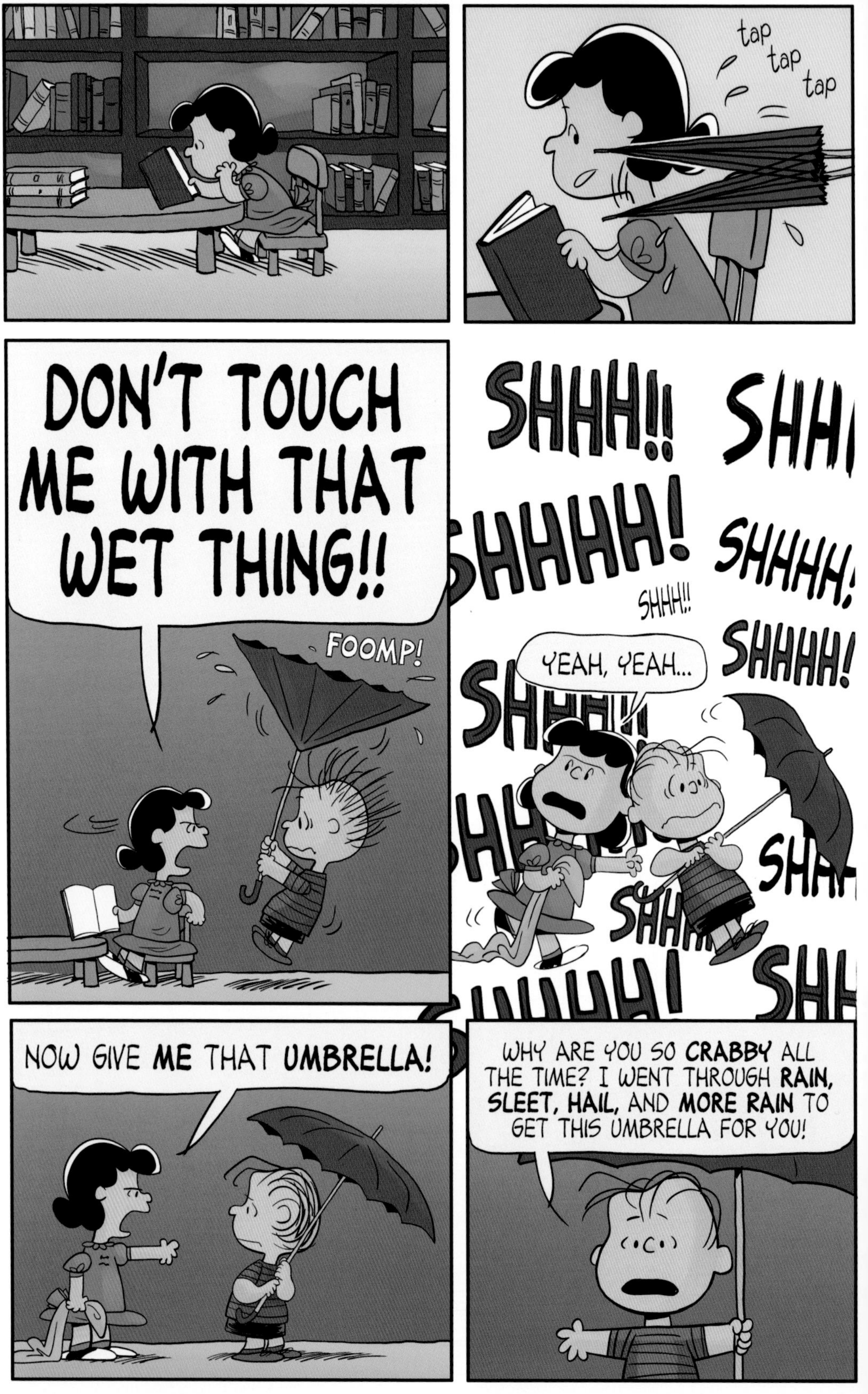
tap
tap
tap
DON'T TOUCH ME WITH THAT WET THING!!
FOOMP!
SHHH!! SHH
SHHHH! SHHHH!
SHHH!!
SHHHH!
YEAH, YEAH...
NOW GIVE ME THAT UMBRELLA!
WHY ARE YOU SO CRABBY ALL THE TIME? I WENT THROUGH RAIN, SLEET, HAIL, AND MORE RAIN TO GET THIS UMBRELLA FOR YOU!

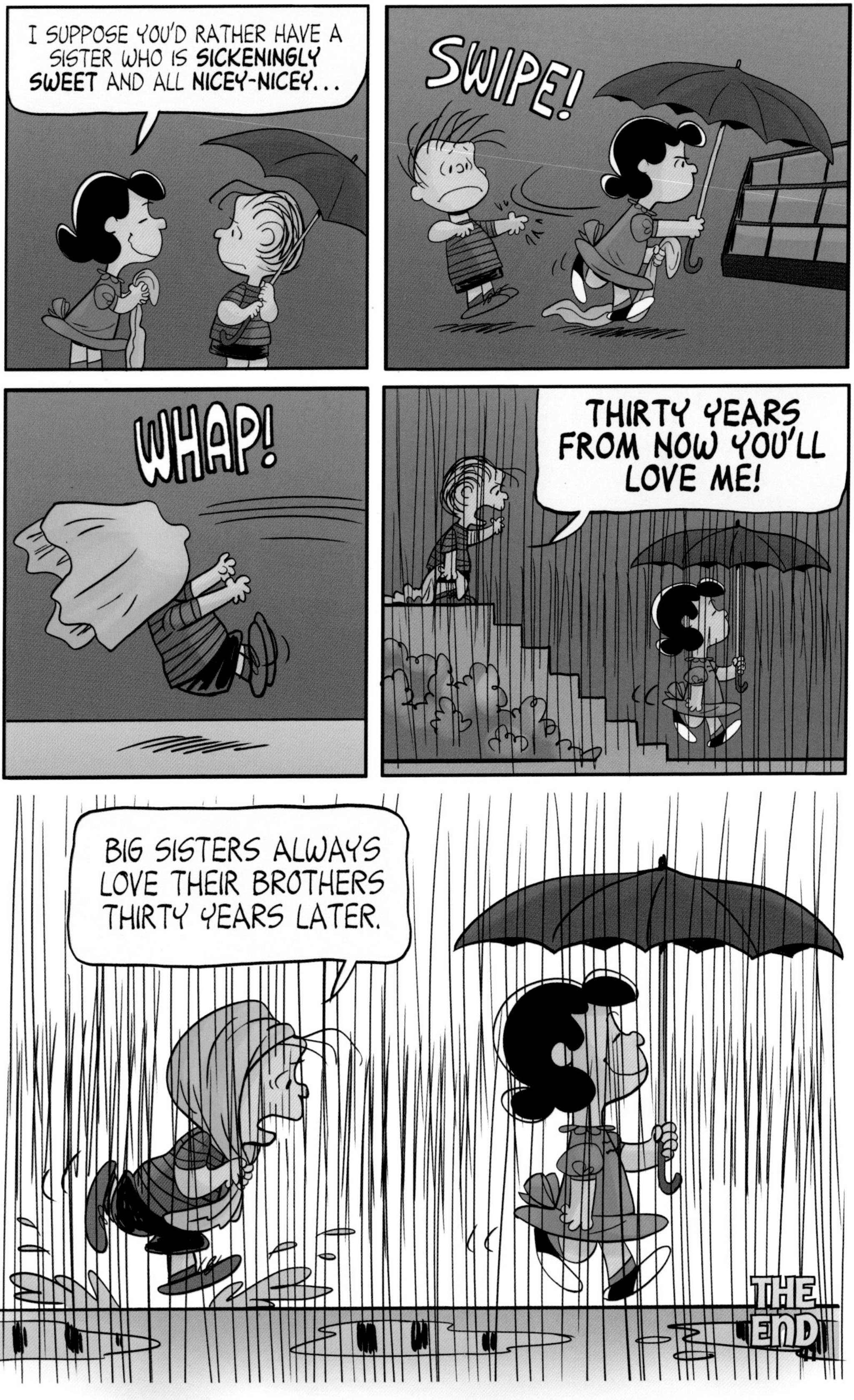
I SUPPOSE YOU'D RATHER HAVE A SISTER WHO IS **SICKENINGLY SWEET** AND ALL **NICEY-NICEY**...
SWIPE!
WHAP!
THIRTY YEARS FROM NOW YOU'LL LOVE ME!
BIG SISTERS ALWAYS LOVE THEIR BROTHERS THIRTY YEARS LATER.
THE END

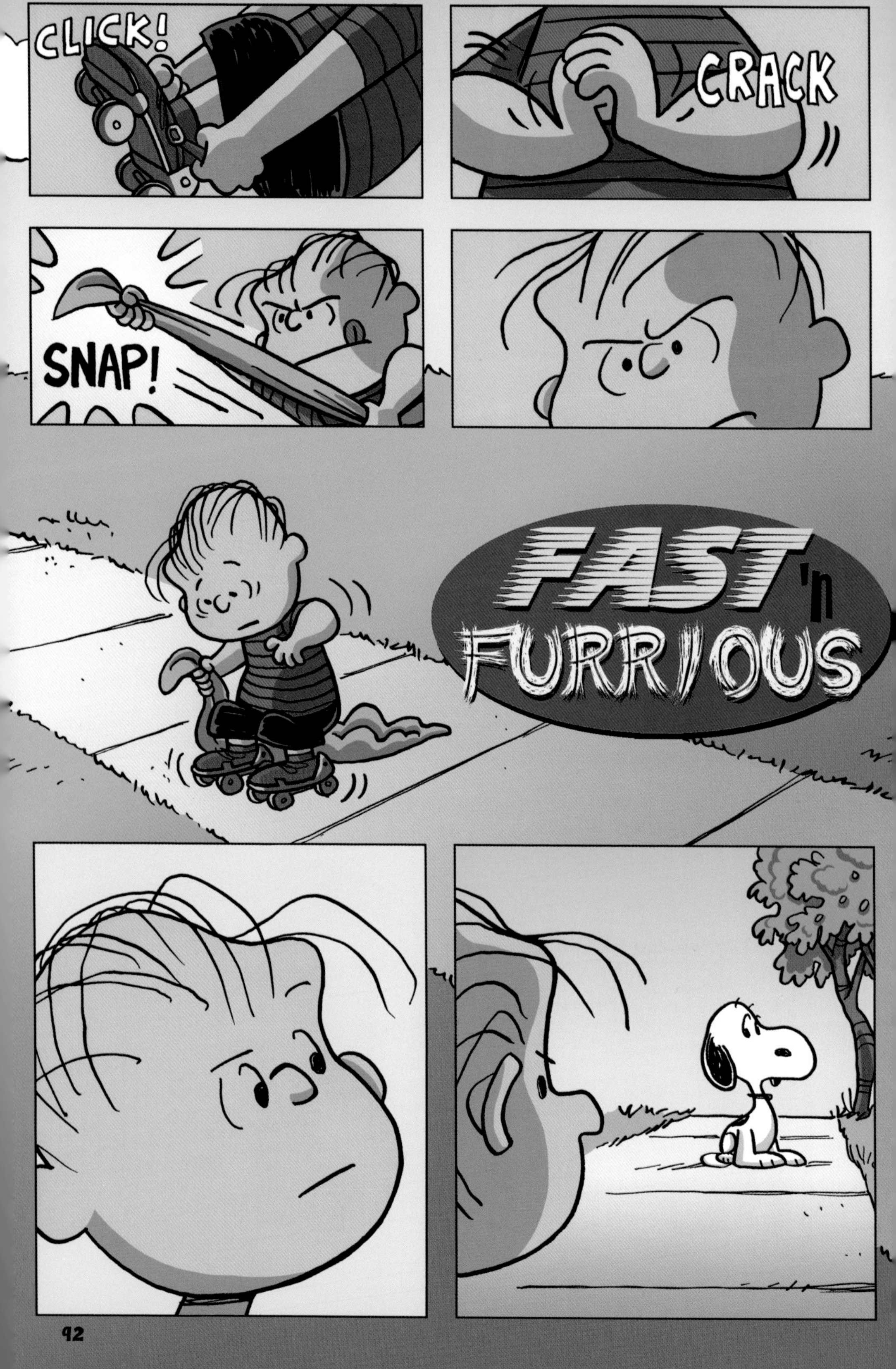
CLICK!
CRACK
SNAP!
FAST 'n FURRIOUS

ZIP!
SWOOP
TROMP
TROMP
TROMP
TROMP
CLOMP
PING!

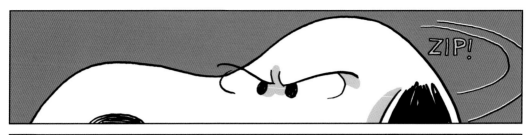

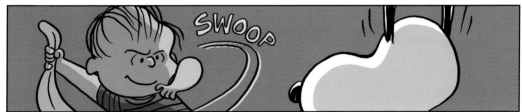

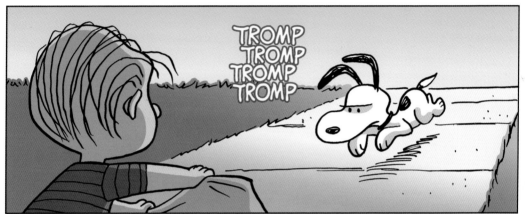

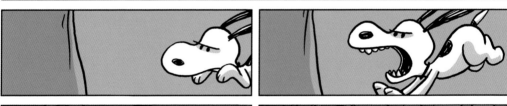

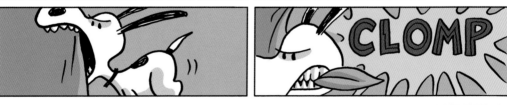

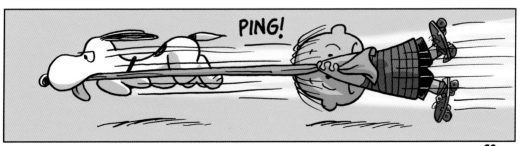

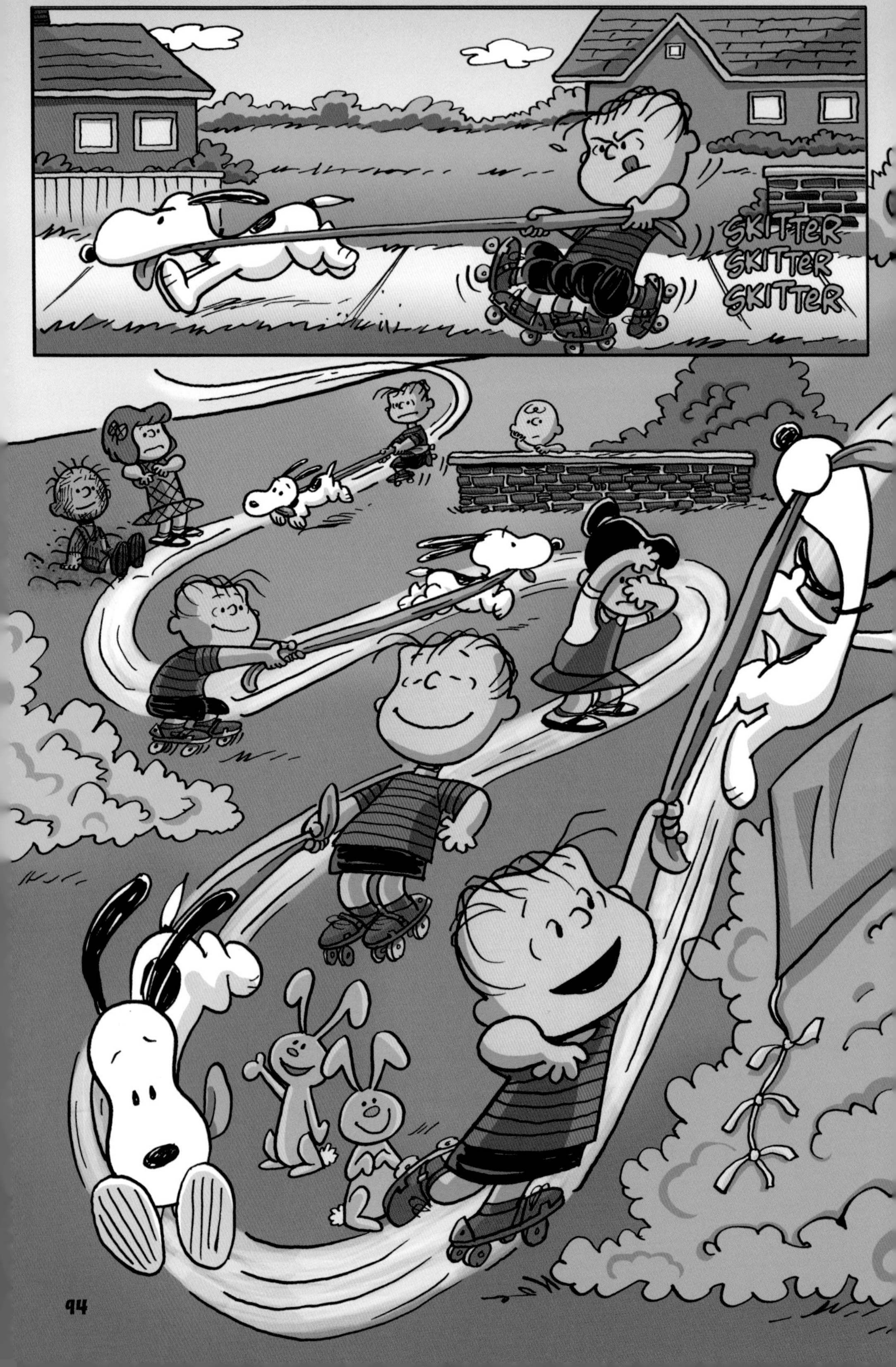
SKITTER
SKITTER
SKITTER

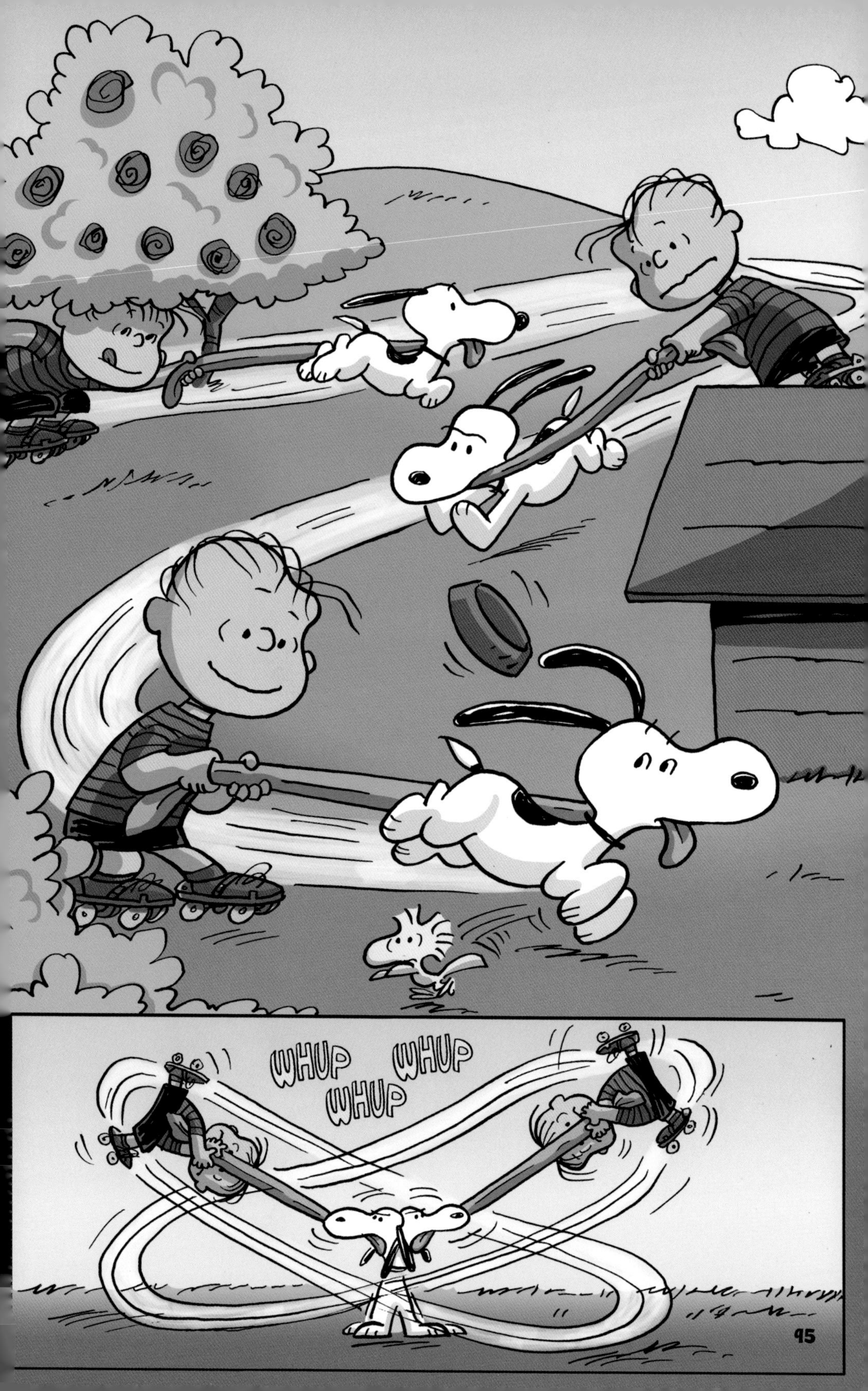
WHUP
WHUP
WHUP

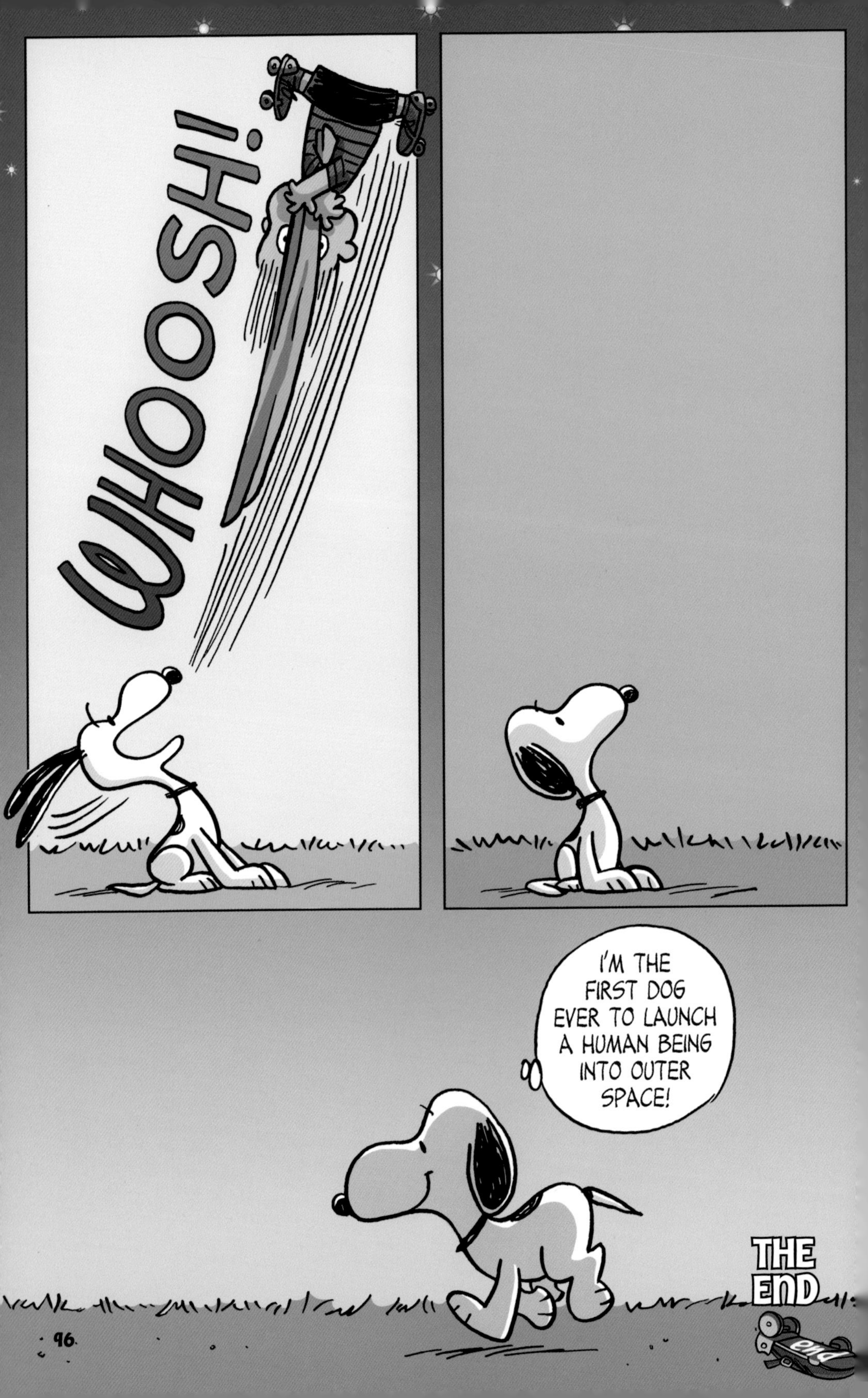
WHOOSH!
I'M THE FIRST DOG EVER TO LAUNCH A HUMAN BEING INTO OUTER SPACE!
THE END

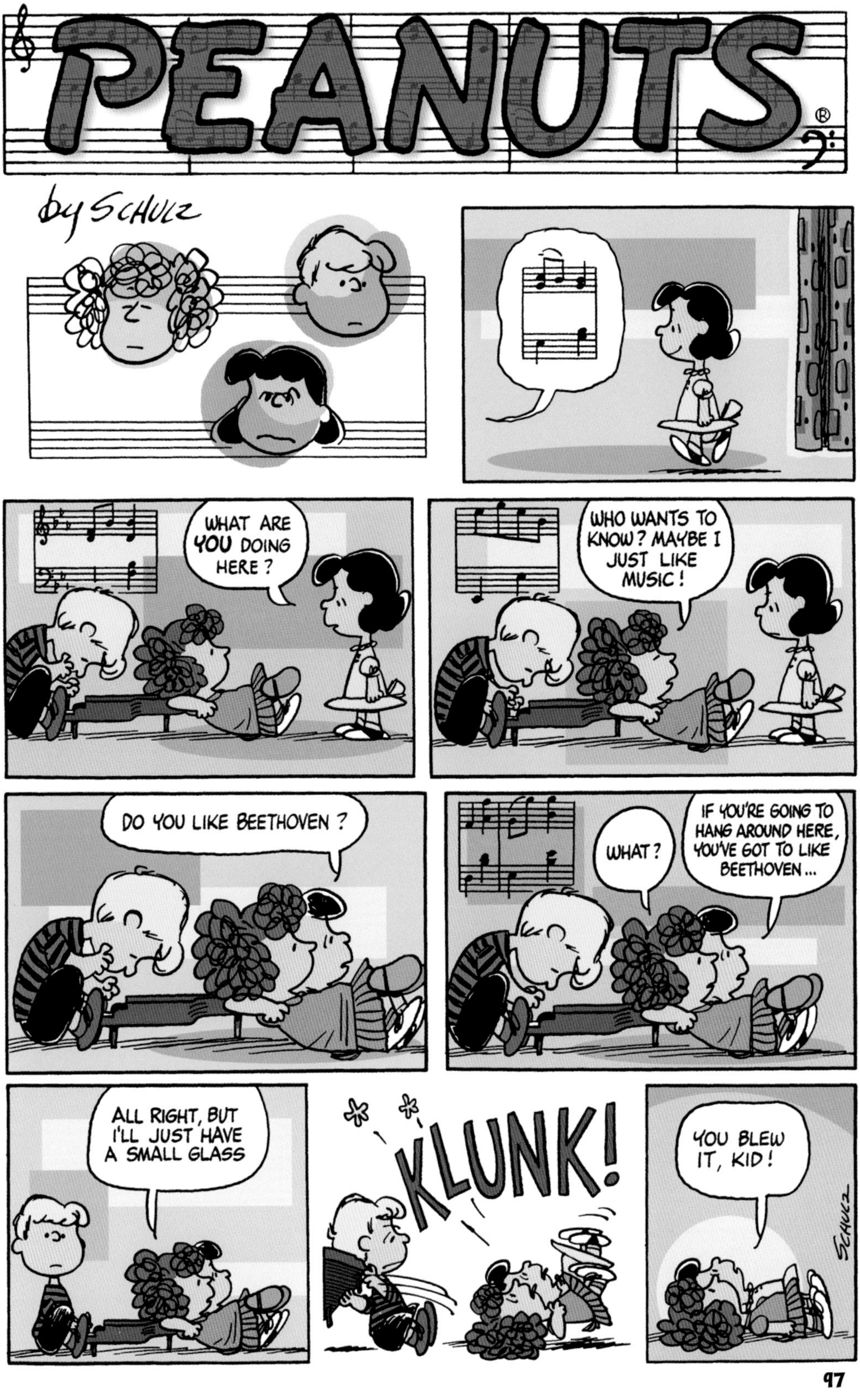
PEANUTS
by SCHULZ
WHAT ARE YOU DOING HERE ?
WHO WANTS TO KNOW ? MAYBE I JUST LIKE MUSIC !
DO YOU LIKE BEETHOVEN ?
WHAT ?
IF YOU'RE GOING TO HANG AROUND HERE, YOU'VE GOT TO LIKE BEETHOVEN ...
ALL RIGHT, BUT I'LL JUST HAVE A SMALL GLASS
KLUNK!
YOU BLEW IT, KID !
SCHULZ

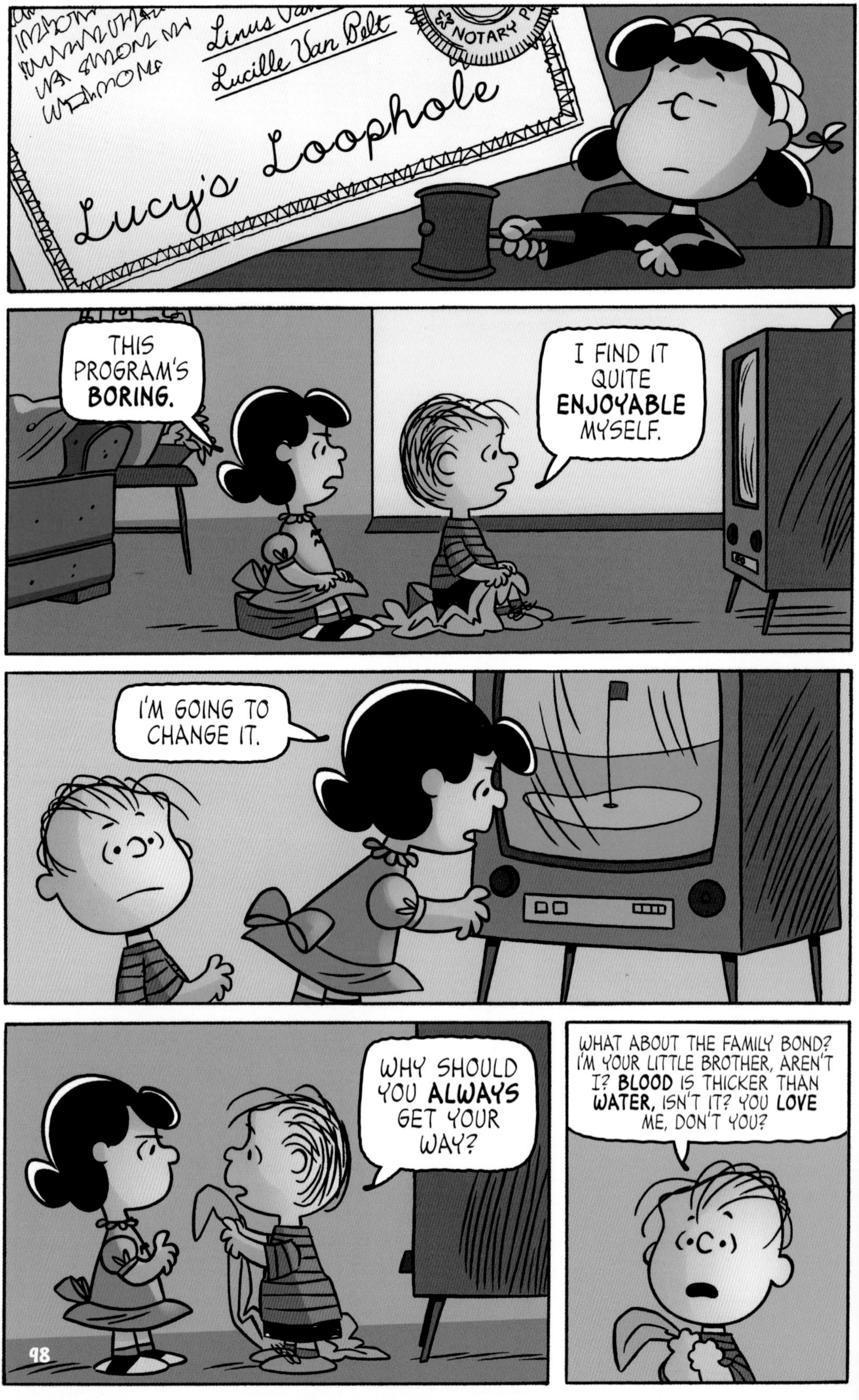
Lucille Van Pelt
NOTARY
Lucy's Loophole
THIS PROGRAM'S **BORING.**
I FIND IT QUITE **ENJOYABLE** MYSELF.
I'M GOING TO CHANGE IT.
WHY SHOULD YOU **ALWAYS** GET YOUR WAY?
WHAT ABOUT THE FAMILY BOND? I'M YOUR LITTLE BROTHER, AREN'T I? **BLOOD** IS THICKER THAN **WATER,** ISN'T IT? YOU **LOVE** ME, DON'T YOU?

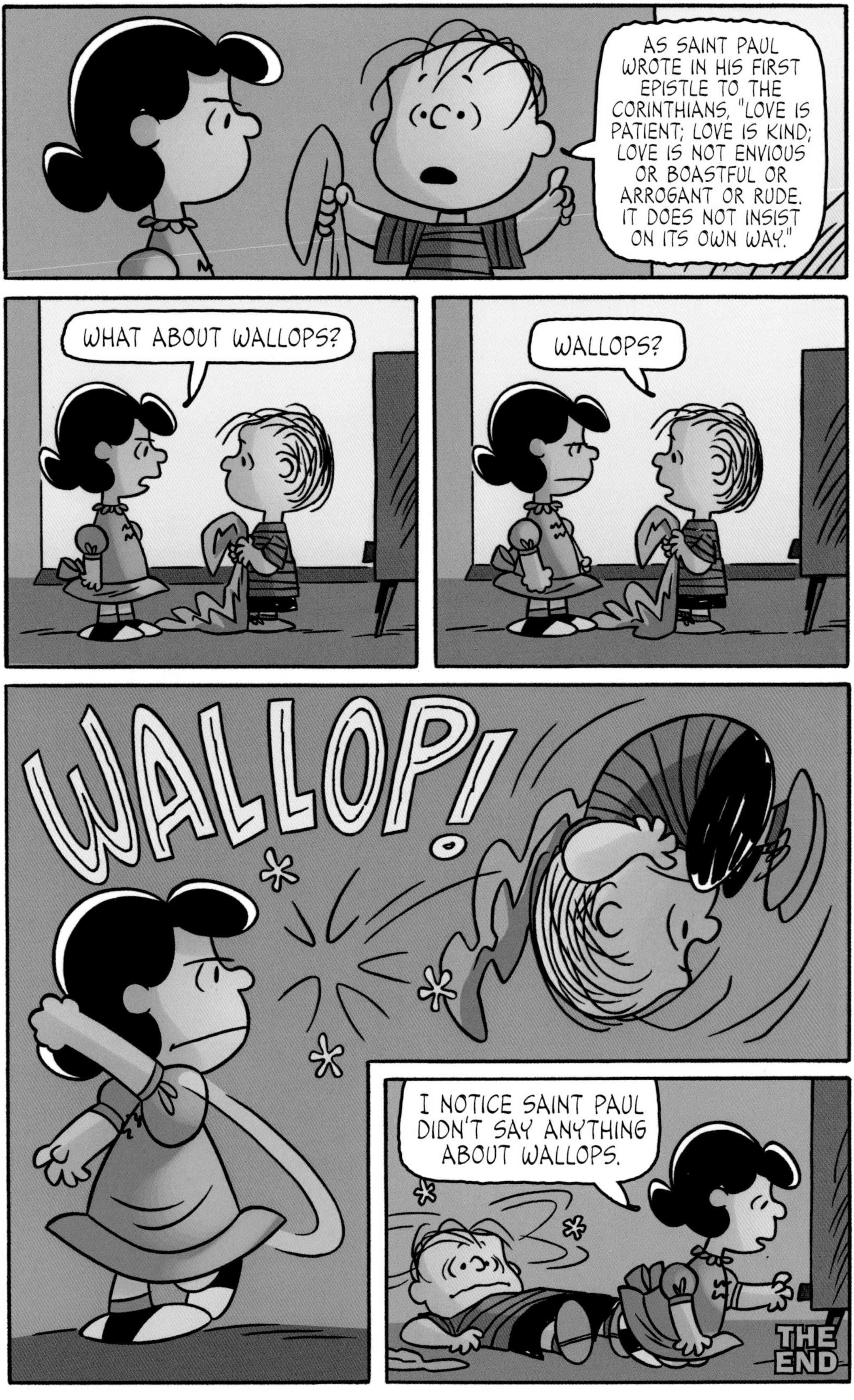

AS SAINT PAUL WROTE IN HIS FIRST EPISTLE TO THE CORINTHIANS, "LOVE IS PATIENT; LOVE IS KIND; LOVE IS NOT ENVIOUS OR BOASTFUL OR ARROGANT OR RUDE. IT DOES NOT INSIST ON ITS OWN WAY."
WHAT ABOUT WALLOPS?
WALLOPS?
WALLOP!
I NOTICE SAINT PAUL DIDN'T SAY ANYTHING ABOUT WALLOPS.
THE END

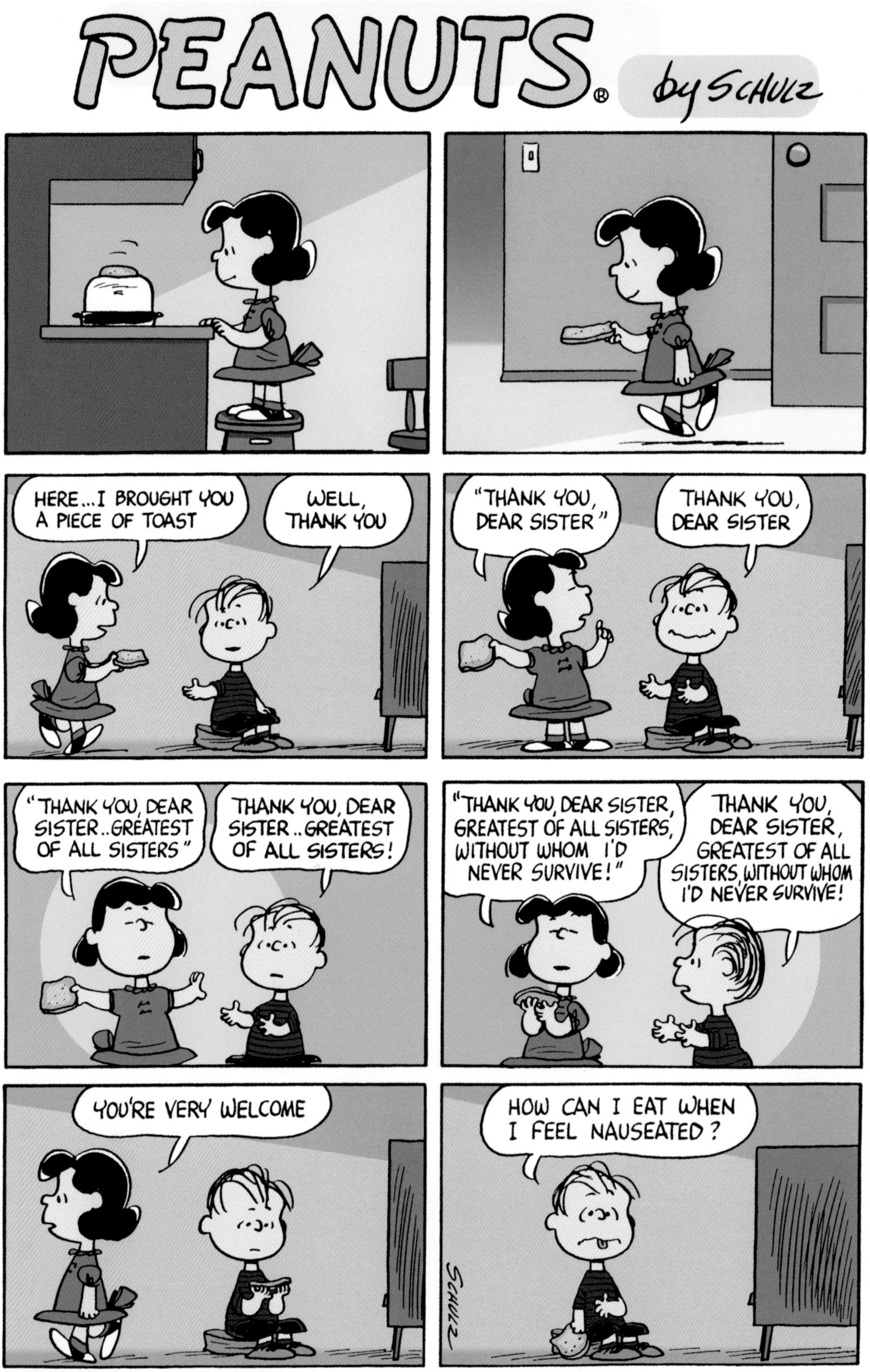
PEANUTS® by SCHULZ
HERE...I BROUGHT YOU A PIECE OF TOAST
WELL, THANK YOU
"THANK YOU, DEAR SISTER"
THANK YOU, DEAR SISTER
"THANK YOU, DEAR SISTER..GREATEST OF ALL SISTERS"
THANK YOU, DEAR SISTER..GREATEST OF ALL SISTERS!
"THANK YOU, DEAR SISTER, GREATEST OF ALL SISTERS, WITHOUT WHOM I'D NEVER SURVIVE!"
THANK YOU, DEAR SISTER, GREATEST OF ALL SISTERS, WITHOUT WHOM I'D NEVER SURVIVE!
YOU'RE VERY WELCOME
SCHULZ
HOW CAN I EAT WHEN I FEEL NAUSEATED?

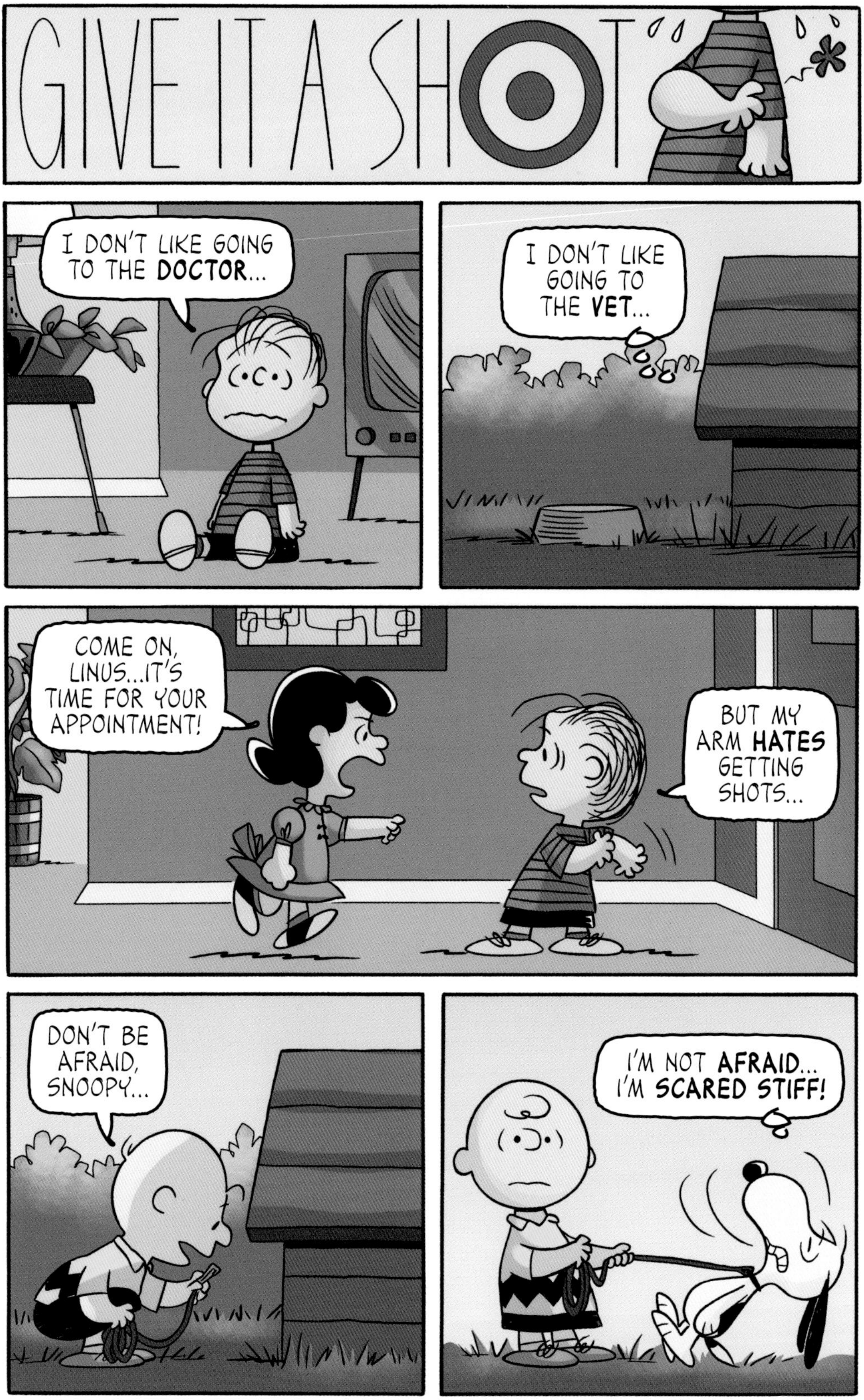
GIVE IT A SHOT
I DON'T LIKE GOING TO THE DOCTOR...
I DON'T LIKE GOING TO THE VET...
COME ON, LINUS...IT'S TIME FOR YOUR APPOINTMENT!
BUT MY ARM HATES GETTING SHOTS...
DON'T BE AFRAID, SNOOPY...
I'M NOT AFRAID... I'M SCARED STIFF!

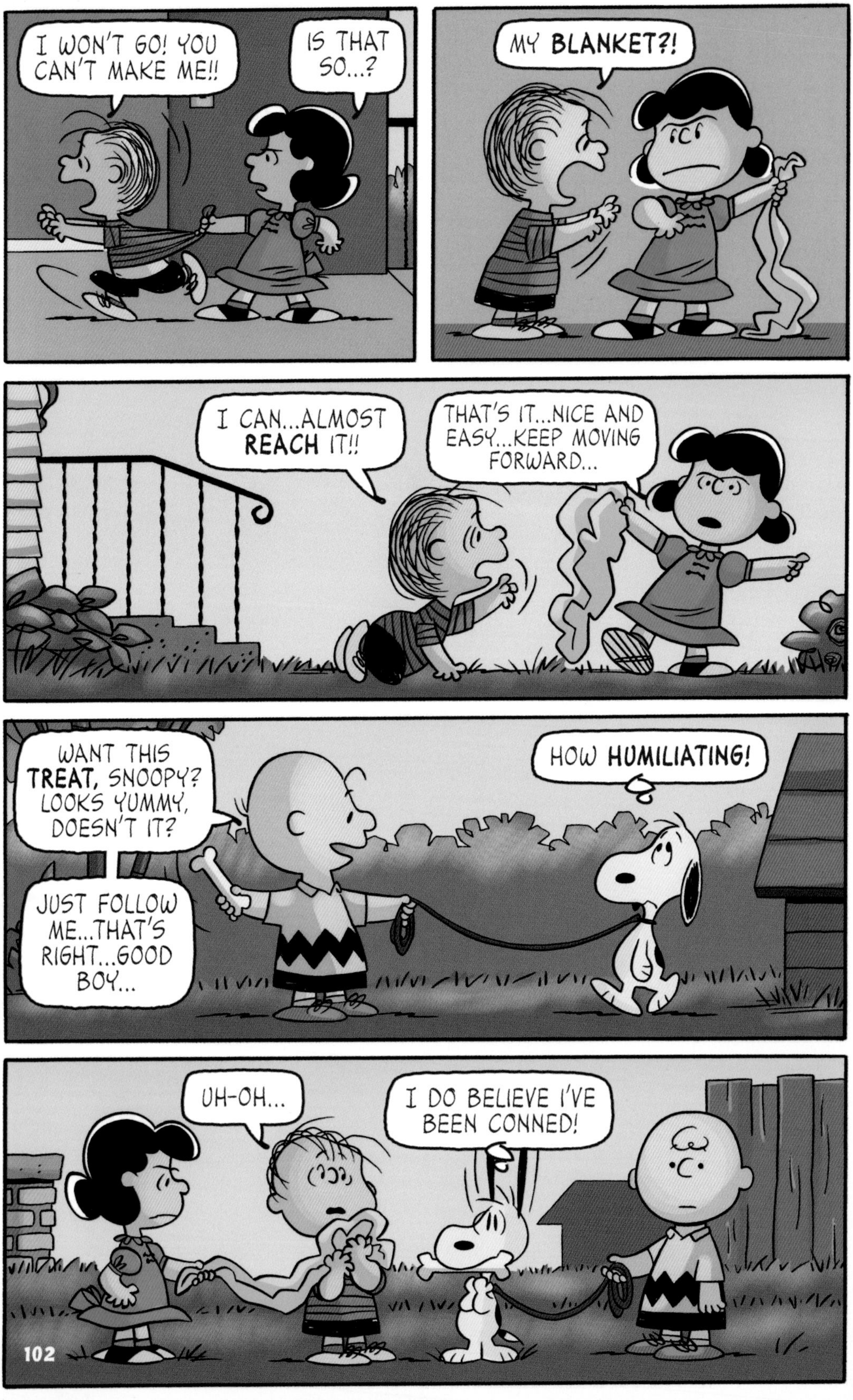
I WON'T GO! YOU CAN'T MAKE ME!!
IS THAT SO...?
MY BLANKET?!
I CAN...ALMOST REACH IT!!
THAT'S IT...NICE AND EASY...KEEP MOVING FORWARD...
WANT THIS TREAT, SNOOPY? LOOKS YUMMY, DOESN'T IT?
JUST FOLLOW ME...THAT'S RIGHT...GOOD BOY...
HOW HUMILIATING!
UH-OH...
I DO BELIEVE I'VE BEEN CONNED!

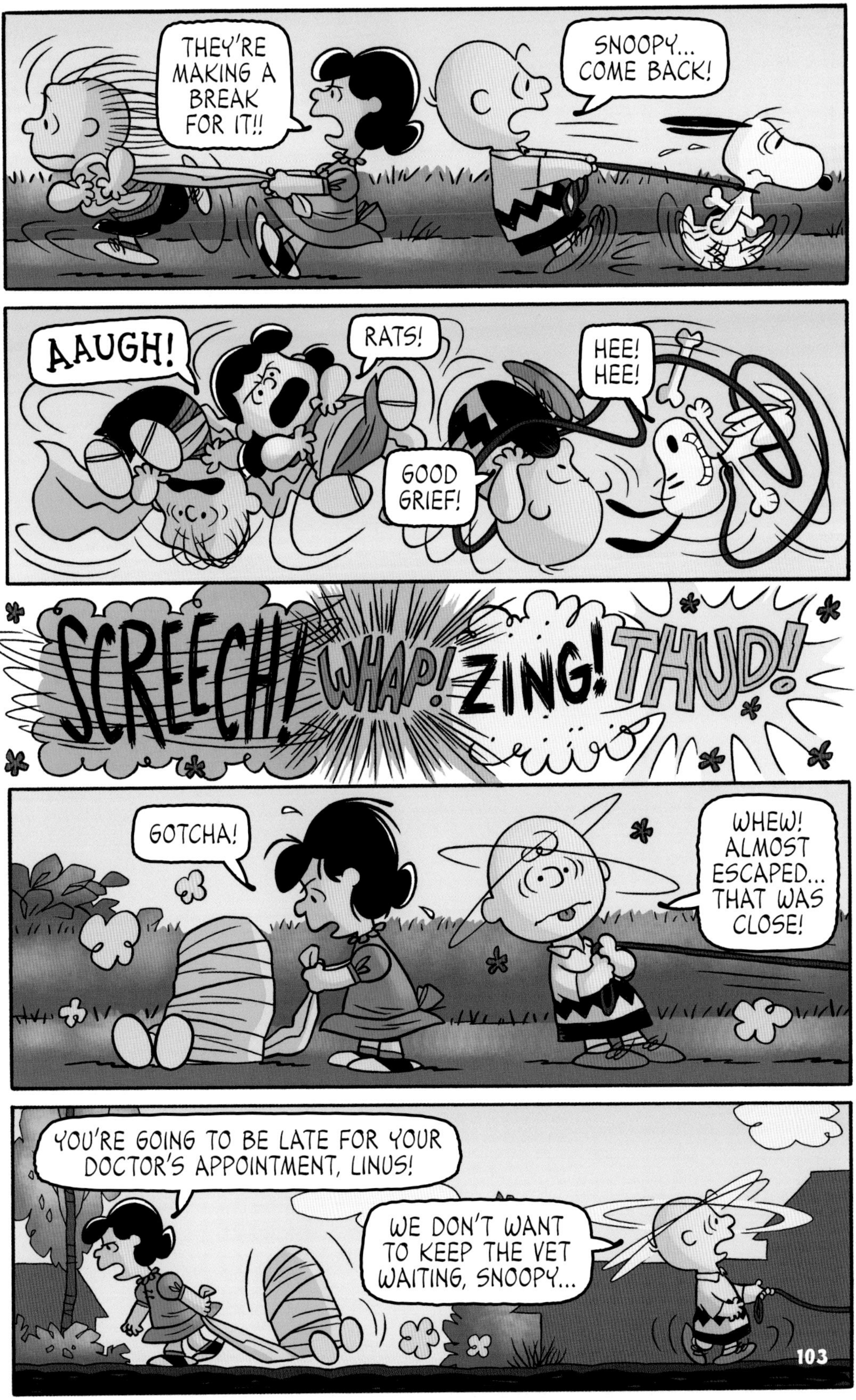
THEY'RE MAKING A BREAK FOR IT!!
SNOOPY... COME BACK!
AAUGH!
RATS!
HEE! HEE!
GOOD GRIEF!
SCREECH! WHAP! ZING! THUD!
GOTCHA!
WHEW! ALMOST ESCAPED... THAT WAS CLOSE!
YOU'RE GOING TO BE LATE FOR YOUR DOCTOR'S APPOINTMENT, LINUS!
WE DON'T WANT TO KEEP THE VET WAITING, SNOOPY...

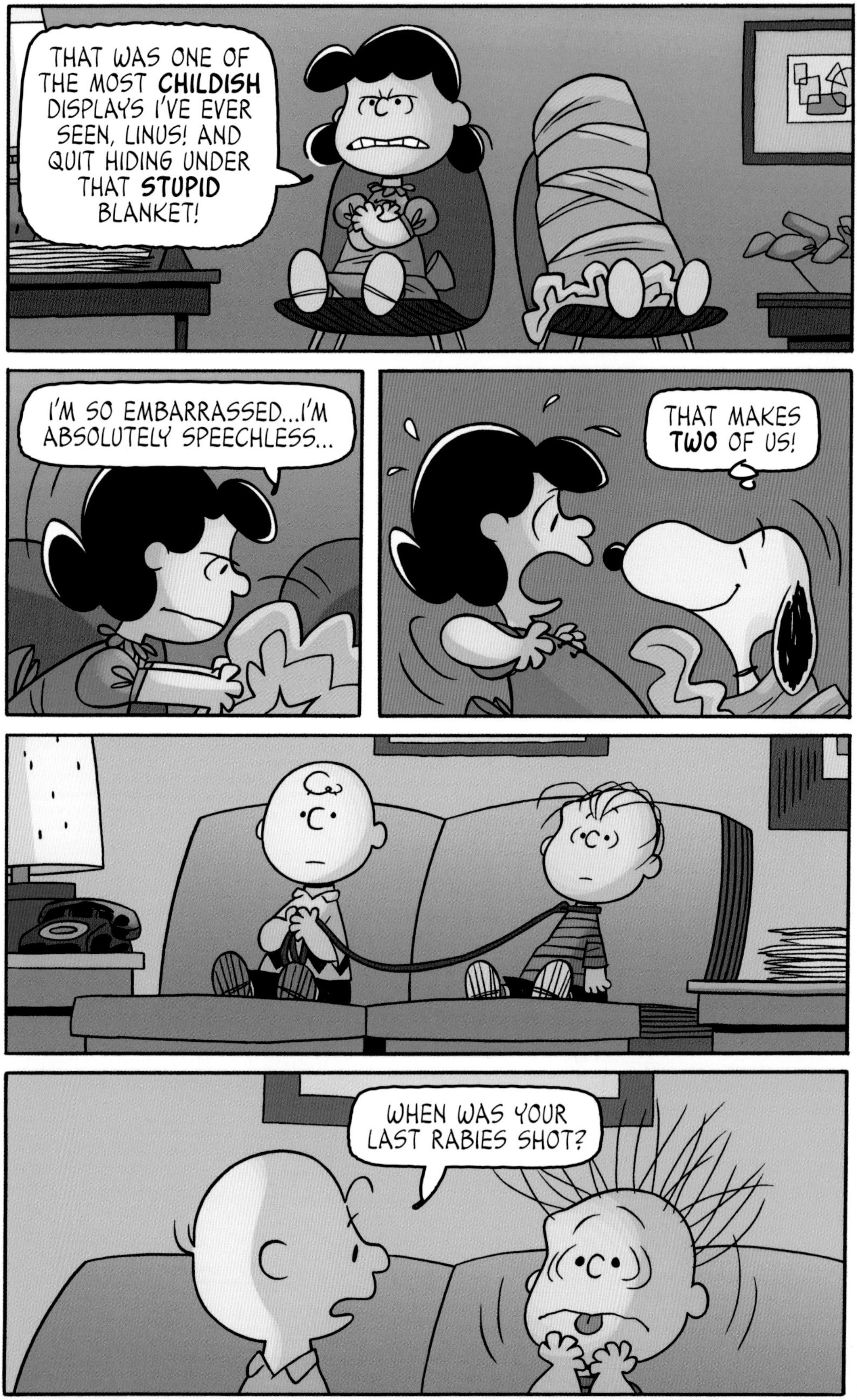
THAT WAS ONE OF THE MOST **CHILDISH** DISPLAYS I'VE EVER SEEN, LINUS! AND QUIT HIDING UNDER THAT **STUPID** BLANKET!
I'M SO EMBARRASSED...I'M ABSOLUTELY SPEECHLESS...
THAT MAKES **TWO** OF US!
WHEN WAS YOUR LAST RABIES SHOT?

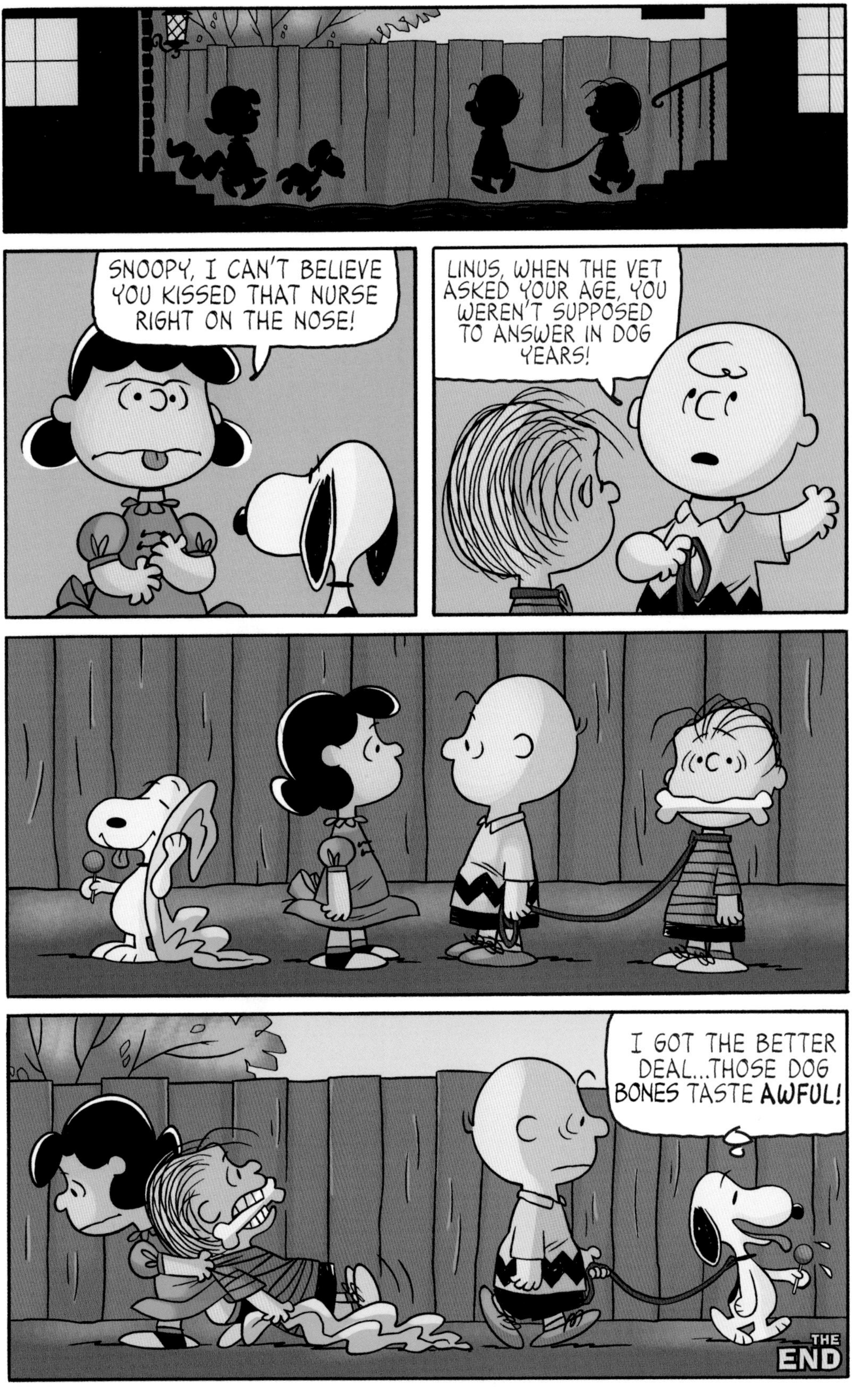
SNOOPY, I CAN'T BELIEVE YOU KISSED THAT NURSE RIGHT ON THE NOSE!
LINUS, WHEN THE VET ASKED YOUR AGE, YOU WEREN'T SUPPOSED TO ANSWER IN DOG YEARS!
I GOT THE BETTER DEAL...THOSE DOG BONES TASTE **AWFUL!**
THE END

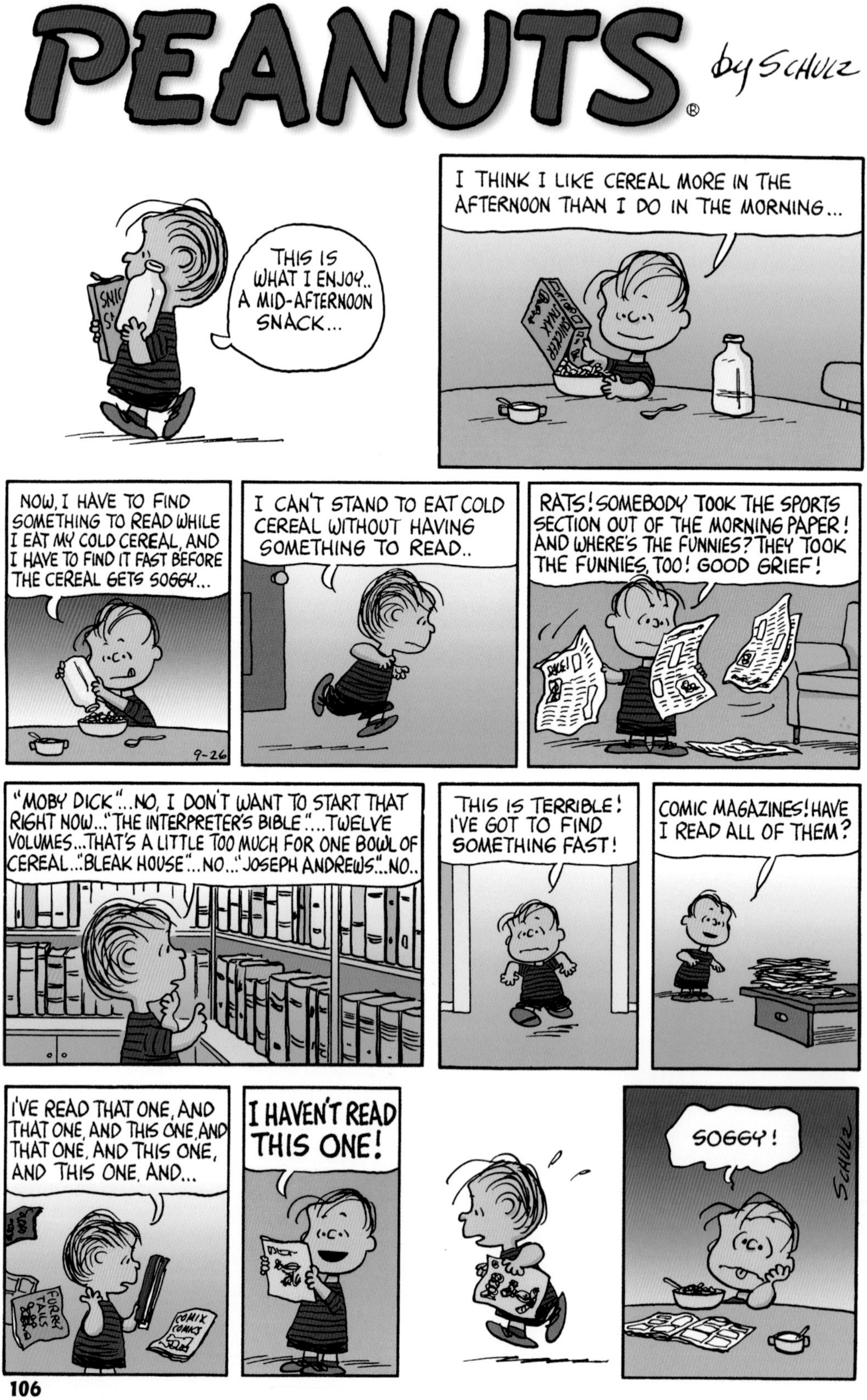

PEANUTS
by SCHULZ
THIS IS WHAT I ENJOY.. A MID-AFTERNOON SNACK...
I THINK I LIKE CEREAL MORE IN THE AFTERNOON THAN I DO IN THE MORNING...
NOW, I HAVE TO FIND SOMETHING TO READ WHILE I EAT MY COLD CEREAL, AND I HAVE TO FIND IT FAST BEFORE THE CEREAL GETS SOGGY...
9-26
I CAN'T STAND TO EAT COLD CEREAL WITHOUT HAVING SOMETHING TO READ..
RATS! SOMEBODY TOOK THE SPORTS SECTION OUT OF THE MORNING PAPER! AND WHERE'S THE FUNNIES? THEY TOOK THE FUNNIES, TOO! GOOD GRIEF!
"MOBY DICK"...NO, I DON'T WANT TO START THAT RIGHT NOW..."THE INTERPRETER'S BIBLE"...TWELVE VOLUMES...THAT'S A LITTLE TOO MUCH FOR ONE BOWL OF CEREAL..."BLEAK HOUSE"...NO..."JOSEPH ANDREWS"...NO..
THIS IS TERRIBLE! I'VE GOT TO FIND SOMETHING FAST!
COMIC MAGAZINES! HAVE I READ ALL OF THEM?
I'VE READ THAT ONE, AND THAT ONE, AND THIS ONE, AND THAT ONE, AND THIS ONE, AND THIS ONE, AND...
FURRY TAILS
COMIX COMICS
I HAVEN'T READ THIS ONE!
SOGGY!
SCHULZ

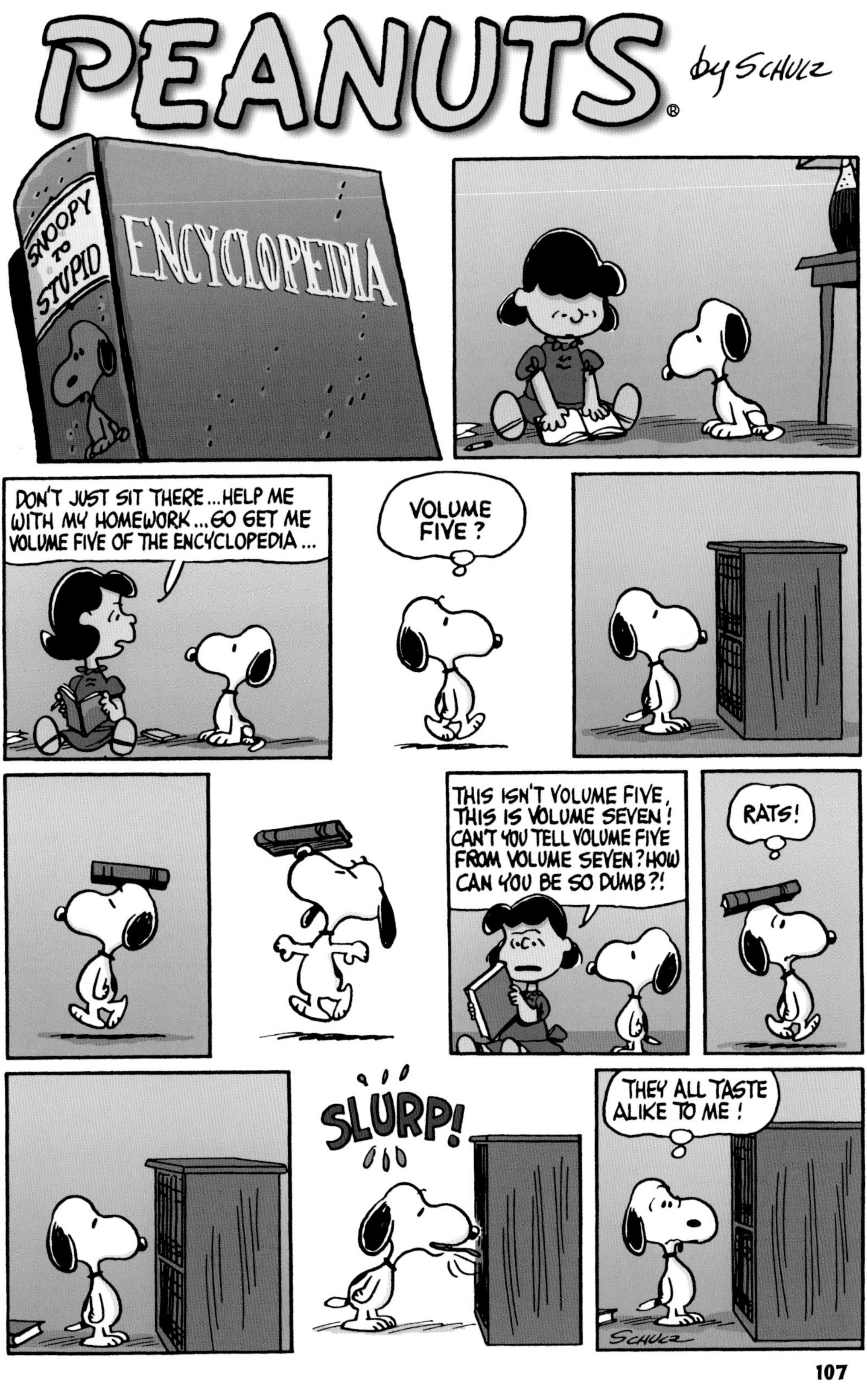
PEANUTS
by SCHULZ
SNOOPY TO STUPID
ENCYCLOPEDIA
DON'T JUST SIT THERE...HELP ME WITH MY HOMEWORK...GO GET ME VOLUME FIVE OF THE ENCYCLOPEDIA...
VOLUME FIVE?
THIS ISN'T VOLUME FIVE, THIS IS VOLUME SEVEN! CAN'T YOU TELL VOLUME FIVE FROM VOLUME SEVEN? HOW CAN YOU BE SO DUMB?!
RATS!
SLURP!
THEY ALL TASTE ALIKE TO ME!
SCHULZ

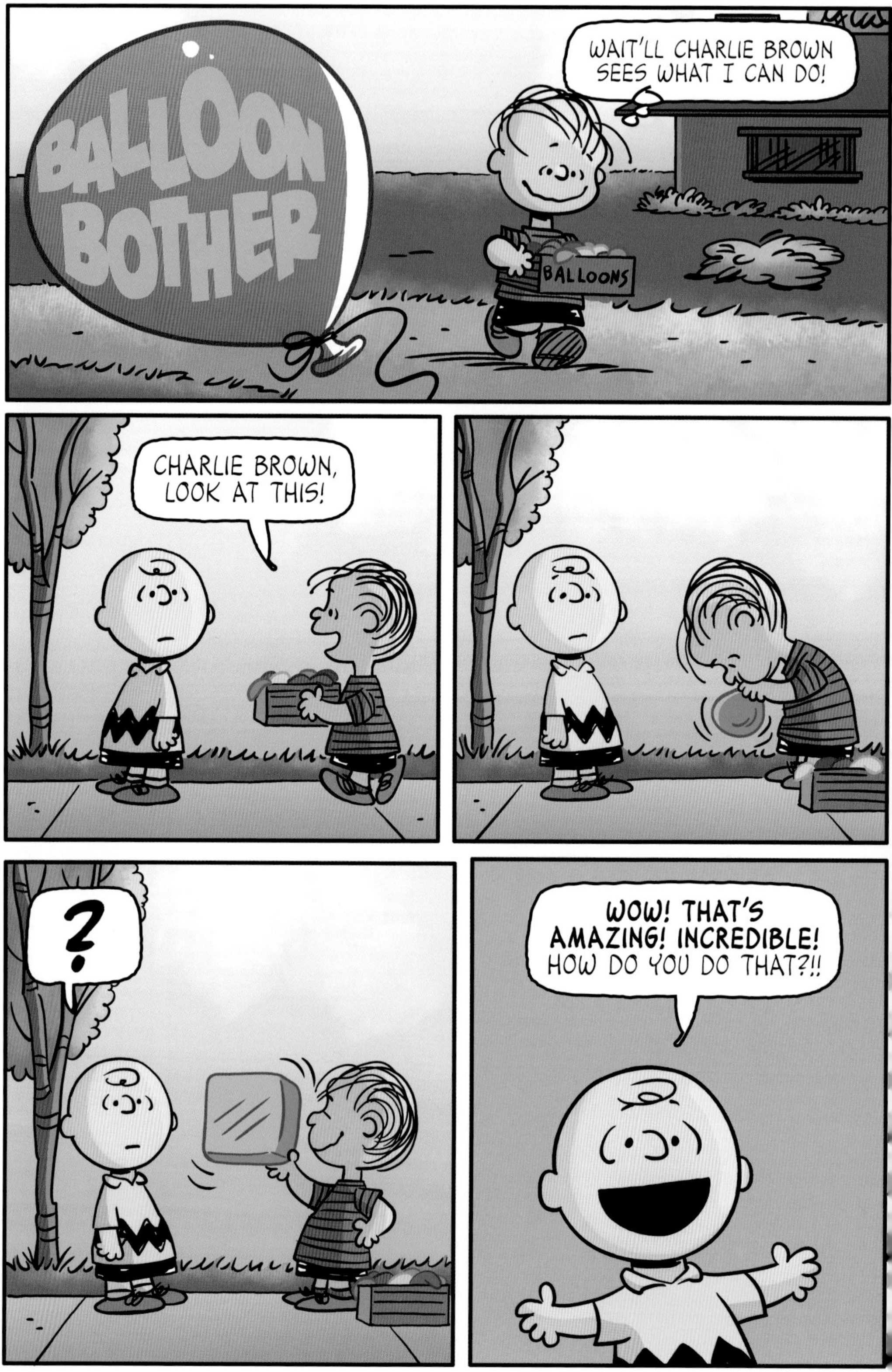
BALLOON BOTHER
WAIT'LL CHARLIE BROWN SEES WHAT I CAN DO!
BALLOONS
CHARLIE BROWN, LOOK AT THIS!
?
WOW! THAT'S AMAZING! INCREDIBLE! HOW DO YOU DO THAT?!!

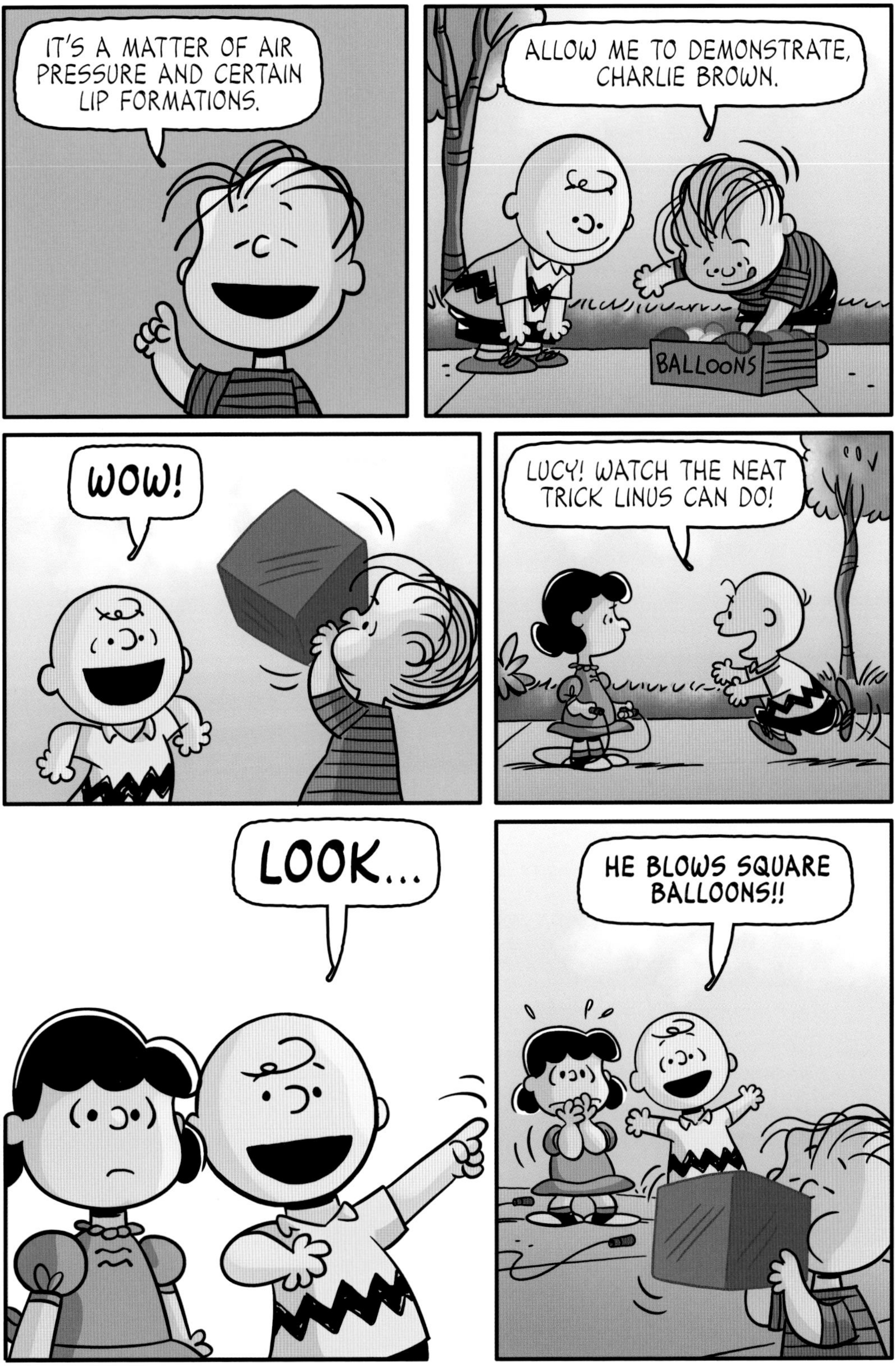
IT'S A MATTER OF AIR PRESSURE AND CERTAIN LIP FORMATIONS.
ALLOW ME TO DEMONSTRATE, CHARLIE BROWN.
BALLOONS
WOW!
LUCY! WATCH THE NEAT TRICK LINUS CAN DO!
LOOK...
HE BLOWS SQUARE BALLOONS!!

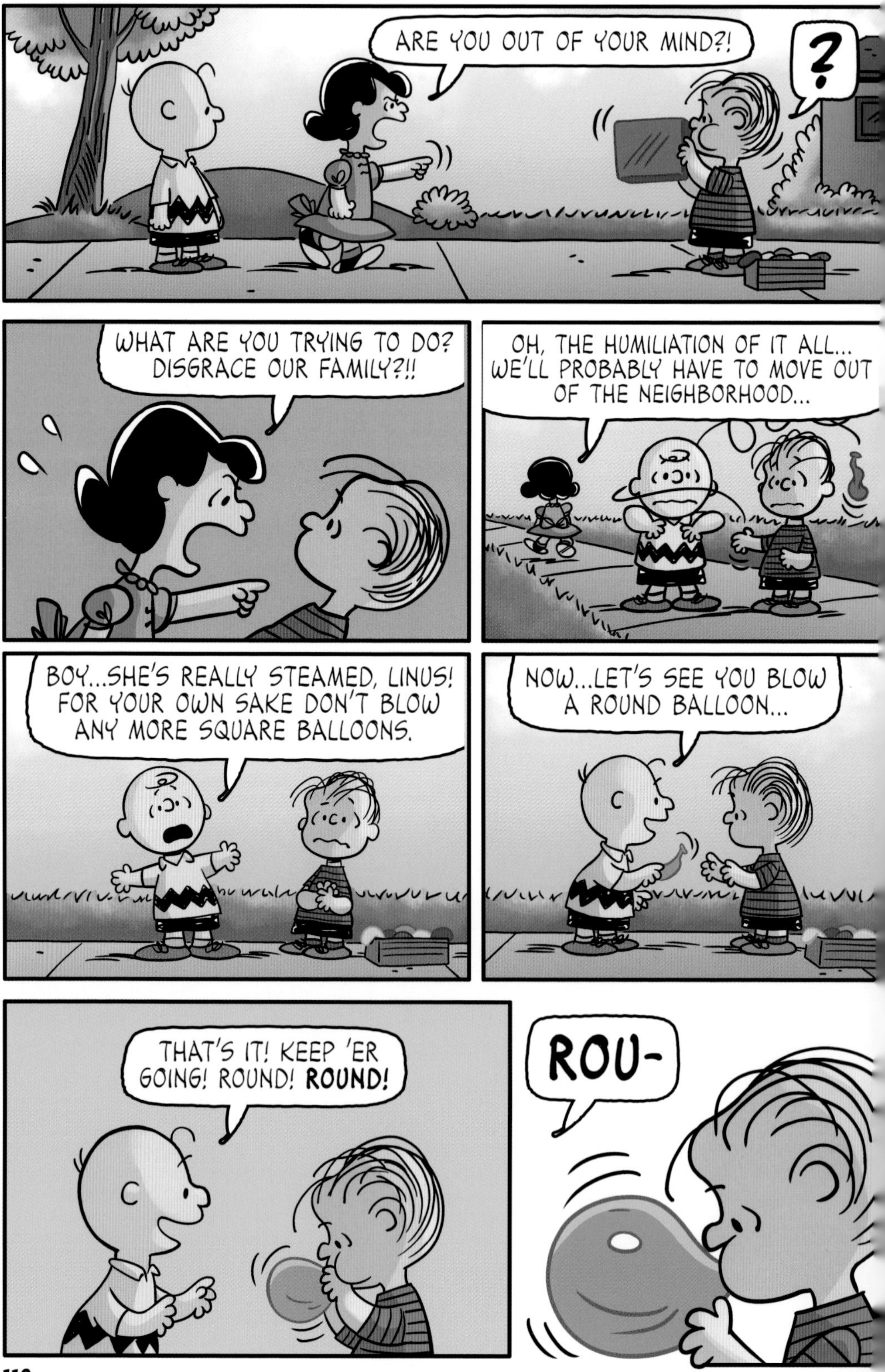
ARE YOU OUT OF YOUR MIND?!
?
WHAT ARE YOU TRYING TO DO? DISGRACE OUR FAMILY?!!
OH, THE HUMILIATION OF IT ALL... WE'LL PROBABLY HAVE TO MOVE OUT OF THE NEIGHBORHOOD...
BOY...SHE'S REALLY STEAMED, LINUS! FOR YOUR OWN SAKE DON'T BLOW ANY MORE SQUARE BALLOONS.
NOW...LET'S SEE YOU BLOW A ROUND BALLOON...
THAT'S IT! KEEP 'ER GOING! ROUND! **ROUND!**
ROU-

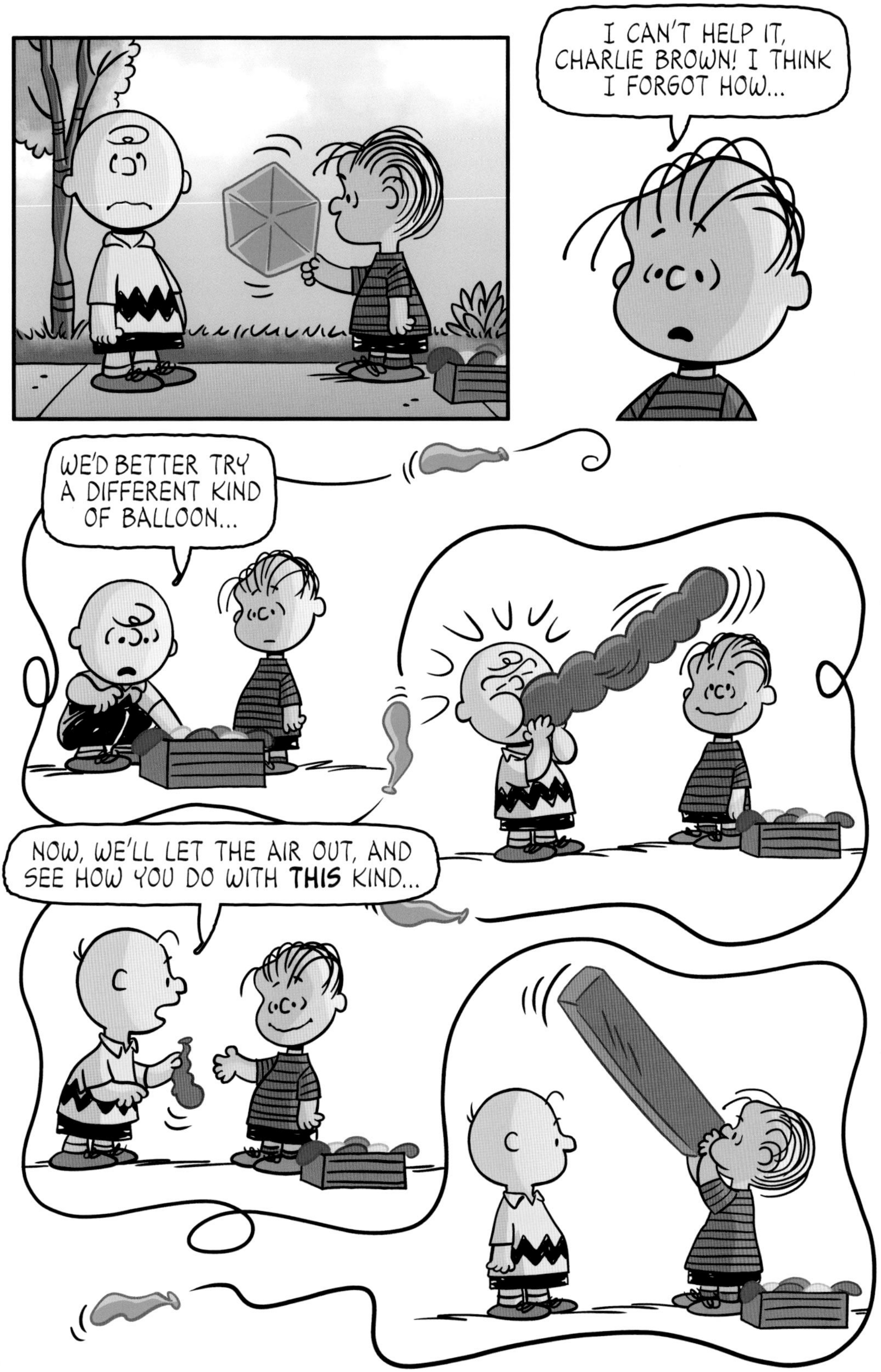
I CAN'T HELP IT, CHARLIE BROWN! I THINK I FORGOT HOW...
WE'D BETTER TRY A DIFFERENT KIND OF BALLOON...
NOW, WE'LL LET THE AIR OUT, AND SEE HOW YOU DO WITH **THIS** KIND...

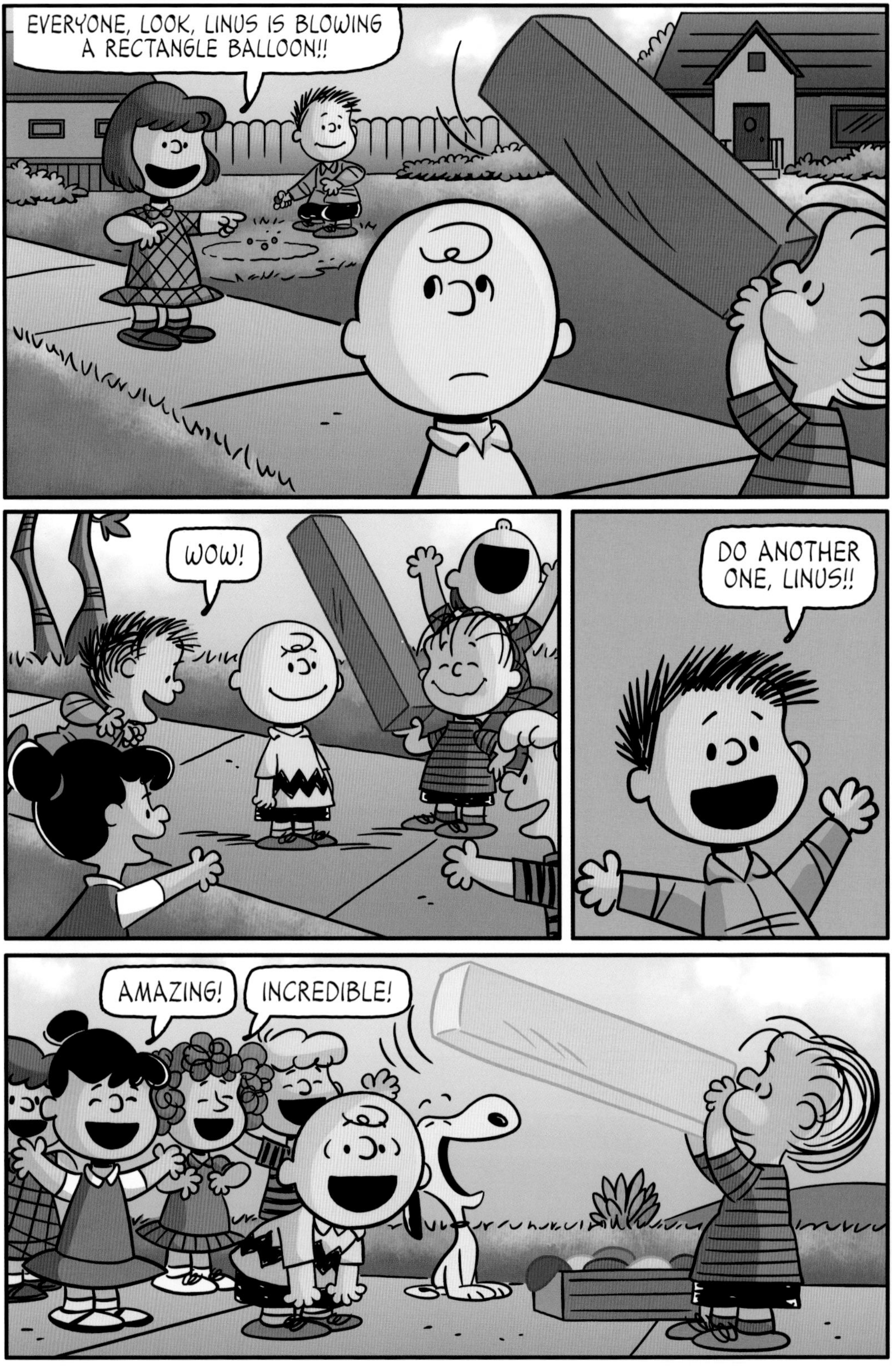
EVERYONE, LOOK, LINUS IS BLOWING A RECTANGLE BALLOON!!
WOW!
DO ANOTHER ONE, LINUS!!
AMAZING!
INCREDIBLE!

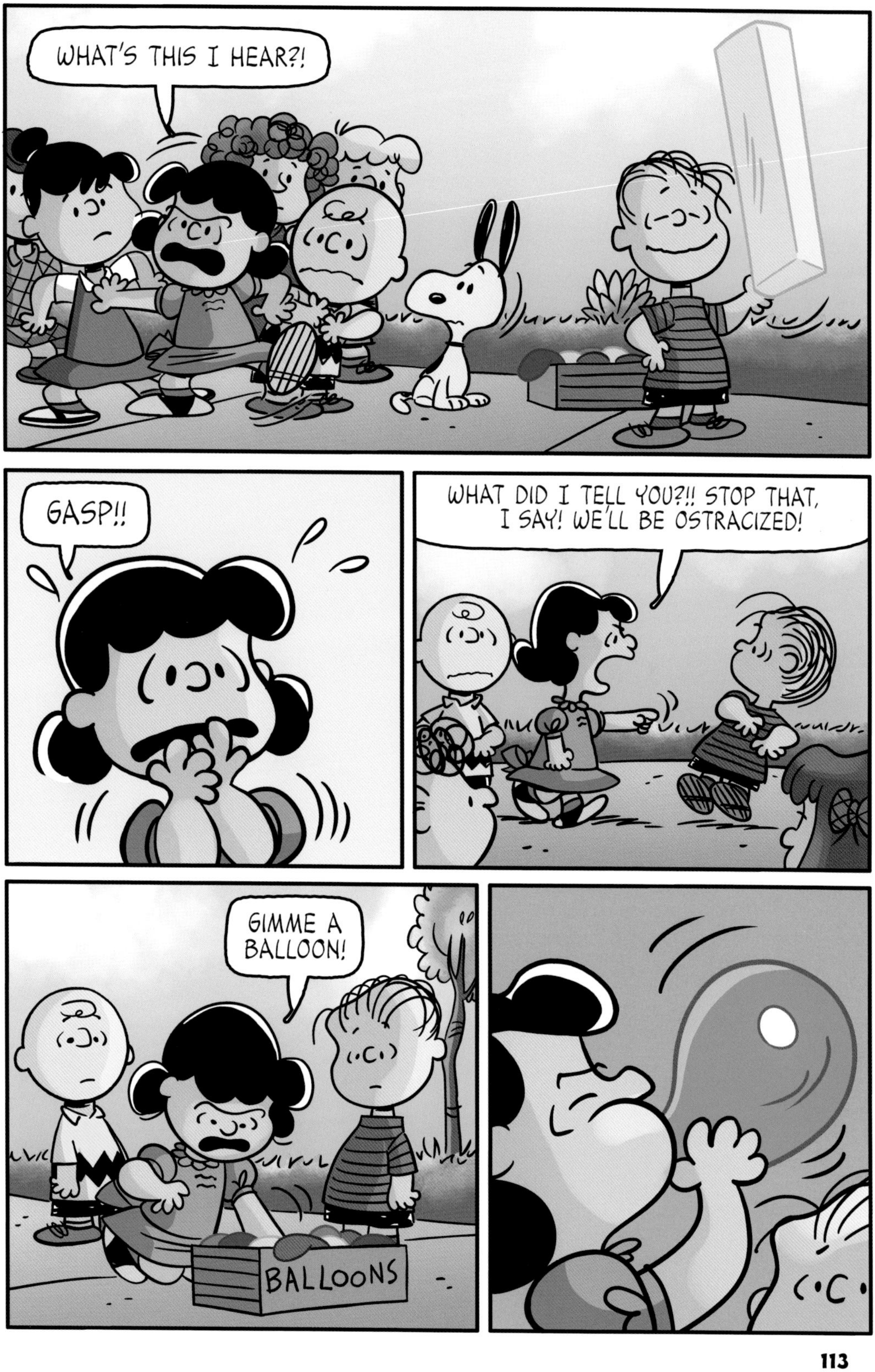
WHAT'S THIS I HEAR?!
GASP!!
WHAT DID I TELL YOU?!! STOP THAT, I SAY! WE'LL BE OSTRACIZED!
GIMME A BALLOON!
BALLOONS

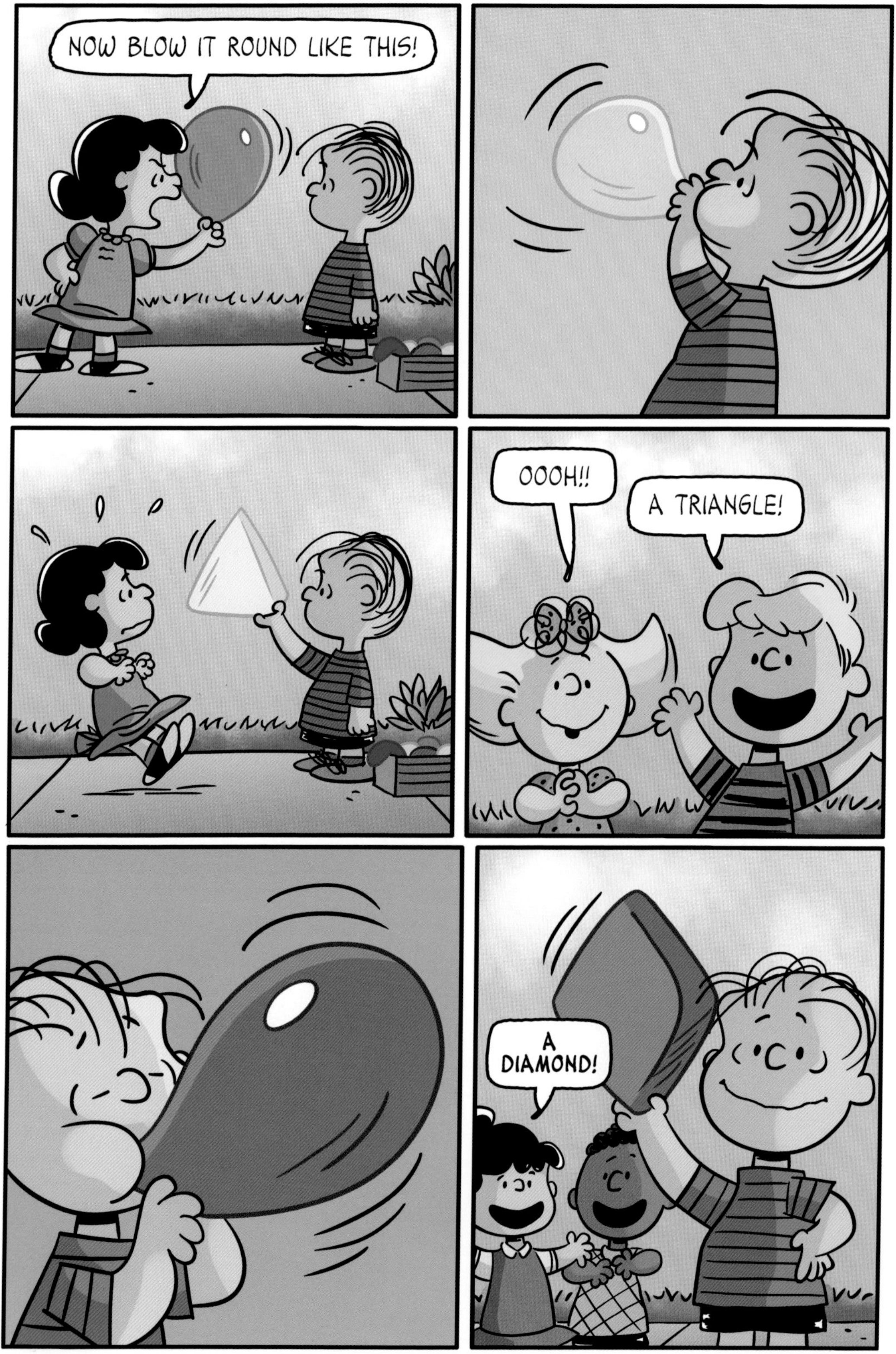
NOW BLOW IT ROUND LIKE THIS!
OOOH!!
A TRIANGLE!
A DIAMOND!

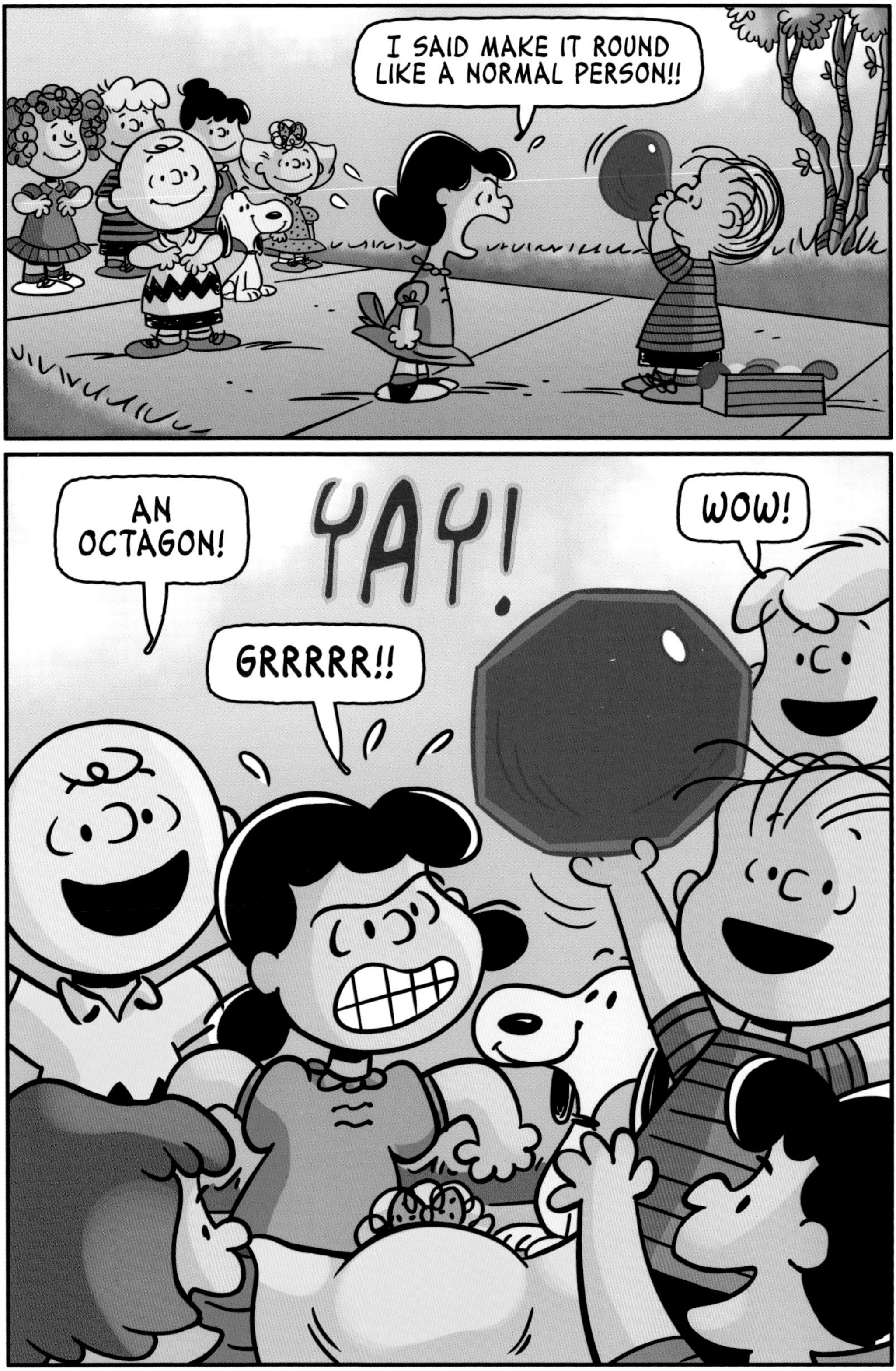
I SAID MAKE IT ROUND LIKE A NORMAL PERSON!!
AN OCTAGON!
YAY!
WOW!
GRRRRR!!

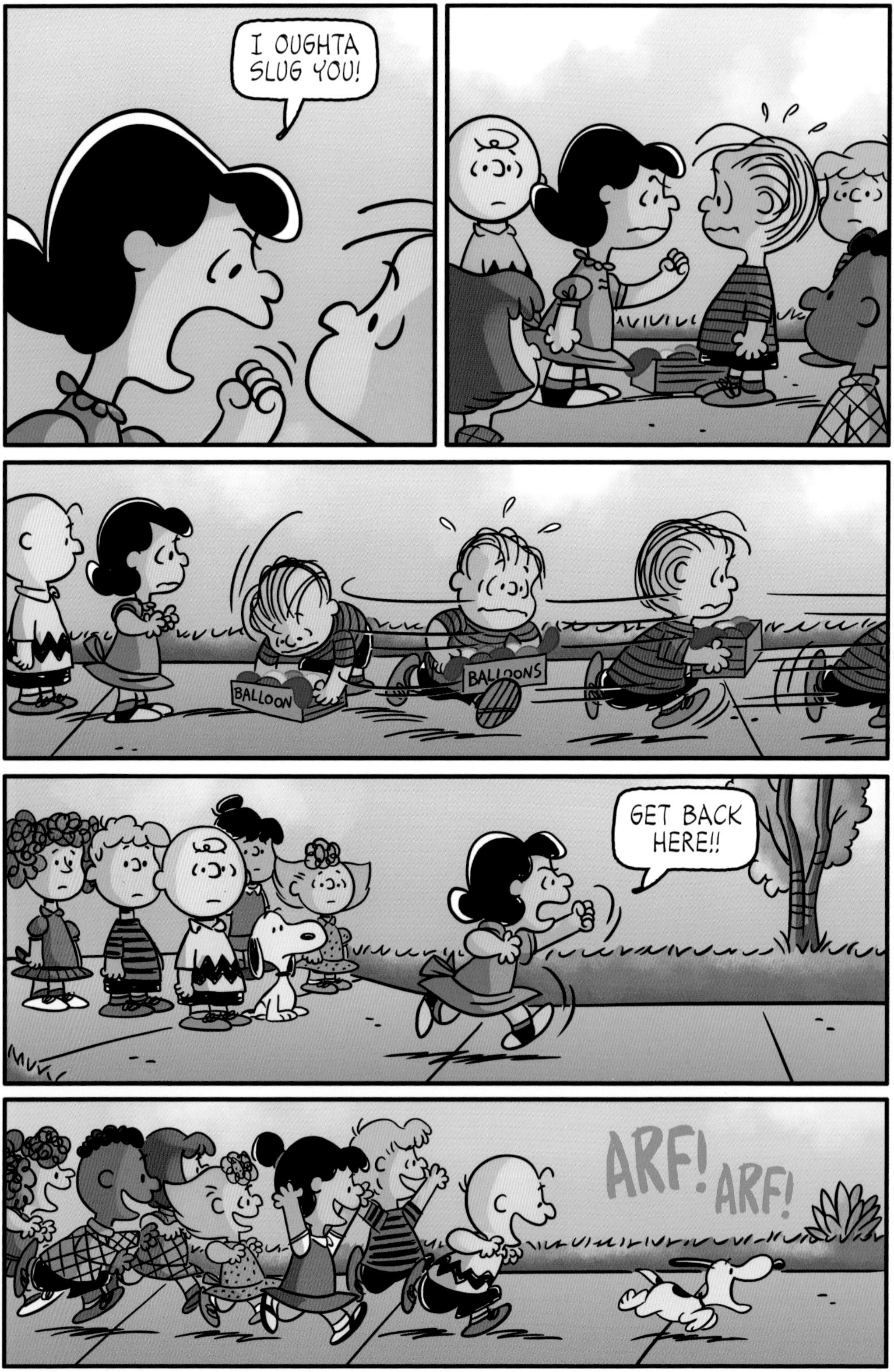
I OUGHTA SLUG YOU!
BALLOON
BALLOONS
GET BACK HERE!!
ARF! ARF!

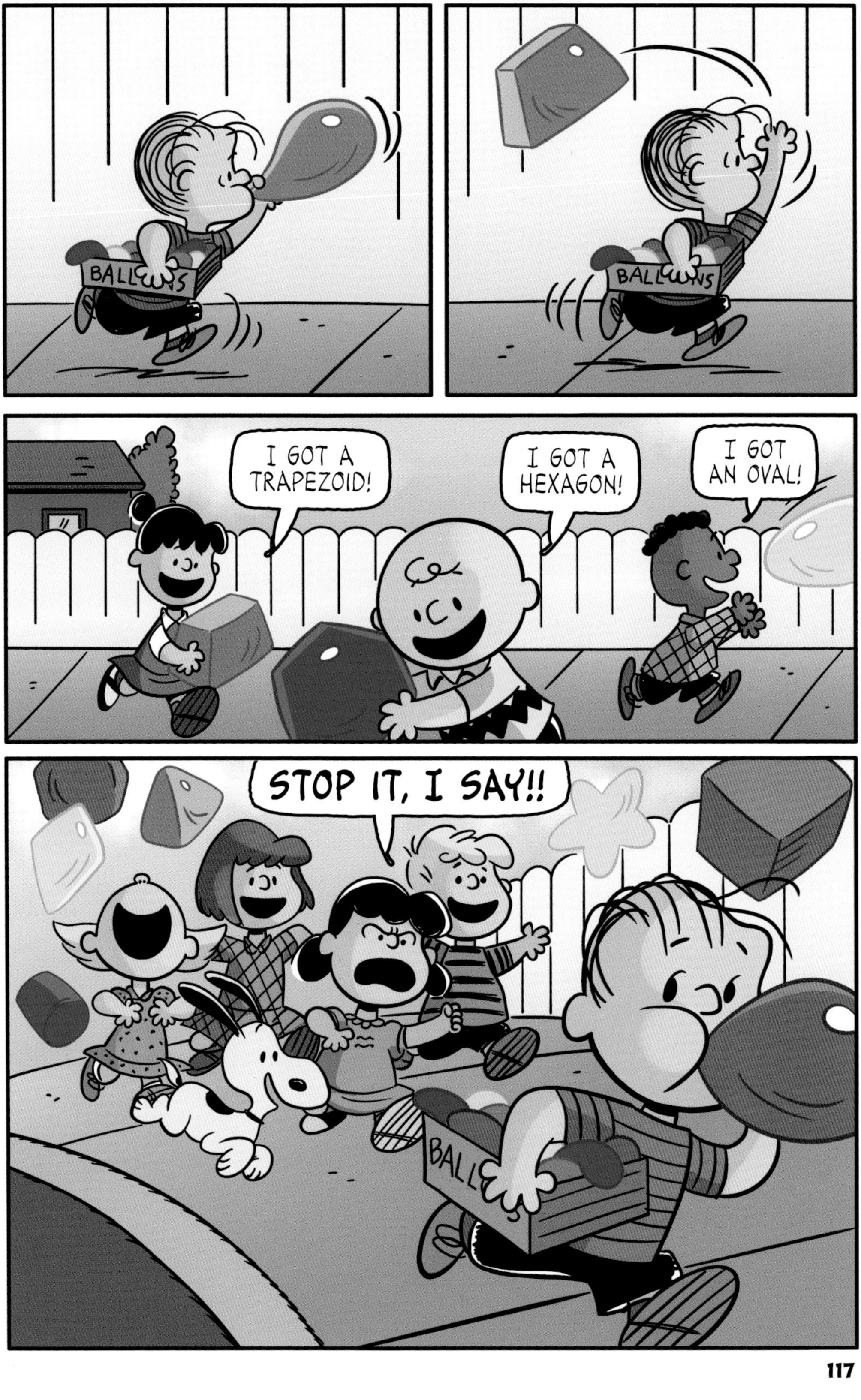
BALLOONS
BALLOONS
I GOT A TRAPEZOID!
I GOT A HEXAGON!
I GOT AN OVAL!
STOP IT, I SAY!!

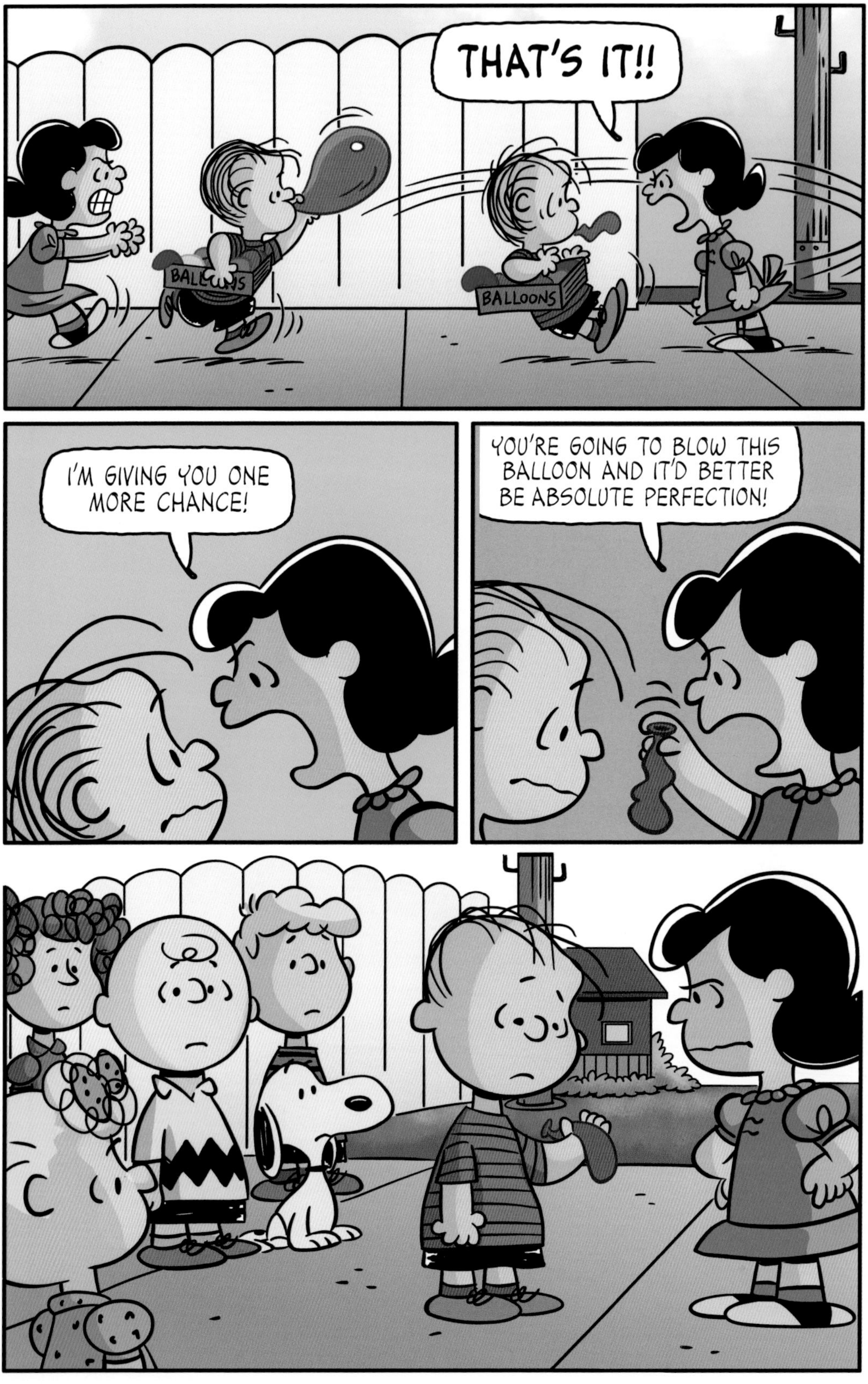
THAT'S IT!!
BALLOONS
BALLOONS
I'M GIVING YOU ONE MORE CHANCE!
YOU'RE GOING TO BLOW THIS BALLOON AND IT'D BETTER BE ABSOLUTE PERFECTION!

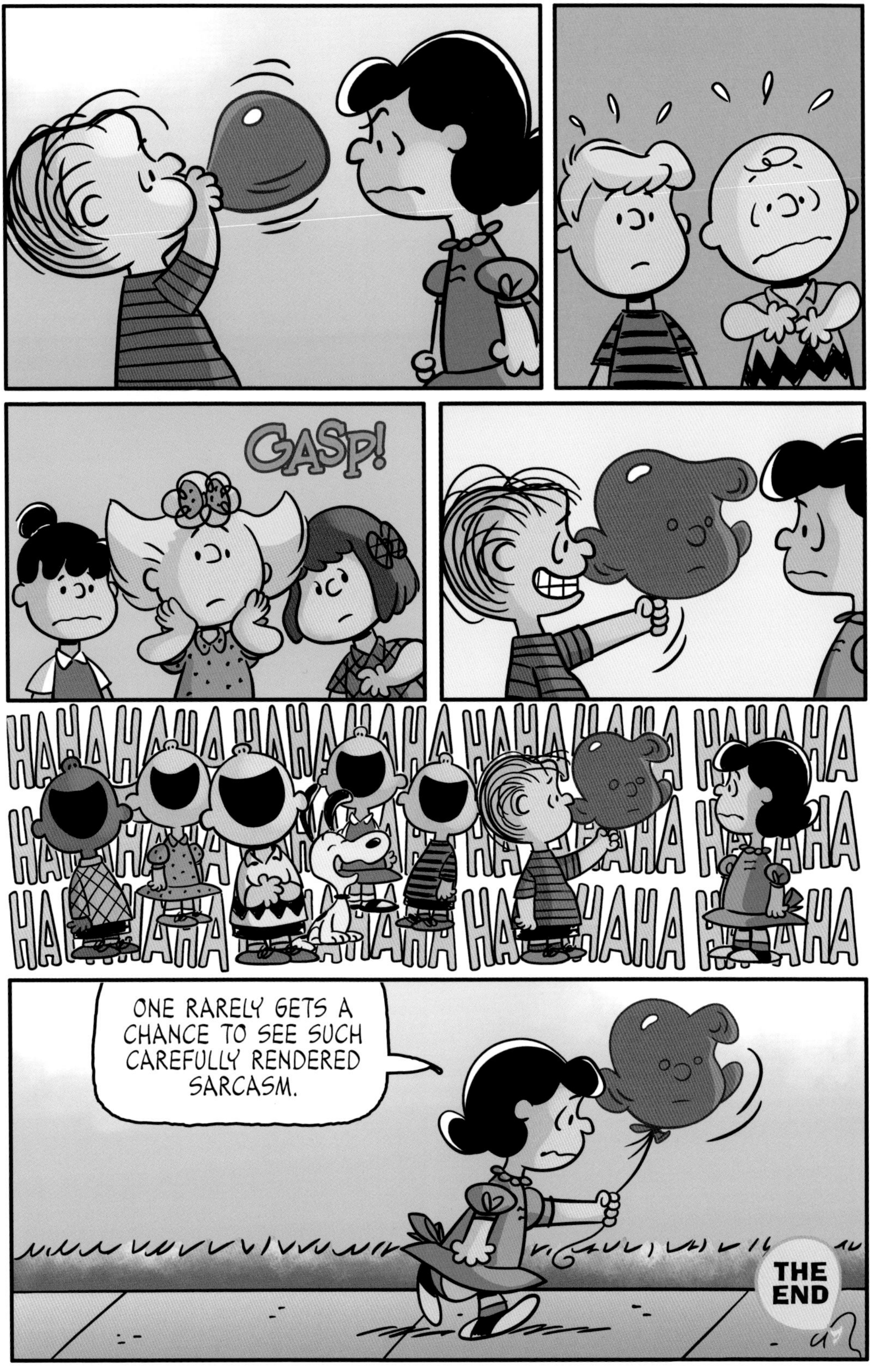
GASP!
HAHAHAHA HAHAHAHA HAHAHAHA HAHAHA
ONE RARELY GETS A CHANCE TO SEE SUCH CAREFULLY RENDERED SARCASM.
THE END

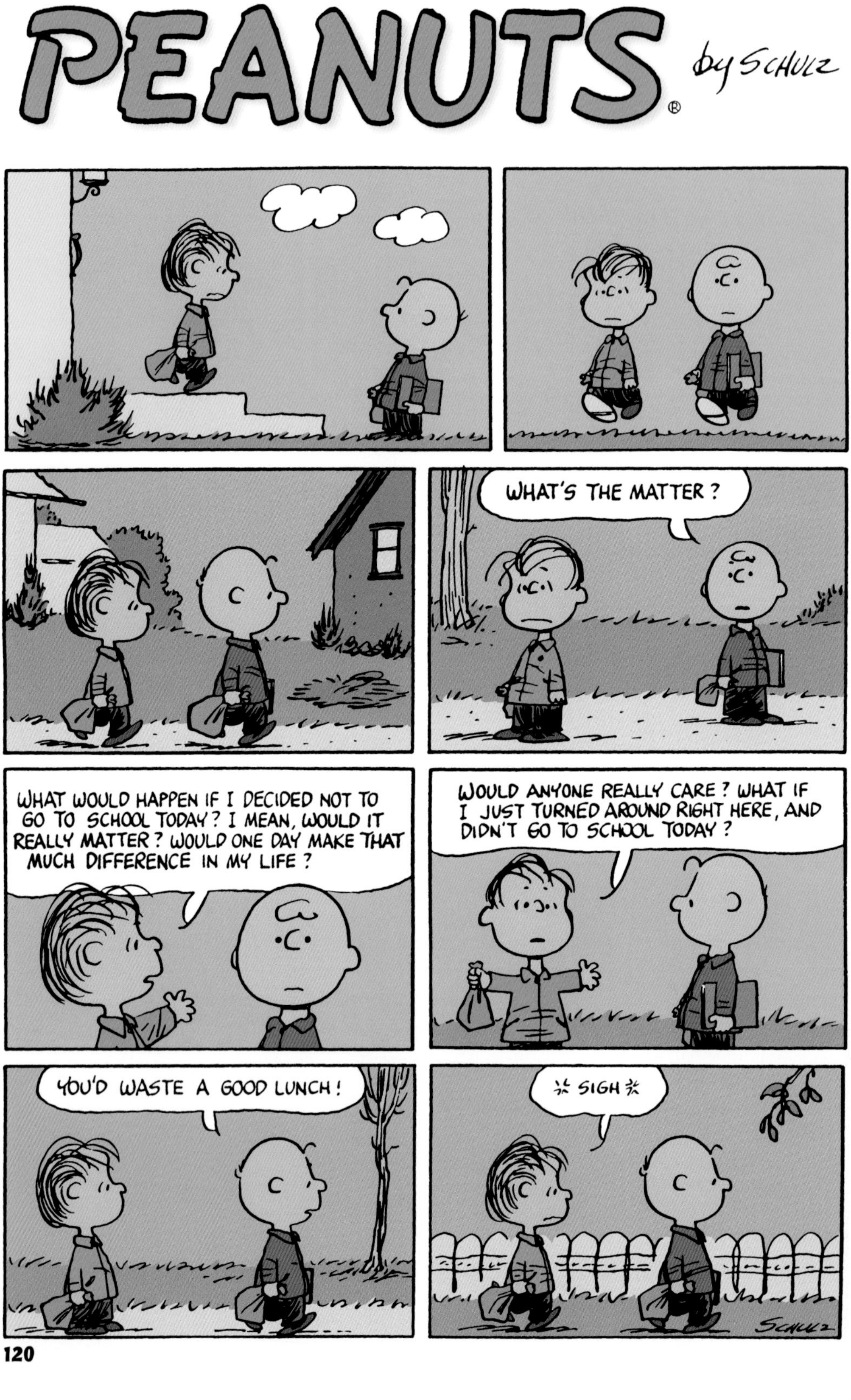
PEANUTS
by SCHULZ
WHAT'S THE MATTER ?
WHAT WOULD HAPPEN IF I DECIDED NOT TO GO TO SCHOOL TODAY ? I MEAN, WOULD IT REALLY MATTER ? WOULD ONE DAY MAKE THAT MUCH DIFFERENCE IN MY LIFE ?
WOULD ANYONE REALLY CARE ? WHAT IF I JUST TURNED AROUND RIGHT HERE, AND DIDN'T GO TO SCHOOL TODAY ?
YOU'D WASTE A GOOD LUNCH !
SIGH
SCHULZ

EWE FIRST

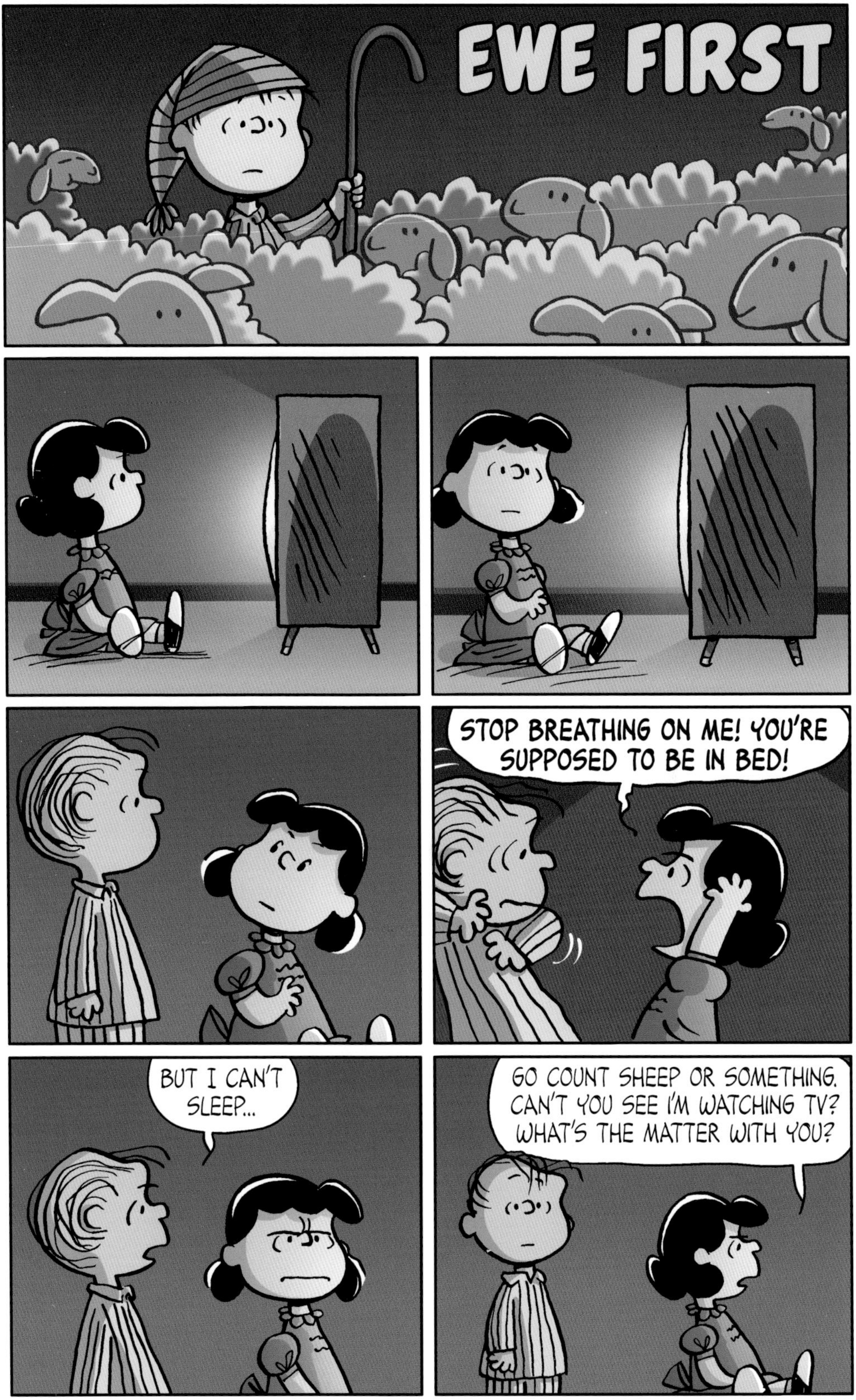
STOP BREATHING ON ME! YOU'RE SUPPOSED TO BE IN BED!
BUT I CAN'T SLEEP...
GO COUNT SHEEP OR SOMETHING. CAN'T YOU SEE I'M WATCHING TV? WHAT'S THE MATTER WITH YOU?

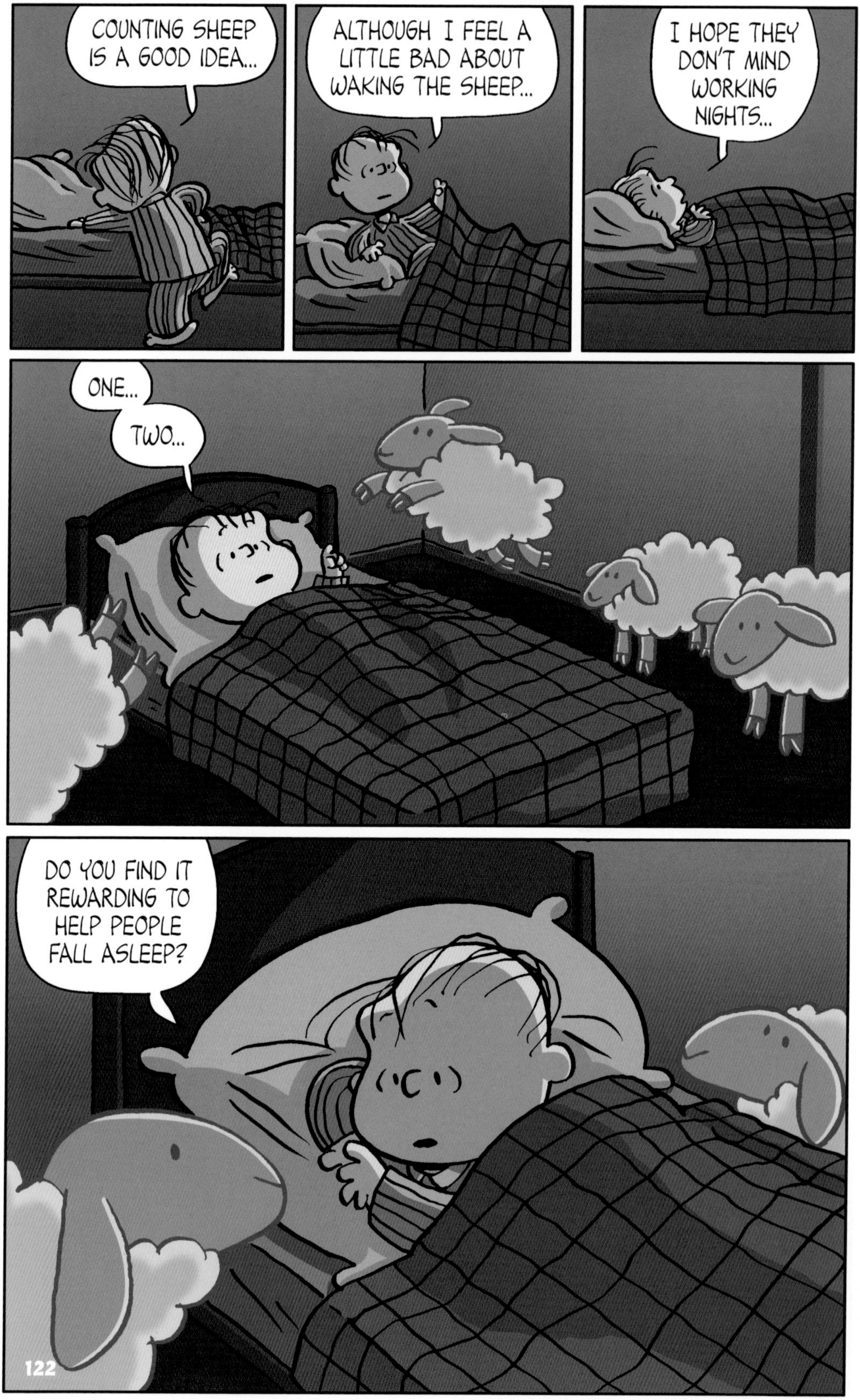
COUNTING SHEEP IS A GOOD IDEA...
ALTHOUGH I FEEL A LITTLE BAD ABOUT WAKING THE SHEEP...
I HOPE THEY DON'T MIND WORKING NIGHTS...
ONE...
TWO...
DO YOU FIND IT REWARDING TO HELP PEOPLE FALL ASLEEP?

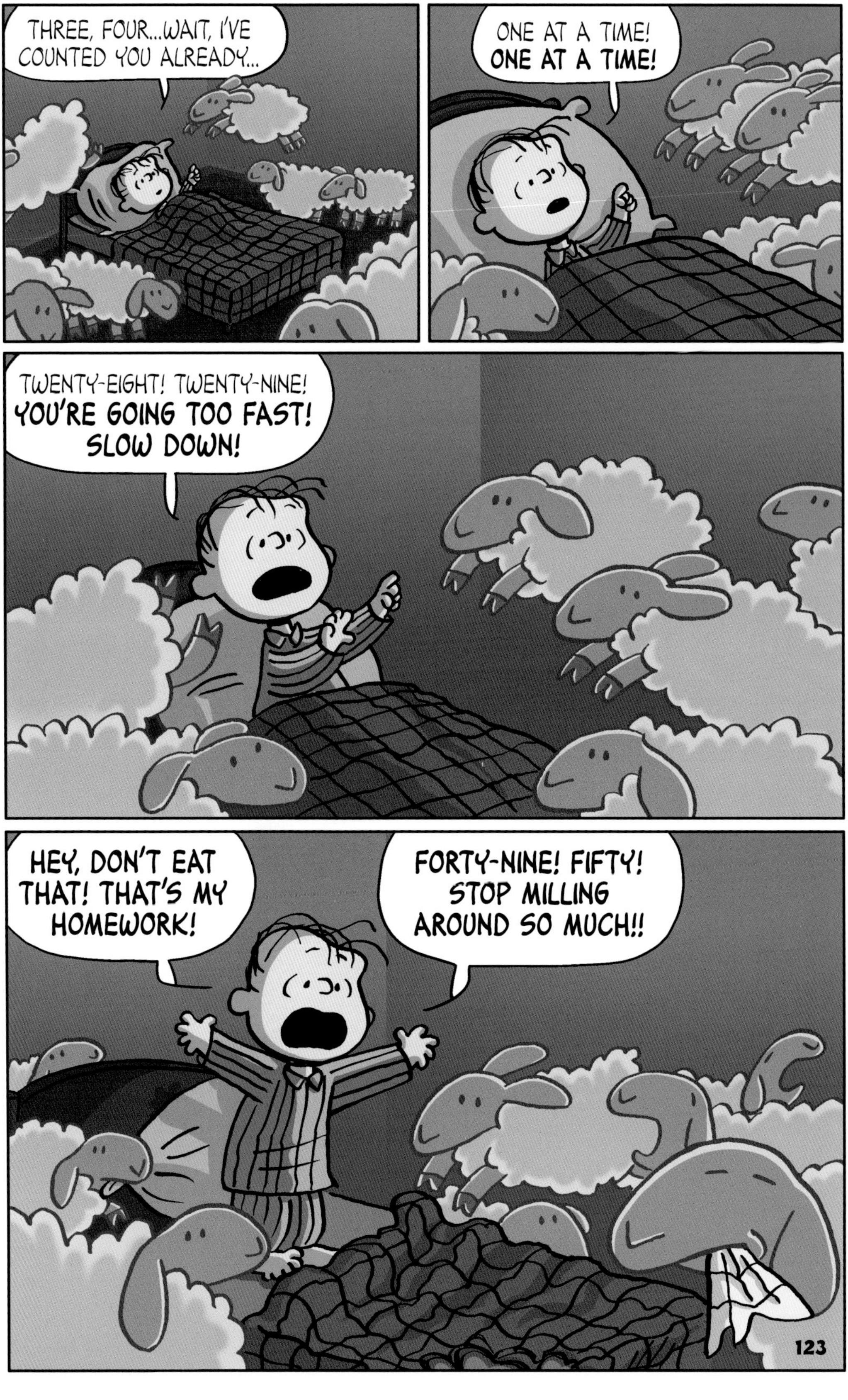
THREE, FOUR...WAIT, I'VE COUNTED YOU ALREADY...
ONE AT A TIME! ONE AT A TIME!
TWENTY-EIGHT! TWENTY-NINE! YOU'RE GOING TOO FAST! SLOW DOWN!
HEY, DON'T EAT THAT! THAT'S MY HOMEWORK!
FORTY-NINE! FIFTY! STOP MILLING AROUND SO MUCH!!

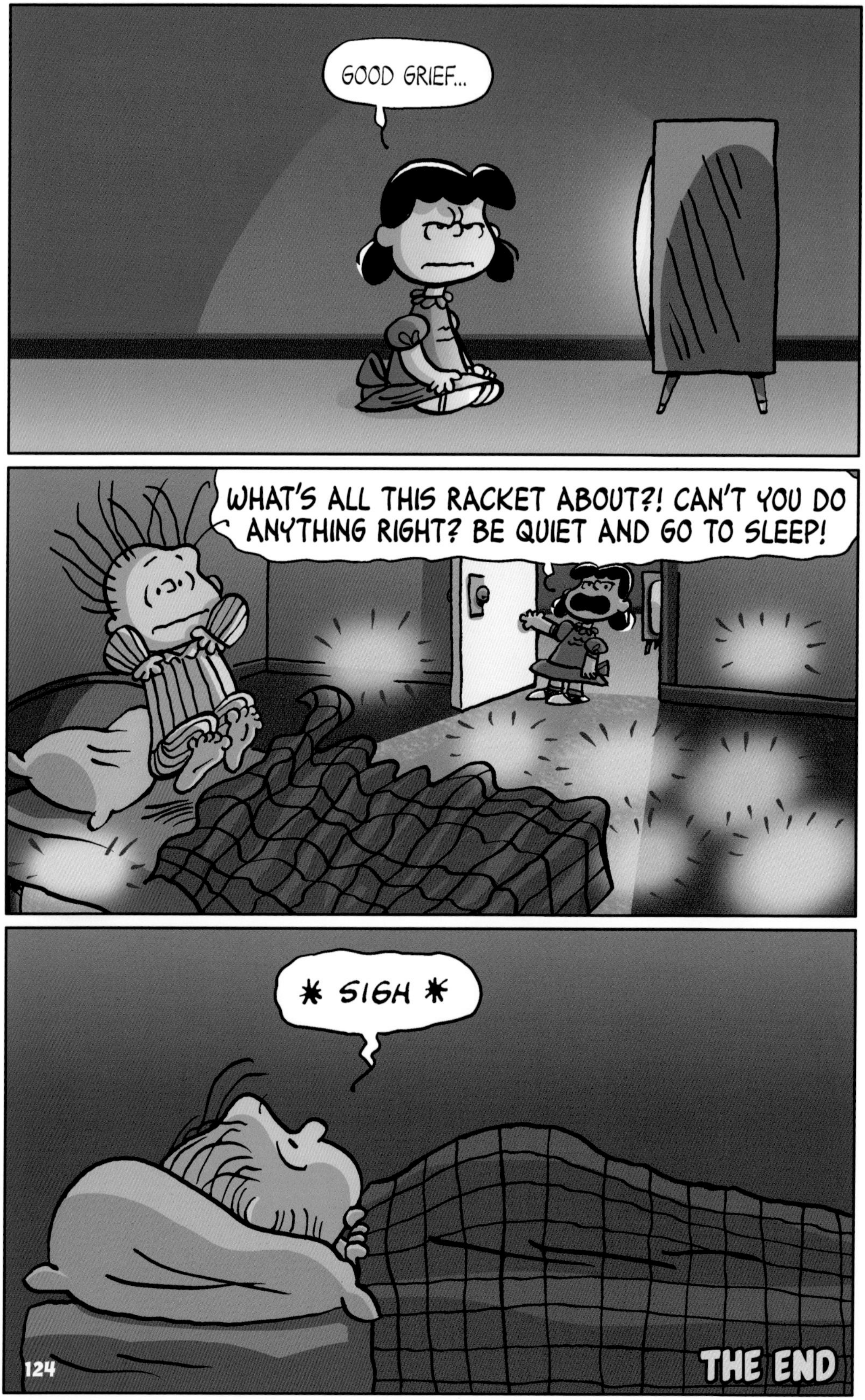
GOOD GRIEF...
WHAT'S ALL THIS RACKET ABOUT?! CAN'T YOU DO ANYTHING RIGHT? BE QUIET AND GO TO SLEEP!
* SIGH *
THE END

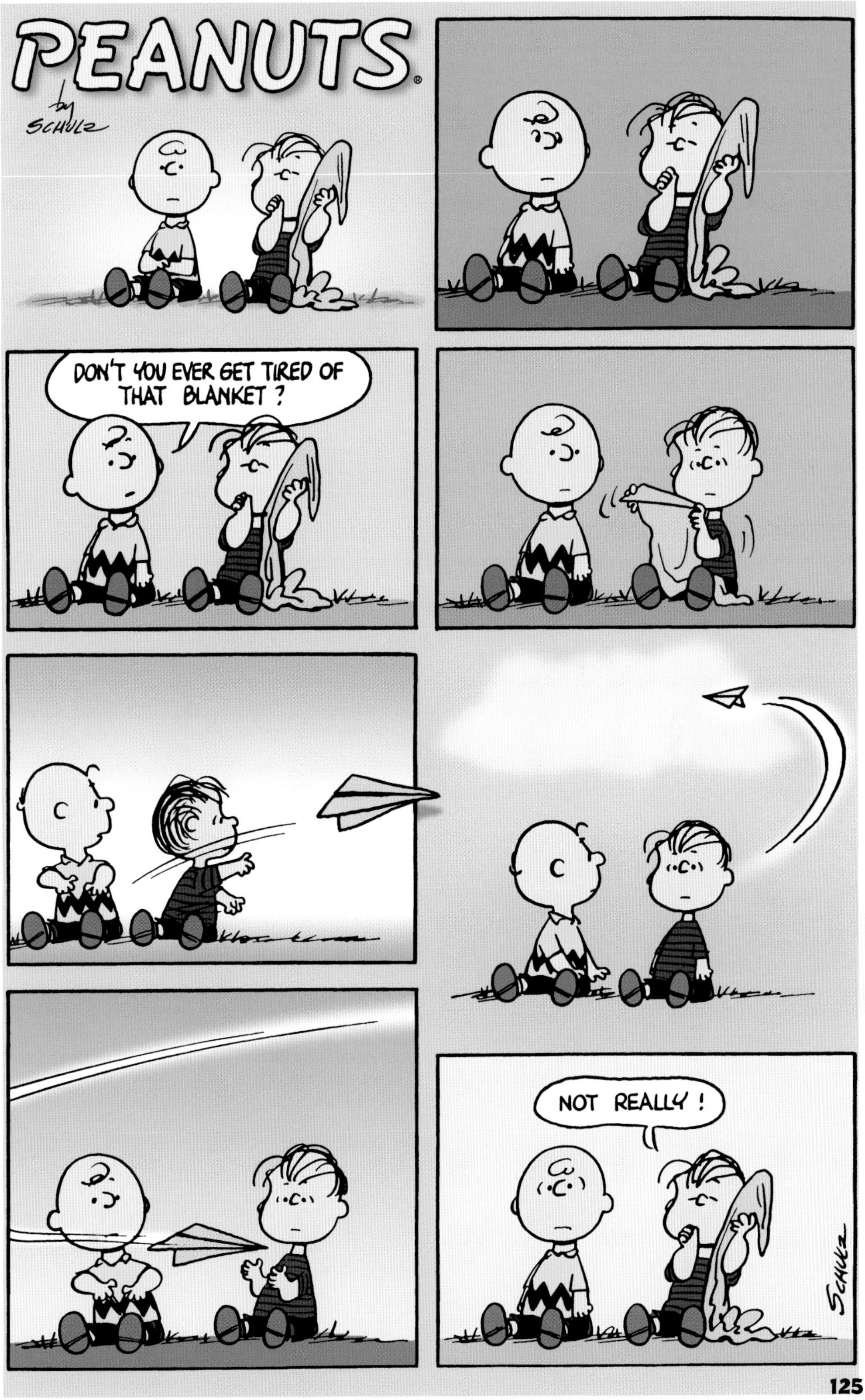
PEANUTS
by SCHULZ
DON'T YOU EVER GET TIRED OF THAT BLANKET ?
NOT REALLY !
SCHULZ

Security Blanket Science

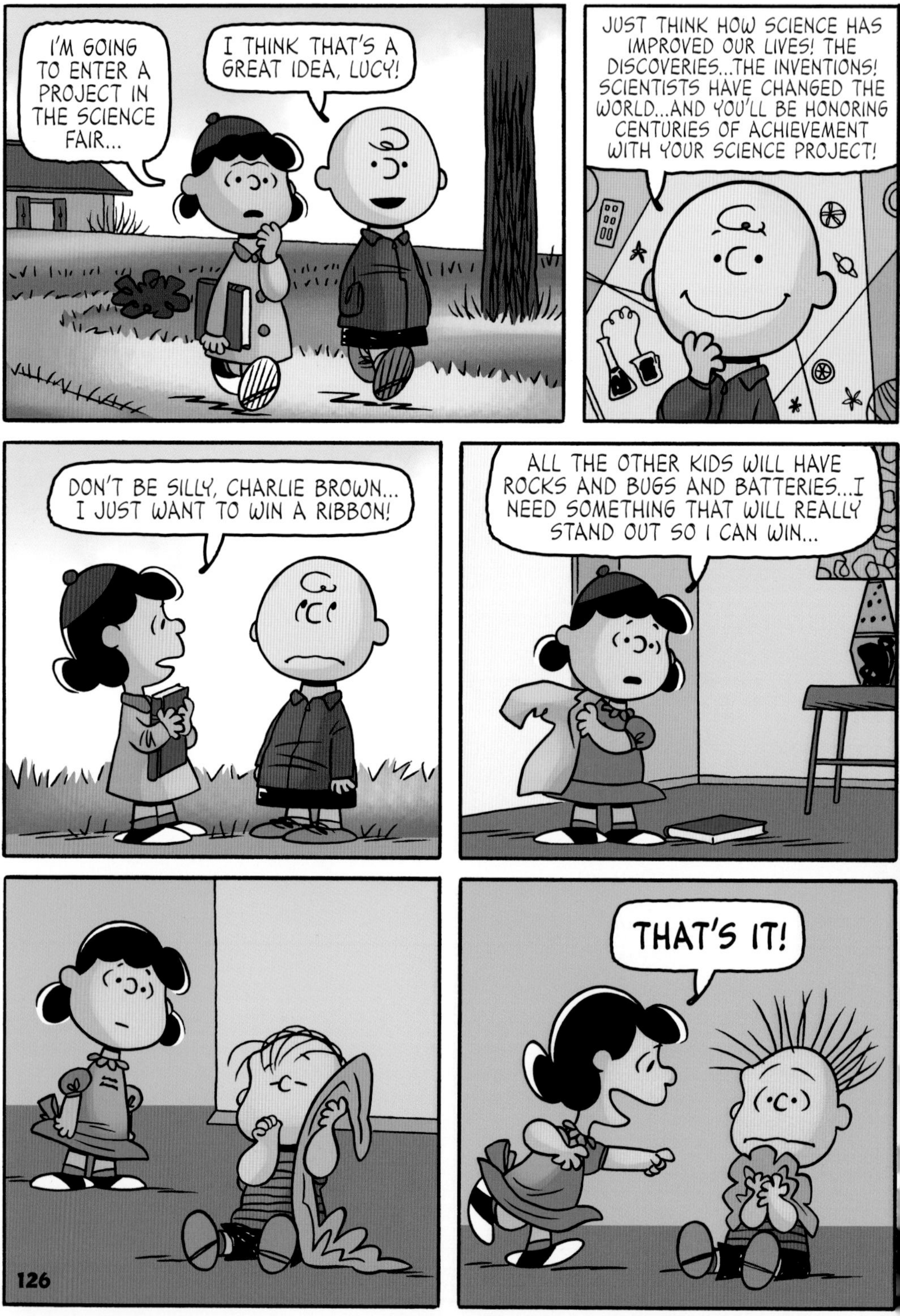
I'M GOING TO ENTER A PROJECT IN THE SCIENCE FAIR...
I THINK THAT'S A GREAT IDEA, LUCY!
JUST THINK HOW SCIENCE HAS IMPROVED OUR LIVES! THE DISCOVERIES...THE INVENTIONS! SCIENTISTS HAVE CHANGED THE WORLD...AND YOU'LL BE HONORING CENTURIES OF ACHIEVEMENT WITH YOUR SCIENCE PROJECT!
DON'T BE SILLY, CHARLIE BROWN... I JUST WANT TO WIN A RIBBON!
ALL THE OTHER KIDS WILL HAVE ROCKS AND BUGS AND BATTERIES...I NEED SOMETHING THAT WILL REALLY STAND OUT SO I CAN WIN...
THAT'S IT!

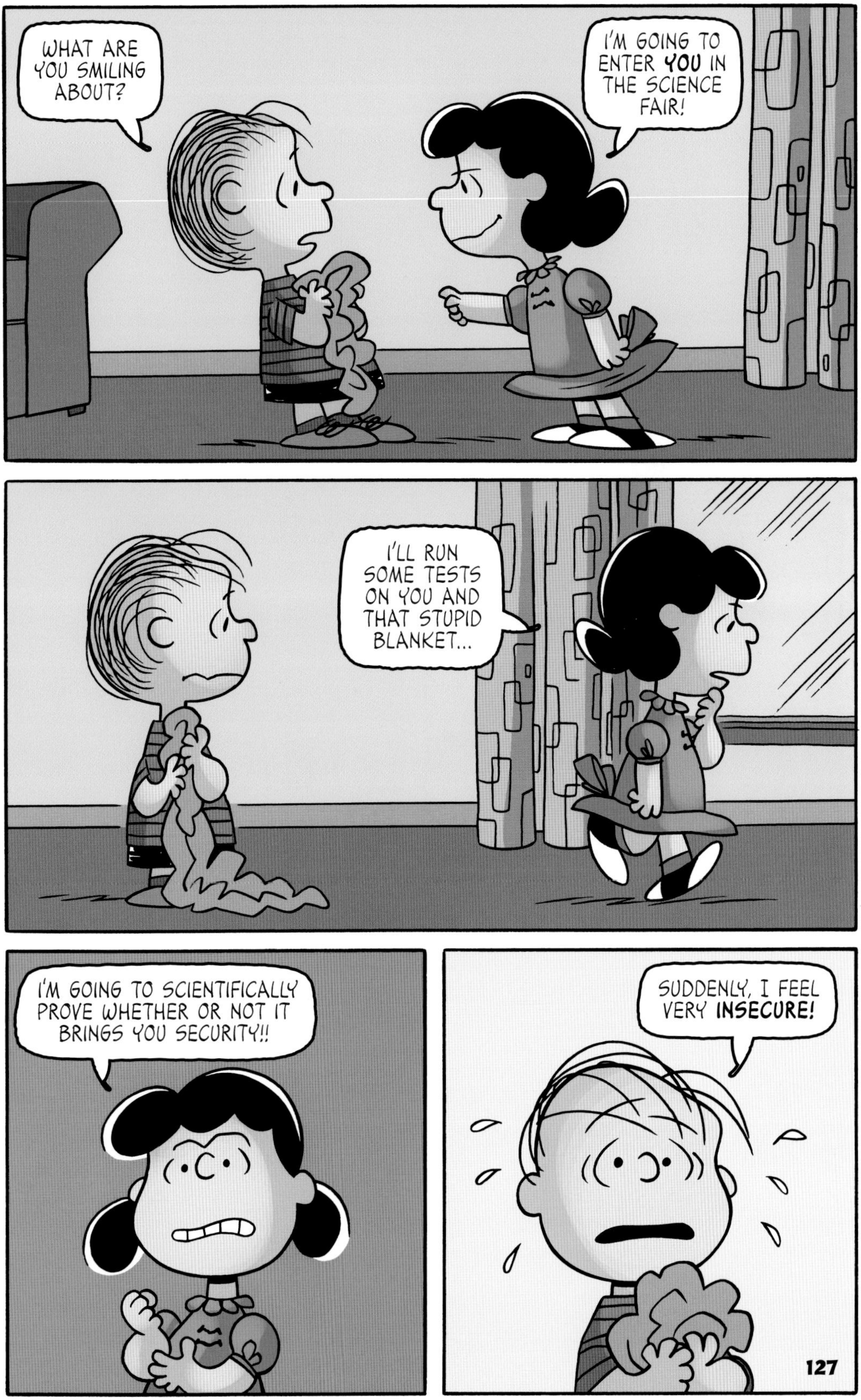
WHAT ARE YOU SMILING ABOUT?
I'M GOING TO ENTER **YOU** IN THE SCIENCE FAIR!
I'LL RUN SOME TESTS ON YOU AND THAT STUPID BLANKET...
I'M GOING TO SCIENTIFICALLY PROVE WHETHER OR NOT IT BRINGS YOU SECURITY!!
SUDDENLY, I FEEL VERY **INSECURE!**

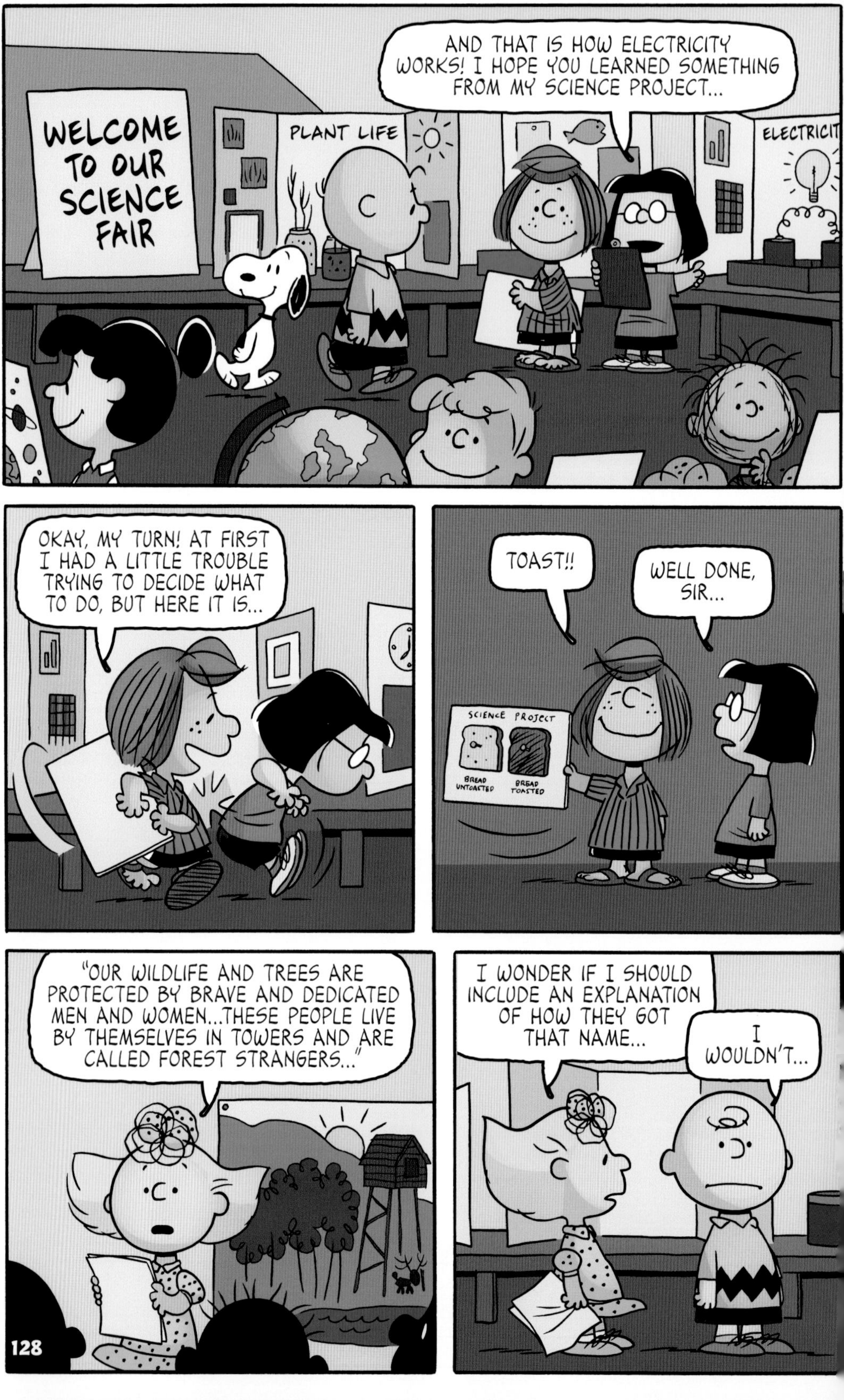
AND THAT IS HOW ELECTRICITY WORKS! I HOPE YOU LEARNED SOMETHING FROM MY SCIENCE PROJECT...
WELCOME TO OUR SCIENCE FAIR
PLANT LIFE
ELECTRICIT
OKAY, MY TURN! AT FIRST I HAD A LITTLE TROUBLE TRYING TO DECIDE WHAT TO DO, BUT HERE IT IS...
TOAST!!
WELL DONE, SIR...
SCIENCE PROJECT
BREAD UNTOASTED
BREAD TOASTED
"OUR WILDLIFE AND TREES ARE PROTECTED BY BRAVE AND DEDICATED MEN AND WOMEN...THESE PEOPLE LIVE BY THEMSELVES IN TOWERS AND ARE CALLED FOREST STRANGERS..."
I WONDER IF I SHOULD INCLUDE AN EXPLANATION OF HOW THEY GOT THAT NAME...
I WOULDN'T...

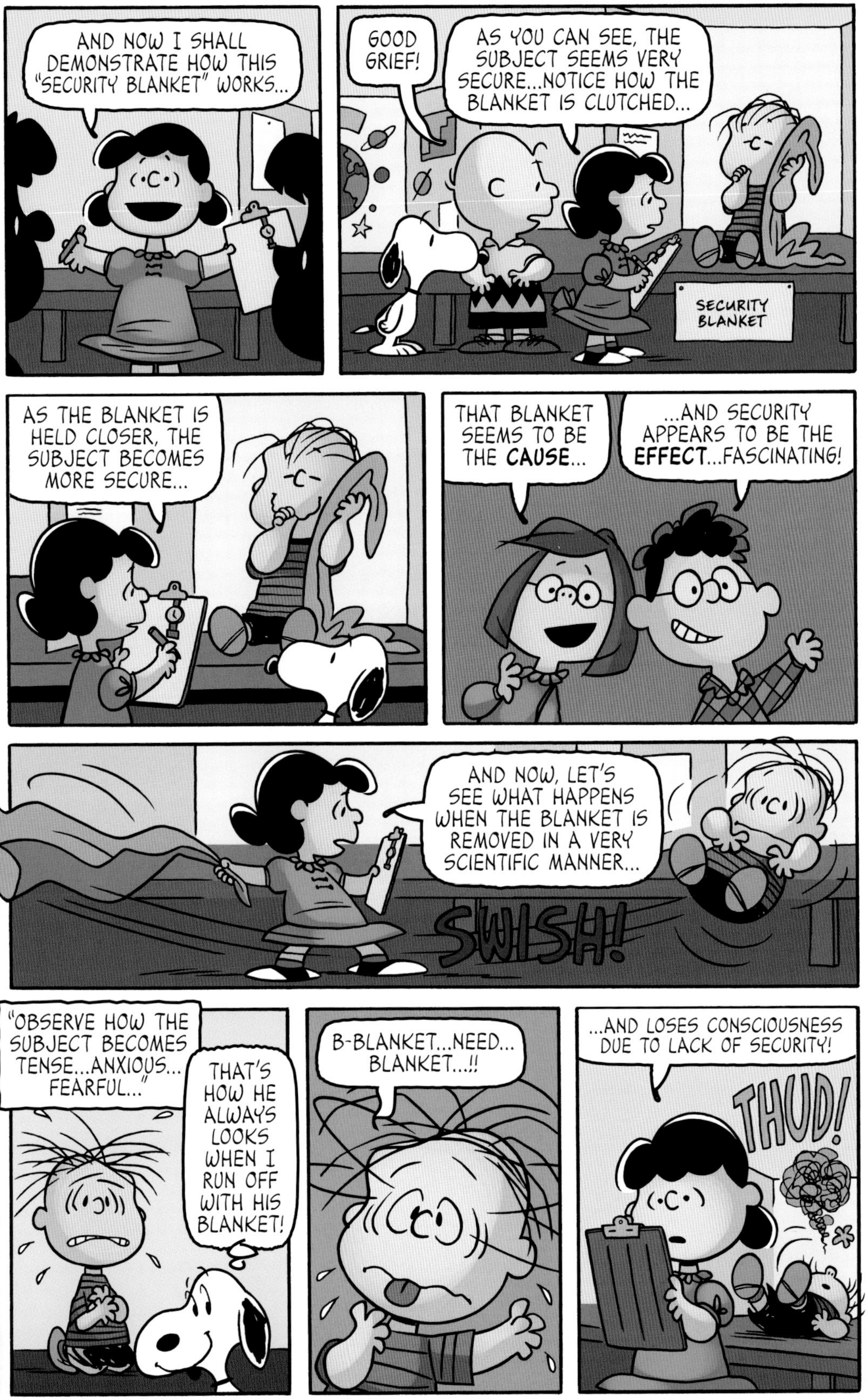
AND NOW I SHALL DEMONSTRATE HOW THIS "SECURITY BLANKET" WORKS...
GOOD GRIEF!
AS YOU CAN SEE, THE SUBJECT SEEMS VERY SECURE...NOTICE HOW THE BLANKET IS CLUTCHED...
SECURITY BLANKET
AS THE BLANKET IS HELD CLOSER, THE SUBJECT BECOMES MORE SECURE...
THAT BLANKET SEEMS TO BE THE **CAUSE**...
...AND SECURITY APPEARS TO BE THE **EFFECT**...FASCINATING!
AND NOW, LET'S SEE WHAT HAPPENS WHEN THE BLANKET IS REMOVED IN A VERY SCIENTIFIC MANNER...
SWISH!
"OBSERVE HOW THE SUBJECT BECOMES TENSE...ANXIOUS... FEARFUL..."
THAT'S HOW HE ALWAYS LOOKS WHEN I RUN OFF WITH HIS BLANKET!
B-BLANKET...NEED... BLANKET...!!
...AND LOSES CONSCIOUSNESS DUE TO LACK OF SECURITY!
THUD!

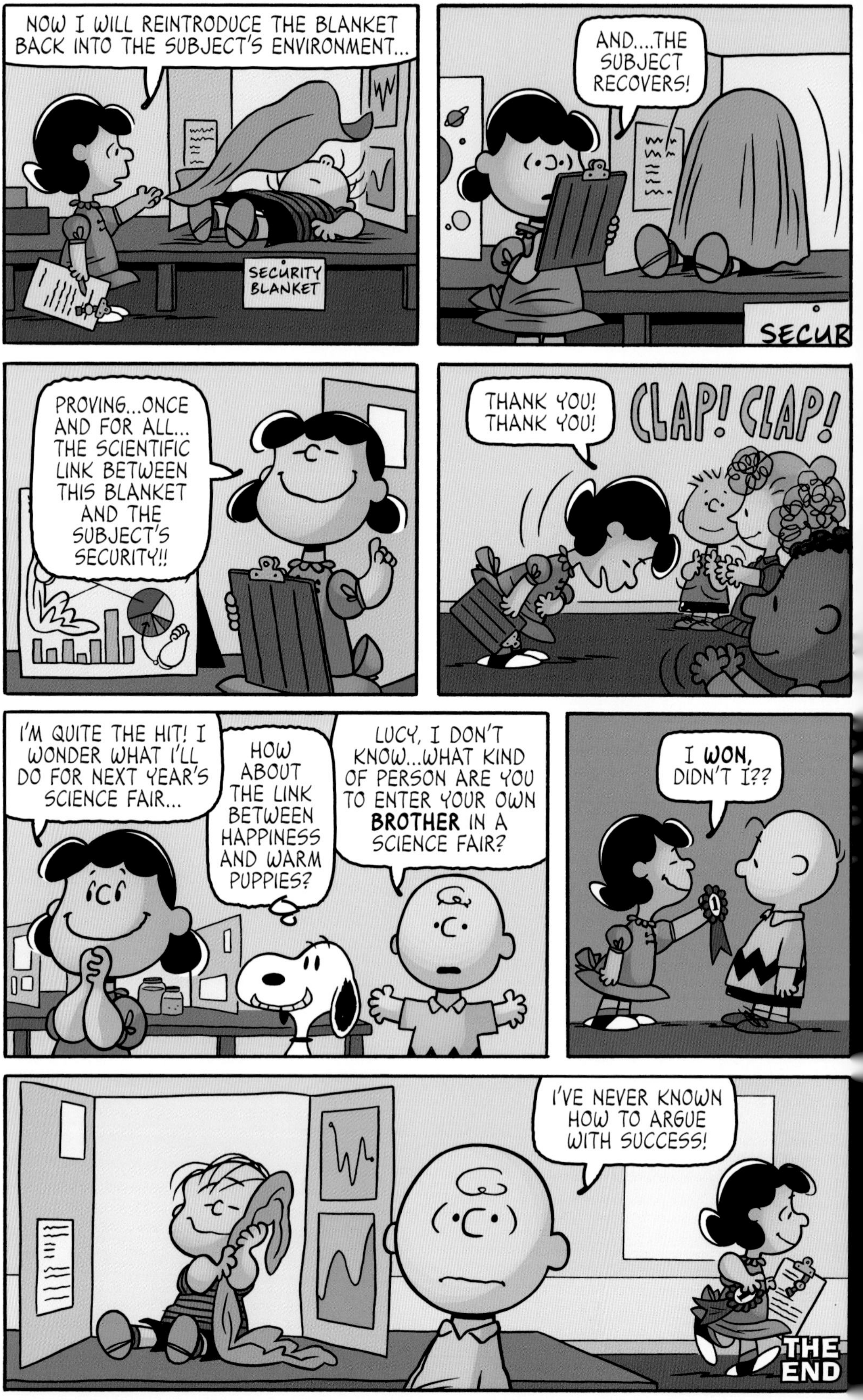
NOW I WILL REINTRODUCE THE BLANKET BACK INTO THE SUBJECT'S ENVIRONMENT...
SECURITY BLANKET
AND....THE SUBJECT RECOVERS!
SECUR
PROVING...ONCE AND FOR ALL... THE SCIENTIFIC LINK BETWEEN THIS BLANKET AND THE SUBJECT'S SECURITY!!
THANK YOU! THANK YOU!
CLAP! CLAP!
I'M QUITE THE HIT! I WONDER WHAT I'LL DO FOR NEXT YEAR'S SCIENCE FAIR...
HOW ABOUT THE LINK BETWEEN HAPPINESS AND WARM PUPPIES?
LUCY, I DON'T KNOW...WHAT KIND OF PERSON ARE YOU TO ENTER YOUR OWN **BROTHER** IN A SCIENCE FAIR?
I **WON,** DIDN'T I??
1
I'VE NEVER KNOWN HOW TO ARGUE WITH SUCCESS!
THE END

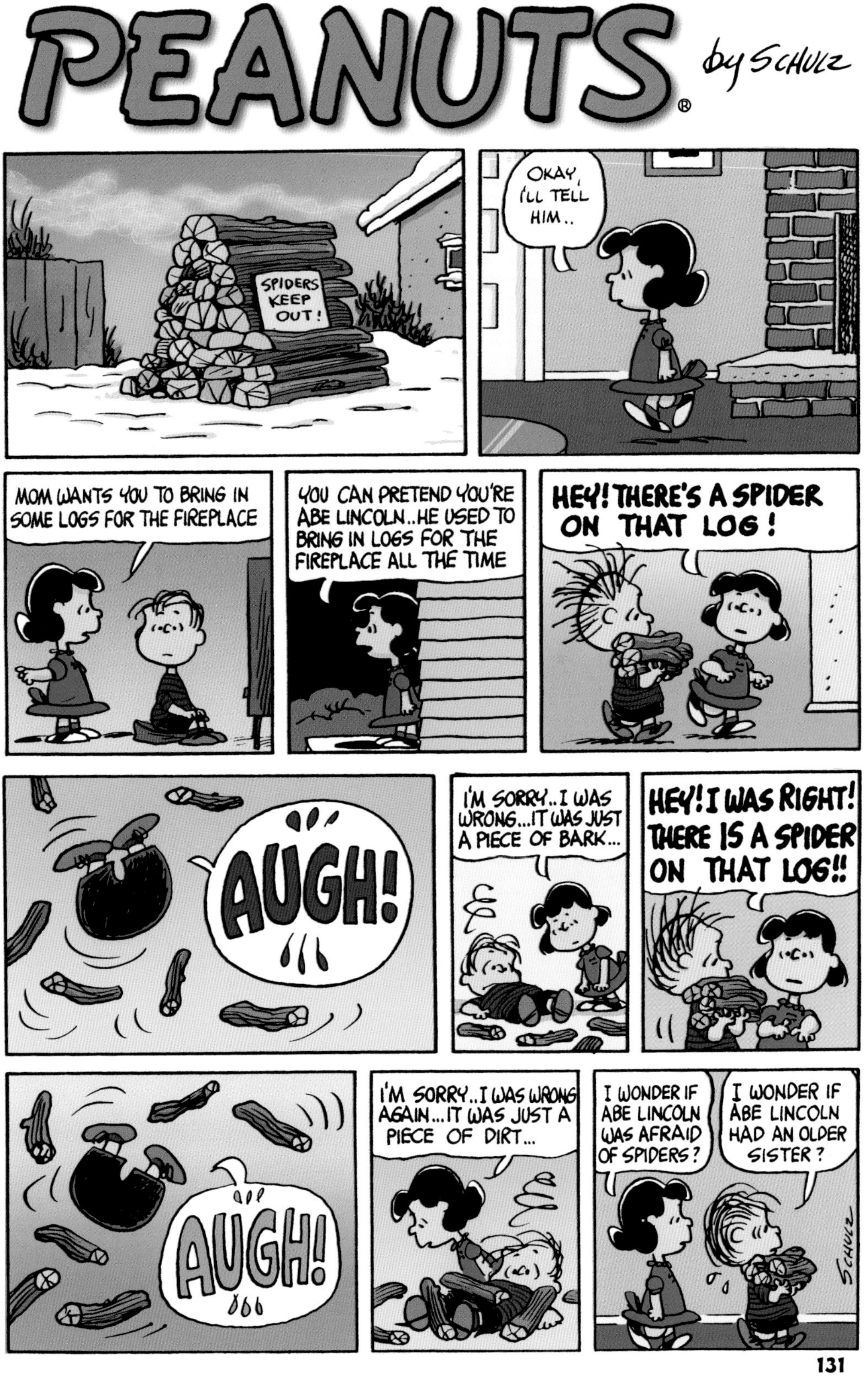
PEANUTS
by SCHULZ
SPIDERS KEEP OUT!
OKAY, I'LL TELL HIM..
MOM WANTS YOU TO BRING IN SOME LOGS FOR THE FIREPLACE
YOU CAN PRETEND YOU'RE ABE LINCOLN..HE USED TO BRING IN LOGS FOR THE FIREPLACE ALL THE TIME
HEY! THERE'S A SPIDER ON THAT LOG!
AUGH!
I'M SORRY..I WAS WRONG...IT WAS JUST A PIECE OF BARK...
HEY! I WAS RIGHT! THERE IS A SPIDER ON THAT LOG!!
AUGH!
I'M SORRY..I WAS WRONG AGAIN...IT WAS JUST A PIECE OF DIRT...
I WONDER IF ABE LINCOLN WAS AFRAID OF SPIDERS?
I WONDER IF ABE LINCOLN HAD AN OLDER SISTER?
SCHULZ

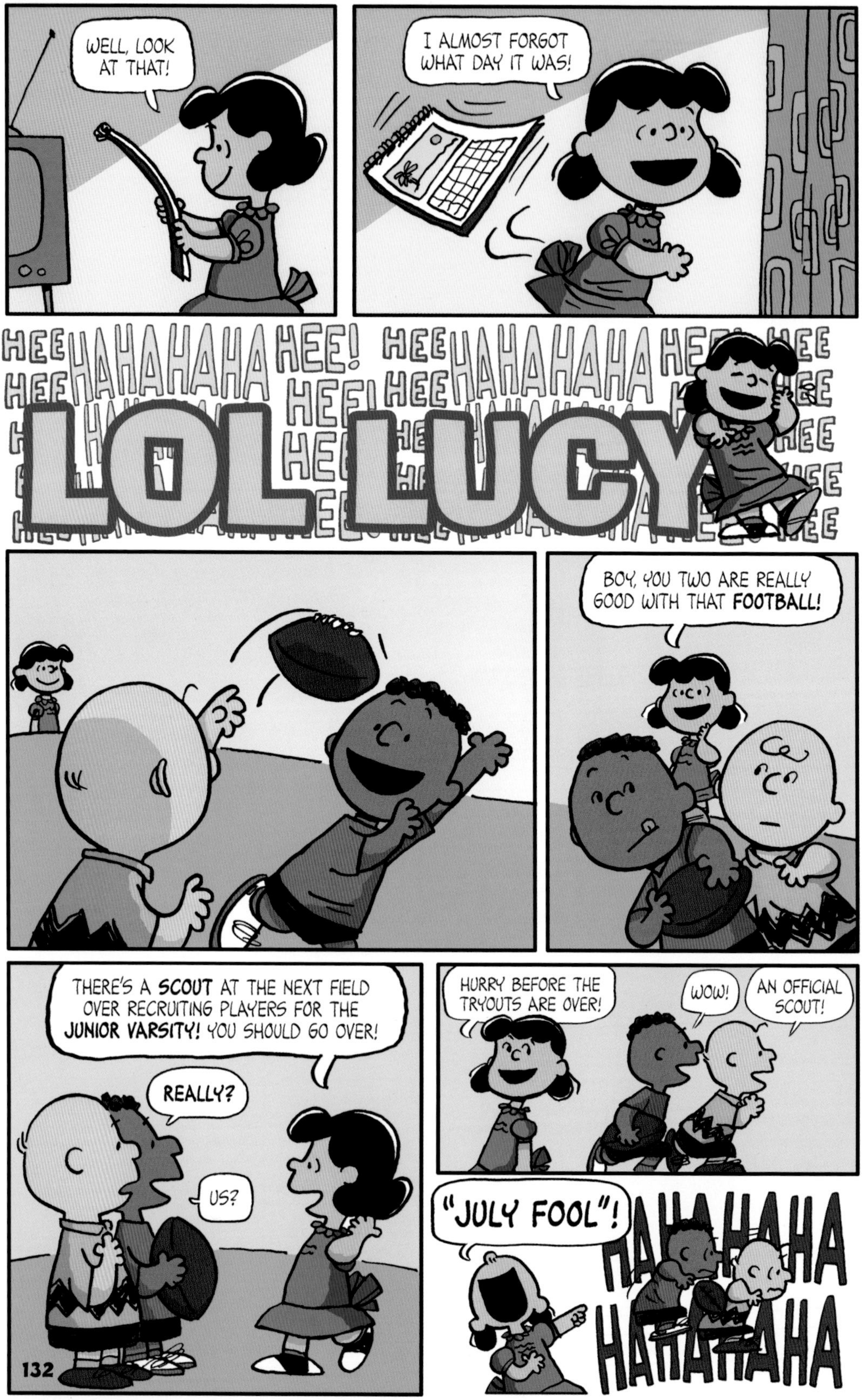
WELL, LOOK AT THAT!
I ALMOST FORGOT WHAT DAY IT WAS!
HEE HAHAHAHA HEE! HEE HAHAHAHA HEE HEE
LOL LUCY
BOY, YOU TWO ARE REALLY GOOD WITH THAT **FOOTBALL!**
THERE'S A **SCOUT** AT THE NEXT FIELD OVER RECRUITING PLAYERS FOR THE **JUNIOR VARSITY!** YOU SHOULD GO OVER!
REALLY?
US?
HURRY BEFORE THE TRYOUTS ARE OVER!
WOW!
AN OFFICIAL SCOUT!
"JULY FOOL"!
HAHAHAHA
HAHAHAHA

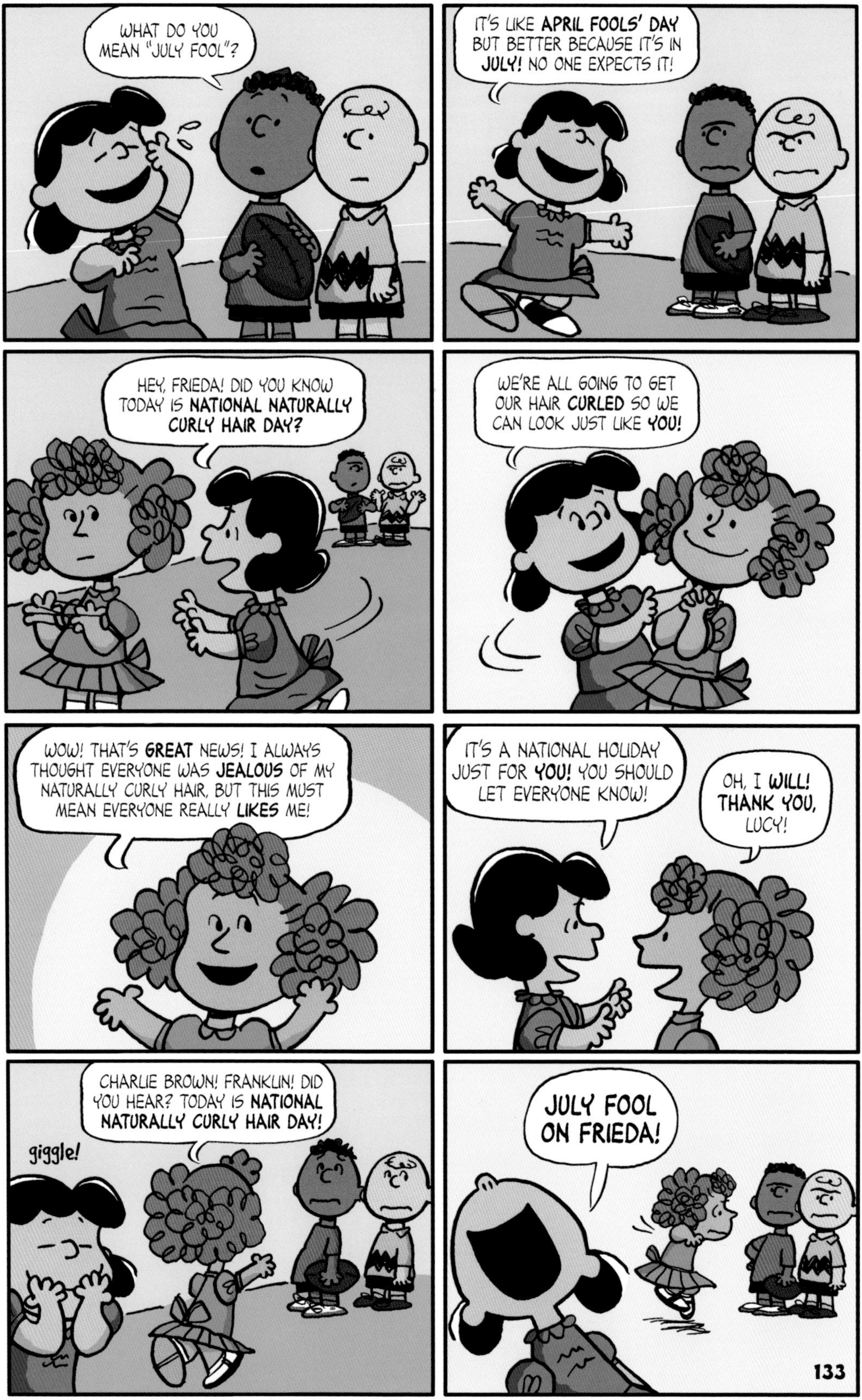
WHAT DO YOU MEAN "JULY FOOL"?
IT'S LIKE APRIL FOOLS' DAY BUT BETTER BECAUSE IT'S IN JULY! NO ONE EXPECTS IT!
HEY, FRIEDA! DID YOU KNOW TODAY IS NATIONAL NATURALLY CURLY HAIR DAY?
WE'RE ALL GOING TO GET OUR HAIR CURLED SO WE CAN LOOK JUST LIKE YOU!
WOW! THAT'S GREAT NEWS! I ALWAYS THOUGHT EVERYONE WAS JEALOUS OF MY NATURALLY CURLY HAIR, BUT THIS MUST MEAN EVERYONE REALLY LIKES ME!
IT'S A NATIONAL HOLIDAY JUST FOR YOU! YOU SHOULD LET EVERYONE KNOW!
OH, I WILL! THANK YOU, LUCY!
CHARLIE BROWN! FRANKLIN! DID YOU HEAR? TODAY IS NATIONAL NATURALLY CURLY HAIR DAY!
giggle!
JULY FOOL ON FRIEDA!

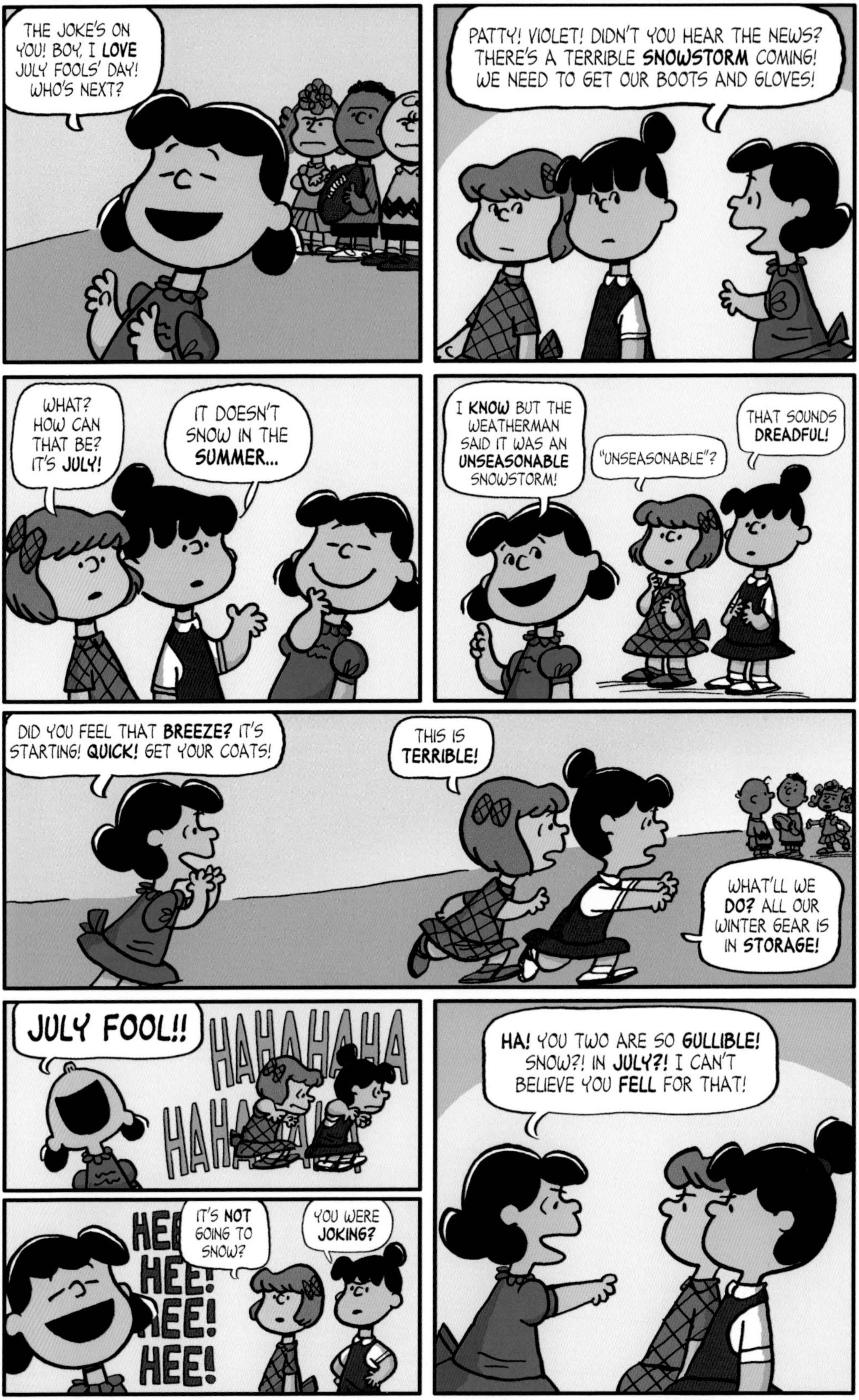
THE JOKE'S ON YOU! BOY, I LOVE JULY FOOLS' DAY! WHO'S NEXT?
PATTY! VIOLET! DIDN'T YOU HEAR THE NEWS? THERE'S A TERRIBLE SNOWSTORM COMING! WE NEED TO GET OUR BOOTS AND GLOVES!
WHAT? HOW CAN THAT BE? IT'S JULY!
IT DOESN'T SNOW IN THE SUMMER...
I KNOW BUT THE WEATHERMAN SAID IT WAS AN UNSEASONABLE SNOWSTORM!
"UNSEASONABLE"?
THAT SOUNDS DREADFUL!
DID YOU FEEL THAT BREEZE? IT'S STARTING! QUICK! GET YOUR COATS!
THIS IS TERRIBLE!
WHAT'LL WE DO? ALL OUR WINTER GEAR IS IN STORAGE!
JULY FOOL!!
HAHAHAHA
HAHAHAHA
HEE! HEE! HEE! HEE!
IT'S NOT GOING TO SNOW?
YOU WERE JOKING?
HA! YOU TWO ARE SO GULLIBLE! SNOW?! IN JULY?! I CAN'T BELIEVE YOU FELL FOR THAT!

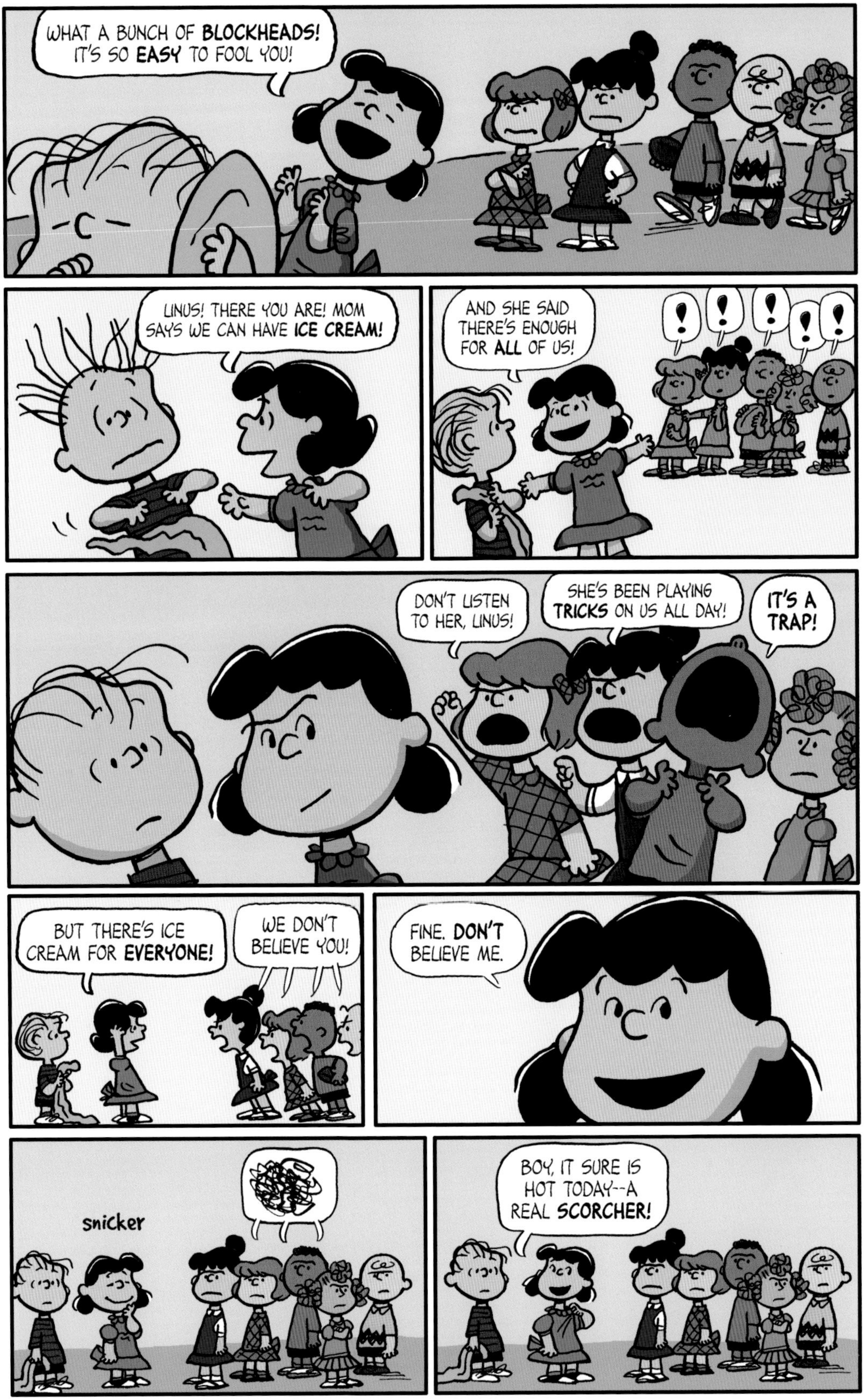
WHAT A BUNCH OF **BLOCKHEADS!** IT'S SO **EASY** TO FOOL YOU!
LINUS! THERE YOU ARE! MOM SAYS WE CAN HAVE **ICE CREAM!**
AND SHE SAID THERE'S ENOUGH FOR **ALL** OF US!
!
!
!
!
!
DON'T LISTEN TO HER, LINUS!
SHE'S BEEN PLAYING **TRICKS** ON US ALL DAY!
IT'S A TRAP!
BUT THERE'S ICE CREAM FOR **EVERYONE!**
WE DON'T BELIEVE YOU!
FINE. **DON'T** BELIEVE ME.
snicker
BOY, IT SURE IS HOT TODAY--A REAL **SCORCHER!**

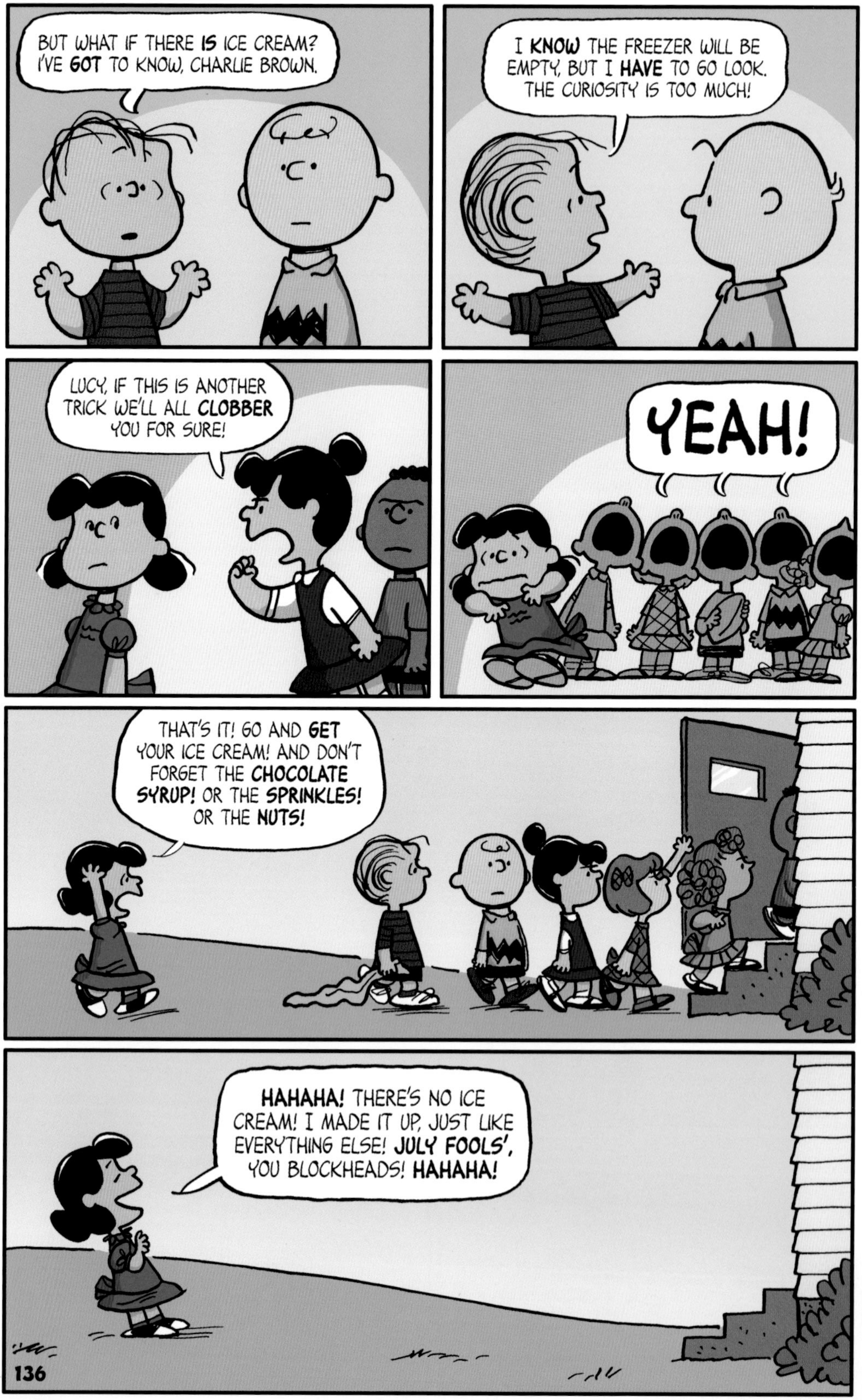
BUT WHAT IF THERE IS ICE CREAM? I'VE GOT TO KNOW, CHARLIE BROWN.
I KNOW THE FREEZER WILL BE EMPTY, BUT I HAVE TO GO LOOK. THE CURIOSITY IS TOO MUCH!
LUCY, IF THIS IS ANOTHER TRICK WE'LL ALL CLOBBER YOU FOR SURE!
YEAH!
THAT'S IT! GO AND GET YOUR ICE CREAM! AND DON'T FORGET THE CHOCOLATE SYRUP! OR THE SPRINKLES! OR THE NUTS!
HAHAHA! THERE'S NO ICE CREAM! I MADE IT UP, JUST LIKE EVERYTHING ELSE! JULY FOOLS', YOU BLOCKHEADS! HAHAHA!

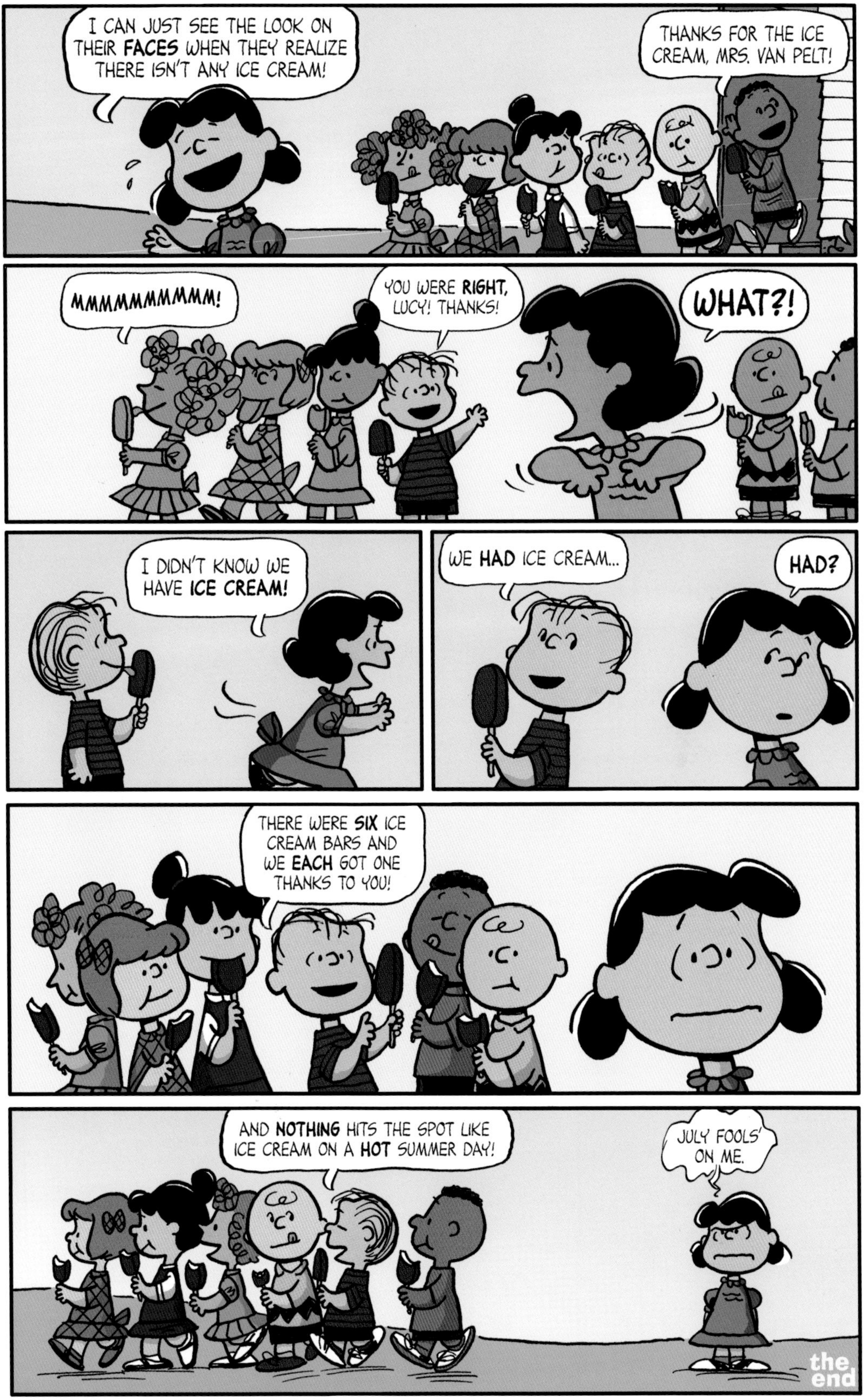
I CAN JUST SEE THE LOOK ON THEIR **FACES** WHEN THEY REALIZE THERE ISN'T ANY ICE CREAM!
THANKS FOR THE ICE CREAM, MRS. VAN PELT!
MMMMMMMMMM!
YOU WERE **RIGHT**, LUCY! THANKS!
WHAT?!
I DIDN'T KNOW WE HAVE **ICE CREAM!**
WE **HAD** ICE CREAM...
HAD?
THERE WERE **SIX** ICE CREAM BARS AND WE **EACH** GOT ONE THANKS TO YOU!
AND **NOTHING** HITS THE SPOT LIKE ICE CREAM ON A **HOT** SUMMER DAY!
JULY FOOLS' ON ME.
the end

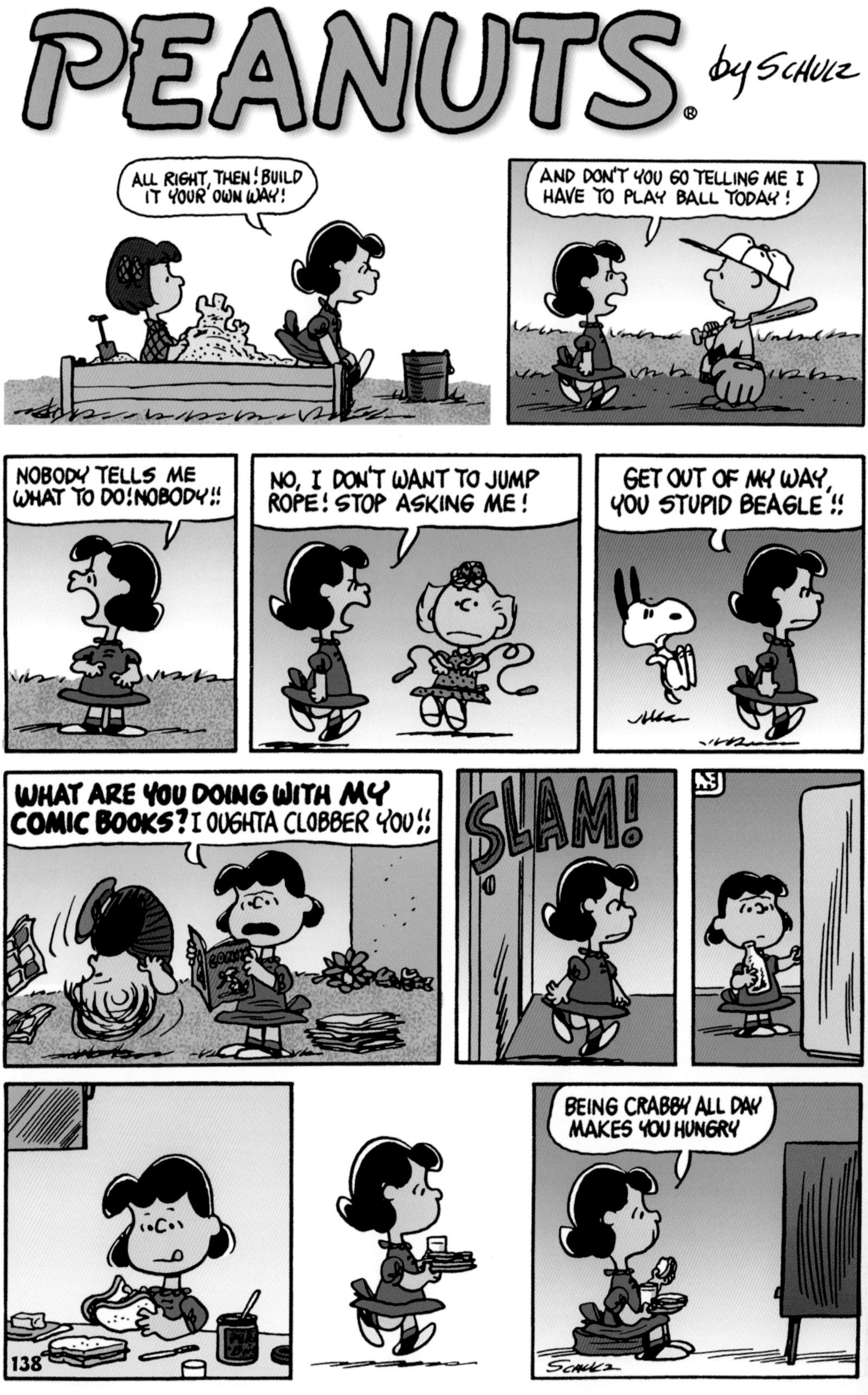
PEANUTS
by SCHULZ
ALL RIGHT, THEN! BUILD IT YOUR OWN WAY!
AND DON'T YOU GO TELLING ME I HAVE TO PLAY BALL TODAY!
NOBODY TELLS ME WHAT TO DO! NOBODY!!
NO, I DON'T WANT TO JUMP ROPE! STOP ASKING ME!
GET OUT OF MY WAY, YOU STUPID BEAGLE!!
WHAT ARE YOU DOING WITH MY COMIC BOOKS? I OUGHTA CLOBBER YOU!!
COMIC
SLAM!
BEING CRABBY ALL DAY MAKES YOU HUNGRY
SCHULZ

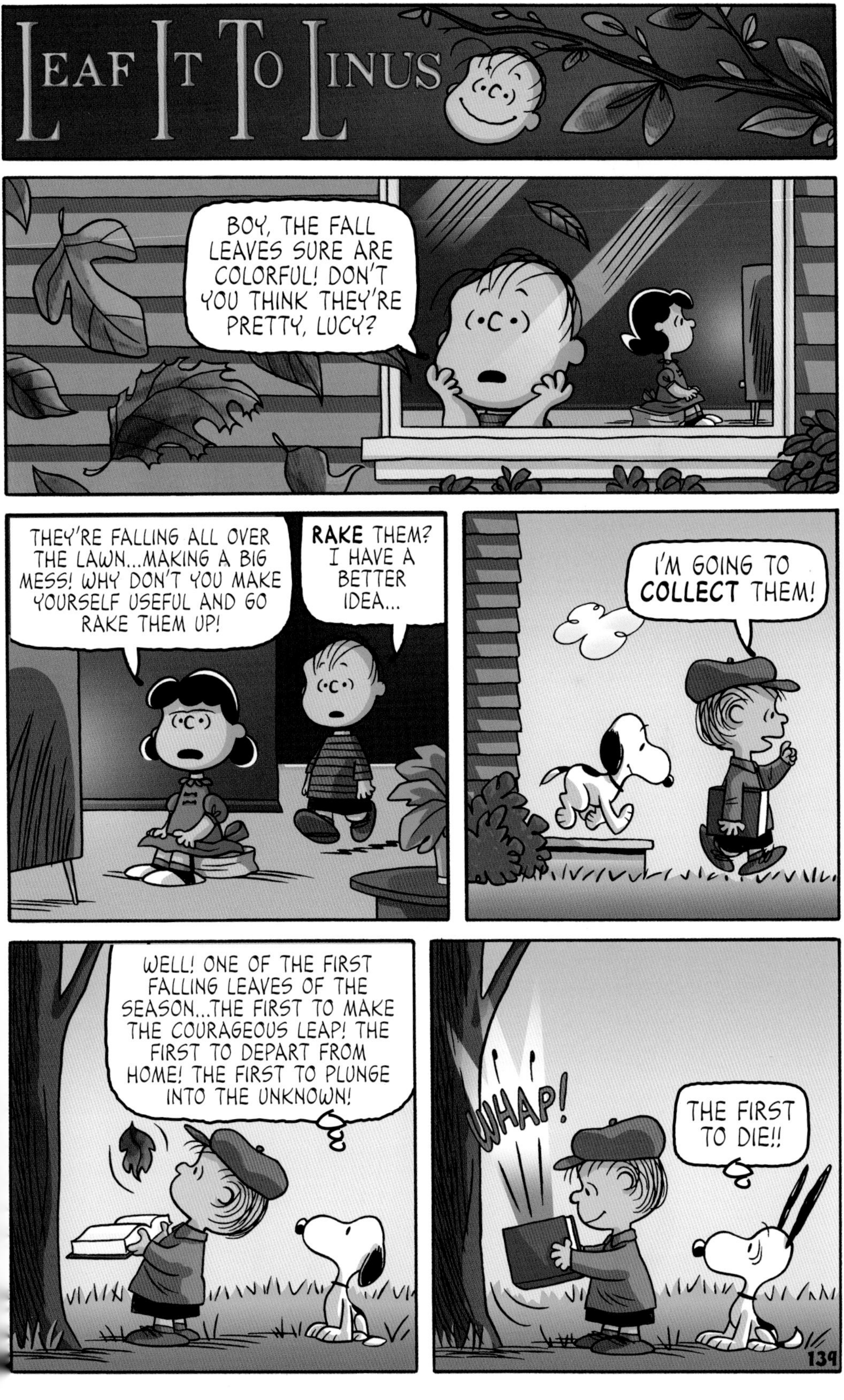
LEAF IT TO LINUS
BOY, THE FALL LEAVES SURE ARE COLORFUL! DON'T YOU THINK THEY'RE PRETTY, LUCY?
THEY'RE FALLING ALL OVER THE LAWN...MAKING A BIG MESS! WHY DON'T YOU MAKE YOURSELF USEFUL AND GO RAKE THEM UP!
RAKE THEM? I HAVE A BETTER IDEA...
I'M GOING TO COLLECT THEM!
WELL! ONE OF THE FIRST FALLING LEAVES OF THE SEASON...THE FIRST TO MAKE THE COURAGEOUS LEAP! THE FIRST TO DEPART FROM HOME! THE FIRST TO PLUNGE INTO THE UNKNOWN!
WHAP!
THE FIRST TO DIE!!

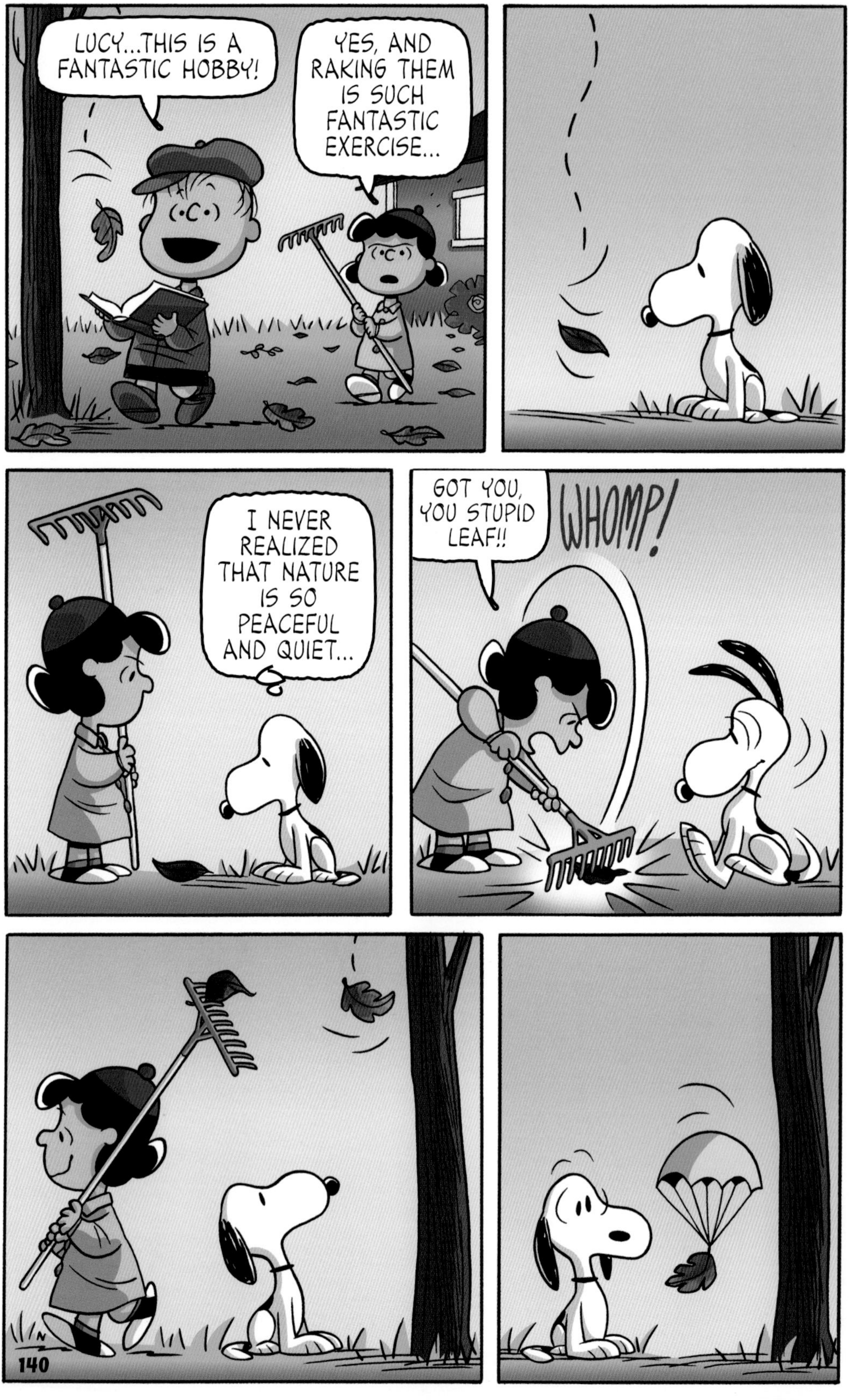
LUCY...THIS IS A FANTASTIC HOBBY!
YES, AND RAKING THEM IS SUCH FANTASTIC EXERCISE...
I NEVER REALIZED THAT NATURE IS SO PEACEFUL AND QUIET...
GOT YOU, YOU STUPID LEAF!!
WHOMP!

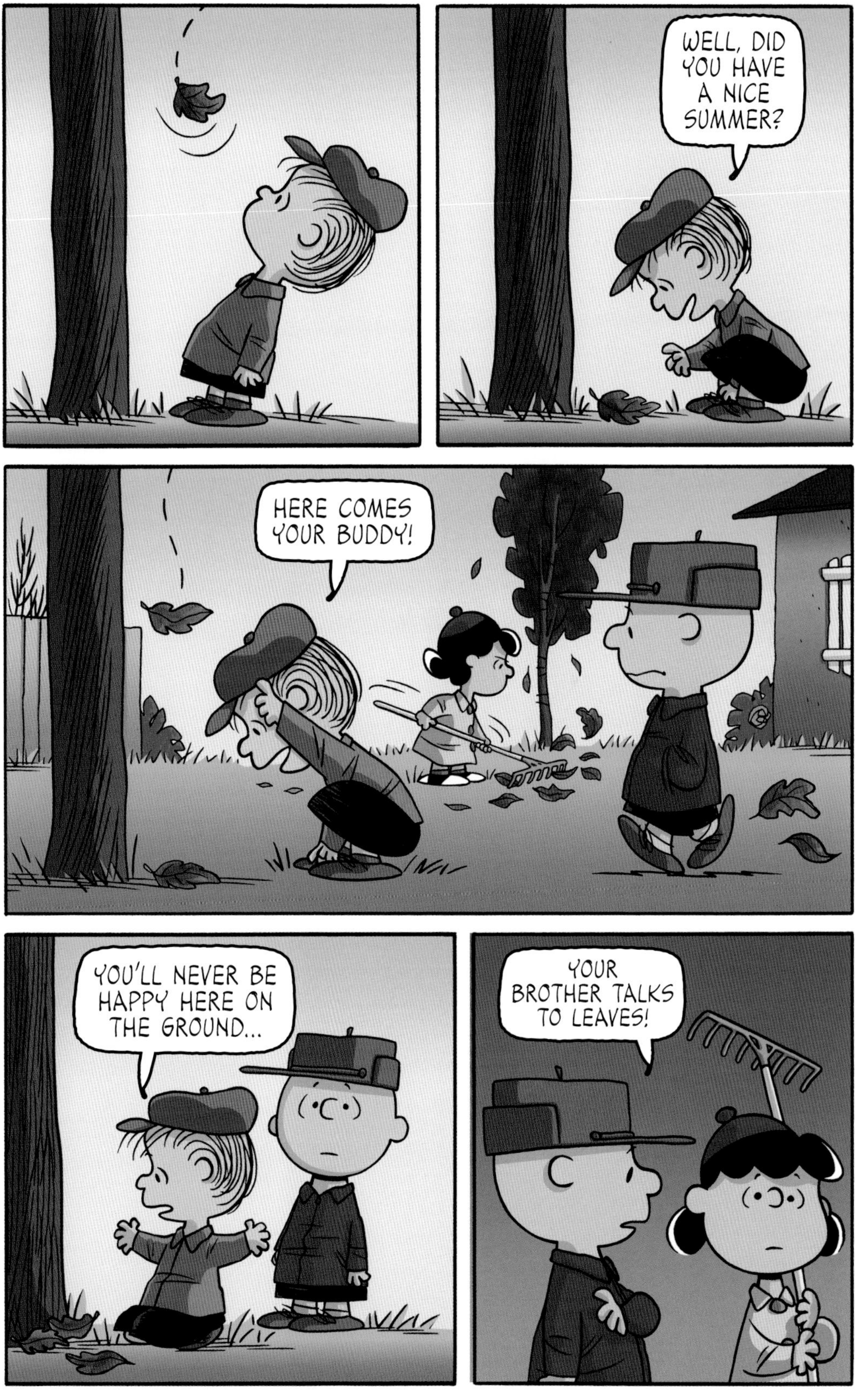
WELL, DID YOU HAVE A NICE SUMMER?
HERE COMES YOUR BUDDY!
YOU'LL NEVER BE HAPPY HERE ON THE GROUND...
YOUR BROTHER TALKS TO LEAVES!

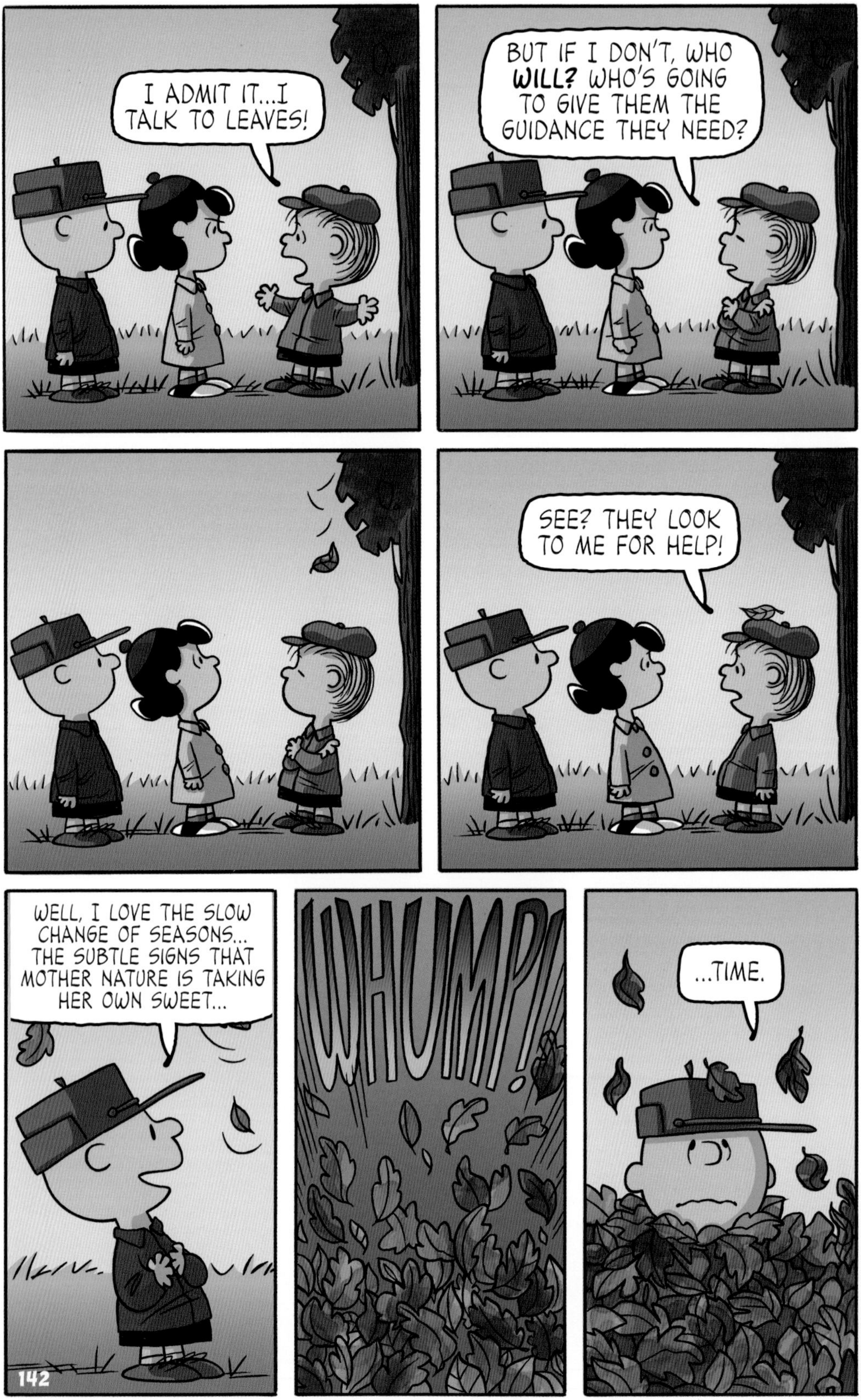
I ADMIT IT...I TALK TO LEAVES!
BUT IF I DON'T, WHO **WILL?** WHO'S GOING TO GIVE THEM THE GUIDANCE THEY NEED?
SEE? THEY LOOK TO ME FOR HELP!
WELL, I LOVE THE SLOW CHANGE OF SEASONS... THE SUBTLE SIGNS THAT MOTHER NATURE IS TAKING HER OWN SWEET...
WHUMP!
...TIME.

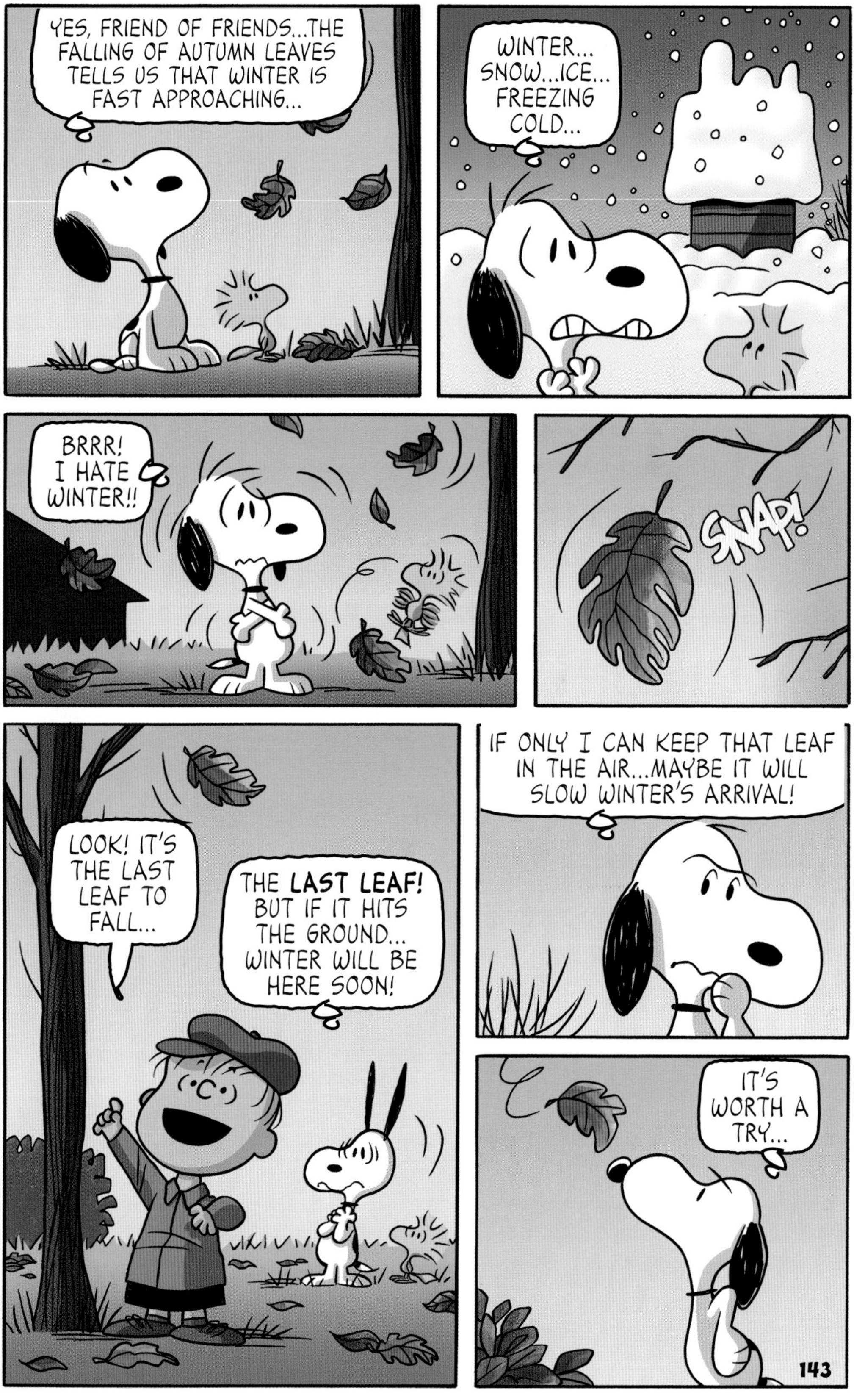
YES, FRIEND OF FRIENDS...THE FALLING OF AUTUMN LEAVES TELLS US THAT WINTER IS FAST APPROACHING...
WINTER... SNOW...ICE... FREEZING COLD...
BRRR! I HATE WINTER!!
SNAP!
LOOK! IT'S THE LAST LEAF TO FALL...
THE **LAST LEAF!** BUT IF IT HITS THE GROUND... WINTER WILL BE HERE SOON!
IF ONLY I CAN KEEP THAT LEAF IN THE AIR...MAYBE IT WILL SLOW WINTER'S ARRIVAL!
IT'S WORTH A TRY...

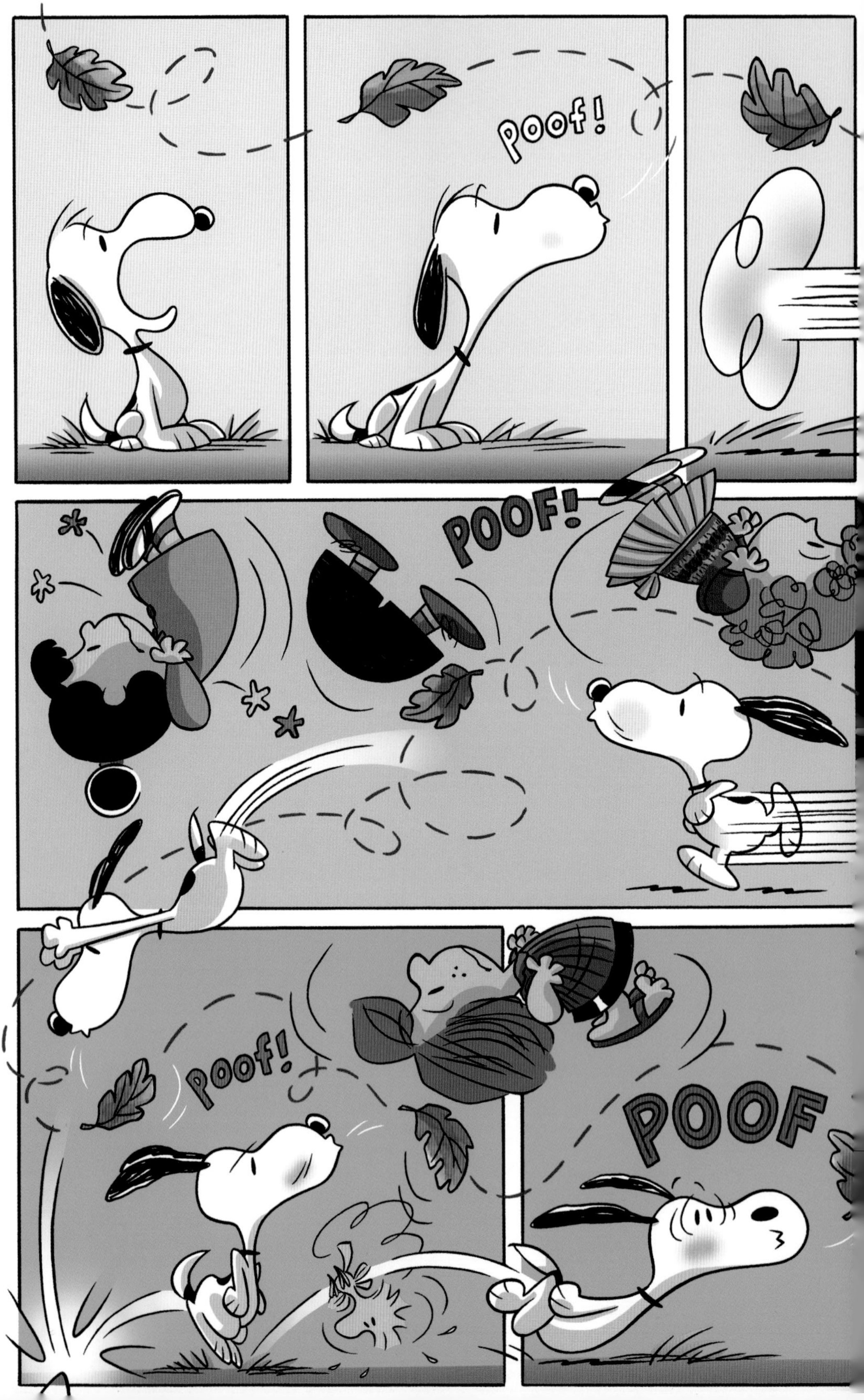
poof!
POOF!
poof!
POOF

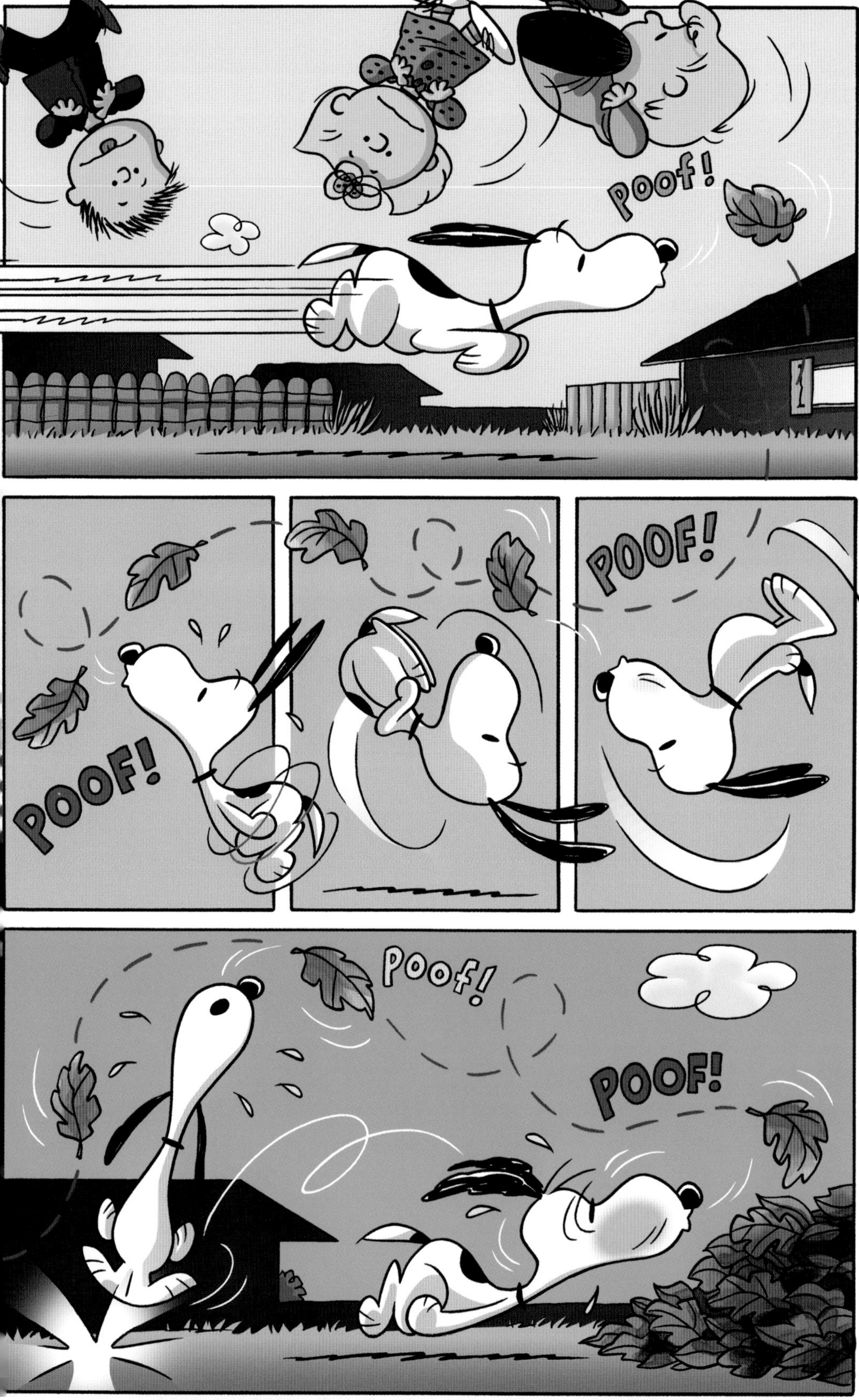
poof!
POOF!
POOF!
poof!
POOF!

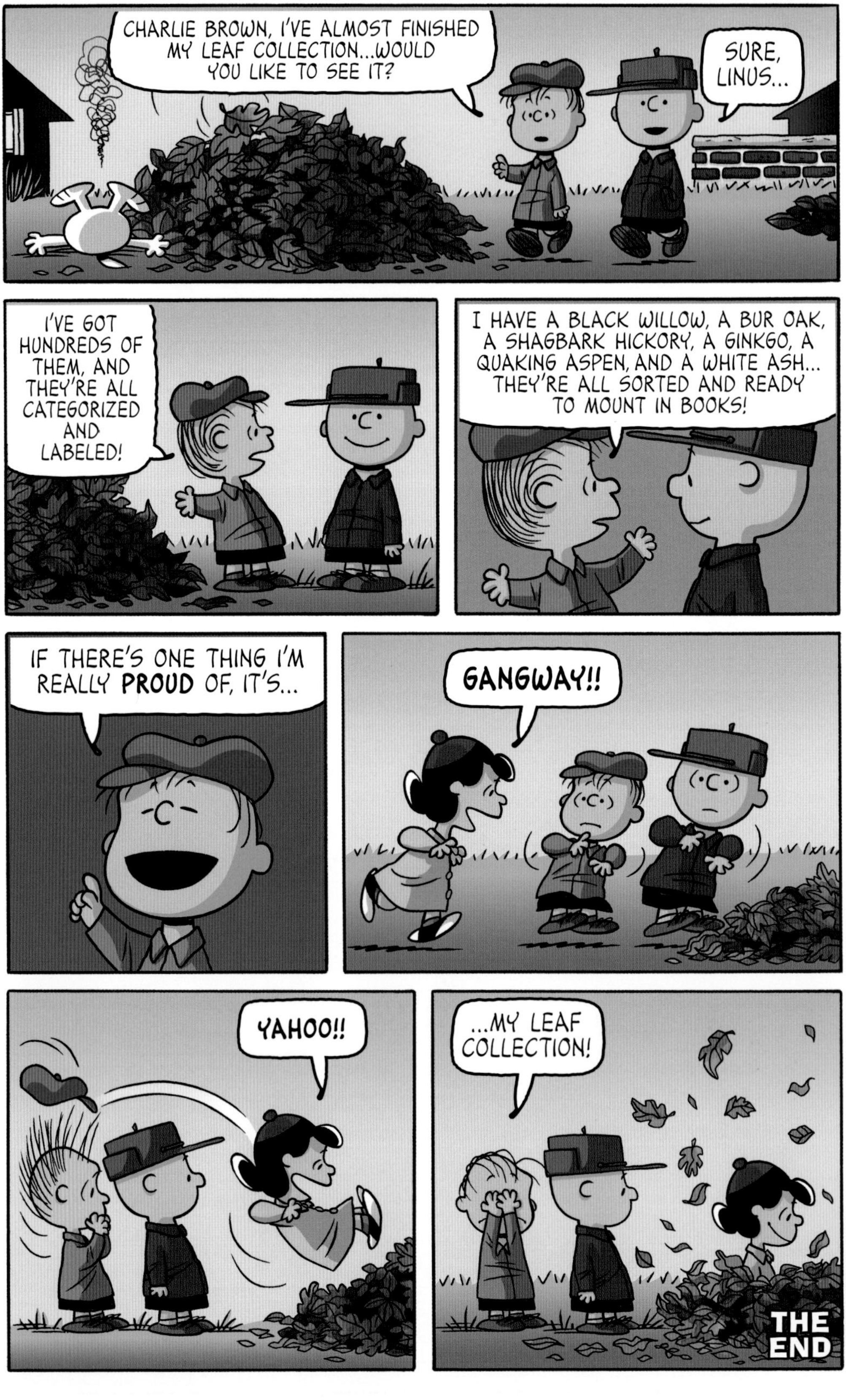
CHARLIE BROWN, I'VE ALMOST FINISHED MY LEAF COLLECTION...WOULD YOU LIKE TO SEE IT?
SURE, LINUS...
I'VE GOT HUNDREDS OF THEM, AND THEY'RE ALL CATEGORIZED AND LABELED!
I HAVE A BLACK WILLOW, A BUR OAK, A SHAGBARK HICKORY, A GINKGO, A QUAKING ASPEN, AND A WHITE ASH... THEY'RE ALL SORTED AND READY TO MOUNT IN BOOKS!
IF THERE'S ONE THING I'M REALLY PROUD OF, IT'S...
GANGWAY!!
YAHOO!!
...MY LEAF COLLECTION!
THE END

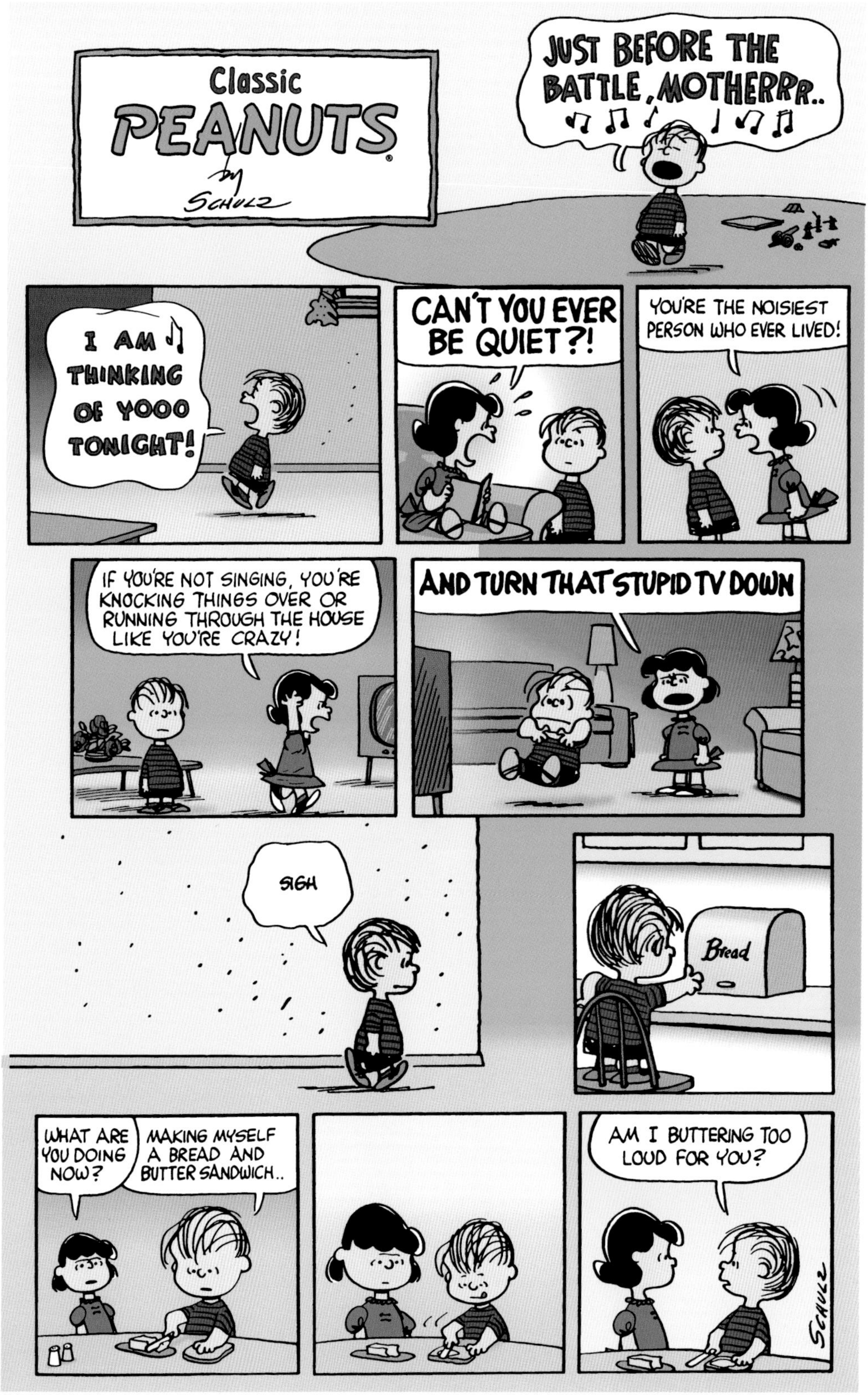
Classic PEANUTS by SCHULZ
JUST BEFORE THE BATTLE, MOTHERRR..
I AM THINKING OF YOOO TONIGHT!
CAN'T YOU EVER BE QUIET?!
YOU'RE THE NOISIEST PERSON WHO EVER LIVED!
IF YOU'RE NOT SINGING, YOU'RE KNOCKING THINGS OVER OR RUNNING THROUGH THE HOUSE LIKE YOU'RE CRAZY!
AND TURN THAT STUPID TV DOWN
SIGH
Bread
WHAT ARE YOU DOING NOW?
MAKING MYSELF A BREAD AND BUTTER SANDWICH..
AM I BUTTERING TOO LOUD FOR YOU?
SCHULZ

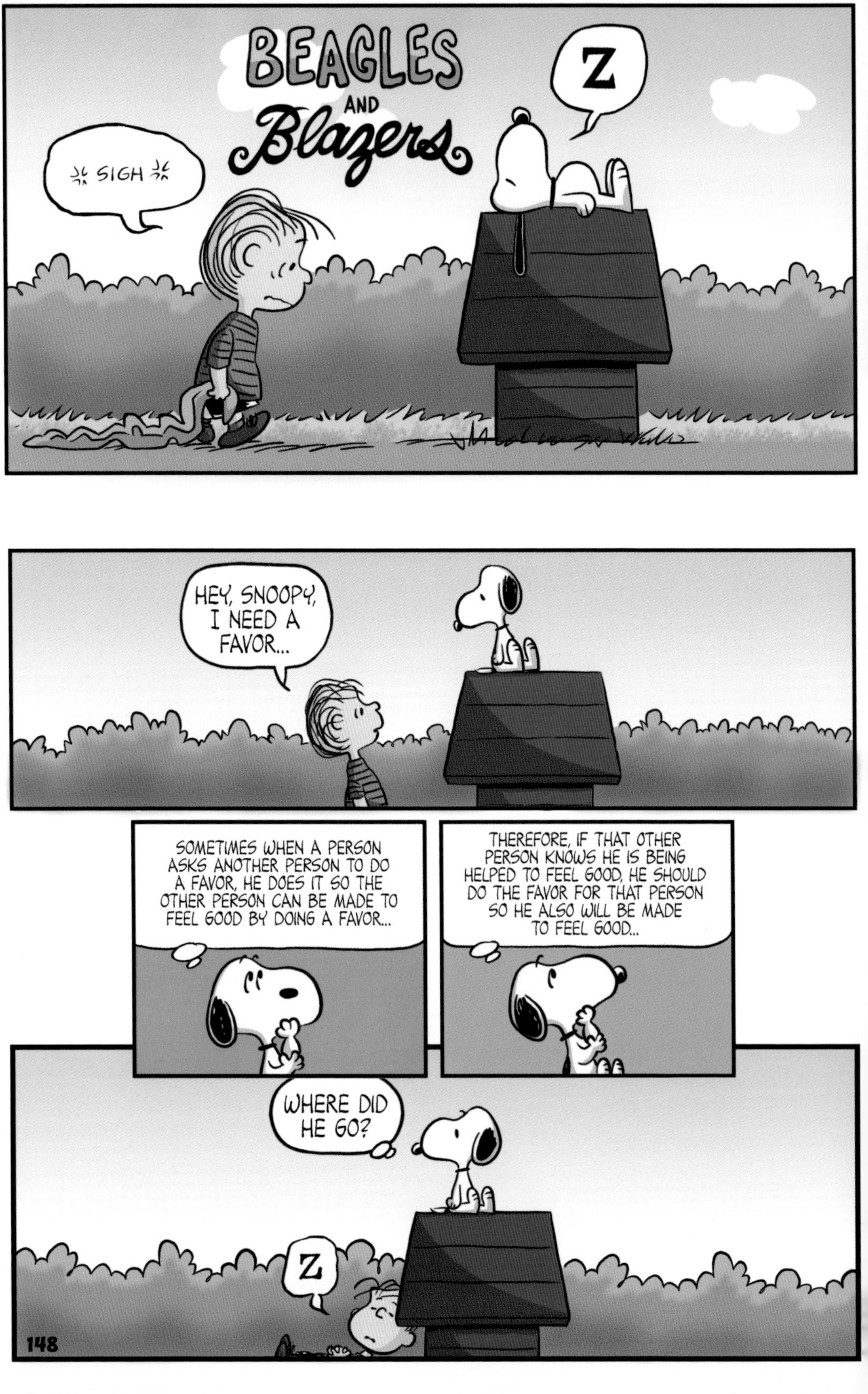
BEAGLES AND Blazers
Z
SIGH
HEY, SNOOPY, I NEED A FAVOR...
SOMETIMES WHEN A PERSON ASKS ANOTHER PERSON TO DO A FAVOR, HE DOES IT SO THE OTHER PERSON CAN BE MADE TO FEEL GOOD BY DOING A FAVOR...
THEREFORE, IF THAT OTHER PERSON KNOWS HE IS BEING HELPED TO FEEL GOOD, HE SHOULD DO THE FAVOR FOR THAT PERSON SO HE ALSO WILL BE MADE TO FEEL GOOD...
WHERE DID HE GO?
Z

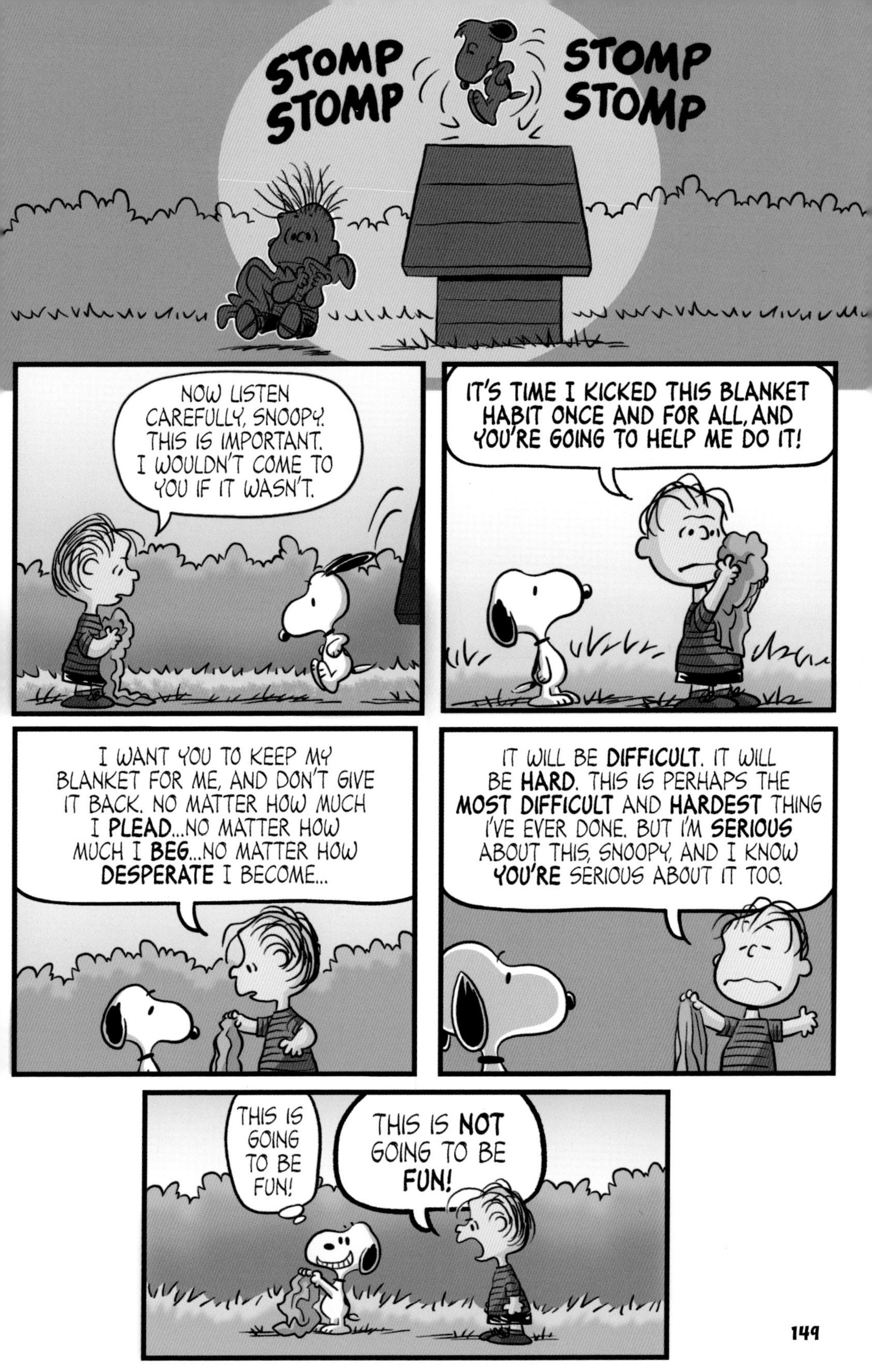
STOMP STOMP
STOMP STOMP
NOW LISTEN CAREFULLY, SNOOPY. THIS IS IMPORTANT. I WOULDN'T COME TO YOU IF IT WASN'T.
IT'S TIME I KICKED THIS BLANKET HABIT ONCE AND FOR ALL, AND YOU'RE GOING TO HELP ME DO IT!
I WANT YOU TO KEEP MY BLANKET FOR ME, AND DON'T GIVE IT BACK. NO MATTER HOW MUCH I PLEAD...NO MATTER HOW MUCH I BEG...NO MATTER HOW DESPERATE I BECOME...
IT WILL BE DIFFICULT. IT WILL BE HARD. THIS IS PERHAPS THE MOST DIFFICULT AND HARDEST THING I'VE EVER DONE. BUT I'M SERIOUS ABOUT THIS, SNOOPY, AND I KNOW YOU'RE SERIOUS ABOUT IT TOO.
THIS IS GOING TO BE FUN!
THIS IS NOT GOING TO BE FUN!

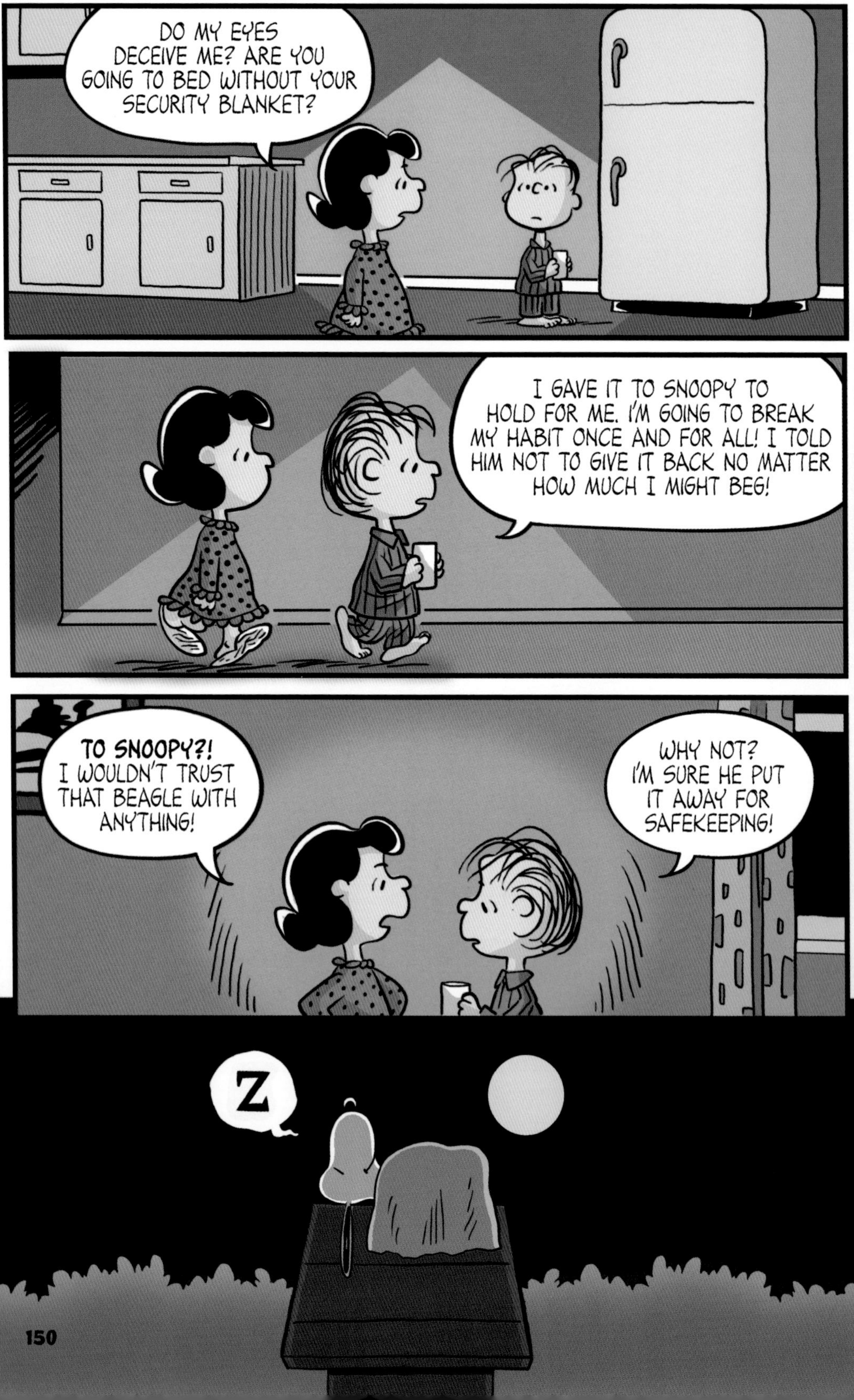
DO MY EYES DECEIVE ME? ARE YOU GOING TO BED WITHOUT YOUR SECURITY BLANKET?
I GAVE IT TO SNOOPY TO HOLD FOR ME. I'M GOING TO BREAK MY HABIT ONCE AND FOR ALL! I TOLD HIM NOT TO GIVE IT BACK NO MATTER HOW MUCH I MIGHT BEG!
TO SNOOPY?! I WOULDN'T TRUST THAT BEAGLE WITH ANYTHING!
WHY NOT? I'M SURE HE PUT IT AWAY FOR SAFEKEEPING!
Z

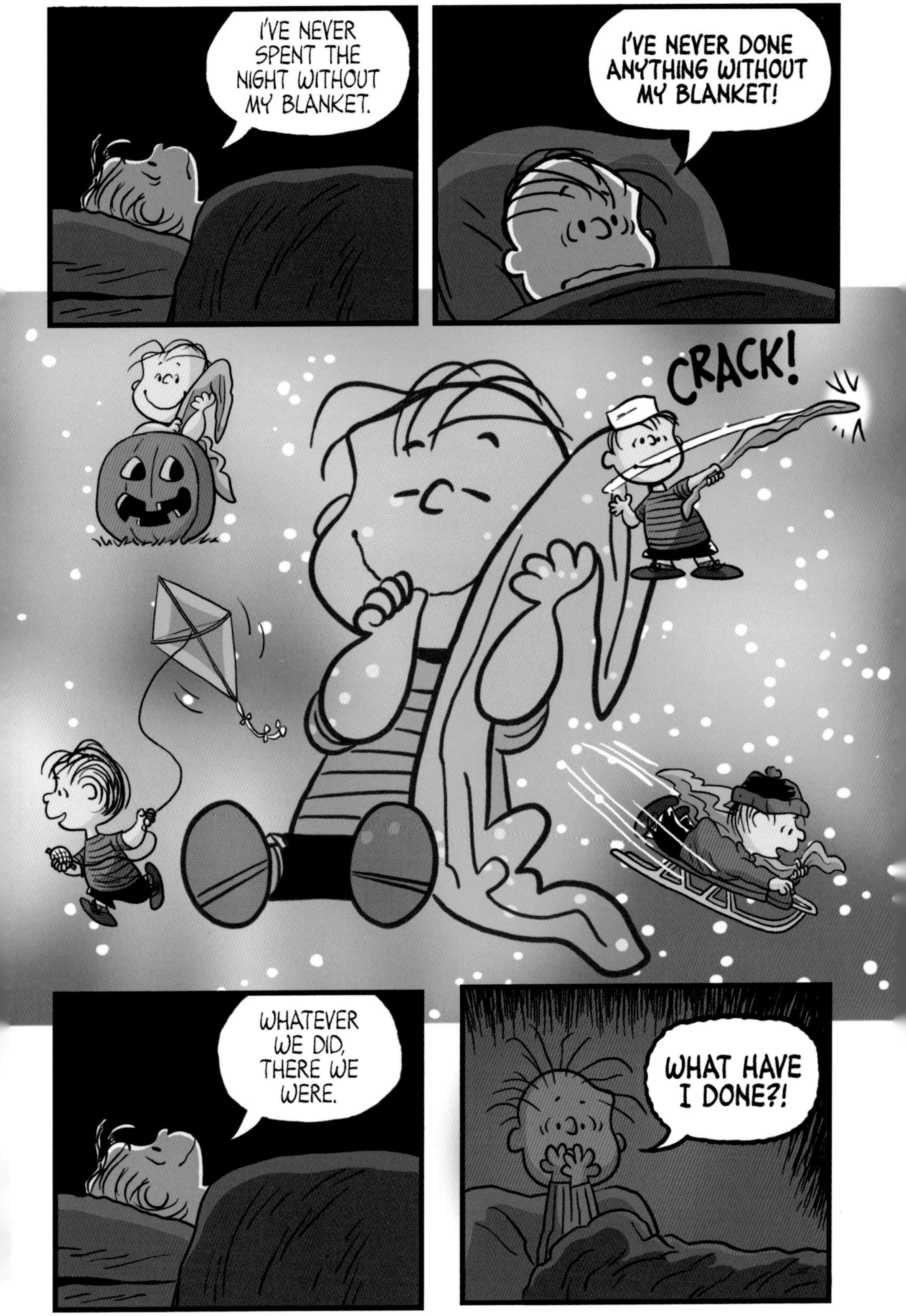
I'VE NEVER SPENT THE NIGHT WITHOUT MY BLANKET.
I'VE NEVER DONE ANYTHING WITHOUT MY BLANKET!
CRACK!
WHATEVER WE DID, THERE WE WERE.
WHAT HAVE I DONE?!

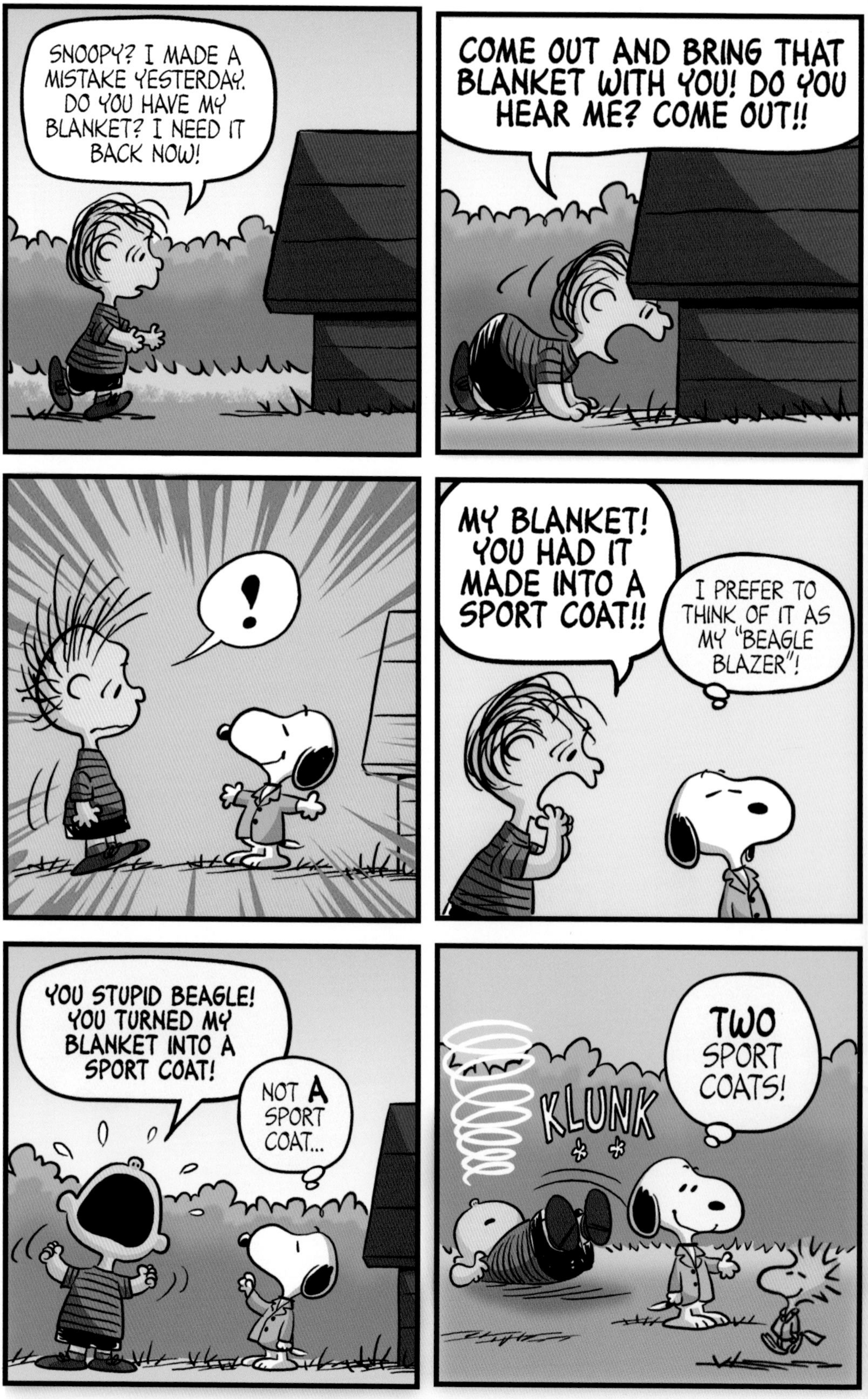
SNOOPY? I MADE A MISTAKE YESTERDAY. DO YOU HAVE MY BLANKET? I NEED IT BACK NOW!
COME OUT AND BRING THAT BLANKET WITH YOU! DO YOU HEAR ME? COME OUT!!
!
MY BLANKET! YOU HAD IT MADE INTO A SPORT COAT!!
I PREFER TO THINK OF IT AS MY "BEAGLE BLAZER"!
YOU STUPID BEAGLE! YOU TURNED MY BLANKET INTO A SPORT COAT!
NOT A SPORT COAT...
KLUNK
TWO SPORT COATS!

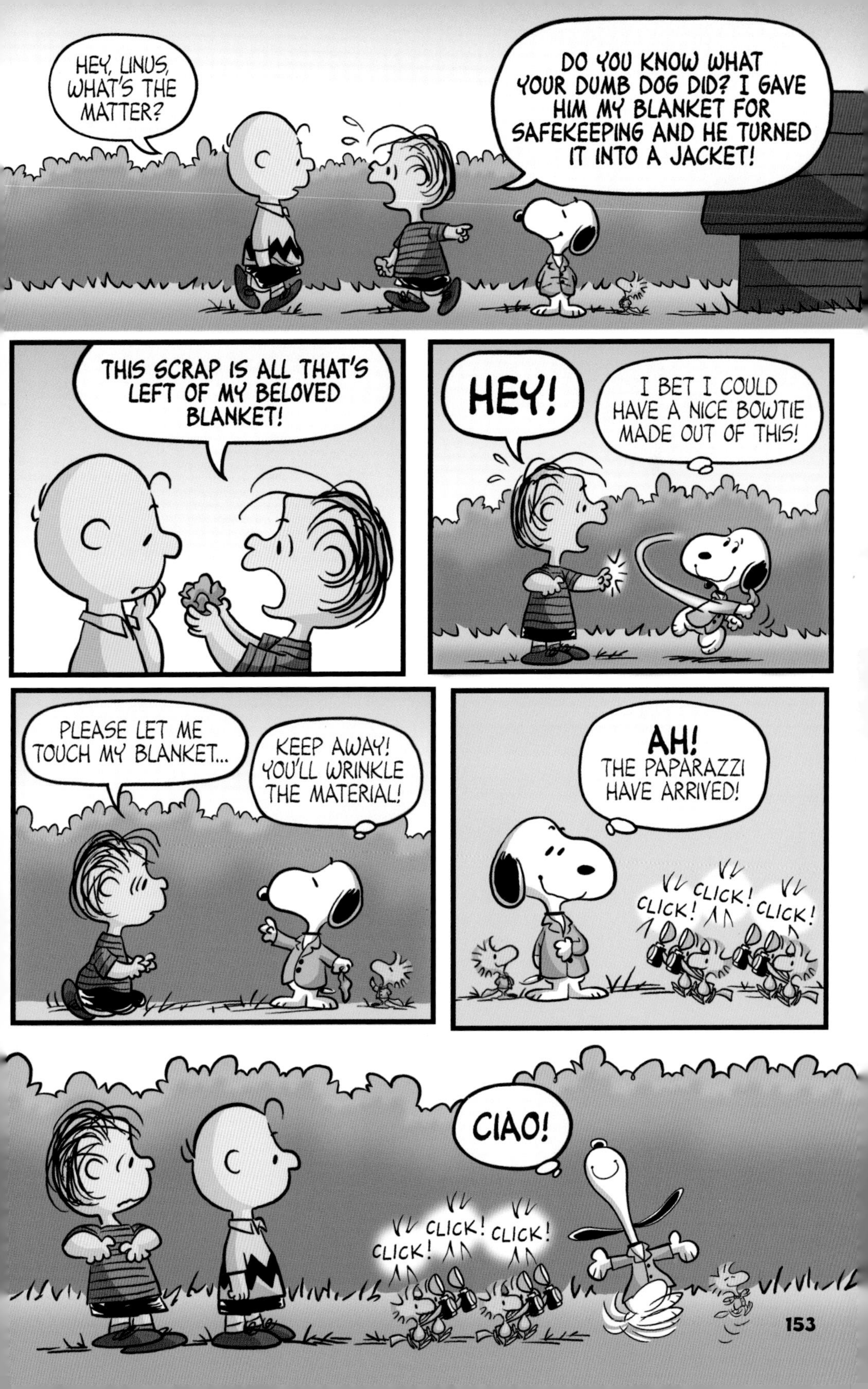
HEY, LINUS, WHAT'S THE MATTER?
DO YOU KNOW WHAT YOUR DUMB DOG DID? I GAVE HIM MY BLANKET FOR SAFEKEEPING AND HE TURNED IT INTO A JACKET!
THIS SCRAP IS ALL THAT'S LEFT OF MY BELOVED BLANKET!
HEY!
I BET I COULD HAVE A NICE BOWTIE MADE OUT OF THIS!
PLEASE LET ME TOUCH MY BLANKET...
KEEP AWAY! YOU'LL WRINKLE THE MATERIAL!
AH! THE PAPARAZZI HAVE ARRIVED!
CLICK! CLICK! CLICK!
CIAO!
CLICK! CLICK! CLICK!

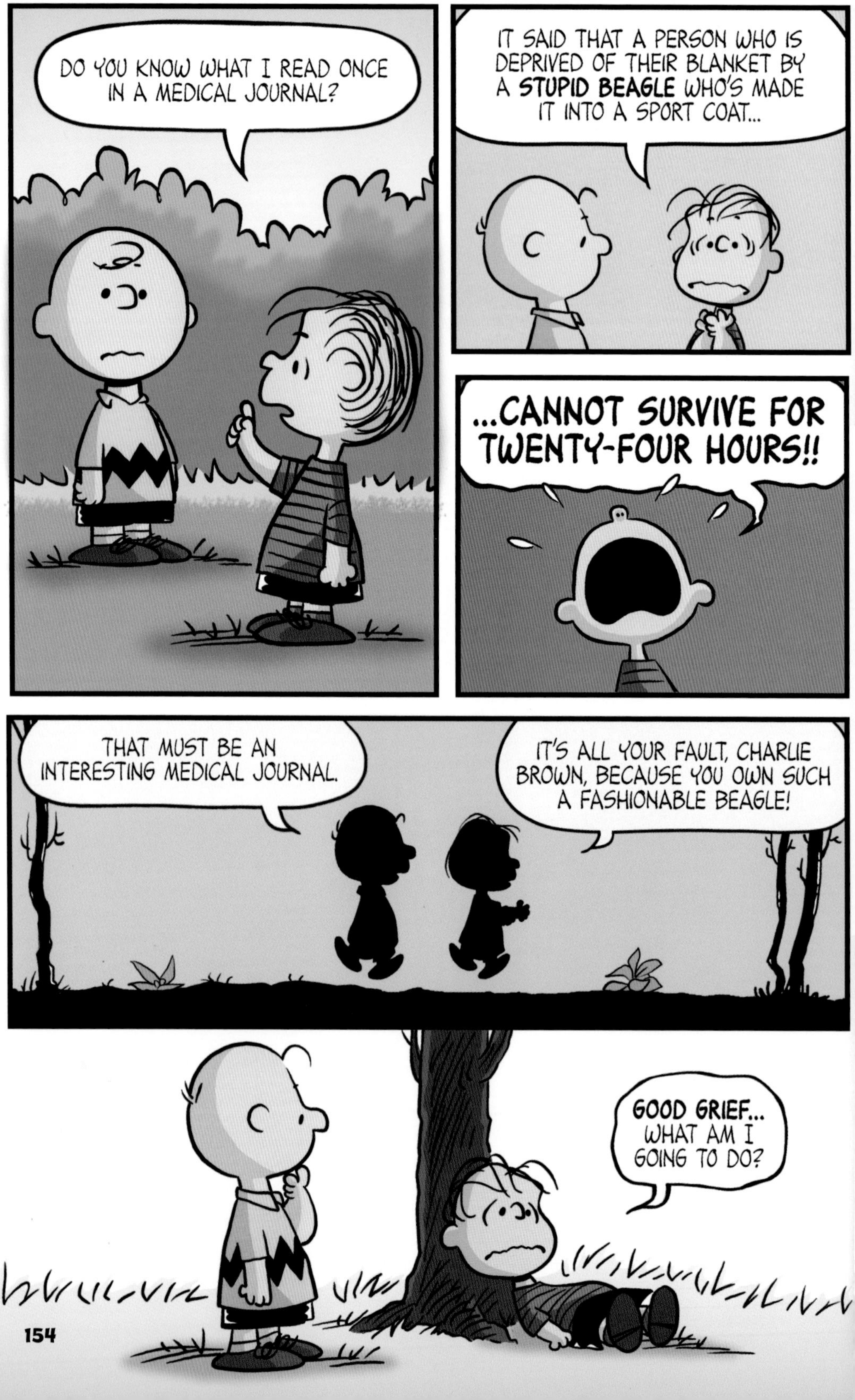
DO YOU KNOW WHAT I READ ONCE IN A MEDICAL JOURNAL?
IT SAID THAT A PERSON WHO IS DEPRIVED OF THEIR BLANKET BY A **STUPID BEAGLE** WHO'S MADE IT INTO A SPORT COAT...
...CANNOT SURVIVE FOR TWENTY-FOUR HOURS!!
THAT MUST BE AN INTERESTING MEDICAL JOURNAL.
IT'S ALL YOUR FAULT, CHARLIE BROWN, BECAUSE YOU OWN SUCH A FASHIONABLE BEAGLE!
GOOD GRIEF... WHAT AM I GOING TO DO?

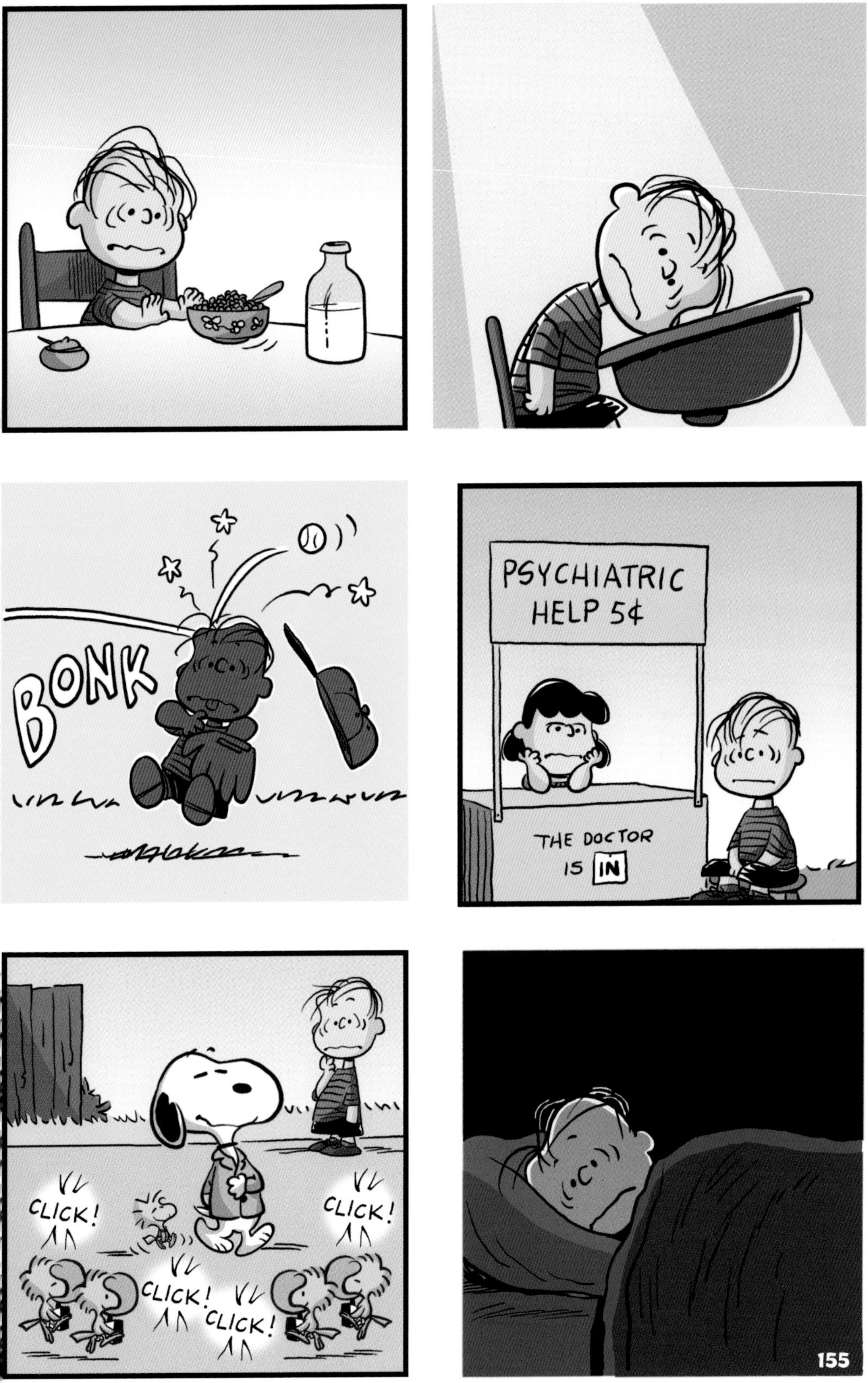
BONK
PSYCHIATRIC HELP 5¢
THE DOCTOR IS IN
CLICK!
CLICK!
CLICK!
CLICK!

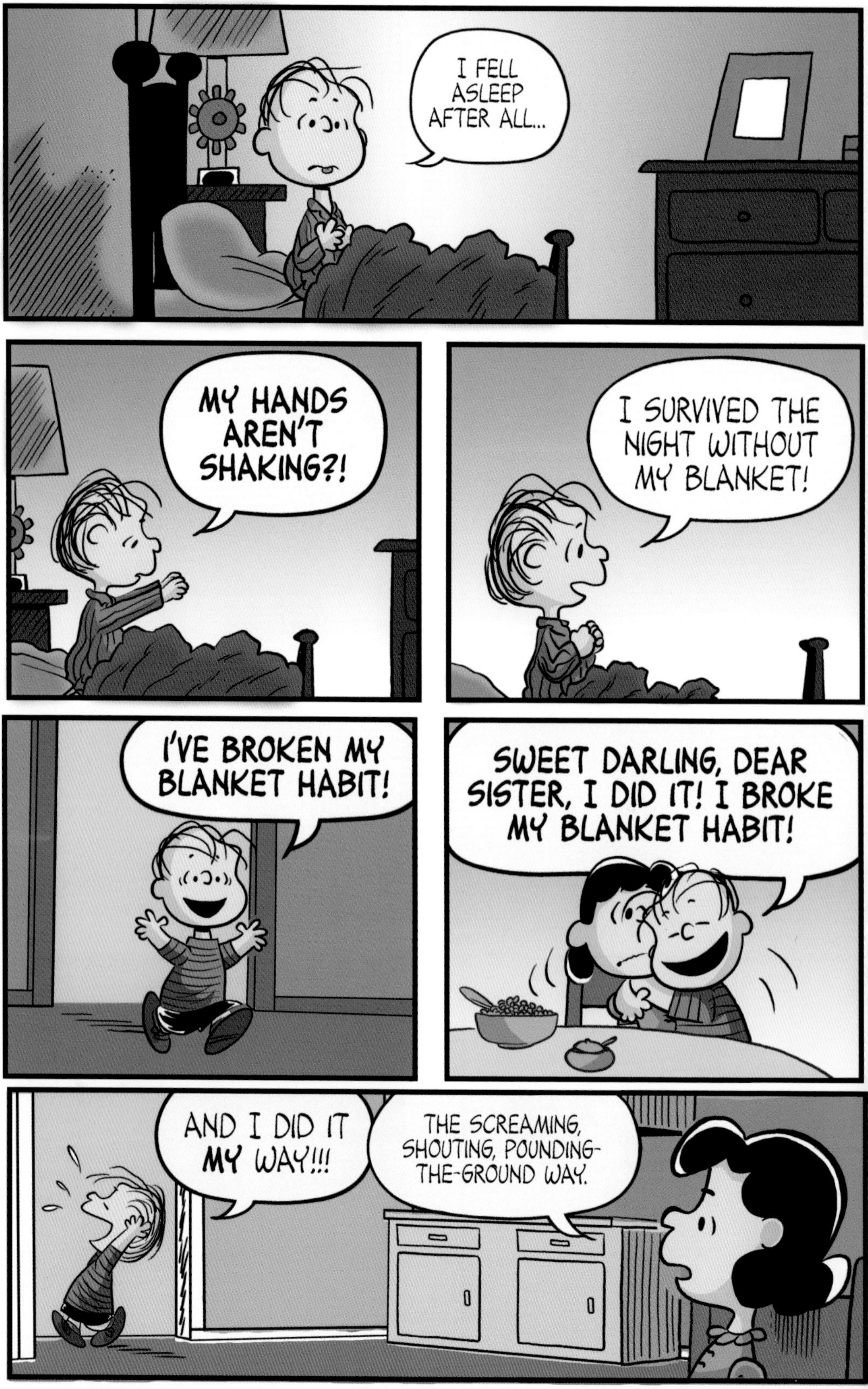
I FELL ASLEEP AFTER ALL...
MY HANDS AREN'T SHAKING?!
I SURVIVED THE NIGHT WITHOUT MY BLANKET!
I'VE BROKEN MY BLANKET HABIT!
SWEET DARLING, DEAR SISTER, I DID IT! I BROKE MY BLANKET HABIT!
AND I DID IT MY WAY!!!
THE SCREAMING, SHOUTING, POUNDING-THE-GROUND WAY.

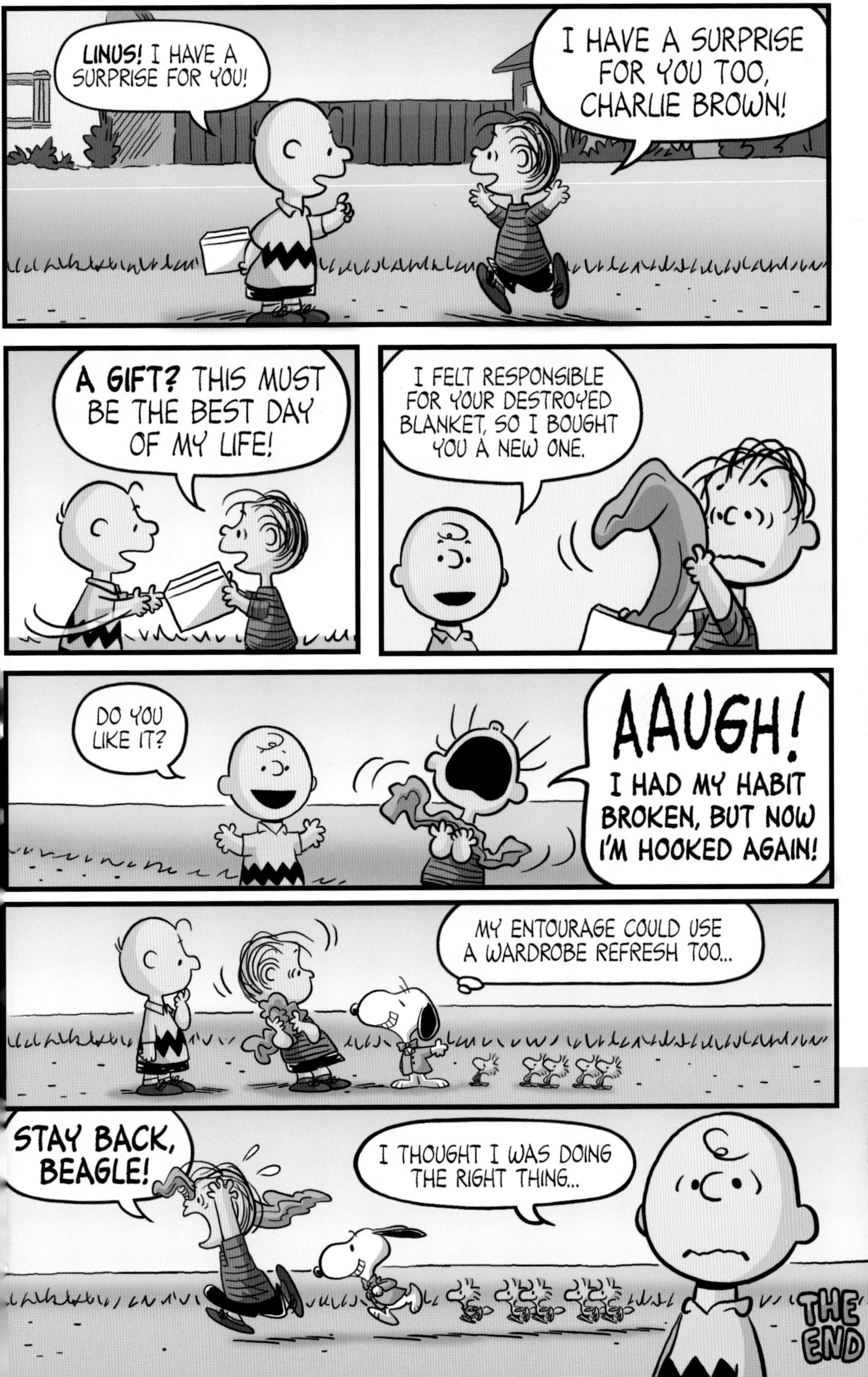
LINUS! I HAVE A SURPRISE FOR YOU!
I HAVE A SURPRISE FOR YOU TOO, CHARLIE BROWN!
A GIFT? THIS MUST BE THE BEST DAY OF MY LIFE!
I FELT RESPONSIBLE FOR YOUR DESTROYED BLANKET, SO I BOUGHT YOU A NEW ONE.
DO YOU LIKE IT?
AAUGH! I HAD MY HABIT BROKEN, BUT NOW I'M HOOKED AGAIN!
MY ENTOURAGE COULD USE A WARDROBE REFRESH TOO...
STAY BACK, BEAGLE!
I THOUGHT I WAS DOING THE RIGHT THING...
THE END

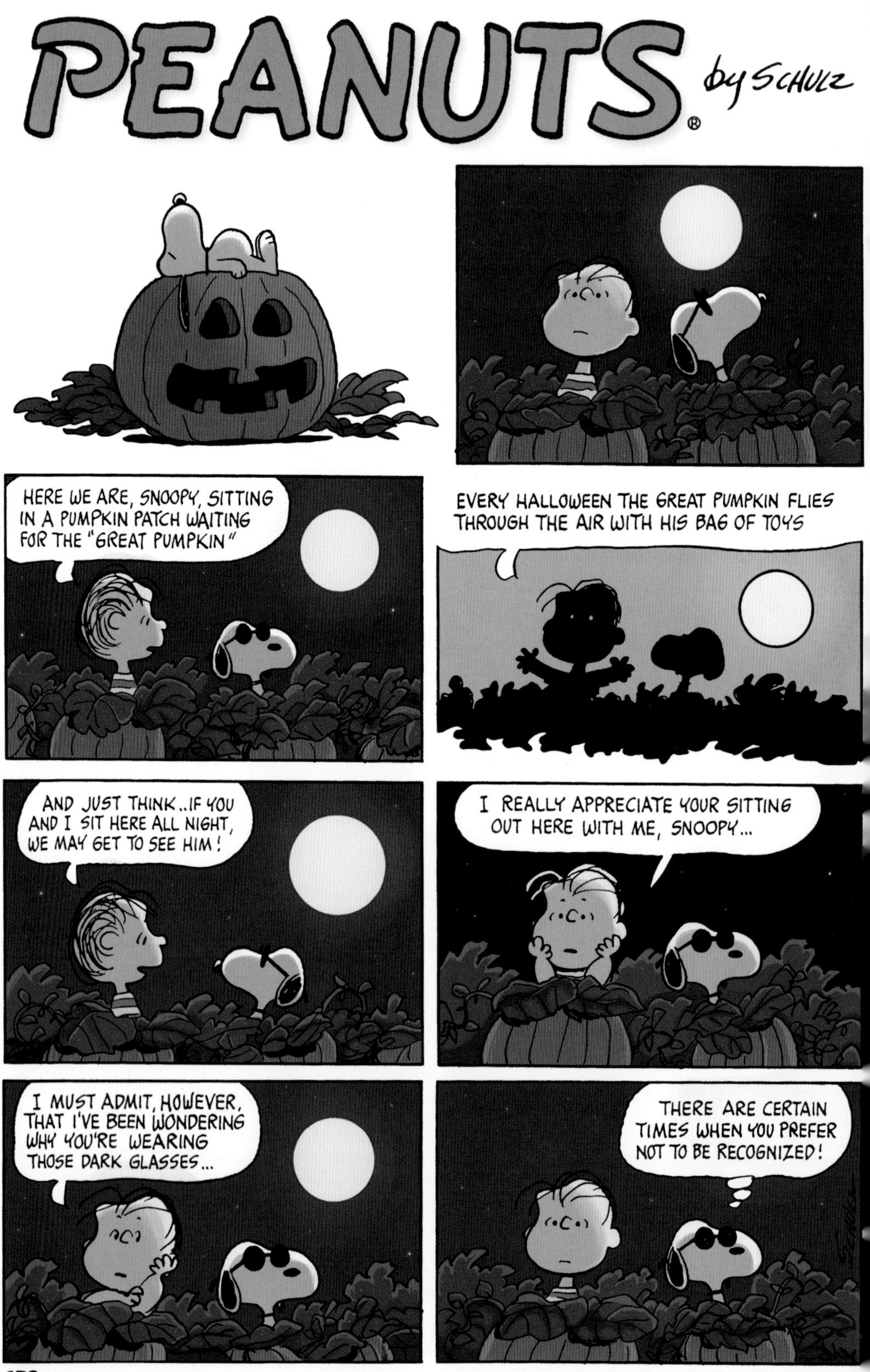
PEANUTS
by SCHULZ
HERE WE ARE, SNOOPY, SITTING IN A PUMPKIN PATCH WAITING FOR THE "GREAT PUMPKIN"
EVERY HALLOWEEN THE GREAT PUMPKIN FLIES THROUGH THE AIR WITH HIS BAG OF TOYS
AND JUST THINK..IF YOU AND I SIT HERE ALL NIGHT, WE MAY GET TO SEE HIM!
I REALLY APPRECIATE YOUR SITTING OUT HERE WITH ME, SNOOPY...
I MUST ADMIT, HOWEVER, THAT I'VE BEEN WONDERING WHY YOU'RE WEARING THOSE DARK GLASSES...
THERE ARE CERTAIN TIMES WHEN YOU PREFER NOT TO BE RECOGNIZED!

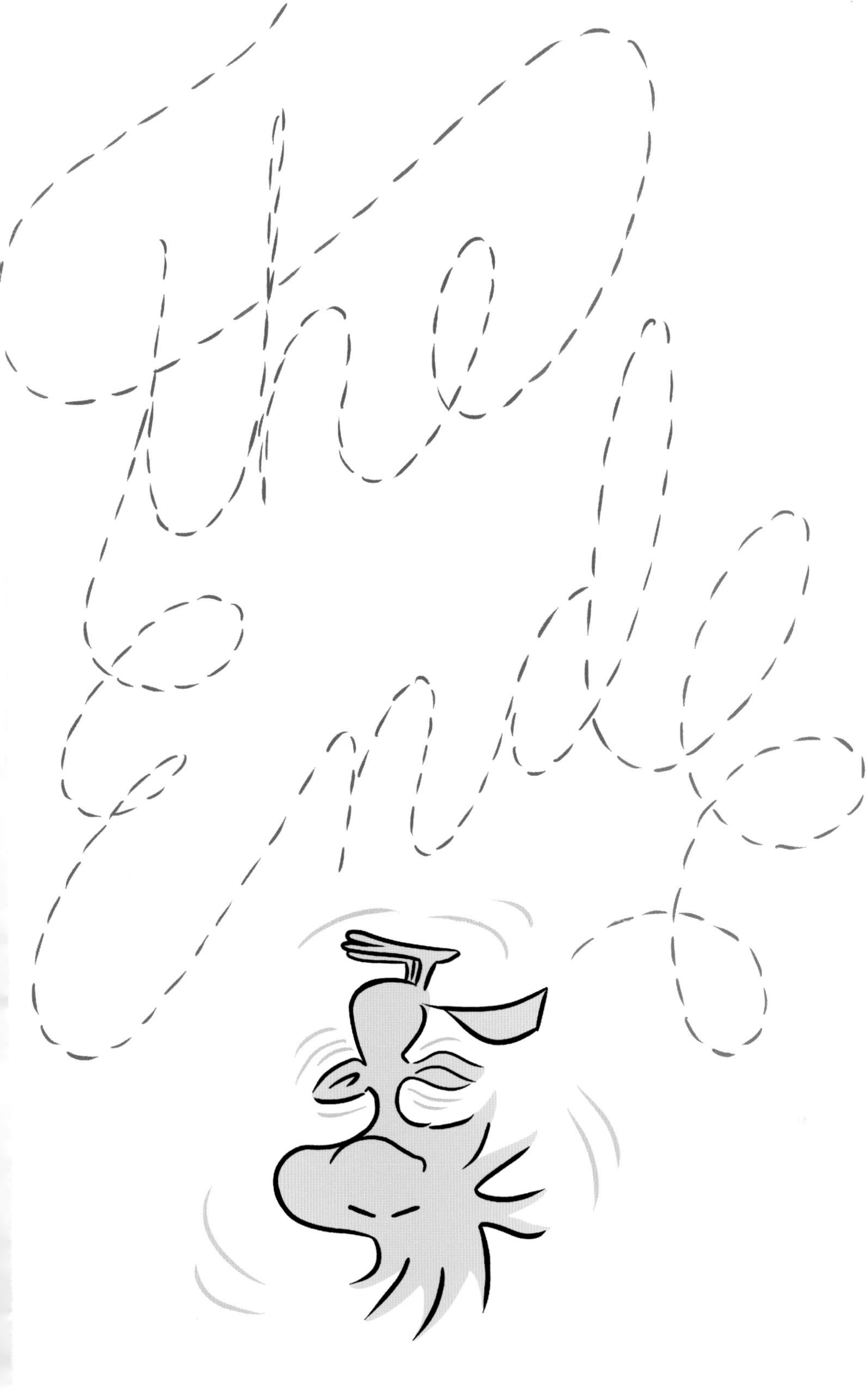
The End

Charles M. Schulz once described himself as "born to draw comic strips." He was born in Minneapolis, and at just two days old, an uncle nicknamed him "Sparky" after the cartoon horse Spark Plug from the *Barney Google* comic strip. Throughout his youth, Schulz and his father shared a Sunday morning ritual reading newspaper comics. After serving in the army during World War II, Schulz's first big break came in 1947 when he sold a cartoon feature called *Li'l Folks* to the St. Paul *Pioneer Press*. In 1950, Schulz met with United Feature Syndicate, and on October 2 of that year Schulz's comic strip *Peanuts* debuted in seven newspapers. Schulz would go on to write and draw *Peanuts* for the next fifty years, and create cultural icons in Snoopy, Charlie Brown, and the rest of the Peanuts gang. At its height, *Peanuts* appeared in 2,600 newspapers across 75 countries and in 21 languages. Charles Schulz died in Santa Rosa, California, in February 2000—just hours before his last original strip was to appear in the Sunday papers.